MAJESTIC

SHADOWS SERIES
BOOK FOUR

SAM BLOOD

Edited by Alicia Lee
Cover Illustration by Lindsey Wakefield
Cover Design by Jenna Brockett

First Published by Blood Enterprises, 2021

Text copyright © Sam Blood, 2021
All rights reserved.

ISBN: 978-0-473-47989-3

www.samblood.com

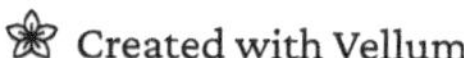 Created with Vellum

This book is dedicated to Tutu James Holly. I wrote the beginnings of Majestic during a month of seclusion in a bungalow on an island in Laos. Tutu is the stray kitten who befriended me and kept me company. Rock on, Tutu!

CONTENTS

LAST TIME, IN 'BOOK THREE: CAMERON'...

Griffin has been preparing to complete the mission of his Mum, Melissa Cameron, to connect the Shadow and human worlds. Working alongside him are Griffin's big brother Calvin, the CEO of Cameron Technologies and Griffin's legal guardian; Calvin's velociraptor Shadow Zephyr; and Mr Falco, who used to masquerade as Griffin's therapist. Their aim is for all humans and Shadows to meet their counterpart, the missing half of them that completes them, by activating nine different Stations around the world. Each of these Stations will open an enormous portal, a gateway between the human world and the Shadow world. However their mission is thwarted when a Rip spontaneously opens in the sky above Auckland City. Two formidable pterodactyl Shadows fly through and destroy the tower of Cameron Technologies. Griffin and the team escape to the labs beneath the building in a last bid to activate the stations. Instead they're surrounded and the controls are destroyed by human soldiers, who blame Griffin and the team for conspiring with Shadows to organise the attack.

Griffin strongly suspects that his nemesis Raven is really behind the destruction of Cameron Technologies. Once an intelligent teenager who was friends with Calvin and Griffin's Mum, Raven killed Melissa Cameron and was banished to the Shadow world, where he formed the human-hating Empire by using the faerie Shadow Hanna as his puppet Empress.

Griffin is separated from the others as they flee for their lives from the human authorities. He ends up in his family's cemetery, and finds himself standing in front of a stone statue of Phoebe, who was the human counterpart of the leader of the Resistance in the Shadow world, Ember. Phoebe was also Raven's best friend, before she banished him to the Shadow world. As Phoebe lay dying, Cirrus had transformed her into stone using his unique power, memorialising her. But as Griffin touches the statue it transforms back into a living, very real Phoebe. Unfortunately, she's still bleeding out and going into shock, the last ten years having passed for her in the blink of an eye. Zephyr finds them, healing Phoebe's wounds just in time. The three of them reunite with Calvin and Mr Falco at a safe house in the city. Calvin is overwhelmed at seeing Phoebe alive again, the dead girl he never stopped loving. Griffin also discovers that Calvin in his darkest moments had occasionally wished Phoebe had survived instead of Griffin that night ten years ago. Already feeling used by Calvin, this poisons the relationship between the Cameron brothers even further. The reunion is short lived as human soldiers storm the safe house, capturing Calvin, Zephyr and Mr Falco. Phoebe and Griffin go on the run together, the two of them on their own now, managing to escape New Zealand airspace in a jet belonging to Calvin.

Griffin and Phoebe feel lost and defeated, seeing no way to complete their mission now that the worlds' governments have confiscated the stations along with all of the Camerons' assets. However, Phoebe recalls a memory from when she was working for Melissa Cameron, which leads her and Griffin into carrying out a heist on Cameron Technologies in New York. Together they manage to recover a file which reveals that Melissa had in fact built a back-up station on an island near Bermuda, from where all the portals can be activated. They resolve to head there and connect the worlds once and for all.

Meanwhile, over in the Shadow world... Eclipse, the powerful dragon-parrot who replaced Cirrus when he died, is being held prisoner by Ember, the leader of the Resistance. This is due to the death and destruction he caused shortly after his birth, when he was intoxicated by his immense power and determined to conquer the world. Now humbled, Eclipse is struggling to come to terms with his identity. He still has the memories of Cirrus, the Shadow who died, and Eclipse wonders how much of him is still influenced by Cirrus Eclipse doesn't feel accepted by other Shadows, who view him as an abomination and not a true Shadow. Eclipse's one desire is to reunite with his human Griffin, the only one who cares for him in the entire universe. Eclipse makes a vow in honour of Griffin not to kill, as Griffin considered life sacred, and Eclipse wants to live in line with the Shadow Griffin believed he could be.

Eclipse escapes Ember's prison, mimicking her power for himself - the power to create and control flame. Eclipse's ability allows him to copy the powers of others, though he can only hold one Shadow's power at a single time. During his break-out, Eclipse encounters Hanna, the imprisoned ex-Empress who was once

Cirrus' nemesis, and they form an alliance to escape. This involves eluding the new Empress Galvanize, a psychotic insectoid now serving Raven in Hanna's place. Galvanize seeks to kill Hanna, jealous of her as Raven's favourite, and plans to bring Eclipse to Raven for an unknown purpose. Empress Galvanize and her Empire now only control a portion of the Shadow world, and are locked in civil war with Ember and her Resistance; the rest of the world is separated into neutral zones, who are yet to vote on whether to pledge their allegiance to the human-loving Resistance or the human-hating Empire. Eclipse is vulnerable to Galvanize's agonising toxic sting, and Hanna and Eclipse only narrowly escape with their lives.

A Rip opens in the sky above Sanctuary City, and humans attack the Shadow city in a similar strike to the one that occurred in the human world. Eclipse and Hanna are unable to cross through the Rip themselves before it closes, but are still tortured by their deepest desire to find and be with their respective human counterparts. Hanna reveals that the Underworld beneath the Islands of Sun and Moon holds the secret to crossing over to the human world, and her and Eclipse form a temporary truce to journey there together.

In their voyage to the Islands of Sun and Moon, Eclipse and Hanna arrive in the city of Midnight Crafters. Hanna shows Eclipse the squalor of where she lived as an abused child before Raven rescued her. The pair discover that the Resistance has followed them in an attempt to capture them both and bring them back to Sanctuary - triggering a massive air battle above Midnight Crafters between the ships of the Empire and the Resistance. There are high casualties of both soldiers and innocent citizens, and Eclipse blames Hanna for not caring about those she was once responsible for as Empress. Eclipse and Hanna shelter from the battle in a flat, where they are welcomed by three friendly students named Celeste, Frigga and Merida. However Empress Galvanize locates them, ordering Celeste and the students who sheltered Hanna and Eclipse to be taken. Hanna breaks off one of Galvanize's stingers, enraging her, in an effort to escape. But with the Resistance forces obliterated, Eclipse and Hanna are surrounded by the Imperial army. Digging down deep, Eclipse summons Ember's power, projecting himself as a flaming giant. This buys him and Hanna enough time to escape across the ocean, winging their way into a storm in an attempt to lose their pursuers. Hanna clings to Eclipse as he flies across an impossible distance. Seeking their humans they journey toward the sacred Islands of Sun and Moon, where Shadows have been forbidden to set foot for millennia...

1

UGLY DUCKLING

Eclipse

I feel something warm and soft beneath me. Something that better be land. Muscles struggling, I claw my way up and out of the ocean, shaking water from my feathers like a drowned spirit. My eyes flicker open, stinging with salt.

Well, well. Hello, paradise.

I'm crouched in a lavish bed of warm golden sand. Crystal water laps the shore around me. Dotting the beach are fragments of ancient stone ruins, engraved with strange markings. Further inland from the beach is dense forest, with verdant green foliage, including ferns curling in ornate patterns. The sun's just starting to set, illuminating the island in the soft light of early evening.

If this place wasn't sacred, it would be covered in luxury resorts. It belongs on a postcard.

It's almost laughable to think that I just flew an unimaginable distance through a hellish storm, chased by forces sent by a psychotic insectoid Empress. Pursued by flying warships that fired bolts and projectiles to try and strike us out of the sky, before they themselves were struck by lightning or consumed by the monstrous sized waves that reached toward the sky in hungry strokes.

We made it, I think fuzzily. We actually made it.

Every part of my body aches in exhausted agony. Grimacing, I flick my tail to make sure it still operates. The arrow-head tip traces patterns in the wet sand grains, before the ocean rushes in, obliterating them. I scoop the sand up in a claw, let it pour through my clenched talons. It feels so good to be on solid ground. I stretch my crest high, the feathers frayed and heavy with water.

A wind blows through the branches out onto the beach, as if the forest is breathing. It carries this familiar scent, something I can't place. As the wind rustles through the leaves and plays with the sand, blowing it in mini-whirlwinds out towards the water, I swear it sounds like a hissing voice.

"*Ciiiiiiirrrrruss...*"

My blood turns cold.

"No. No," I mutter, shaking my head. I stare warily into the forest, unnerved. I must be imagining it. But perhaps that's what scares me more. That the demons are on the inside, and they're not done with me yet.

I have to keep it together. We are so close.

We.

"Empress?" I croak, looking around the shoreline. She must be nearby, but I can't see her. As I search, uncertainty quickly turns to dread. "EMPRESS?"

She has to be here. The idea that she somehow didn't make it is... unthinkable.

Could she have drowned, out there at sea? With me too exhausted to notice as she plunged beneath the ocean, her pleas for help lost in the water?

I feel my heart palpitating, a strange anxiety encroaching at the thought of her being dragged beneath the freezing waves.

An idealistic, optimistic part of me had hoped that I could save Hanna's soul by helping her find her human. Have I failed her instead? Have I led her to her death for nothing?

Finally we've made it across the ocean to the Islands of Sun and Moon, thanks to the information Hanna found. The entrance to the Underworld, and to our humans, must be nearby. But an overwhelming loneliness crushes my chest. Strangely, without someone to share the end of the journey, it might as well not be real. It feels like I might as well be back in my cage.

My exotic surroundings feel like they're mocking me. Without knowing exactly where the entrance to the Underworld is, really I've just washed up in a beautiful prison. A false promise.

Besides, what right do I have to push on, to find my human without Hanna? The idea of a happy ending feels tainted, and I feel an apathy setting into my bones. The idea that I might find Griffin again feels too good to be true, a prize I definitely haven't earned if you count the death and destruction I've caused in my brief lifespan. Helping Hanna find her human was meant to be my redemption, my ticket through the metaphorical pearly gates. My way of earning my human, of becoming worthy of Griffin. I realise that now, more clearly than I've articulated it to myself before.

I launch into the air, beating my wings to rise above the treeline, higher, and higher. I take in the dizzying view laid out before me. Steeling myself, I scan for any sign of Hanna.

The lush canopy stretches out across the entire island. I can make out the second island in the distance, and the strait that separates the two. The Islands of Sun and Moon nestle into each other like two halves, like yin and yang. The long, slender tail of the other island curls around the end of this one far to my right.

My gaze is drawn far into the distance. Across the treeline, out over the water and at the far side of the opposite island. The structure rises tall enough to draw the eye even from this far away.

It's a massive palace, timeless and ancient simultaneously. It could equally be a castle, or a cathedral of unprecedented scale. Something about it certainly does convey a sense of religion, or worship. Grey stone protrudes upward and outward from it in undulating towers high into the sky, slender bridges connecting them like strands of spider web. The random layout of the tallest towers seems to defy gravity. Parts of it have crumbled into ruin. But the thing about it which really strikes awe into me is harder to fit into words. The entire palace exudes an intimidating influence, a cold aura, as if it sings with the voices of long lost souls.

I shake my head, laughing at myself inwardly.

Architectural appreciation? Poetic fancy? I must be more delirious from the journey here than I realised. Something about that distant palace does haunt me though. I can't help but feel hypnotised by its almost supernatural sway.

But there are no signs of Hanna. An epic, desolate sense of isolation sets in. I'm stranded, alone, the only living being in the middle of an endless ocean.

Defeated, fatigued, I fall aimlessly back toward the shore, like a leaf on the wind.

There's a rustle in the trees and I look sharply in its direction. Scanning the treeline as if hunting for prey. These islands were meant to be uninhabited.

Unless... the voice I heard on the wind before wasn't inside my head. Unless I'm not really alone.

But then a Shadow emerges from the leaves, striding out onto the sand. She looks like a human girl with long dark hair, still wearing the casual clothes she borrowed from the students in Midnight Crafters. She'd easily pass as a human, if it wasn't for the large wings emerging from her back like a violet butterfly.

Relief floods through me, the strength of it surprising me.

Hanna's alive.

More than that, she looks strangely happy. On her shoulder she's resting a spear carved from a wooden branch. Pierced at the end of it is a baked, wild salmon, artfully blackened around the edges.

Mad, I light down beside her. I try to hide my frothing anger, even though I'm tempted to fling her back into the trees with a single claw for putting me through that. Hanna screws up her nose as my heavy wingbeats send sand flying into her face.

"How you doin', big bird?" Hanna asks jovially.

"I thought you were dead," I say in a disappointed tone. Secretly, my chest is still pounding.

"Sure," Hanna responds. "Or that I'd left you and abandoned you here, right? Pretty pointless though. We're on the Island of Sun. There's nowhere to run away to, other than the island next door. We're marooned, you shmucklehead."

"The Empire will know this is where we were headed."

"These islands are sacred, remember? Strictly off-limits, since earliest memory. Even I feel queasy breaking a taboo like that. Our only way now is forward, to the Underworld." Hanna brightens. "Or, how about we divvy the islands up, one each? I can start my civilisation, you can build your own. We can grow trade and commerce... see who wins the inevitable war for resources..." Hanna slips the toasted salmon off the end of her spear and hurls it at me. I snap it up, catching it in my beak like a seagull.

"My civilisation would annihilate yours, Empress," I say through the mouthful of flesh. It's my nickname for her, even though she's been dethroned. I enjoy how much it riles her. I swallow the fish. My starving stomach welcomes it. "Any more of those?"

"What, you're asking me for help?" Hanna puts a hand to her heart, as if touched. "You want to benefit from my survival skills?"

"Please, don't make a scene," I sigh. "I flew us an extremely long way. I know this is hard to believe, but I *am* only mortal."

"Well, we do still have a ways to go yet, and I'm not journeying into the human world on an empty stomach. Come on, let's get some grub. I still have to spear the fish one at a time, but I *have* been building a net." Hanna waves towards the forest. "The fish get one look at your face, you'll scare them right into it."

"Witty," I congratulate her. "So, what's that haunted

carnival attraction on the other island?" A shiver runs through my feathers just from mentioning it.

"Aeyu."

"*Aeiou?*" I laugh. "Did they just use every vowel in the alphabet?"

"No, bird-brain. *Air-yoo*. It was built further back than anyone can remember, in a time of legend. It stands directly over the entrance to the Underworld. That's where we're headed. The only way off these islands now is through there."

Griffin, I think. I feel a rush of exhilaration at how close we are, along with sensing an entire host of new nerves.

What do I know about the human world? Nothing, despite everything Cirrus ever collected from it. Their world is a mystery to us. Cirrus imagined it as heaven, based on his foggy but happy childhood memories from growing up there. But he spent most of that time underground, in the labs beneath Cameron Technologies. He never really got to know the human world. And now that I've seen the evil some groups of humans are capable of after that attack on Sanctuary, now that I've found out that Raven was human too... what if the human world is just as dysfunctional as this one? What if it's *worse*?

Oblivious to my thoughts, Hanna turns and vanishes back into the greenery. I take a last look around at the primal, prehistoric shore with its jutting stone ruins, at the eternal water stretching out behind us under the soft light of finality. Then I follow after Hanna, slender tree trunks cracking under my passage as I carve my way after her.

Beneath the canopy is a different world - tropical exotic flowers decorate the undergrowth in rich colour, and strange insects mimicking their predators lie in wait on branches and fern fronds.

"It was a mistake, you know," Hanna says out of nowhere. "Leaving Galvanize alive."

I recall the psychotic insectoid Empress, her writhing mandibles like those of a green wasp. I remember my failure to save Celeste and the other students, the ones whom Galvanize had ordered to be disposed of.

Celeste had been a real character. A meerkat with the pink plumage of a flamingo, she hadn't hesitated to offer their flat to hide us from the authorities. She'd even tried to offer Hanna and I peer mediation when she sensed the fight we were going through. She hadn't been scared of me like everyone else in this world, hadn't cared that I was different. For a moment, it had felt like Hanna and I could have lived there with them, living normal lives. Instead of hunted and reviled both by Empire and Resistance.

I'd thanked Celeste for those magic moments by standing by, watching her and friends be captured and sent to a dark fate at Galvanize's pleasure.

I feel a burning inside of me.

"You know that I've vowed..." I begin coldly.

"Not to kill anyone," Hanna cuts me off. "Yeah, very gallant of you."

"That's why you're my favourite travelling companion," I smile sarcastically. "The way that you mock me for not murdering people."

"Galvanize is a psychopath."

"Look who's talking," I remind her. "I suppose I just prefer the devil I know."

"She'll go on to kill countless others," Hanna shoots at me. "She's turning my Empire into a ruthless dictatorship."

"Whereas before..."

Hanna holds up a hand before I can call out her hypocrisy.

"One that's prepared to brutally kill or torture anyone who's even associated with anything it disapproves of. I used fear to keep people in line, for the greater good. She uses it because she enjoys it."

"Galvanize won't stay in power long," I say dismissively, though there are problematic stirrings beneath my words. "Her advisors will get tired of her unpredictable behaviour and laughable leadership and turn against her. If she does harm to the Empire's reputation in the long run, that can only be a good thing."

"And what if the majority of Shadows choose to side with the Empire instead of the Resistance?" Hanna challenges me. She flies up to hover level with my head, dodging the branches of the canopy brushing past us. "If Galvanize rules this entire world like I did, who will be able to stand up to her then?"

"What do you want from me?" I seethe.

"Me? Nothing. Just to point out that by not killing Galvanize, thousands more will die. Maybe more. Inaction can be the worst form of evil. I'm tired of your moral superiority shtick. You don't get to just opt-out so you can try and feel like the good guy."

I try not to show it, but her words stir doubts that plagued me during my long flight across the sea. I'd had a long time to reflect on the chaos and bloodshed we'd left in our wake back in Midnight Crafters. Not from our own hands, technically, but like Hanna says... we could have tried to stop Galvanize. Even with her entire army against us, we could have interfered in the giant sky battle between the Empire and the Resistance, tried to save the lives of Shadows on both sides. But we hadn't. That was a choice we made, and one we're going to have to live with. I just wish I had some idea if it was the right one, and if any of these infuriatingly complex moral dilemmas would be clearer to Griffin than they are to me.

"I appreciate another 'grey morality' reality check," I simply say to Hanna, rolling my eyes. "Now, can we just go fishing and have a good time?"

We've finally reached a river that looks promising enough. Across the flowing water from us is a broken stone statue, eroded by time. Once it must have stood there as a proud sentinel, a guardian to greet new arrivals to the island. Now split in half, a human head and torso eerily lies there in the long grass. Its face stares up at the canopy. The lower body still stands, composed of coiling octopus tentacles. The statue has a heavenly, divine slant to its depiction, like a tribute to some deity.

"Half human, half Shadow," I say, narrowing my eyes as I study it. "Like you."

"Not like me," Hanna mutters.

"What's it meant to be?" I ask, prickling with curiosity.

"Didn't you ever hear the legend of the Majestics? Didn't Cirrus, in his memories?"

I shake my head.

"Majestics were mythical beings from our earliest legends, supposed to be part human and part Shadow. They were angels, essentially. Guardians who protected the Underworld. Ancient Shadows believed this was the final resting place of every Shadow's soul when they died. The Majestics were the shepherds of those souls."

"Cirrus probably would have read those legends - if

your Empire hadn't burned every single one of them," I say dryly. "Half human, half Shadow? I bet those were the first books to get burned in the Empire's schools."

I move closer to get a better look at the depiction of the Majestic. Shadows and humans, as a single being. My heart hurts as I think how much that's all Cirrus ever wanted. To find Griffin, and never be separated from him again. To find the missing half of himself... and never let it go. I have just never seen it depicted so literally - a Shadow and a human, actually fused into the same body. I understand the appeal of the myth to ancient Shadows all too easily. I suppose in all of our evolution we've never really changed all that much. The fear of being alone can be overwhelming.

I realise that despite her words, Hanna and I are both staring at the fractured statue with longing.

Breaking from her trance, Hanna jabs her spear into the river, testing the content of the waters. Further upstream, a short waterfall has wild salmon leaping and splashing through a torrent of foam.

"Stand at the mouth of that." Hanna retrieves her net from some bushes. It's masterfully woven, I have to grudgingly concede, weaved from some of the flax bushes we passed.

She sees me looking, and winks, grinning fiercely.

"Like you've said before, I hunted Cirrus and Griffin down in Kashlak forest. I know how to disguise myself, how to pass by undetected in the real world, how to hunt and cook on an open fire and find shelter when I need it. What survival skills do you have, what with your whole six months of personal life experience?"

Searching for a comeback but coming up empty, I reach the top of the waterfall and spread my wings to cast a shadow over the water. I mean to look quietly dignified, but I just feel like a dumb behemoth pigeon instead.

"Now!" Hanna shouts, breathless with the exhilaration of the hunt. "Do your scary thing."

"Scary thing?" I say dubiously.

"*'I'm Eclipse, fear me, bow to me!'* All that jazz."

I perch on the low wall of rocks, with foam surging past both of my feet. Taking in a breath, I roar as loud as I can muster. The sound echoes off the trees, driving out across the island. I snap with my beak at the spray of water, trying to catch the fish in mid-air. It feels like a game, and I can't help but enjoy it. I lift a foot to snatch a fish, but I've under-estimated my weariness from crossing an entire ocean in flight. I lose my balance unexpectedly, falling over the waterfall to splash into the river below.

Erupting fully from the water, I shake myself off, sending water in all directions. I hear Hanna laughing, and it surprises me. It's a bright, happy sound. A sound I didn't think she could make.

Suddenly, Hanna's laughter cuts.

"Eclipse," she says in warning. I turn to see what she's looking at.

We're surrounded.

The small forest clearing is surrounded by Shadows who have appeared as silently as the wind. They stand there, unmoving, staring at us.

"Uninhabited my arse," I say to Hanna. "What the hell are they doing here?"

"Stay back," Hanna warns them. "I have an Eclipse, and I'm not afraid to use it."

I rotate my head slowly, taking in the strange Shadows. At first I think there's only twenty, but then I see that the forest is full of them - enough to make it an army, if they were actually armed. Some of them are wearing brightly coloured feathers, bands and straps made from flax and reed. Others have clothes or ornaments that look like they're made of repurposed plastic and trash.

An electric blue frog with bark for clothing and a hippogriff with the front half of a toucan step apart, allowing a feline Shadow to stride to the front. She surveys us shrewdly, exuding such calm certainty and self-possession that I know at once that she must be their leader.

The feline Shadow appears fearsome, even though she looks like she's still in her teens. She's a wildcat with dappled fur of brown and black. White spots shine like trapped moonlight in her dark fur. She stretches her formidable claws languorously, her fierce green eyes piercing us. It feels like they see right through us.

This is their home. And the shamed ex-Empress and 'The Beast' Eclipse have stumbled right into it.

But then the wildcat grins, and gestures grandly with her paws.

"Welcome," she intones theatrically, "to the Islands of Sun and Moon!"

I blink. I turn to Hanna, and she looks just as stunned as I do.

"Come again?" I say.

The wildcat jumps down the incline to stride past Hanna, coming to where I stand in the river. She holds out a paw to me, retracting her curved claws. Ignoring Hanna quite blatantly.

"Hey man, I'm Joni," the wildcat grins up at me. She must be young, but there's swagger to her, a confidence in how she handles herself. She talks with a crackling energy, never wanting to stand still. "We're always happy to have new arrivals!"

Trying not to smile, I raise a single talon to shake her tiny paw.

"It's an honour," I say seriously, "and a privilege."

The others are whispering excitedly, clustering in tightly to get a better look at us.

"We didn't mean to intrude into your home," Hanna says carefully. "We're just passing through."

As I look around us though, I feel a flutter of realisation. These Shadows aren't staring at me in hatred and fear like they were in Sanctuary City. Instead they're staring at me as if I'm a long lost brother... and at the same time as if I'm something new. The emotion on their faces is one I can't quite place.

Is it actually possible they don't recognise who we are? How long have they been here? Hanna had said that no Shadows had stepped foot here for a very, very long time.

"You've gotta stay!" Joni is insisting. "Tonight there's the festival. There's going to be dancing, and drinks and feasting..."

"A festival?" I ask, intrigued. "Celebrating what?"

Joni shrugs.

"Okay, you've got us there. We don't know. We have a festival most nights." She grins sheepishly.

"Come on, Eclipse," Hanna says, amused. "Who are we to pass up a festival? Besides, this could be our last night in the Shadow world."

I shoot her a warning look. On edge, I study the faces of the Shadows surrounding us, but none of them seem to have reacted to what Hanna just said. Only a few of them mutter to each other, mainly looking slightly confused. Joni doesn't even blink.

They clearly want us to stay for the night. And remembering Celeste and her student friends back in Midnight Crafters, the last Shadows who enjoyed spending time with us, guilt compounds my desire to stay just a little longer. We failed to save them, and now, best case scenario, they're rotting in an Imperial cell somewhere. The least we can do is be the guest of this strange, rag-tag community for a night.

So that's how we end up strangely being led in a cheerful procession of a loose collection of island-dwelling Shadows toward the tip of the island. Many of them are excited to talk to us. Some of their children even come up to us to ask for autographs - not that they know who we are, I don't think, just because being strangers makes us... special, somehow.

The children beg for me to crane my head down, and when I do they place a long chain of alternating coloured flowers around my head like a crown. I blink, stymied, flushing at the kindness of the gesture.

"Who are you?" Hanna asks, looking across the vast numbers of Shadows moving through the trees. There are even more now than there were before, others joining us now that they can see we're not a threat.

"We're Shadows."

"Clearly," I say, "but are you from the Empire, the Resistance, or one of the Neutral Zones that hasn't declared yet for either side?"

"We're from everywhere," Joni says readily. I'm struck by her self-possession for someone so young, and how the others clearly look to her with trust and respect. Although thinking about it, she's about the same age as Hanna... around sixteen years or so. "We're everyone who's fleeing this stupid, wasteful civil war. We've got refugees from the Empire, Resistance, the Neutral Zones... We don't focus on our differences here on the island, we all want the same things. All of us took to the water in makeshift rafts and boats to escape our collapsing cities and countries. All in the hope of finding survival. No, more than that, a brighter life for our families, on some other shore." Joni's voice turns steely. "Some of us lost people we loved to the water on the way here. But we made it. More and more refugees wash up here every day. You're hardly the first."

"This island is sacred, taboo," Hanna says slowly, uncertainly. "Most Shadows wouldn't dream of stepping foot on it. It's drilled into all of us from childhood."

Joni shrugs, her tail flicking.

"It's given us a home. Somewhere the world can't touch us. There's nothing like a place where you feel like you belong, somewhere you can feel in your soul. They all feel they've finally found that again here. We have peace, with plentiful food and resources. It felt like a gift, that if it was meant for anyone it was meant for us. But..." Joni pauses.

"What?" I ask suspiciously.

"There's always strange happenings on the Island of Moon, in that palace across the water. Strange sounds carry across to us in the night. There's something... off about that place. We can feel it in our guts. That's why we're not living there in the lap of luxury. Some of us believe it's cursed, and not just the superstitious ones. Yesterday... some of our people went missing." Her lively energy drops for a moment, a grimness passing across her face. She glances at the others, troubled, then drops her voice to a murmur, so that only Hanna and I can hear. "It was like our people were sucked into thin air. Only one of them has reappeared so far, talking about things that sound impossible."

I feel a sudden tingling of excitement. Hanna was right. The entrance to the Underworld must be here, our way through to the other side. We're so close.

Hell, what am I going to say to Griffin? I exhale, anxieties playing in the corner of my mind like silhouettes on the wall of a cave. The answer to that isn't important right now, I scowl broodingly.

"But don't let that put you off this place," a child butts in jauntily, cutting through the tense silence. She beams. "The bananas that grow here are like, super-good. Really creamy and sugary."

"Damn, I really wanted out of this place," Hanna mutters under her breath. "But nobody told me there was *bananas.*"

Then the child is suddenly shoving a banana in Hanna's face, beaming. Hanna freezes, then smiles back, accepting the banana. I laugh. As soon as the child happily turns away again, Hanna glares at me.

"Are your people here for or against humans?" I ask Joni curiously. I'm hoping that the free Shadows of this world will decide to open themselves up to the humans, to no longer buy Raven's lies that they were a disease.

Joni shrugs her feline shoulders.

"Some Shadows here fear them, some still tell whispered stories of the day when humans will arrive from the other world to save us all." She delivers this as if she's trying really hard not to roll her eyes. "But most of us don't care."

"You... don't care?" I say, dumbstruck.

"Come on, man, we just want food and shelter. For our friends and families back home to be safe. These humans, these aliens from another world..." She looks troubled again. "We know nothing about them. They didn't arrive to save us when our countries were falling apart. If we hadn't taken action ourselves, if we'd just waited around for humans...we would have died. I mean, that's only how *I* feel. I try to be a representative here. It's not about just me."

My head is still struggling with this when Hanna taps the side of my leg.

"Bird-brain," Hanna says, grinning. "Look up."

I look above us and breathe in in wonder.

The trees here grow taller than the others, stretching high above me into the sky. Walkways spiral around the ancient trunks. Emerald fireflies flicker through the trees, and weave around the arching wooden walkways between them. And perched in the branches around our heads, lit by the slowly creeping sunset, are homes. Houses shaped like lanterns that glow with golden light. Some of the structures supporting the houses look hand-built, while in other places it looks as if the bark of the tree has warped organically, growing itself intentionally into sheltered alcoves and pockets along the trunk to offer shelter and protection. Rope swings and sleeping baskets hang down from the branches, suspended beside the homes. An entire village in the treetops. Extra walkways and shelter have been added from rubbish and makeshift items, including tattered commercial signs advertising Stormbrew and TV shows. All of which must have washed up on the shores of these islands, happily repurposed by the refugees.

Filtering through the forest comes the rhythm of dance music, building slowly. I can make out the pumping sound of drums, the sound of wooden instruments and flutes. Modern music made from the most ancient of materials, infused with a sense of wild joy and abandon.

Hanna laughs at my expression, and there's joy in hers.

"You should see your face," she chortles. "Eclipse fancied himself an Emperor. But in all of Cirrus' memories, that little dragon-parrot never made it outside of White Isles. There's an entire *world* out here. This? This is only a glimpse of it. There are so many wonders that you haven't seen yet." Her voice grows passionate, and her eyes mist with nostalgia. "The golden glitter of the frosted Mountains of Hope. The sunlit glades with singing fawns in Olympia... I visited all of them. I miss them so much." She looks up at the tree houses and smiles in admiration, her smile like starlight. "But I've never seen this place. There are so many magical secrets squirreled away in this world. Even if I travelled all my life I'm not sure if I'd have a chance to see all of them."

I take in her expression. The wonder she has for her own world. It's a wonder that she always seems to be trying to suppress, to hide under the toughness of her edgy persona.

She's about to leave this world, all of her people... behind.

"Perhaps..." I say tentatively, "Perhaps we'll have a chance to come back and explore it all with our humans."

Hanna's smile falls.

"Perhaps," she says quietly.

The Shadows in the hanging village above us are streaming down the ladders and wooden walkways. Dropping down to the forest floor to join onto our posse. Then we hang a left toward the very tip of the Island of Sun. We surge out of the tree line and over a sand dune, a beach revealed down before us.

There are small huts dotted here and there, and I see what may be volleyball nets, and an outdoor stage where a band plays instruments made from shells and hand-carved wood. Crowds of refugees are already dancing in a throng to the music, illuminated by flashing rainbow lights from the dangling lanterns overhead. The music plays out across the sand and over the waves, a kind of joyous mania gripping the Shadows.

It makes me think of how Cirrus was never invited to dance at school discos when he was growing up in his own world. It also brings back memories of a dance party Cirrus witnessed at Winghold, before the place burnt to the ground.

Hanna and I get caught up in it. I can't describe it. It seems ludicrous, ridiculous. We're two of the most wanted fugitives in the Shadow world. But suddenly we're caught up in the music, in the sound, in this rising fever... and before I know it we're dancing. I've never danced in my entire life. But we dance with Joni and her people, flailing their tentacles, wings and appendages too unique to name in a furry, in a throng of scales and fur. Hanna and I catch ourselves laughing. I feel so far from that horrible prison which I escaped from in Sanctuary. It feels so strange... to feel like I belong.

A full moon hangs over the island. As the night moves onward in a strange hypnotic dance of light and colour, Hanna and I find ourselves moving away from the sound and the sweaty bodies. She has a blanket draped over her shoulder, and she's drinking some sort of sweet nectar cocktail, while I sip mine through a reed straw straight from a colossal coconut. Joni's people foraged it - the normal sized ones hadn't been doing much for me.

We walk a safe distance from the party. The night air is cool, the soft sand feeling good as it swells between my talons. I perch on a low sand dune with Hanna sitting beside me, nursing our drinks as we stare out across the dark, infinite expanse before us, streaked with silver.

A warm ocean breeze sweeps its way up the beach, rustling my feathers and Hanna's wings. It's soothing, bringing the smell of the salt air to mix with the scent of wood smoke. The night sky is brimming with stars, a dreamscape pierced with glittering light. Hanna's face is covered in dark stains from snacking on the vine of hyleberries beside us.

"What?" Hanna asks, looking at me sideways.

"Hmm?"

"You're smiling." she says suspiciously.

"Just..." I grin, "the Empress and Eclipse, hanging together at a beach party. Utterly absurd. No one would believe it."

"A temporary truce," she corrects me, but the corner of her mouth threatens to bend into a smile as well, and the next moment she's chuckling too.

"Your face is an absolute mess," I say, laughing. "It's appalling. How do you even get juice on your forehead?"

"Oh, I'm sorry, am I embarrassing you?" She chucks a handful of berries up at me playfully. I manage to snap one in my beak.

Hanna looks out at the ocean as our perverse fit of

giggles subsides. "You know? I had fun tonight," she says, staring almost longingly out beyond the crashing waves.

"I thought you weren't capable of having fun."

"That's not true," Hanna snorts. "I've had lots of fun in my life."

"Oh really? Was that when Raven was training you to be the Empress, keeping you locked up like his little pet?"

"I had friends my own age."

"Any who weren't terrified of being strung up in the dungeons by Raven if they talked back to you?"

Hanna is lost for a comeback.

"You don't... know me," she mutters.

"I remember you saying that the most fun you ever had was being on the run from the Empire with Cirrus and Griffin. Being shot at. Hiding your own identity. If that's your idea of fun, clearly you've never had any."

"So now you're a fun expert?" Hanna scoffs. "You've spent most of your life in prison."

I look back in the direction of the festival, watching the Shadows dance joyfully in the flashing lights. It's so simple. Living their lives through these small acts of happiness.

"You know, I told Ember I'd gladly burn this world to the ground if that's what it took to find Griffin," I say, hardly believing I'd said that only a day or so ago. Has it only been that long? "But this place... it isn't so bad. I'm not saying there aren't a few Shadows in it though who I'd love to tear to pieces."

"Arseholes are universal," Hanna agrees.

I look down at the faerie, sitting nearly beside me on the dune. The two of us just sitting in admiration of the moon.

"Did you really try to be a good leader?" I ask, the question burning in me too intensely to ignore. "When you ruled this world..." What do I want to ask her? "Did you really *try* to make their lives better?" I finally say.

"I did," Hanna says, depressed. "I thought I had. Along with Raven I united this world's nations together. We stopped their warring and infighting. I introduced the new technologies Raven designed, tried to usher in the dawn of a healthier, more connected future. And I succeeded, even if it's still haphazardly and unevenly distributed. My entire time growing up I thought it was my life's purpose to make the lives of Shadows better. Happier."

"Does that include hating humans?"

"Raven told me that everyone needs a monster in the closet," Hanna responds, her gaze lost deep in the ocean. "Something to fear to keep them in line. But I still read the old myths when he wasn't paying attention. Raven was human, and he was my everything. They couldn't be so bad, I figured. They could even be something good. I think helping Raven to teach this world otherwise may have been my greatest mistake."

I see a haunted look come across her face, her lips pressing tightly together. I'm getting better at reading her. There's something coming, something she's scared to ask. So I wait for it to come.

"Do you... do you see Cirrus?" Hanna whispers, so quiet I can barely hear her. I look down at her in shock. Her voice trembles. "You said you have some of his memories. Can you ever... hear him? Talk to him?"

"No," I lie.

Hanna nods, then bows her head, pulling her knees in to her.

"If you do... tell him, tell him I'm sorry," she says. I see a tear streak down her cheek. "He and Griffin were the only friends I'd ever had. The way I felt about Griffin... I did things I never thought I'd do. I ruined everything. But I didn't mean for Cirrus to die. I'd do anything, anything to take that back. I had a chance, a chance to change. To not be the bad guy. Instead I did whatever I thought it would take to get Griffin back. I see Cirrus all the time. In my dreams." Her gaze is haunted.

The night grows darker. One million stars burn only more brightly against the inky black above.

I move my eyes from the stars above down to Hanna to see that she's fallen into an uneasy sleep. She slumbers beside me, violet wings splayed outward in the sand, looking so small. Fragile.

Gently, I pull her blanket over her with my beak to cover her from the wind.

A small pebble falls to the sand beside us. Looking down from the dune I see Joni standing on the beach, beckoning expressively for me to join her.

The waves are breaking against the shore, violently flurried by a strong wind. As I join Joni, I can see the Shadows making their way back from the festival through the trees, to the warm bungalows that await them. With their friends, their families. Something aches in my chest.

"I'm not used to being summoned for secret rendezvous," I say. "We've really enjoyed the party, but if this is meant to be a romantic thing, I'm sorry. I didn't mean to mislead you."

Beneath her fur, I think Joni is flushing.

"What? No. That's not what I'm... oh, you're messing with me."

"I am," I smile. "What did you want to talk about?"

"Just that... I'm guessing, you've realised that you're different," Joni tells me.

"What?" I say, miming shock. "That's why everyone keeps staring at me? Wow. Thanks for solving that one, it's been bugging me."

"You're special," Joni continues. "Can't you see how my people have been looking at you? Not like you're something strange or threatening. I know you've seen it. They're looking at you like you're hope."

It's true, I realise, feeling strange. I hadn't given it a name, but I had seen something in their eyes I hadn't seen elsewhere.

"Hope? Why?"

"Don't you believe you were sent here for a reason?" Joni asks.

I'm tongue-tied for a moment.

"I came to these islands to fulfil a promise to someone," I finally say. "A promise I mean to keep." Griffin's face hovers before me, but it's murkier and more indistinguishable than it's ever been. Like I'm clinging onto an idea of a thing, the ghost of a memory, while the actual thing feels strangely removed from me.

"You're trying to go to the human world, right? That's what the Empress said." Joni catches my look. "Yes," she says with a roll of her eyes, "I actually recognise her too. Even out of the ridiculous makeup and clothes. Look Eclipse, you're no stranger to pain, but you could heal a lot of it. You have no idea of the impact you could have." Joni's voice is intense. She stares at me with something I am not used to seeing. Is that hope again? Belief?

But I snort, shaking my head.

"From the moment I was born I dreamed of having an *'impact'*. This world doesn't want me."

"Maybe not. But it needs you. Haven't you ever had faith that you're part of a greater design? That you were given this body, these powers, for a reason?" Joni challenges me. She wriggles her ears in frustration. "For a giant Shadow, you think so small. You get burned once, so you run away from your home world."

"I'm a freak of nature," I say in a low voice. Bitterly. "Your little club only treats me as if I'm one of the family because your people don't know about the things I've done. This world is not my home. Nor my responsibility."

"This world is in your *blood*. You're part of us, and we're part of you. Wherever you choose to go," Joni says softly. "But I hope you stay. My people... they're scared. They don't know how to fight. They party to forget what they've left behind. But we can't hide here forever. I spent so much time just trying to help them escape the civil war, to save them. Now I can feel it in my bones that the world will reach us no matter where we run to. I need to teach them to fight. To own the power that they have inside themselves, to do something to try and make this world just. But I don't know how to do that. I feel... I feel like you do. Like together, we could show them the way. Help me, Eclipse. Please. Be a part of something that matters."

I stare down at Joni longingly... and fearfully.

"You're asking me to... what are you asking?"

"Eclipse?"

I turn quickly to see Hanna walking down toward us. For some reason, I feel weirdly guilty. Anxious, even.

"They want me to stay," I say, self-conscious. "To 'make a difference.'"

"I heard,' Hanna says, sounding confused. "But we can make a difference by getting back to the human world. By helping Griffin to unite Shadows and humans together."

But Griffin... Griffin hasn't come back for me, I think painfully. Why not? Why am I going to such lengths for him, after I already nearly lost my life? Maybe he's changed his mind. Maybe he still misses Cirrus too much. Whatever I do for him, I can never live up to the memory of his dead Shadow. The Shadow who died for me to be brought into life.

But these Shadows are prepared to be my family. They could be.

And what if uniting humans and Shadows doesn't work? What if all of the problems blossoming across the Shadow world right now are too deep? What if even with their humans, Shadows can't just change who they are overnight? We have to admit there's a chance that joining the worlds will just be putting a Band-Aid on an arrow-wound.

It's farce. Hanna and I are right on the eve of victory, of finally being with our humans. I know the old wisdom that it's always darkest before the dawn, but thick clouds of doubts are whispering to me, corroding my faith in Griffin and our connection, causing me to question everything.

I don't trust myself to speak for a moment. I'm taken by surprise, thrown by the conversation with Joni against my expectations. Not so long ago I dreamed of conquering this world. Now one young refugee Shadow says she believes in me and it feels too good to be reality.

"But what if we could?" I ask Hanna slowly. "Make a difference here? What if that is what we're meant to do?"

"Sorry?" Hanna says, equally thrown.

"Griffin and his team could be working to connect the worlds at any moment. Why not stay with Joni's people and help them to take back some of what they lost, while we wait for Griffin to open the gates between the worlds? Maybe you were right about Galvanize. Right about us not having an option to just stay out of everything going on in this world right now. We could stay and do something that matters."

"Not her," Joni says coldly. I look down at the dappled cat, her arms folded tightly. Her voice is firm. "She can't stay here. The offer was for you, Eclipse. Just you."

"Why?" Hanna demands, even though she already knows.

"Seriously? You think I didn't recognise who you were?" Joni says, disbelieving. "You're the Empress, or you used to be. You turned this world into something unspeakable. The darkness, the sickness in our society, whatever you want to call it... you're the one who introduced it, who helped it to grow. You've committed horrible acts."

My crest flares, and I ruffle my feathers intimidatingly.

"You think I don't know that?" I challenge Joni. "I know first-hand what she's capable of."

"Eclipse..." Hanna starts.

"She tortured Cirrus, all right?" I say, my voice dangerous. Hanna snaps her mouth shut. "She tried to split Cirrus' connection with Griffin so she could make Griffin her human instead of his." I take a sinister step toward Joni and she staggers backward, suddenly frightened. "Hanna tortured Cirrus' mind, all out of her own misdirected loneliness and messed up fantasy. She's selfish. Imperfect. Dangerous. But once upon a time, she really did care about the Shadows of this world. And she's someone you want on your side, not the other one."

"The others won't accept her once they figure out who she is," Joni says, meeting my gaze. She's quivering, prey before a predator. "I'm sure some of them already have. She has the right to be our guest for a night, especially as she was your companion. But the night's done. She's not one of us."

"So you blame her for all your problems? She fought hard as the Empress to make your lives better," I smoulder. "Yes, the Empire did unspeakable things, but Raven is the one you have an issue with. Not her. Understand?"

"*Eclipse.*" Hanna is hovering in my vision now on her violet wings, illuminated in the moonlight. Her face is brave, determined. "Don't worry about me," she says, her voice hard. "Really, it's fine. They're right. It doesn't matter what I intended to do as Empress. Just that I grew the sickness at the heart of this world. I made it worse. I'll go on to find my human, alone. I've always worked better alone." She smiles, and there's pain in it. "The entrance to the Underworld is in Aeyu Palace if you change your mind. Stay. Be happy. Dance. For tonight, at least... don't worry about tomorrow."

Hanna looks at me, and it's a haunted look. I don't understand what's going on in her untameable brain, if she's angry, or hurt, or if she just doesn't care about being shunned by these refugees as much as I do.

But her shoulders look heavy as she takes to the night's sky, flitting off into the silvery moonlight, away over the trees toward Aeyu Palace.

"I was wrong to take it out on you, Joni," I say quietly. "Your people are lucky to have you."

"She poisons everything around her," Joni says softly as we watch her go. "You shouldn't trust her."

"I know," I say, hushed, feeling strangely lonely as I watch Hanna flit away into the night, "like how you shouldn't trust me either. Except for some reason you can't explain... you do."

I bound away from Joni and lunge into the air. I flap hard, my powerful wings lifting me so I'm quickly above the island. I need my own space, to breathe, to try and find some kind of perspective. Clouds have been moving in, a gale blowing out across the islands. I lose myself in them. It feels like a different realm up here, closer to the spirit world, somehow apart from everything down below.

Confused, tormented, I try to clear my head. I don't know why Hanna's abrupt departure shook me. I think of her role in Cirrus' death. Whether it was her experimenting on Cirrus that had caused it, or something that had come from Griffin's own darkness when he murdered Nugwai that night, Hanna was still connected to Cirrus' fate. And through that, my birth. Cirrus had died because of me too. I *replaced* him to come into this world. And even if that was unintentional, it's a scar, a burden that I'll always carry. It's something which Hanna shares with me, which will always tie us together. I hadn't realised it until now, now that I'm up here alone in the air. My sense of guilt at Cirrus' death is overwhelming. I imagine Hanna flying alone through the darkness to that strange, intimidating palace that guards the Underworld. I think of the refugee Shadows trying to sleep in their makeshift beds down below, trying to forget the world that they lost. The homes that they were forced to flee from for their own safety, in a civil war that none of them chose.

What would Cirrus have wanted, if he was forced to choose? Would he have wanted Griffin, the human he loved, or would Cirrus have wanted to find a family in the world that had been so reluctant to accept him. Zephyr had tricked and abandoned him so many times over. Cirrus had been so misused by the Empire, by everyone he had known. Would he have longed for Shadows to belong with just as badly? What are the parts of Cirrus that Cirrus would have wanted to honour and protect?

I know what he chose, though. He chose Griffin, and now Cirrus is dead as a consequence.

But I'm not Cirrus, I'm Eclipse. And I suppose that means I have to make my own meaning for myself.

Feeling an awful rending in my chest, I finally drop down below the cloud.

I fly away from Joni and her people, into the night. Following in the direction Hanna left, on course toward the Island of Moon and Aeyu Palace. I fly toward Griffin, my counterpart, the human who Cirrus loved... and died for. And I fly after Hanna, the only person I really know.

That's when I hear the sound that makes my heart lurch in my chest. A rattle that echoes through the trees, and splits the silence of the island. A sound I heard for the first time in the skies of Sanctuary City.

Guns. Guns with bullets in them. The sound comes from where lights glow like fireflies in the canopy behind me. Joni's camp in the trees.

With a rush I remember the human helicopters slowly rotating toward me, the killer steel prepared to be unloaded into my skin. I remember the flaming bomb sites across Cirrus' home city.

And following the sound of bullets comes a hauntingly familiar cry.

"Hanna!" I scream, and my voice echoes out across the island's canopy and over the ocean. Fear floods through me. I divert my course, flying hard back toward the camp, hoping against hope that I'm not too late.

2

THE GREAT UNKNOWN

Griffin

I move along the wall of my bedroom, examining the drawings and crayon scribblings from my childhood. One of the pieces of paper stands out to me - two curving brackets covered in green glitter, with a sparkly gold star in the centre. I trace my finger along the pathways of glitter forming a peculiar symbol:

(*)

"What does this mean?" I ask. Curiosity piqued, I turn to my Shadow. A green feathered cockatiel with the lower body of a dragon, his crest sticks up high into the air, making him look cheeky.

"You don't remember?" Cirrus says uncertainly. The voice he

uses when he realises that there's still things about our childhood that I don't recall, that I'm still remembering everything about our friendship.

"I'm sorry," I say, and mean it. "Remind me."

"It was our thing. You'd draw it for me whenever you wanted to make me feel better, or I would whenever I wanted to comfort you. We said it was two arms - or wings - with a star of specialness in the middle. Your Mum called it a Mental Hug."

I look at my Shadow, raising an eyebrow.

"We were five," Cirrus shrugs, embarrassed. I grin at the dragon-parrot, as his tail swishes back and forth. Like he's a cross between a cat and a demented gargoyle. I feel strange, like a little kid waking up blurry eyed on Christmas morning. Overwhelmed, puzzled, but above all...

"What?" Cirrus asks softly, even though he can see the answer in my mind.

"I'm happy," I say, smiling at him.

"Griffin!"

Someone's shouting my name. The dream peels away, becoming just that. A dream.

No...

Mumbling reproachfully, I try to bury myself back into it, to remember the feel of being there, of having Cirrus right there beside me, as real as I am. Breathing, and very much alive. Every part of me hurts with missing him.

"Grif, talk to me! Are you okay?"

Phoebe. It's Phoebe. That's strange. She sounds worried for some reason. Why all the drama? It sounds as if her voice is coming from a very long way away anyhow.

"Grif, if you don't wake up, I swear I'll..."

Finally, I open my eyes wide, startling her.

"Boo," I grin, delirious.

Phoebe doesn't find it funny. I'm shocked to see there are tears in her eyes. She grabs me by the shirt, pulling me out of my seat and dumping me on the floor of the jet. Pinning me down, she starts madly clubbing me with both hands.

"I'm sorry, I'm sorry!" I cry under the onslaught, rapidly coming back to reality. Trying and failing to defend myself against the pummelling.

"DO YOU WANT TO DIE FOR REAL?" Phoebe says, furious.

"Okay, okay, it wasn't funny, I'm sorry!"

Then as quick as her anger flared she's suddenly getting off me and storming away, down the length of the jet. Disorientated, I try to remember where the heck I am.

We're still on the jet. Obviously. But we've stopped moving. In other words, we've landed. Through the windows it's black outside, probably night time, which doesn't help me to get a sense of our surroundings.

Did we make it? To the island?

My head feels sore, and I touch it gingerly. My hand comes away with blood. I must have banged it against something. I'm guessing we had a rough landing. That explains why I'm feeling all dazed and goo-gah in the brain.

I bolt upright, and my head swims. I grit my teeth.

"We were followed," I say as it hits me. Our hasty landing on the island near Bermuda, the screaming of the engines...

"There were other jets," I say, remembering. I cringe as I heave myself up. "They followed us to the island. Maybe they'd even been tracking us from New York."

Phoebe is further down the aisle from me, stuffing items into our packs. We already changed during the flight. I'll miss our fancy party attire from New York, but now Phoebe and I are dressed in tight black combat suits. Perfect for a stealth mission. Phoebe looks deadly, a hunting knife sheathed in her belt. While Phoebe's outfit is a good fit, mine's clearly for someone bigger than I am.

"Stop playing dumb. I'm not in the mood for more games," she says, her voice tight.

"Seriously, Phoebe, I think I might have a concussion or something. Just... fill in the gaps, who were the jets following us?"

"How am I meant to know?" Phoebe snaps. "The US Military, or whatever international strike team the human world has put together to track down anything to do with Camerons or Shadows... hey, this is your messed up future, I'm just a visitor here, *remember*? I'm just lucky I managed to get the jet autopilot to land this thing and in one piece. Get up, we have to get going."

I'm on my feet. As long as I don't discover I really do have a delayed concussion, I don't feel too banged up. And the urgency in Phoebe's tone is getting through to me. I look around the jet. It's big enough for a full chartered flight of passengers, and I've always thought of it as a luxury doomsday bunker for the sky, everything you need crammed into a single aircraft. But the scope of it just adds to the sense of loneliness. Phoebe and me the only passengers aboard.

"Wait. Those other jets followed us here, to the island," I say, the true fudgestorm we're in starting to sink in. "Maybe they know about the station now. Maybe they're trying to get to it and take it over like all the others, before we can get there to activate it. We *have* to beat them there."

"Now you're getting it." Standing, Phoebe chucks me my pack, hard. I grab it. She tosses me a pair of night goggles too, then folds her arms, as if she can't stand to have them idle.

I look at her, and for a moment I force myself to imagine how I'd feel if Phoebe had died during the landing, and I was left all alone. Suddenly I feel terrible for my *'boo'* line, acting as if playing dead was all a joke.

"I'm sorry," I say softly, stepping closer to Phoebe. "For messing with you. I'm okay, really."

"Don't do that again," is all Phoebe says in a low voice. Then she turns. "We've got to go. Now."

It's pretty freaky and unsettling, having our first glimpse of the island by night, knowing that we're pretty much alone on an island in the middle of the Bermuda Triangle. The only exception of course being that there may be some hostile soldiers hunting us, out there somewhere among the tree trunks. If bullets are coming for us, we'll have zero warning, and zero defence. The darkness is our only protection.

Pale trees and disconcerting shapes press in at us as we run through the forest, the island an eerie green through our night vision goggles. We're in one of the most out-of-the-way places Mum could find to stash a secret station if everything went to hell. And went to hell it certainly did.

"You sure your head wound isn't serious?" Phoebe finally asks when we stop to catch our breath. "You seem to be doing okay. Any symptoms?"

"Nope, just one question. Why are the trees all made of spaghetti?"

"Haha. Have you ever noticed you use humour as defence mechanism when crap gets too real?"

"*Your* crap is too real. No, but seriously, I think I'm fine." I frown. "Remind me though, why is your hair blonde?"

"That would be because we each dyed our hair to sneak into Cameron Technologies in New York for a heist. Like, hours ago."

"Right." I nod, and wince. "Yeah, that sounds right. Good, I'm all caught up now."

"Also, heads up, you look like a midget Ron Weasley. Just if you look in a mirror and get a fright."

Phoebe's mood seems to be lifting again. It's suddenly dawning how close we are to the Station. To the end of the road.

"Excited?" Phoebe whispers as we move.

"Excited *and* so scared I might vomit," I say, upbeat.

Phoebe looks at me.

"Why?" she asks.

"Just, Eclipse. What if... there's a chance we were wrong about each other? Maybe I did imagine his voice in my head. Maybe when Cirrus died... my Shadow died. Maybe Eclipse is somebody else's Shadow, and I'm just... lingering here. Like a ghost, when Cirrus is on the other side." I exhale shakily. It feels a relief, saying some of that aloud. "Sorry, there wasn't much humour there. I didn't know how to turn that one into a joke."

"I'm scared too," Phoebe says quietly, "that things will be different between Ember and me. That maybe she's already grieved for me and moved on. But you know what your Mum used to say?"

"What?"

"My connection with Ember, and yours with Cirrus... your Mum said they were the most powerful connections out of the whole team. Something about our telepathic links with our Shadows was at an entire other level of intensity. When Melissa said it, it was like she believed we were special. That we were destined for something."

"Like somehow we were always going to end up tramping across this island?" I say. I mean to be sarcastic, but my voice comes out hopeful. "That it was always going to be us who finished this so that we could meet our Shadows again?"

Phoebe smiles, and shrugs.

"Who knows?"

"So, what's the first thing you'll do in the new world order?" I ask.

"You know? I hadn't really thought that far ahead."

"Oh, yeah," I tease. "Never mind the fact that we're maybe less than an hour away from changing the worlds. What happens after hasn't crossed your mind?"

"All right, Mr I've-Got-Everything-Figured-Out. What will you do?"

I open my mouth, then frown.

"I don't know," I confess. "Get some Burger Max?"

Phoebe laughs.

"Okay. That's our big plan for the new world order, we'll eat some Burger Max with Ember and Eclipse."

Through my goggles I look at her, a green, smiling gremlin.

"You know," I say, "after that funk you were in when I brought you back from the dead... it's good to see you smile."

"I didn't know if I could. So, did you use to go to Burger Max a lot? Before you found out Shadows were real? I don't know anything about your old life, before all of... this."

"Yeah, it was pretty much just hanging out at Burger Max," I say honestly. "Just so I could be around people and feel less alone."

"Wow," Phoebe says. "That's sad. And I begged for food for a living." Phoebe looks sideways at me. "So meeting Cirrus again was an even bigger deal for you, huh?"

"Yeah." My voice breaks slightly. "I just miss the little things about him, you know? How for some reason he had to sing each morning to welcome the sun into the sky. His weird love of alcoholic cereal which I in no way support. And this thing we had, when we were younger. Mental Hugs. I was around him since he hatched. He wasn't just my counterpart, he was my brother." I come to a stop, gasping for breath. We're climbing up an incline, and it's more punishment than I'm used to. I lean against a tree trunk for support.

"Here. Let me look at that," Phoebe says, moving in to check my head wound. She moves my hair out of the way, examining it.

"Am I gonna live, Doc?" I wince.

"Either you're going to die in five seconds, or... it's just a Band-Aid job, no stitches required. I'm going to guess the second." Phoebe takes off her pack to retrieve the first-aid kit. "I'd tell you to avoid exercise shortly after banging your head, if we weren't in a pivotal race with armed soldiers somewhere on the island."

Gently, she plasters the Band-Aid over my wound, smoothing it carefully around the cut.

"Ember was like a sister to me to," Phoebe says. "She

forced me to get over my phobia of fire pretty quick. It was a bit of a crash course really. I'd been terrified of naked flame, ever since…" she trails off.

"Calvin told me about your sister," I say quietly. "What happened with your family. I hope it's okay he told me."

"About how I burnt down our house?" Phoebe smiles grimly.

"About how you got your little sister out of there alive. You saved her."

"Yeah, well… that's not how my Mum saw it," she mutters.

"Is that why you push people away?" I ask hesitantly. "You're trying to protect them, like you did with Anna?"

"Grif, I've failed to protect everyone I ever tried to. My friend Bee, Taylor, Melissa, your whole family…"

"You almost died trying to protect my family."

"And it still wasn't enough," she says simply.

"I bet Ember was proud of you," I say. "Protecting the innocent, fighting for Shadows and humans to be able to live together in peace… just like she does. You two have a lot in common. She's pretty kick-arse too."

Phoebe smiles painfully, tears in her eyes.

"When I thought I was dying, Ember promised me that she'd always keep fighting. That she'd make my sacrifice worth it."

"She fought like hell," I say. "I bet you she's still fighting over there right now trying to make a better universe for everyone. Just like you are, Pheebs."

Phoebe looks at me, taken aback.

"What," I ask, "Is Pheebs a no-go as a nickname? It just slipped out."

"It's just that… it reminds me of someone."

"Is it bad?"

"No." Phoebe smiles. "No, I like it."

We suddenly realise we've spent too long idle, and set off again at a jog. Relying on our night vision goggles to see each other, and to dodge low hanging branches and vines.

"You have no idea what a relief it is to have someone my own age I can actually talk to about this stuff," I say breathlessly. "About Shadows. Calvin, Zephyr and Mr Falco didn't really count. I just want to say... I'm glad you came back."

Phoebe nods. With surprise I see a tear trickling down her cheek. "I'm so sorry you lost Cirrus," she says softly, her eyes reflecting my pain. "Especially when you'd just found him again. I can't imagine what that must have been like. Losing him. Being with him when... I just feel for you so much. I'm here. If you ever want to talk it out."

I nod, but there's a lump in my throat and I can't get the words out. She seems to understand.

"And I'm sorry I couldn't save your family," she manages. "The night of the fire, the night that I banished Taylor. I'm sorry I couldn't save your Mum."

"I'm sorry that we failed to connect the worlds," I say, and I mean it. "After everything you sacrificed."

Phoebe smiles at me.

"Well... this way we get to do it together."

As we reach the top of a rise, I move a low hanging frond out of the way for us - and gasp.

We have a clear view out across the island. The Cam Tech goggles we're wearing having a long range in clear conditions. Further down toward the coast, I can make out an artificial metal structure, overgrown with vines, blurred through the goggles, but unmistakable.

"I don't believe it," Phoebe breathes beside me. "The station. It's real."

I feel a wave of ecstasy, staring down at it. The key to Mum's hopeful vision of the future. The station that can birth a new order, two worlds in harmony. The secret to activating the portals that will help me get Eclipse back from the Shadow world. Undiscovered here until now, placed here by Mum as a backup for a worst case scenario. A scenario just like this one.

Phoebe puts a hand on my shoulder.

"I just want you to know..." she says awkwardly, "Calvin and the others, they're here with us. They're still part of this, and wherever they are, I'm sure they feel it. That we're out here, honouring them."

My smile tightens. Phoebe's trying to comfort me, and I appreciate that. But she doesn't know that was the worst possible thing she could have said. Because now I have to think about my brother again.

Calvin. He's in some high-security human prison somewhere, being interrogated right now. Along with Zephyr and Mr Falco. My feelings are pretty complicated around all three of them, but my big brother especially. And no one deserves to be in whatever horrible hole they're being held right now, but even with that colouring things... just thinking about Calvin still feels like flushing a toxin through my bloodstream, a poisonous anger that's quick to spread to every part of me.

My brother pretended to give me what I wanted more than anything. His love, his respect. He manipulated me just so I'd hack the Oracle device for him. Just so he could take all the credit, and fulfil the promise he made to Phoebe years ago to connect the worlds. Phoebe, the dead girl who had been the only person he'd ever loved.

I remember Calvin trying to use my connection with my Shadow to activate the portals, because he believed his dysfunctional relationship with his own Shadow was too far gone. He'd forced my hand against the controls to activate the portals, so hard that it hurt me, and he didn't even care. Like I was necessary collateral damage.

Mr Falco told me that Calvin had almost let him and me burn along with Mum's lab the night she died. We might have, if Mr Falco hadn't saved us. I hadn't been enough for Calvin to live for. I recall the moment in the safe house, the one which turned out to not be very safe. I remember the moment when I asked Calvin if he had ever wished that Phoebe had survived that night instead of me... and he couldn't honestly answer me to my face.

And the worst part of all of it? How much of myself I still see in Calvin. He's the guy I looked up to the whole time I was growing up. The man I wanted to be some day. The only kind of parent I had.

I've never hated anyone this much, and at the same time the grief that something may have happened to him is enough to make it hard to breathe. It's a storm inside me that's been there since the safe house. Ever present. Tearing me apart at my centre, over and over again.

Suddenly, the tumultuousness inside me seems to leak out into the world around us. I realise the ground beneath us has started to tremble. A rumbling that's running through the entire island.

I turn to Phoebe, both of are in shock, slow to understand what exactly is happening. Both of us unsure if we're in the middle of an earthquake or some kind of attack. Then the very air seems to start brightening, shining, until I cry out in pain and I tear the night goggles from my face. I feel Phoebe grab me, tackling me to the ground. Holding onto her, the two of us trying to shield each other, I jam my eyes closed but the light still sears through my eyelids, brighter and brighter and...

Then it's over. The sense of the very earth rising up beneath us is gone. The island is still again.

Blinking, I open my eyes, waiting for the dancing spots of light to dissipate from my vision. Trying to readjust again to the darkness of night.

"Ummm... Griffin?" Phoebe asks. As we slowly get to our feet, we look around at the bioluminescent ferns surrounding us. Like peacock feathers, circles at their tips glowing with blue ethereal light.

Those definitely weren't there before.

Somewhere in the distance is the boom of thunder. The sounds of a storm encroaching. A storm that I swear didn't exist a minute ago.

That's not all. In the patch of forest illuminated around us, we can make out stone protrusions, ancient worn stone pillars and fragments of ruins, engraved with patterns of triangles and knots that look almost Celtic in design.

"That's not possible," I breathe, blown away.

Can it be?

I'm back.

"Grif... we're here," Phoebe says, grabbing onto me and pulling me close. "We're here, aren't we? We're in the Shadow world," she whispers in wonder. She shakes me to make sure she's getting through to me. "The actual Shadow world."

"I know," I say. Despite my shock, I find myself laughing

at her reaction. Phoebe laughs too, a beautiful sound of pure happiness. She turns to me, and her grin is so dazzling I have to turn away.

But it's pretty quickly becoming clear to me that our change in dimensional address may complicate things.

"I suppose active stations could cause a flux between the worlds in the surrounding area," I say rapidly to Phoebe, trying to make sense of this. I'm reeling. It still feels unreal that suddenly I'm back, that we've left our own dimension entirely behind. We were so close... "As the barrier between the worlds grows thinner, Rips are more likely to tear open. But that means... that means that the secret station is active. When the others were switched online, that one was too."

"It's just waiting for someone to push the final button," Phoebe says, understanding. "Except... it's another world away."

I try to squint back out at where we'd spotted the station down toward the coast. I'm about to pull my goggles back down when suddenly a flare of lightning brings that side of the island into sharp relief.

Our jaws drop. We only see it for a moment, but afterwards the striking shape lingers with us.

Mum's station is gone. Where it had been, now rising up high, high into the sky like a mammoth of medieval engineering, is... a castle. No, a *palace*.

Phoebe and I don't have to wait long for another flash of lightning to reveal more details. The storm is coming in quick and sharp.

The palace is ancient, in a severe state of disrepair, but it still draws the eye to it with an almost supernatural pull.

There's a kind of dark holiness to its spires and rambling, Dr. Seuss-ish towers. The thing is massive, a juggernaut that looms above the canopy on the far side of the island.

"Huh," I say. "That's new."

"So... small problem," Phoebe agrees, as I try hard not to let my hopes sink. "If the station is over in the human world... and we're stuck with this big freaky castley thing... how the hell do we get back over there? Do we just... wait to get dragged back to our dimension again?"

I hear movement suddenly, and grab Phoebe by the arm, pulling her around the back of one of the fragments of broken stone. We squat down behind it, and seconds later a Shadow explodes through the ferns, coming to a slow trot only feet away from us.

It's a unicorn, pearl-white with a spiralling horn of pure silver that glints in the sun. It pauses for a moment like it's caught in headlights, cocking its head to listen. Beside me, Phoebe covers her mouth, overcome. She's staring at the unicorn with transcendent wonder. Tears fall down her cheeks.

I feel her fingers brush mine, caressing the side of my hand.

I don't breathe.

I'm not sure if it's an accident, or if it's the two of us being all alone in the world, suddenly stranded in an enchanting setting with the fate of humans and Shadows in our hands. Maybe it's just not wanting to feel alone, to share this moment with someone. Maybe I'm misreading it and she's just really uncoordinated.

But my heart beating hard, summoning all my bravery, I gently take Phoebe's hand in mine.

She pulls her hand away abruptly, like she's been stung.

The unicorn darts away, scaring us both. It vanishes into the foliage. I wonder if we somehow spooked it, or if it was reacting to something else. Something we can't perceive.

"I wish Gecko was here," Phoebe gushes, the cheerfulness in her voice sounding super forced. "He wouldn't believe it either."

I blink, flushing hard with shame and guilt. I try to not to look too wounded, try to pretend it doesn't hurt to hear her mention Calvin. I know she's feeling guilty, that she's weirded out by what just happened. I mean, so am I! I'm definitely confused.

I know it was wrong, considering that her and my brother were together ten years before. I guess no matter what we face, she can't move on from the old life she knew.

"That was a Shadow," Phoebe's saying. "A real life Shadow, in the Shadow world! Do you think maybe she could have helped us? Could have found a way back to the station on the other side?"

"It's... it's too much of a risk," I say, finding my voice. I swallow. The cogs in my brain turn sluggishly, trying to focus. "If the Empire is still in control here, wherever we are... then I doubt that Shadow would take kindly to spotting two infectious humans running free."

The storm clouds are creeping across the island, lightning flaring, turning the magical wonderland around us into something more hostile. Or maybe that's a poetic exaggeration, and I'm just projecting my internal state onto our new surroundings.

The leaves rustle around us, and a sense of unease creeps through me suddenly. I turn to look back into the branches suddenly, tensed, but I don't see any other Shadows there. Nobody else comes. Still, something about the darkness in them makes me shiver. A sense of being watched.

"Right," Phoebe responds, still somehow avoiding looking at me. "The Empire. Taylor's in charge of this world now. That feels so strange to say out loud."

Silence stands between us for a moment.

"You know, I'm not Taylor," I say, unable to keep hurt reproach from my voice. "I'm not Calvin either. I know you've had bad luck with friends going dark. I know that makes it hard to trust people. But I'm not them."

"You don't know them," Phoebe says automatically. "Either of them, not really. Taylor..."

"Raven," I snap, not in the mood for humanising the man who killed my parents.

"Taylor's not everything you think he is," Phoebe says. Her voice is strangely cold, and she still won't look at me. "You know I nearly died the night Taylor found me? I was in a bad place. My family definitely didn't want anything more to do with me. And I was over the pain of existing. But Taylor and I looked out for each other after that. I fended for him when he was being picked on, he gave me food when I was hungry, even when he was starving himself. On the streets when you have nothing, the people you have is everything. He had so much kindness in him. We both hated the system that put us in that position, we both wanted to find a way one day to make a better world, to see the best that life had to offer instead of the worst. I know it hurt him so deeply that he couldn't give me that. That he couldn't think a way out of our situation for us. Taylor was a dreamer, he lived for the impossible. So you get that it's hard, trying to connect the Taylor I knew with this Raven you keep describing to me. The guilt I feel at banishing him from our world when I was his only friend. Because of me he was alone in a world where humans were hated. Who can even imagine that, what that must have been like?"

I do try and imagine it. I wonder how the hell a human teenager stranded here who had nothing became the ruler of a global empire which had reshaped the world forever within just ten years.

Phoebe's voice softens a fraction.

"I get that you've spent your life hating Raven, wanting justice on the guy who took your parents from you. Hell, just the idea just of ever meeting Taylor again feels like a living nightmare. I imagine facing him, and I... I can't breathe. But I need you to understand, Taylor loved your Mum like his own. He didn't kill her in cold blood. That, at least, was a terrible mistake."

I remember the horrifying figure in black hooded robes, the man who had slashed me with a knife in his underground lair, trying to end me.

"I don't think so," I say, teeth gritted.

"The villain you saw in the Shadow world... I'm just saying that hurt people *hurt* people. Taylor always had a darkness in him. His moral code was a greyer sense of right and wrong. But it was me, his one best friend turning her back on him and banishing him to the Shadow world, which turned him into anger and hate. He was all alone in this alien world, Griffin. That monster that hurt you... I helped make him."

"Phoebe, all of this is on *Raven*, not you!" I snap. I'm shouting now. I know I shouldn't be, but I am. "Stop blaming yourself like you're meant to be this... saint. Raven murdered my Mum."

"Melissa was a terrible accident," Phoebe shoots back, grief in her voice. "And was it really so unexpected what Raven ended up doing to your Dad?"

I stare at her, breath knocked out of me. It feels like I've been punched in the gut.

"*Excuse* me?" I say, hardly believing she just spoke those words.

Phoebe looks stricken.

"I didn't mean... I'm sorry, I didn't mean for it to come out like that."

"What did you mean?"

"We just... we both know how hard it affects you, being forcefully separated from your Shadow, right? When Taylor was a kid, and your Dad stole his Shadow, all of Taylor's fear, all of his confusion and anger... Taylor blamed it all on your Dad. It wasn't right, and maybe you and I would have made different choices in that situation..." Phoebe trails off at my expression.

"What?" I ask, my voice not sounding like mine.

Phoebe looks confused.

"When your Dad became convinced that Taylor's Shadow, Winter, was his, even though he wasn't... your Dad even went into hiding so nobody could... Calvin didn't tell you any of this," she finishes, with the sound of awful realisation.

I don't answer. Wind howls through the trees.

"Oh, God, Griffin..." Phoebe looks anguished. "I am so, so sorry. I really thought you knew... you said Calvin had told you everything."

"You're lying," I say thickly. Hurting that she'd say that,

that she'd even believe it. "Or you're wrong. My Dad was a good guy. Calvin always said I was a lot like him."

"From what I heard he was a great man, Grif," Phoebe says gently. She tries to move closer to me, but I step away. She bites her lip. "He was loving, and kind and funny. Just like you. But... everyone has darkness in them along with the light. And you can't just separate the two out."

"You're wrong. There's a mistake."

"Griffin, I'm not. I was there with your Dad when he died. We found Taylor's Shadow in the basement where your Dad had been hiding out...." She halts abruptly, seeing my face.

All my life I'd thought Mum's death was the main mystery. That the reality of why she was no longer in our lives was the dark secret at the heart of our family. At the core of the company. Then when I came back from the Shadow world, Calvin had told me that Raven had killed both of our parents. Mum and Dad. That had just given me one more reason to hate Raven. To give me someone solid to pour all my unresolved rage into.

All I've ever heard about Alex Grove, my father, is good things. The only photos I've seen of him are always mid-laugh, a guy just full of joy at being alive. A guy who was light, to the darkness that seems to always have weighed down his son Calvin's shoulders.

Phoebe has to be wrong. But... who do I really trust more? Calvin, or her?

Calvin always lies.

"You're saying my Dad was a monster," I say unsteadily. "No..."

"What does that make me? If Calvin and I are descended from someone like that?"

"He was *troubled*. He made bad choices that hurt others. People aren't... good or bad. Your Dad still loved your Mum. He loved you and Gecko. He just wasn't in his right mind at the end."

I'm silent.

Griffin, the idiot. Griffin, the little puppy dog always idolising one of the most twisted families in existence.

My Dad stole a child's Shadow. *Raven's* Shadow.

"We should get going," I hear myself say dully, feeling strange. I hoist my pack over my shoulder.

"Griffin..."

"Come on. We've got two worlds to save, right?"

I traipse off down toward the treeline, toward the palace. After a moment, I hear Phoebe follow.

Both of us freeze at the sound of gunfire. Twisting our heads back in the direction it came from, we listen. There, again. Bullets firing, in the distance. Not close enough to be meant for us, but not far from here. In the same direction that the unicorn had been running from.

"Crap," Phoebe whispers. "The jets that followed us here. They made it.... I guess they got sucked through to the Shadow world too. What do we do?"

"You know what we do," I say. "We make it to that palace, and we find a way to cross back over to the station in the human world before they do."

We start running, the glowing plants illuminating the night, helping us see as we cut through the undergrowth. But even as we hear the sound of gunfire once again, closer this time, all I'm aware of is the feeling of the past moving in on us, haunting the strange Shadow world island around us.

When Raven killed my father, it was revenge. He was a

little kid, acting out of the unbelievable trauma he'd suffered years before.

The closer we get to fulfilling my family's grand legacy, the less I believe my family deserves one. Perhaps it would be better if the Camerons and Groves slowly faded out of existence, forgotten.

Phoebe and I wade through murky water. The forest has slowly given way to a swamp. Thunder booms above. Surrounding us is a low silvery fog, silently creeping over the surface of the black water as if it possesses its own haunted light. Here and there are little hard islands and wide swathes of mud forming a kind of archipelago. Along these islands grow creepy trees with reaching branches, some as dark as the water, some with bark which is the pale white of bone. I shiver, like something is off which I can't place. There's something else too, a sensation that I can't shake. A strange... familiarity.

"I haven't been to Burger Max in ages," Phoebe is saying. She's speaking quickly, her voice strangely bright. "I used to rely on their Summer Saver deals for most of my meals. It made a few coins go a lot further. Also, pretty good spot to sleep out front, in a pinch."

Her voice is a muted droning in the background, like she's underwater. Or maybe I'm underwater. It's cold and dark in my head, like our surroundings. Secret things lie in the darkness in my mind, waiting gleefully to ensnare me.

So this is the clue from the past, Phoebe's dark revelation. The taint on my family's legacy that Calvin was too ashamed to tell me.

I feel scared, the ground falling out beneath me. Reality is just ash around me, and I'm choking on it.

My Dad wasn't the first to be driven mad by the desire to meet his true Shadow. I wanted to meet him for so long. To know what it was like to have a real Dad, not the flawed copy that Calvin resentfully provided.

Dad had left us, he'd left Mum, all because he became obsessed with a Shadow that wasn't his own.

What kind of a man am I becoming? With Calvin and Dad as my role models? I think of Sophie calling me a monster when we broke up. Maybe she was right.

"*Grif*," Phoebe says.

"Sorry?" I mumble.

"I was just... I was talking to you. You weren't answering."

"Oh," I say vaguely. "Sorry."

We have to push on and connect the worlds, I tell myself. I repeat it over and over again, like a mantra. That's all that matters.

I feel the pressure rest on my shoulders like an overbearing weight. Mum is relying on us now. We're on the home stretch. We just have to find a way to cross back from this dimension we're stranded in to our own one with the station, and we have to do it before whoever the gun toting soldiers are who've followed us here stop us.

I think I hear whispering on the air, and turn quickly, but nobody's there. I wonder why the fog seems to emit that dim light, providing a grim ambience that leeches joy from the air. Maybe I'm projecting.

Another shiver runs down the back of my neck. Everything is still, but I feel like something is watching me from out of those trees. As we move along through the black water, the trees growing from the water become denser, and twigs scrape my shoulders like fingers and tear at my hair.

I hear it again. Whispering. I look around us uneasily, between the still, dead trees. Even Phoebe seems unnerved.

"Just the wind," she says, trying to convince both of us. "Anyhow, tell me more about the games you were into. I never played video games. I mean, I did before I ran away from home. But even at Cam Tech we tended to play board games instead. I really like board games. Do you... do you like...? Oh, come on Griffin, I can't stand this."

I turn to stare at her. My brain is finding everything very murky and confusing, struggling to keep a handle on what's happening.

"What did I do wrong?" I ask, numb.

"*Wrong?*" Phoebe says incredulously. "Nothing."

I'm confused.

"Then why are you..."

"*Why?* Because I care about you!" Phoebe says, shocked. "I know I've been pretty shut off up until now, but can't you see that..." She struggles to arrange thoughts into words. "You've been keeping me *sane*, Grif. I know I talked about going at it on my own, but my..." she looks scared for a moment, "...my mind can be my own enemy, sometimes. I'm not sure if I would have made it here on my own. You and I have been through some seriously freaky crap. And having you and your jokes has made things feel... safer. I need my Watson if I'm going to finish this." Phoebe smiles, her eyes wet. "Besides, afterward... scares me. Please don't leave when this is done. I don't have anyone else. Not anymore."

I stare at her, trying to think what I'm meant to say, but

it's like tumbleweeds are blowing through the wasteland that is my brain.

Then I look past Phoebe's shoulder, and I freeze. My gaze has caught on a tree with six knobbly branches.

"What?" Phoebe says, shooting me a look.

I blink slowly. I open my mouth but nothing comes out. On one of the spidery white branches hangs a small wooden doll, dangling there. A winged Shadow, smiling insanely as it looks out with unseeing eyes.

It's a crude mockery, but there's no mistaking who the doll is meant to be.

It's Cirrus.

I stagger backward. Phoebe and I both whirl around, staring out into the fog, heart-rate going at a million miles an hour.

"Phoebe," I say tensely, "there's something out there. I can hear it moving."

"Come on," she says, and we start to step again through the fog. Each tendril of weeds in the water feels like it's a clammy hand as it tangles around my ankles.

I feel like a hand has grabbed and twisted my insides. Hanging from the branches of the trees before us are pale white shapes, blowing gently in the breeze as they wind around on their cords.

"Look," I say, numb. "Are those..."

"Bones," Phoebe whispers with equal dread. "Keep an eye on our backs."

I think I hear a wail through the fog. Or is that the breeze gusting too strongly? I can't be sure.

I feel like we're in a graveyard.

We make our way through the almost-darkness, on the lookout for any movement. It doesn't seem right to talk.

Then I see it. Something pale, flickering amongst the trees. It's enough to know we're not insane.

We're being hunted.

"It's close!" I hiss.

"Run!" Phoebe whispers, and we splash forwards through the silvery fog. I didn't see whatever's chasing us, I don't even get an impression except for every instinct screaming at me that it's something dangerous.

An unearthly whisper runs through the trees, causing ripples along the deathly still surface of the glassy water.

"Something's coming," I gasp.

We splash through the water, navigating between the trees. Phoebe grabs my hand and pulls me along behind her to help me keep up. Just because *she's* some kind of freaking action-hero.

I feel like reality is distorting around us. The trees, the water, this entire forest, is responding to whatever's chasing us, reality rippling around it. Or maybe that's just the primal fear racing through my brain's cortex. It feels like I'm squinting through a swimming pool, sweat pouring down my face despite the chill of the water.

I look over my shoulder, just once, but don't see anything there. Then Phoebe and I take a turn, and I swear that through thick leaves, I see something pale slithering through the tree trunks. Just a flash, like before.

"This way!" Phoebe yells. She's still holding my hand so we don't get separated in the fog. We clamber up onto a muddy bank lined with more of the trees. We make a series of tightly cutting turns and then we duck under a branch... suddenly Phoebe's foot snags on a root. We lose our footing and next thing we're sliding down a muddy slope, through a dense pile of fronds to come to a stop near the foot of a giant tree. Its arching branches and the fronds at its base unexpectedly make for an excellent hiding place.

We've landed with me lying on top of Phoebe. I'm staring into her wide eyes, panting, both of us too afraid to move. There's a sudden silence, where I can hear the slightest twig crunching somewhere else in the forest. We both hold our breath.

I can feel her shivering. Her blonde-dyed hair sticks to her face, a reminder that I must barely look like myself anymore either.

I stare down at the leaves beside my hand, to avoid Phoebe's eyes which are so close they're blurring into one big Cyclops one. The leaves are shiny and brown, like the carapaces of cockroaches.

Both of us are too terrified to venture back out into the swamp, in case the pale demon hunting us is still lying patiently in wait.

Then we hear it.

A hissing. Almost like the rattle of a snake.

It's close. It sounds like it's almost right over our hiding spot, looking down toward us. Maybe, maybe it won't be able to see anything through the fronds disguising us.

Nothing. Then...

The scraping of branches. Something is moving toward us, through the treetops.

I'm scared to even breathe. It sounds like it's right above us.

And I look down at Phoebe, and I'm thinking... I can't leave her here. We can't just wait for whoever or whatever is closing in on us to strike, because then Phoebe will be dead. Both of us will be, and there will be no one left to complete the project. All of it, *all of it*, will be for nothing.

Phoebe meets my intense gaze, looking uncertain, as if she's wondering what thoughts are going on behind my eyes. And I can lie and say it's about the mission, it's about what's best for all the billions of humans and Shadows out there, but really all I'm thinking is one repeating thought.

She has to live.

Despite the trauma of losing home, of losing my brother, in a strange way the twelve hours since then are also the happiest hours I've ever had, second only to my times with Cirrus. Finally being with another breathing person again who gets my weirdness, no matter how aloof she may have acted at first. I think of how odd it is that it makes me so happy to see her happy. I recall her reaction when she thought I was dead in the crashed jet.

I just know that I brought Phoebe back to life, and I'm not prepared to now watch her die. And I've always been good at playing the bigger picture.

"You knew from the start this was your mission," I whisper to Phoebe, barely audible. "*You're* the Sherlock."

She looks at me for a moment, not understanding.

Then, for the first time since I've met her, Phoebe looks totally stunned.

"No." She shakes her head madly. "Grif, that's not what I meant. You have to see Eclipse again. You have to help me finish this, together."

I can see my hand shaking as I place it on her shoulder.

"Connecting the worlds means nothing," I say quietly, "if I lose the only family I have left. The only person I know or care about."

Then I lean in, hugging her goodbye.

Pulling away, I see her panic, real and vivid, in her eyes. Her realisation that I'm really leaving her.

I smile at her. Ignoring the primal instinct for survival that's screaming through me. "It's okay. I wasn't meant to make it to the end," I whisper. "My Mum believed in you, so I do too. Finish this, Pheebs. Finish it for all of us."

Then I crawl away from her, tense, and burst out of our hiding spot, running at full tilt.

"COME AND GET ME!" I scream, clambering over mud, then splashing unexpectedly back into black water. "COME AND GET ME, YOU BLAIRWITCH ARSEHOLE!"

An ancient fear jolts through me, electrifying. An inbuilt sixth sense, like the instinct of prey. A deep knowledge in my bones. I can feel that whatever is stalking me is a natural predator.

Fear is rushing through me, but part of me also feels invincible. At least whatever happens to me right now... it has some meaning. This is larger than just me. Because of this, Phoebe will live. Because of this, there's a chance she can end things.

I can't resist. I risk a glance over my shoulder, to see what's chasing me.

There's nothing there.

Gasping, I come to a sudden halt. Standing in the water, soaked, I feel sick. Like there's been a blow to my stomach.

Tell me it didn't just go for Phoebe. Tell me I haven't abandoned her.

I start to run back to where Phoebe was hiding, backtracking my way through the twisting swamp.

In the last moment, I see what's looming above me.

I only get a fleeting impression before it strikes. A massive tentacle of a tail, like a hungry worm that undulates through the air. Skin as pale as chalk, like a blind creature that dwells in deep rock pools, living its life in perpetual darkness.

Something that isn't a Shadow.

I scream.

"PHOEBE! RUN!"

3
HUMANS

Eclipse

I pump my wings, rocketing over the canopy. Scanning the gaps in the treetops for any signs of Hanna. Waiting with dread for the sound of more gunfire.

Then I hear the screams.

I soon arrive overhead of the treetop village. Some of the golden lantern homes are shredded like balloons. I hover overhead, my wingbeats blowing leaves from trees. My tail traces the air, hungry for a fight. Staring down at the village, I feel my stomach wrench inside me.

The bodies of Shadows are littered below, draped across the bridges and over the spiralling walkway. Families. Children. My blood runs cold.

What kind of a Shadow could have done this?

Down below I can hear screams and sobs from the forest floor. Through the branches I can make out Joni's people fleeing in all directions, a chaotic stampede of fear. But I can't see the cause...

Then I hear the voices.

I spy the very tallest tree of Joni's camp. Its trunk breaks the rest of the tree line, rising into the sky. Beneath its tallest branches the trunk supports a giant circular platform of glass, offering a lookout point across the strait toward Aeyu Palace. The glass shines translucent green in the light of the flaming torches around its perimeter. An awning of ferns and assorted greenery drape down over the platform. It's as if the very bark of the tree is enchanted to warp itself, parts of the husk flowing outward to form overhangs and alcoves to shield from the elements.

Voices are rising up from the staircase that spirals around the trunk. Shouts of pursuit. As I fly toward it, a Shadow emerges up from the stairs to the lookout. She's backing up on the glass platform, paws held wide in a sign of surrender. Even from this far, I can see that her body is shivering in terror.

It's Joni.

While I was busy soul-searching in the clouds, she must have heard the commotion and made a bee-line back to camp.

I fly faster toward the platform.

"Why are you doing this?" I hear Joni shout. Confused and devastated, but equally bold and fearless. "You have me! I'm in charge. Just... stop killing them, I'm begging you. I'm their leader, I'm responsible. You're welcome here too, we can forgive this. We came here because we just want peace..."

Bullets fire. My stomach muscles spasm. I'm too late.

I watch, screaming inwardly, as Joni falls limply to the

platform. Her unseeing eyes staring up at the stars, while her people lie dead below.

Then the gutsy, upbeat wildcat is gone forever, her body staring unseeing up at the stars, as the bodies of her people lie dead below her. The rest fleeing into the forest, certain now that nowhere can ever, ever be safe again.

The owners of guns spread out onto the platform, inspecting the body. I see who's responsible for the slaughter below. My talons clench.

Humans.

I count five in total. Each of them is covered in a black outfit, a reflective visor where their eyes should be.

I land in the thicker foliage of the canopy near the platform, obscuring myself in the leaves and the darkness of night. My talons tremble in shock, making me unsteady on the branch where I perch. This shouldn't have happened, with all of my power. I should have intervened. But it all happened so quickly... and I didn't believe for a moment that it would happen. That the humans were capable of cold-blooded murder. That they could do something this... *inhuman.*

The sound of gunfire has ceased below. From the amount I'd heard, I think these five are the only culprits. The ones who went on a killing spree.

"Did you seriously hear that?" I hear one of the humans say. "She spoke. That was messed up, Ron. This is so messed up."

"Quit it, Amy. They were hostile. It was self-defence."

"Yeah, you seemed pretty bloody sure of that when you started shooting everything that moved."

The human voices sound young. Older than Griffin, but not by much. The thought makes me feel even sicker.

But not as much as when one of the humans pulls a Shadow by the hair into the light, kicking and squirming, revealing he has a hostage.

"Guys. Guys!" I feel like the wind has been driven out of me. The human releases the Shadow, and presses the muzzle of his gun against her head. He stares down at Hanna and her splayed violet wings.

She's alive. Thank God, she's alive, but she doesn't have long.

"Why are you holding onto that one? She attacked us."

"She's still alive. And she's... pretty."

"We know you like it freaky," the tall one, Ron, grins. He seems to be the leader. Strutting over, he stares down at Hanna. I have a mad desire to reveal myself, to scatter the humans away from her and encircle my wings protectively around her. But their guns are all aimed directly at Hanna. If I spook even one of the human soldiers, he could fire by accident and Hanna could be dead. "Those wings really come out of her back, don't they? We've had a panda, a tree, a fairy..." He gestures down at the stairwell they ascended from, "those other arseholes. What a circus."

"She looks so human," the one called Amy says nervously. She sounds sick. "What should we do with her?"

"If her heart is still kickin', we tie her up. Take her back to command as proof, or nobody's going to believe this."

"And how are we meant to do that?" another soldier demands. I study them through the darkness. The soldier in question is wiping blood from his knife off on his pants. "Have you noticed that palace over there? This isn't the same island we followed our target to. We're not *home* anymore, man. We're in hostile territory, and we don't even know how the hell we got here."

"Then we find a way back," the tall soldier shoots at them. "Back to our dimension, or whatever. And we take as many of these monsters prisoner as we can. You dingos don't get it. We're gonna be heroes. The first soldiers to get Intel on the alien scum that attacked Auckland. This is the start of something big."

"Not if I can help it," I say coolly. The branches bend beneath me as I launch myself over the canopy, the platform juddering as my talons grasp the edge of it. I spread my wings wide, signalling I mean no harm.

"Don't shoot," I say, heart thudding. "I'm here in peace."

Facing me are the five humans. They're all screaming at me, their voices conveying their shock. Their faces are hidden by those mirrored visors, reflecting five versions of myself back at me.

The humans aim their guns up at my head. Even though a monster just landed in their midst, they stand their ground. I know from Sanctuary that human bullets can tear through me much easier than any Shadow can.

"Holy crap, *look* at this thing," one of the humans says in terror and awe. His gun is shaking.

"Hey, stay back!" another of them warns. "Or we'll shoot your friend here." He gestures at Hanna's limp form. "Yeah, you understand me, don't you? I told the others your kind were intelligent."

The tallest human steps out casually in front of the others, his weapon aimed at me. The leader, I'm guessing. He's the one carrying Hanna with his free hand, long dark hair hiding her face. Hanna's body has gone limp, the side of her head wet with blood. Her eyes flicker as if she's barely conscious. Slowly, the leader presses the barrel of the weapon against her head, as if a reminder for me not to get any ideas. I lurch, remembering to hold my ground at the last minute. The humans flinch and raise their guns higher.

The tall leader laughs.

"You care about this one, don't you? What is she, your sister? I'm not seeing much of a physical resemblance."

"We are not your enemy," I say hotly, blood pounding. "You're all... you're all confused. I'm a friend to humans. My name is Eclipse." There are tears in my eyes. Maybe they thought that the members of Joni's tribe were the enemy. The Shadows that now lie slaughtered below us, throughout the suspended camp. Perhaps these humans were too scared, too trigger-happy. Perhaps... they do not understand the horror they've committed.

The humans do not respond. They're hesitating, eyeing me and my immense size. Perhaps trying to judge how much of a threat I am.

I shrug my wings, unsettled by the eerie silence, combined with the devastation around us. Just like Cirrus, I've always held humans in high esteem, like they're guardian angels like Griffin, watching over us. The humans' faceless helmets reflect my own image back at me. I feel a deep sense of unease. They feel like hollow people.

I think of what Hanna said about Raven being human. That the same darkness I've seen in Shadows can live in humans as well. That they suffer from the same emptiness that we Shadows do.

"Griffin Cameron is my human," I try again. I'm trying not to stare at Joni where she lies in the middle of the platform. I'm trying not to let my voice tremor when I can barely keep it straight. "My counterpart. Perhaps you know him?"

"Griffin Cameron?" one of the humans mutters. "The terrorist?"

"What the hell's a counterpart?"

"Shut up, Amy. I'm running this dialogue," the tall soldier says.

I don't understand. Terrorist?

"Eclipse, huh?" I cannot see, but it feels like the tall soldier is grinning. "Hell, this is fantastic. We can bag both of you."

"Shut the hell up, Ron," Amy mutters. "Have you seen how friggin' big this thing is?"

"If he tries to move, we'll kill his friend here. He cares about her. Look, you can tell."

"You're psycho."

"Are you disobeying orders now?" the tall soldier demands. "Is that how you're playing this?"

"No," Amy mutters, shifting awkwardly. She raises her gun again, keeping it fixed on me.

These are humans. *Humans.* I think of all the posters Cirrus collected. All of the games he played, the magazines and human books he treated like prized possessions. The human world he had dreamed of visiting.

"Leave her alone," I say. I want to be threatening, but I think I just sound confused. My whole body feels like it's vibrating, this tension building inside of me.

The tall human laughs. His laughter is cruel. No, it's ordinary - as if someone just told a joke. What makes it evil is how casual he is about the gun he has pressed to Hanna's face.

"Interesting," he says. "From what I've seen, you don't have any feelings at all. Your kind will happily destroy a building full of humans. I've seen the footage, you know. I saw the falling bodies." He presses the muzzle into Hanna's wound, and she cries out. My left foot lurches forward in an involuntary step.

All of the humans fix their guns on me, tensing. If I move, I could be shredded.

They're meant to be our friends.

"Please. Let her go," I say. Blood sings in my ears. Everything looks sickly in the green light that seems to exude from the glass platform beneath our feet. "What do you want from us?"

"Lie down," Ron commands. "We're going to tie you up and take you back to our superiors. You're going to tell us how to get back to our world. Cooperate, and no one needs to get hurt."

"How much rope do we have?" another soldier asks doubtfully, sizing me up.

Hanna lurches to life suddenly, knocking the muzzle away with her tied hands. Then she rolls back and swings her legs around to kick the tall human hard between his legs. He groans and stumbles. The other humans switch their guns toward Hanna, and she flings a cloud of stinging hornets at them. They swear and contort, trying to shake the insects free. Still, the hornets' stingers seem unable to penetrate the thick, black suits the humans wear.

I know that Hanna has bought me a moment, but I still don't know if I can bring myself to...

Then the lead human kicks Hanna in the side of the head. She cries out, her hornets falling to the ground as if they're dead, legs prone in the air. The tall human calls her something unspeakable.

I black out. It's a strange feeling. I don't pass out, but I'm not as certain about what is going on around me. This numbness, this darkness takes hold of me, protecting me from the deep hurt in my chest. I'm not aware of anything, until what feels like an infinity has passed.

When the numbing darkness retreats, I look around me in confusion. That's when the puzzle falls into place.

Three of the five human bodies are strewn around the glass platform. Two of those are still on fire, burnt and blackened, golden flames still licking at their backs. I turn to see a fourth body slowly slide and fall from an over-hanging branch behind me, hitting the platform with a heavy thud. The fifth soldier is nowhere to be seen.

The wind is gusting off the edge of the platform and out into the emptiness below. The glass of the platform is now cracked and riddled with bullet holes that weren't there a minute ago. But the platform holds. And if any of the bullets touched me... I cannot feel them.

"Oh God," I whisper. I stare down at the blood on my talons. Surely I can only have blacked out for a few seconds.

I stagger forward, spotting Hanna lying there, unmoving. I rest a talon against her bare neck. She has a pulse, like the heartbeat of an insect. The relief at feeling one, however faint, is overwhelming.

She must have heard the sounds of gunfire. Hanna turned around, came back to try and help these Shadows at her own risk. These Shadows who had rejected her. She cares more for other Shadows then she wants me to know. Somewhere inside her is the instinct to still try and protect the people of her world, no matter who they are.

In grief, I move to Joni. She's so still, now beginning her eternal sleep. Respectfully, gently, I close her lids with the tips of my talons.

Joni had more conviction and more compassion for others in her left paw than I have in my entire body.

I survey the human bodies surrounding us. I can feel Cirrus rising inside me, and part of me is terrified of what he will think, that he will scream at me, call me 'monster' - and that maybe he'll be right.

How could they do this? Cirrus asks inside my head, a mournful cry. *Why would the humans kill all these Shadows?* And lastly: *What have we done?*

And then I fall to the ground moaning, convulsing. A dark shroud rises, the memory of the last few seconds revealing itself. I remember beserking, I remember the fierce sense of justice, of revenge as I fell on the humans and tore them asunder like prey.

I killed them. These humans are meant to be our answer. They have Shadows of their own in this world. Shadows who are waiting to be reunited with their other halves.

But I killed their humans in seconds. I broke my promise to Griffin in the worst way.

"Please..." a voice says faintly. I look around, and then realise it is coming from one of the soldiers. One of the humans is still alive. Her voice belongs to the one called Amy. Her helmet is off, and she is crying.

I lean over her to look closer. She opens her eyes, tight with pain. She looks up at my face.

"Please," Amy whispers. "I'm cold. It's so very cold."

I should say something. But I don't know what to say. The entire world is receding around me, and the humans Cirrus spent his entire life hunting for are as bad as the Empire.

"Don't be afraid," I say, my tongue feeling clumsy.

"I just want to see my family again. I told them... I told them I'd be there for Christmas this year."

I encircle the human with my wing, shielding her from the cold winds brushing the treetops. Trying to keep her warm. The human known as Amy doesn't make a sound, and when I peek under my wing, I see her staring up lifelessly at the golden, feathered shroud around her.

I have a distant sense of crouching on the glass platform, amongst the dead bodies of humans and Shadows, shuddering uncontrollably. I hear a voice, but it feels far away. Someone's tiny hands are touching me, soft, gentle. Trying to calm me.

"You're okay, Eclipse," Hanna is saying. I glare down at her, savage, terrifying. She's staring up at me, eyes wide and afraid. But instead of backing away she runs a hand comfortingly over my feathers. "Eclipse, you saved me," she says, her voice breaking. "It's okay. It's going to be okay."

4

THE ROOM

Griffin

I lurch upright. My head swims. The last thing I recall is running through the swamp with Phoebe, using myself as a distraction so that she could escape and finish our mission. I hadn't really expected to ever open my eyes again.

I'm in... a bed.

Wait, that doesn't make sense. How long have I been out? My pulse races. Stranger than that, I'm wearing a pair of soft, flannelette pyjamas. Okay. That strikes me as even more sinister. That someone undressed me without my knowledge. I feel a deep squirm of unease in my gut.

Looking around, I take in my surroundings, squinting as my eyes adjust to the near darkness. The only light that exists is cast by flickering fireplaces.

I'm confused. I'm staring at a lot of human teenagers.

For a minute, I wonder if I'm back in my own world, but our surroundings don't make sense either.

"He's awake," a girl says from the top of a bunk bed beside mine. Then I turn to see a boy who can't be more than ten standing beside my bed. He prods my forehead with a finger.

"Wakey-wakey," he says. He has an English accent. I look around. I count thirteen other kids in the room, mostly teenagers. All of them are wearing the same uniform: white and blue chequered flannelette pyjamas.

I swing my legs out of the bed and press my bare feet against cold, hard wood. Raising myself slowly to my feet, I make my way around my bed to get a better look at where I am, supporting myself against the bunk above mine.

We're in some kind of large, long hall with walls of oak, and strips of diamond-patterned wallpaper between the slats of wood. Symmetrically running along on either side of the room are six bunk beds, twelve in total. They all have clean white sheets, like hospital beds. Set into the walls between the beds are tall mirrors, their black frames twisting into claws at the corners.

"Hey! I'm Rihäm," a girl on the top bunk says warmly. "Meet the pyjama club. You've already met little Marty, poor tyke. He's from London. These two chill dudes are Woo-Min and Nam, then the Flemish Gals, Anke and Sien..." Anke and Sien wave cheerfully from a nearby bed. "That's Ula... oh and there are our two Kiwis - Jade and Peach Tree."

"It's Petry," one of the New Zealander's rolls her eyes. "Call me Georgia."

"Right, Georgia Peach Tree. That's what I said." Rihäm shrugs, smiling sheepishly at me. "We've been locked in here a while. There are a lot of inside jokes for you to catch up on. Oh, and then there's the dude with the cool loner vibes over there."

I look across the room and see a guy clearly older than the rest of us, casually reclining against the wall with his arms folded. He smiles sardonically, his face curtained by his dark long hair. He looks slender, wiry but there's something about his sureness and calm that makes me think he might be good if we get into a fight.

What's happening to me? I've only just woken up, and I'm thinking which of these kids would be the most capable in combat. Going to the Shadow world really screwed me up. Or you know, it could have been the constant diet of violent videogames before that.

Actually, no. Definitely the Shadow world.

"What's your name, Mr Too-Cool-for-School?" I ask the dark-haired young man reclining against the wall. He's easiest the oldest here, eighteen or even in his twenties maybe.

"Toby," he says breezily, seemingly totally unfazed by our predicament.

"He speaks," Rihäm mutters. She points. "Anyhow, over here we have the American Sorority. Patty, Julia and April. They only just arrived."

"We were having an amazing holiday diving the reefs in Bermuda," Patty gushes. She frowns. "This is not how we wanted our holiday to go. Freaking... hole in the sky."

"Wait," I say, trying to keep up. "So you were brought here through Rips, all of you?"

"Rips?" Patty asks, puzzled.

"Yeah. Like... these tears in reality?"

"Seems like it," Rihäm says. "We're from all over. But

each of us was sucked through some sort of... rip, like you said. That's all we remember. Then we were all drugged, or knocked out somehow... and brought here."

"So you all came here from the human world," I say slowly, trying to piece my new situation together. Wherever we all are now, we have to find a way to break out. Phoebe may still need my help, might be in danger. I have no idea how far I am from her now.

"I wish I had brought my book," Nam comments, clearly trying to sound upbeat. "Or maybe a fun group game."

"Excuse me, we don't have time for a gossip session." April swallows, scared. She looks like a petite doll, pretty with big cartoonish eyes. She looks utterly at odds with our sinister surroundings.

At each end of the hall is a roaring fireplace, the smoke escaping up ancient stone chimneys. Painted at both ends of the hall are a pair of eerie, piercing blue eyes. An eye on either side of each fireplace. And the way the brow seems to contort, shaping the eyes, makes them look like they're fixing us in their wide fury.

I shiver.

"Yeah, we know," Jade says, in a comfortingly New Zealand accent. "They're hella creepy."

It takes me another moment to realise what exactly is nagging me about the room.

It doesn't have any doors. It's a room without any way out.

"We're all meant to be asleep," April whispers urgently. "Those are the rules. No talking after lights out."

"I don't want to sleep!" Marty wails, the little English boy running into April's arms. "Sleep is bad."

"What happens?" I ask urgently. "Where are we? What happens after lights out?"

"Your guess is as good as ours," Rihäm shrugs.

"Or better. What do you know that we don't?" Ula asks suspiciously, eyes narrowing at me. She's speaking in a quavering whisper, like she's scared about who might be listening.

"You're in the Shadow world now, it's a parallel reality to the one we all come from. Each of you came through a sort of... tear, in between the worlds. Now sssh, I'm thinking of an escape plan."

Ula shuts her mouth, and looks surprised that she did.

I look quickly around the room, urgently checking each face. No Phoebe. A feeling of loneliness sets in, but I shake it off. It's good that she's not here. That means she wasn't captured. But did she manage to get away from the entity that found me in the swamp?

"Where are we?" I press.

Toby shrugs.

"All of us have only been here for a few days at the most. Newbies like you arrive all the time. But usually they're here when we wake up in the morning. I have no idea how you came in - it was so dark most of us didn't even realise you'd appeared on the bed there."

"So why are there only fourteen of us?" I say, with a slow, sneaking suspicion.

"Good question, Kiwi boy," Rihäm says. "Another New Zealander, right? Only place that ridiculous accent could possibly be from. '*Would you like some fush and chups?*'"

"That was a terrible imitation. Why only fourteen?"

"That's what happens after ten pm," one of the Flemish girls, Sien, says uneasily. The others trade fearful glances.

"Every night, they come to take someone. We never see them. I think they put something in the air to make us stay asleep. When we wake in the morning, another person is always gone."

There is a long, grim silence. I start pacing furiously.

So all these kids came here straight from my world. Each of them were sucked through a Rip in the last three days. That's a lot of Rips. Unless there is more of them now. I think of the one that transported Phoebe and me here. Over the last few days our team had been weakening the barrier between worlds to prepare for the opening of the portals, so that could be the cause of all this.

"I came here with a girl," I say. I feel truly scared for a moment. "Has anyone else been...?"

They look at each other, checking with silent glances.

"No," Rihäm says finally.

"No," Toby repeats, looking at me curiously. "We haven't seen anyone like that."

"You guys," Sien hisses. "We don't all want to get in trouble. If we're not asleep when they come..."

"We're *always* asleep when they come," the one called Georgia vents. She tosses her dark brown hair across one shoulder, glowering at Sien. "Each night they come and abduct one of us. How could these monsters possibly escalate things more?"

"Monsters?" I say.

Georgia hesitates, then nods.

"I know this might sound crazy," she says in a rush. "But that's who's keeping us in here. Monsters, real ones. One of the guys that used to be in here, Patrick, he swore that he remembered landing in an empty paddock before he was taken. That this kind of... *monster* caught him and took him prisoner. Marty says he saw some kind of dead *bird* standing over his bed in the middle of the night, but none of us saw it. The others just told him he had a nightmare." Her voice trembles but she presses onwards, defiant of her own fear. "And then there's whatever made April freak."

"What?" I say.

"You would have freaked too," April mutters. She looks haunted. I remind myself that her and the American girls only just arrived here before me. I'm not the only newbie.

"April, tell him," Sien presses.

"I didn't just... black out like the others did," April says reluctantly. She tries to put on a tough act, but I can see the raw fear in her. "Something came for me. I saw it. Something that wasn't human. It was pale and unnatural, and the way it moved... it was something that shouldn't exist."

With a flash I remember what I witnessed in the forest, before I was taken. Something that didn't even seem like a Shadow.

"She only just stopped gibbering to herself," Anke says. "She was a wreck when she woke up."

"Because we're meant to be asleep. You said it yourself, those are the rules. If you guys get into trouble, they can't blame me!" April says, trying to sound angry, but it trails off in more of a whimper. She buries her head under her pillow.

I'm examining the oak walls, feeling with my fingers for any fixture, any hidden passage which might be where the captors enter at night to steal away the prisoners.

"You won't find anything new," Georgia says. "Everybody that's been through here has searched this place a thousand times."

"The sleeping gas they use on you at night-time," I say, quickly calculating. "Have you tried resisting it before?"

"We've tried wrapping blankets around our mouths to keep it out," Ula says. "But we always pass out eventually, and we wake up when the lights are back on."

I tap the pattern of black-and-white diamonds painted across the wallpaper between two bookshelves.

"These ones aren't decorative like the others. I think this is where they inject the gas. Help me cover them, we should be able to block them."

Most of the kids look sceptical, but the breezy loner, Toby, strides over to where I am. He eyes it doubtfully, but when he runs his finger along it where I did, he looks surprised. "You might be right. Nice going, kid. Come on, you lot!" he says briskly, grinning with excitement. His voice is clear and commanding. "You heard our new saviour. We have to move fast. Get those duvets, check if the opposite wall has them too. If they do, keep those duvets pressed against them."

"Search for any others in this twisted purgatory that we might have missed," I add. "Have you tried shattering the mirrors? We could use something sharp for weapons."

One of the Americans, Julia I think, shakes her head.

"We tried. They're unbreakable."

"Okay," I say quickly, "break the bunk beds then. See if you can kick out the rungs of the ladders and sharpen them into weapons. When they come in tonight, you're all going to be pretending to be asleep until the right moment. Then we'll swamp our captors and overwhelm them, got it? Go, go!"

The others all burst into action, stripping down their beds, tearing off the blankets to press them against the walls. I feel like the light from the fireplaces is dying lower, because all I can see now is a bundle of dark moving shapes, and on all sides I can hear the frantic, scared breathing of children.

I stride to the middle of the room, turning to squint to all of them. I have to make sure they're ready for this.

"I know you're all scared," I say urgently as they tend to their tasks. "It's okay to be scared, use that energy. But you have to listen to me. Those creatures who put you in here are called Shadows. They're not all evil. My best friend was... *is,* a Shadow. He's this weird mix of a dragon and a parrot. It sounds mental, but when I'm with him I can hear his thoughts. We understand each other without even speaking."

Some of the kids are staring over at me, transfixed. I wish I could read their expressions better.

"What happened to him?" Patty asks in a small voice.

"He died," I say, swallowing. My voice hardens. "But that doesn't have to happen to us. I don't know who stuck us in here, but they're going to regret it. You're all ready to be soldiers. Trust me, you have no idea of what you're capable of. And I want you to be alive long enough to discover what that is." I'm surprised by the passion in my own voice. I really believe they can do this, and they need to as well. "I chose to come to this island, because I'm on a very important mission. And I need all of your help. I have to break out of here, and the fate of this world and our world depends on it."

"If you're on a mission, how did you get stuck in here with us?" I hear one of the American girls state doubtfully. She doesn't believe me.

"Because I saw it too," I say to April. "What you saw. It

caught me." I remember the swamp, the creepy reaching trees and the whispering. Seeing it, while also not perceiving it. As if its form was beyond my mind's own comprehension.

"Really?" April breathes. She's actually moved closer to stare at me. "What did it look like to you?"

I remember the feeling that reality was rippling around us, distorting in the presence of that being. I remember my scream of horror, as I looked up in shock and awe. The heavy weight that seemed to settle on me.

I don't answer.

April looks at me even closer, and frowns suddenly.

"Do I know you from somewhere?"

"Nope." Hurriedly, I turn away so I'm facing away from April and the other American girls. As the most recent kids in here, they're also the most likely to have seen my face on the News. Griffin Cameron, in league with the evil Shadows. If I get recognised, there's no way the kids are going to listen to me. More likely they'll think I'm behind all this and tie me down to torture me for information. Fear can be a powerful motivator.

That's when I hear something. I can't be entirely sure, but it sounds like a sinister creaking in the darkness. Everyone instantly goes still.

"They're coming," April whispers.

5

GOING GENTLY

Eclipse

I'm passed out for a long time, and it's a sad, numbing sleep. When I wake, the world is illuminated by cold daylight. I realise I don't know how long it's been.

The air smells like rain. We're still on the high lookout, the glass platform above the forest where I confronted the humans. But their bodies are gone now. Joni's too. If it was Hanna who cleared them up, I'm not sure whether she did it for hygiene's sake or to spare me from looking at them. The thought that Hanna might think about my feelings is surreal, and it feels too farfetched to be true. On top of that, someone has built a soft, comfortable makeshift nest from fern fronds and branches around me.

I turn toward the high reaching palace of Aeyu on the Island of Moon. It's so close. Its heaven-reaching towers seem to glisten in the morning light, like they're made from ice rather than stone. Beneath it is the Underworld, Hanna says - and my way home to Griffin. The sky is growing slowly darker, erasing the morning light as gargantuan thunderheads move in toward us across the sky. So high above the canopy, it looks like the clouds are charging toward us, unfurling across the sky with peals of thunder. I listen to the reverberations, feeling them rock the glass beneath me. The island across the strait begins to grey with sheets of rain.

If we're going to make it to the palace, we best do it now. Lightning flashes briefly out over the island's canopy, confirming my thoughts.

Hanna places down a big leaf in front of me, and I start. A stack of wild salmon sits on the leaf, all freshly cooked.

"Empress," I say weakly. She avoids meeting my eyes, turning to leave me to eat. I stare at her, feeling wounded. "Hanna."

Slowly, I raise myself back up to my feet. Hanna is striding to the other side of the platform, and she is staring across the strait at the palace on the opposite island, darkened by the rain clouds. She stares at it as if it's a beacon.

"Joni's people," I say, my words sounding rough. "Are they all right?"

"A lot of them are dead," Hanna says, huddling into herself. "The humans panicked, went trigger-happy. Instead of fighting, most of the Shadows ran. They're scattered around the island. I took Joni's body to them, so they could give her a proper burial."

I absorb this, feeling cold. These Shadows had accepted me. This could have been my home.

"I was supposed to protect them," I say, past a lump in

my throat. "How can humans do something like this? They were meant to save us."

Hanna turns to me, glaring.

"What?" I say, straightening. The world still feels foggy around me. "Why are you angry? I saved you."

"I didn't need you to save me, okay?" she blasts at me, arms folded tightly. "You had to go and break the golden rule Griffin gave you, not to kill anyone."

I shudder thinking of what I did to the humans, feeling another rise of nausea.

"They were going to hurt you."

"So what?" Hanna challenges me, mad. "What does it matter? Why did you come after me?"

"Wait, no," I say, growing mad myself. "You don't get to do this. How about *'Thanks, Eclipse, I would have died if it wasn't for you?'* even just an *'I owe you one?'*"

"You were supposed to stay with Joni's people," Hanna says, livid. "She offered for you to stay. You know it's what you really wanted. A home. Why did you leave them to follow me?"

"How did you know that?"

"Don't lie to me. I know when you're lying."

I shrug, self-conscious.

"If you weren't allowed to stay with Joni's community, I wasn't going to either. It wasn't fair. Besides, we have an alliance, right?"

Still no answer.

"I wish things had happened differently," I say, my crest falling. Does she hate me for what I just did? Have I done something so dark that even the Empress herself can't come to terms with it?

I need her to understand. I need one person to be able to forgive me for what I did.

"I wish those humans were still alive," I whisper. "How I can face Griffin now if I have to tell him the truth? And if I try and hide it from him, the noise from it will be so loud in me that he'll see it no matter what. I can't lie to him." My voice breaks. "But if I hadn't stopped them, you'd be dead right now. And you are the only person I have really known in my entire life. The only person I have gotten to know for myself, and not just from Cirrus' memories. You might think your life is worthless, but I know we're both here for a reason. That's why we're still alive. So let's do what we came to this island to do. Let's cross over, together, and finally be with our humans."

Hanna stares at me, nostrils flared, eyes cold. But her eyes are not quite meeting mine. They stare off to the side of my face, into empty space.

I still don't understand why she's this angry at me. I stand, lost and forlorn.

But then I look carefully at her eyes, and see the tears glistening there. Finally, understanding sets into me, like a terrible poison absorbed through the skin.

The wind blows around us, flicking droplets of hard, freezing rain. Thunder booms again, filling the cold silence.

I think of Hanna's attempt to lose me in Sanctuary and her breakdown when Raven didn't send anyone to the Domain to save her. I remember having to prise the information she'd found on New Redemption about the Underworld from her, and how reluctantly she'd agreed to an alliance.

I think of us holding hot chocolates in Celeste's apartment seeing the life we could have had, and laughing together in the dunes surrounded by Shadows who were just happy to be themselves as they were, and my heart pains me deeper than I had known it could.

Hanna poisons everything around her. You shouldn't trust her.

Suddenly the furious tears, her inability to look me in the eye, all make sense.

Numb, I look out toward Aeyu, so sinister and forbidding. I wonder what really awaits me there.

I am aware of Hanna staring at me now suspiciously. She can tell that something has changed. She's taut as a bowstring, waiting for my reaction, suspicion slowly setting into her that I *know*.

She could have killed me while I slept, if that's what she really wanted. Hanna wants me alive, but for what purpose I do not know.

But mainly I just feel sadness. I deserve this. I killed Cirrus. I killed innocent Shadows in the Battle of Sanctuary, and now these humans' blood is on my talons. No matter how hard I try, Eclipse the bloodthirsty conqueror is still a part of me. It's my programming, and I cannot escape it, always looping me back toward who I am really am.

My destiny is tied to Hanna's. Since I found her in her cell, I've felt that if she could find a way to be redeemed, if she could find a brighter way forward for herself after so much darkness... that would be a sign that perhaps there was hope for me too. We rise together, and we fall together.

"Eclipse?" Hanna asks, voice uncertain.

"We should get going," I say dully. She looks surprised to see me slump, deflating. The sky is crying. The rain is falling thickly now, clumping my feathers together, wilting the crest feathers trailing down the back of my head. But I don't make any move to escape the rain. "It would be a shame to come all this way, and not finish what we intended to."

Hanna stares at me, her expression enigmatic.

"Right," she says, hesitant. Still trying to decipher my melancholy. To know if I really know.

I shuffle to the edge of the platform and throw myself off it. My wingbeats are half-hearted as I lift into the sky, riding through another encroaching storm. Storms seem like a regular occurrence in these islands. Riding the air toward the beautiful palace that seems to exude dread, I hear Hanna falling in behind me. If there's any kind of storm going on in her own head and heart to match my own, all I can hear is the hiss and thunder of the one we're approaching.

I don't know why I care about Hanna so much despite everything. Even though she doesn't seem to give a care about me, I suppose she's all I have, the only one who understands me. Even if she used that to manipulate me all this way, to manoeuvre me into this moment.

I know it's ludicrous, twisted. But I'm done fighting. I'm finished struggling to find my place and my purpose. Griffin may never even want to see me again if he knows I killed his own kind, I think shamefully.

If Hanna is taking me to my grave, if this helps her in some way, if it's what she really wants... then I won't deny it to her. I'll follow her no matter how this ends. I'm too invested in her not to. I'm too tired not to.

Hanna's a good Shadow in her heart. Or she once was, before she was corrupted. She needs to see that good is still inside her, to believe it. She'll make the right decision.

And if not... maybe this is what I deserved all along.

．．．

Lightning burns white as we fly across the water. Aeyu Palace grows closer and closer. My spirits strangely lift at the thought that this is it. We finally made it. Griffin is so close I could almost touch him. But at the same time the moment is tainted by the bitter sweetness that maybe I was never meant to reach him... and perhaps I never will.

I wonder what it would be like, to cross into the human world. Would we keep exploring deeper and deeper into the Underworld, until we are in this world one moment and over there in the next? Or would we be sucked into the human world just from getting closer to Aeyu, as Joni had said some of her Shadows were, as the humans probably were as well. As if a curtain had temporarily lifted between the two worlds?

We fly through the intermittent darkness, thunder rumbling and rain beating us backward in sheets. The Island of Moon is now below us. I can almost feel myself in the human world, can almost see Griffin running across a green summer field, ecstatic to see me. I can almost hear him making his obscure human-culture gaming references.

Aeyu's towers rise high into the sky, somehow as terrifying as they are breath-taking. Below us, a mighty river twists through the trees. Its current swollen with the rain, it thunders over the rocky cliffs surrounding the base of the Aeyu. Then the water winds its way around Aeyu Palace in a moat of surging rapids, before heading out to the ocean. I feel it again - there's something coldly enchanting about the palace, something you cannot resist but be pulled towards, like a magnet. Its reaching towers are brought into stark relief with the flashes of lightning, and the bridges like strands of spider web sway in the growing winds of the storm.

As we fly into the thick black cloud, sailing through darkness, I hear something all around us. A strange whisper running through the air.

Like something breathing.

I shiver with foreboding.

"What is it?" Hanna shouts. She looks unnerved, breathing unsteadily. She's pale. Still, it sounds as if talking seems to calm her, to keep her distracted.

"I don't know."

But as we descend down toward the palace which holds the entrance to the Underworld, the wind rises in a scream, and I hear something in it again. The same sound I swear I heard when I first woke on the beach.

"*Ciiiirrrruss...*"

6

AEYU PALACE

Griffin

"Everyone, get in your beds," I hiss. The darkened faces are staring at me in terror from all around the wide room.

I hear it again.

Creeeeak.

"When they come in," I press on, "we'll force our way out the way they come in. Toby, I want you at the front with me. Being... tall and all."

"You've got it, boss," Toby says.

"But where's the door?" April hisses, confused. "Where have they been coming in?"

"Not doors," I say, my voice falling to the barest of whispers. "The mirrors." To punctuate my statement, there's a definite creaking, and we all fall silent. Most of the kids lie flat on their beds, while Toby and I stand deathly still like statues. My eyes slightly adjusted to the dark now, I scan the tall, ancient mirrors fixed to the walls, spaced between each of the bunk beds. Waiting.

Only to see the mirror beside April's bed slowly sliding open.

The mirror is swinging subtly like a revolving door. Only the faintest creak comes from it. The hairs on the back of my neck stand on end. Moving quickly across the space, I flatten myself against one side and Toby stands sentry on the other.

Then the mirror slides fully open, and I can make out a clawed foot slowly extending out from behind it. I watch with bated breath as the foot feels its way down to the floor. Not a foot. A claw. Sensing, feeling, it places itself down on the hard wooden floor. I swear the temperature of the room just dropped several degrees. I try to quieten my breath, but I can see a plume of steam emerging from my mouth in the flickering firelight.

Then our captor steps through completely, eyeing the still, slumbering forms of the human teenagers in their beds.

It's not the being who took me hostage. It's hard to see in the dark, but I get the impression of something feathered, humanoid. Two beady eyes glitter in the firelight. Something deep inside me recoils at the sight of the Shadow before me, though I can't say why.

The Shadow cocks its head to the side suddenly, as if it's heard something.

"Now!" I shout, fear giving me strength. I lunge forward, bringing a broken shard of wood from one of the beds downward. The Shadow turns unnaturally fast and sweeps my weapon aside with its talons, revealing its enormous wings.

I hear the crackle of ice, and suddenly realise I can't move my feet. I try to rip them free from the floorboards but it's like they're immobilised with fear. My skin burns with cold, and I realise my feet are actually frozen to the wood. Helpless, like a fly tangled in a web.

The creature hisses, raising a clawed hand up to my throat. There's cries and shouts from the beds as the other kids spring into action, throwing aside sheets to reveal their own weapons from beneath the blankets. They rush the feathered Shadow. He turns in surprise, fixing them with those beady eyes. I can see some of them, shivering, and on their legs I can see black ice spreading out across their skin, locking their limbs into place.

"What do you want from us?" Georgia screams at our jailer. Tears streak down her cheeks, and she's clutching little Marty protectively.

"Please," April begs. "Just let me out. Let me out of here. My Mum will be wondering where I've gone…"

Then Toby steps out from the other side of the mirror and brings his length of wood down at our captor, wielding it like a baseball bat. He strikes hard and true, and the Shadow makes a horrible sound, like a horse's scream ending in an injured whimper. I feel the ice locking my feet in place melt.

"Come on!" I yell to the others. The mirror the Shadow entered through is already closing, rotating at its centre to close the gap. It's about to lock into place and trap us in here indefinitely. I grab Toby's wooden weapon off him and run up to the mirror, wedging it long-ways between the mirror and the wall. The mirror halts, jammed, but then the wood starts to splinter under the fierce pressure of the mechanism. The mirror is determined to lock us in.

There's no way to stop it clamping shut. All of the other kids are still frozen in place, their eyes angry or pleading. We need someone on the outside.

Toby throws himself through the gap just as the wooden wedge creaks warningly.

"Come on!" he screams, reaching for me.

I make a split second decision.

"I'll come back for you!" I shout at the other kids. "I promise."

Then I throw myself through the gap just as the wooden weapon snaps. I grab Toby's arm as he pulls me through, narrowly missing getting jammed between the mirror and the wall. The mirror shuts behind us and I hear bolts locking into place.

Turning, I urgently slam myself back into the mirror, but it will not move. And whatever it's made from is unbreakable. Examining it, I see a small scan pad. Fudge. The creepy feathered guard must have some sort of key card. I wonder if it's trapped in there on the other side, if the card only works from here.

The thought of that Shadow makes my hands shake uncontrollably, as if there's still something about it I can't place my finger on.

"We need to find another way in," I say.

Toby is warily surveying the stone hallway we now find ourselves in. It's like a passage from some Gothic castle.

That's it. The crumbling giant palace that me and Phoebe had spotted across the island; that's where we are, where we've all been taken.

Which means... that right on the other side, another

world away, we are standing right where my Mum's portal facility should be. The station which is the key to opening the doors between the worlds.

I'm just one universe away is all. Right GPS coordinates, wrong dimension.

Where the hell is Phoebe? Did she make it to the human side? Or did something horrible happen to her out there on the island?

I wish Eclipse was here.

Then I feel it. Just like I felt it in the swamp with Phoebe. A sense of creeping familiarity, like an urge to return home. It's like a call, rippling through the wind, pulling me into it. Something is compelling me.

"It's coming," I gasp. I hesitate, eyes on the back of the mirror. But right now we have no idea how to release the others from the room. And if we die, their only hope of breaking out dies with us. "Run!"

"But the others..." Toby protests.

"We can't help them if we get thrown back in there!"

The two of us sprint down the palace hallway and turn tightly. The stone around us is cracked and crumbling, yet has a timeless feel to it. There are silvery cobwebs in artistic patterns hanging between the nooks and crannies, strands hanging from the ceiling. The air is cold. I don't mean to get hysterical or let my imagination run away, but it feels like the stones sing with the cold voices of lost souls. The ghosts of all this palace's previous inhabitants.

Or maybe it's the ghosts of the children who have been taken from that room.

I shake the thought from my head. We are going to get the others out alive. It just means now there's an unexpected bonus side mission to the main one that brought Phoebe and me to the islands.

"Thanks for holding the mirror open for me," I gasp as we run.

Toby grins cockily beside me, then turns solemn. "Seriously Grif, we're in this together. I'm not going anywhere."

I smile a small smile. A tiny pinprick of hope glows to life in my chest. It feels safer having Toby here with me. Older, smarter. He seems more friendly than Calvin, more relying on emotion and gut instinct than cold logic. Despite everything, I suddenly feel less alone.

We hurtle through the palace's corridors, zigzagging like rats in a maze. Primal fear forces us onward as we race to escape whoever trapped us here... and whoever is hunting us right now.

It's on us now, just the two of us. Me and my new pal Toby, who I barely know. We have to find a way to cross back over to the human world, and open up the portals once and for all. But if whatever was in the swamp hunts us down first... we'll be dead, and there will be nobody left to complete Mum's project. Or to save those kids.

It's hopelessly infuriating. The Shadow world has this giant freaky palace of nightmares, rather than the station my Mum built. If I was to cross over now to my own world, I wouldn't be running through a corroded palace but the futuristic metal corridors of the station, and I'd be minutes from completing my family's destiny.

How do I get back to the other side? Will the air crackle around me like it did the first time, and suddenly I'll be in the human world instead of here? Or do I need to be looking for some kind of Rip on the island, like the one that cracked open in the sky beside Cameron Technologies and started all of this?

Toby and I hit a railing at the top of a stairwell and stop, at eye level with a massive hanging chandelier of crystal. It emits a blue, icy flame from the candles contained within it.

We're staring down at a grand ballroom, pillars decorating its fringes. It reminds me of the one from the dance scene in *Beauty and the Beast*. Actually, it makes me think of a straight-up post-apocalyptic Disney palace; The Happiest Place On Earth, if it was forgotten over the years and started crumbling around the edges. I have the feeling that it might have been a fantastical wonderland once, but has since witnessed terrible events, the memories of which have been absorbed into the very body of this place.

The floor we are on has a circular balcony so onlookers can survey the ballroom below from any angle. Two curving stairways lead down to the level below, and we take the one on the left. Letting gravity speed our descent, as I take the steps two at a time.

The grand ballroom branches into four other passages, like spokes on a wheel.

"It's coming for us," I exhale, a shiver rippling down my spine. "I can feel it."

"Which one?" Toby says. He seems quite happy to be my loyal number two and let me make the calls.

"Lucky Dip," I say, and run for one on the passage on our left hand side. We bolt through the passage. Toby is slightly ahead, being far more fit than me and in possession of longer legs. We hit a door, but luckily it's unlocked. Toby jerks it open and ushers me through, following behind me.

I'm disorientated for a moment. We're rushing through a dark chamber full of machinery, blinking with crimson sinister lights. Our surroundings rush past me in a mad mess but I don't even have a moment to fully comprehend it, just focused on putting as much distance between us and the nameless horror pursuing us as possible.

Another door, a foyer, a pair of wide palace doors... together Toby and I heave the heavy doors open, then spin around to jam them shut behind us. I'm breathing heavily. But we're finally outside, standing on rough rocks in the light of day. I breathe in deeply. The wind whips around us.

"Come on, this should do it." Toby bends down to heave on a broken tree trunk, as if deposited here by a storm. I help him, hauling as we use its heavy weight to block the doors.

Then we turn and run wildly across a shoreline made of large black rocks, dodging around reeds and rock pools. Here and there the odd tree sprouts upward, deformed and strange. A river flows past the rocky shore, out toward the ocean, forming a moat for the palace. But maybe there's a chance we can swim across.

I'm disorientated from our race from darkness into the glaring cold light. I turn to look over my shoulder to see if our pursuer is still on our heels...

Up behind us towers the enormous palace, every turret and spire out-matched by another that rises even higher.

"Do you have a family that's worried about you?" I ask Toby suddenly, thinking of Calvin.

"No. Orphan. And a loner by nature. You?"

"Same," I say. "On both counts."

"So. What made you want to become a radical world-changing terrorist?" he asks bluntly.

I look at him sharply, but he's smiling wryly.

"I was a newbie in that room too," Toby says with a

grin. "I'm more up to date with world events than most of those kids were. I know what those monsters... sorry, what those *Shadows* did to Cameron Technologies, back in our world."

"That wasn't meant to happen. Shadows aren't like that. Not most of them. We were trying to make things better."

"I get that. Most people don't, but... I do. I know that you and your brother have been treated as scapegoats for the whole mess. So, why the career choice? From working at a burger joint to trying to bring interdimensional creatures to our reality?"

I grin back at him.

"I guess it started because of my big brother, mainly," I confess.

"Ah, yes. Those big brothers can be pretty self-righteous."

"I didn't say he was self-righteous."

"You said it with your tone," Toby says, amused. "The great Calvin Cameron. That's a pretty big reputation to live up to."

"Don't mock him," I say, more defensive than I intend to be. I pant as I leap from one jagged rock to the next, forcing my way onward. My mood darkens. "He's been taken captive because of... what they're blaming us for."

"You're right," Toby says, shrugging. "I just got the impression that the guy could be a pain in the arse."

"Well, yeah," I exhale, wrapping my arms around myself to stay warm. "No arguments there. But he's blood. No matter what he does, he'll still always be my brother." Maybe I say it in an effort to convince myself more than Toby.

'Did you... did you ever wish that she'd survived, instead of me?' I'd asked Calvin. I remember his silence.

I fight the memory away. No time for self-pity, Grif. Two worlds are relying on us right now. And Eclipse and Phoebe are out there somewhere, waiting. Don't let them down.

Suddenly Toby's hand shoots out to grab my shoulder. My foot slips and I struggle to regain my footing, nearly getting washed away. Pebbles roll out into the river before me. I totter on the edge, at risk of being swept out to sea. I'd been too occupied with my thoughts, and the drop came quicker than I'd expected.

The current of the river is wild. Rapids swirl and crash past us, a deadly barrier that seems to run wide and deep. The water surges and washes over the rocks, filling them with feathery white foam around my feet, hungry for foolishly brave souls.

My swimming idea seems less plausible now that we're seeing the water up close. I look across at the trees up on the steep bank opposite, trying to think of some other way of crossing. Is Phoebe still out there somewhere, running and hiding? I wonder. Or has she found a way back across to the human world, leaving me in the Shadow world all alone?

"What's our game plan?" Toby asks.

"What matters is survival. Finding a way to cross. Nobody will rescue the others back in the palace if we're taken too. Then, I have to find a way to cross over into the human world. There's a station over there, the trigger to connecting the two worlds. That's the best thing we can do to fix this madness."

"Another one of those portal buildings?" Toby asks as we move along the shore, hunting for a way to cross the river. "I thought the News said all of Cameron Technologies' property was seized and shut down."

"There's one station they don't know about. One my Mum built in secret, as a back-up."

"A secret interdimensional portal facility? Wicked," Toby says, grinning. He actually looks like he's having a whale of a time, joking like we're doing a team bonding exercise and not running for our lives. "So, Cirrus, this... this Shadow of yours you said died. What was he like? You two were really friends?"

Toby's still scanning the riverside for ideas of how to cross. Meanwhile I've gone still, something playing in the back of my brain. There's something nagging me I can't let go of, a mental chew toy that I just can't leave alone.

I watch Toby from behind as he goes still too. Slowly Toby straightens, dropping his characteristic slouch. The bouncy energy calms, replaced by a sense of calm self-possession.

"What gave it away?" he says, without turning. It sounds like he's smiling.

"I never told you that my Shadow was called Cirrus," I say quietly.

"Somehow you avoided that?" He laughs. "Holy crow. You were testing us all from the start." Turning, Toby grins. His smile still has the same genuine warmth. "Damn it! We were having so much fun together." He tosses a stone over his shoulder, out into the river.

"Who are you?" I demand. My hands are tight fists, nails digging into my palms.

There's this kind of fierceness to his smile too, I realise. A sadness and a rueful joy. Like he's smiling at a joke that I haven't gotten yet, waiting for the penny to drop. The young man looks at me through his long, dark hair, and for the first time I notice the burns concealed beneath it. Burns quite similar to Phoebe's.

The answer comes over me. My heart has turned to ice.

The island is quiet around us, other than the spray of the river.

"I have missed you so much, Griffin," Raven says.

I move forward to shove him into the river, blood singing in my ears.

When suddenly I'm lifted from the ground by an invisible force, and flung backward.

I strike against a rock and cry out, but no bones break. Shocked, outraged, I look up to see what attacked me...

I gasp. It's the second time I've seen it, but only the first that I've had a real good look. I'm unable to look away. There's something awful about it, a dark divinity that compels me. I feel a sense of primal awe mixed with petrified terror.

At first I only get the faintest impression of a great being. A being that twists though empty air like a spider clambering down its invisible web toward its captured prey. I seem to be able to make out more of it if I look at it from the corner of my eye, rather than straight on.

I make out a human torso ending in powerful scaled legs. A massive tail like a hungry white worm. Its pale arms are swollen at the ends into broad claws like spades. It's something monstrous, something... draconic.

Every instinct in my brain is screaming too. Like how prey knows to fear its natural predator.

Whatever this *thing* is, some part of me strangely thinks straight away: this isn't a Shadow. It's something more.

Then I'm on my feet, and I'm running. I run with everything I have. I fly back across the rocks toward the palace. Hunted by an entity whose very existence seems to disobey the laws of physics. I can hear Raven's laughter.

"You can't hide," I hear him yell, and I can tell he's grinning. "This is my home!"

I'm nearly at the palace doors again when suddenly my body starts disobeying me. I come to a complete halt, my muscles trembling like they're paralysed in terror. A fly in a web that it can't even perceive.

I hear footsteps behind me.

"You did always love hide and seek," Raven speaks softly in my ear.

7
FUSION

Eclipse

I struggle to land in front of the epic palace as we're buffeted by howling gales. Rain runs from the tips of my feathers.

Up above us, lighting flares, illuminating the ascending towers and levels that lead up into the sky like a juggernaut above us. Aeyu. The gateway to the Underworld, and our ticket to crossing over to the human realm. To Griffin.

Hanna looks like a little drowned violet butterfly, wings beating against the rain. My own feathers are slicked back from the water. Suddenly I recall I still have Ember's flame to heat my feathers. My feathers glow with fiery light, trying to warm some life back into me.

As I do I can't help but think of Ember. The happier memories of our conversations during my imprisonment. The bad memories too, of the fight which led to me stealing her power and abandoning her. I still don't know if she's alive, or if she died in the battle above Midnight Crafters. Part of me aches at the thought. I hope she was never there at all. That she's safe. I'm still hurt, I'm still angry at Ember for keeping me caged for so long, but I've seen too much over the last couple of days to keep hating her any longer. I just appreciate that I can keep her memory alive through the flame running through me - even if it is a stolen gift.

A large pair of wooden doors stand in front of us. Hanna is heaving on the handles, but they refuse to move.

"Stand aside," I say, and charge. I slam into the doors and they thunder open, wood splintering and cracking.

Hanna zips in behind me, vanishing into the dark of the palace. It feels so good to be out of the cold and the wet as I enter. So good that it takes a moment to see our surroundings for what they are.

We're in a cavernous chamber. It's completely dark, apart from the glow and blinking of futuristic lights that you wouldn't usually expect in your run-of-the-mill abandoned ruin. The low crimson glow of the equipment feels unquestionably sinister.

It's impressive how many giant pieces of technology, blinking lights, cold glaring monitors and pulsing pistons are arrayed throughout the space. They come together to form the prime feature that attracts all of the attention; a machine that looks as if it is breathing like a living entity, a giant artificial organism of metal and glass.

We hear wails. Cries that send chills like cold needles into my spine.

"Well, we've definitely found something," I say, looking sideways at Hanna.

Drawn to the source of the distress, we see what the

machine is really doing, and suddenly it's like something from a nightmare.

I'm staring at a young human girl, trapped in part of the machine. I've barely digested this before a clawed robotic arm grasps her, hauling her screaming out of a suspended cage. I detect a symmetry to the movement and realise that on the other side, mirroring the human youth, a Shadow is being hauled out of a second cage. The Shadow resembles a shivering plant bulb with a tail arching over her head, ending in a simple flower blossom. The mechanical fingers clamp around the Shadow like pincers. It trembles in pain. Then the robotic arms manoeuvre to drop human and Shadow each into a large pod of dark rubber. It all happens in a single moment of insanity, before Hanna and I can even react.

We hear the flower Shadow and her young girl shouting, before their screams cut off completely.

Hanna and I cry out in unison. Roaring enough to shake the dark palace chamber, I lunge toward the machine to tear open the rubber pods and release them...

"NO!" Hanna warns me.

"You want to just leave them in there?" I accuse her.

"Eclipse, look, it's too late," Hanna says, pale. "Whatever is happening to them right now... it's already started. Interrupting it could hurt them irreversibly. Maybe it's even helping them. Some kind of... surgery."

"Yes, this place looks like it's all about making people feel better," I say scathingly.

Hanna flies forward toward a blinking control panel at the base of the machine, searching it for some indicator of the nature of what we're witnessing.

I scan the machine for clues as to its purpose. Thick

tubes wind from the two pods to a third containment pod. Beneath that sits a transparent glass pool filled with red liquid.

A crystal orb suspended from the stone roof turns white. Inside of it, two silhouettes come into focus, displayed side by side. The outlines of the plant Shadow and its human girl. The silhouettes begin to circle each other, spiralling before flowing together, fusing into a new shape. Merging into a single silhouette.

The third pod beneath the first two starts to jerk, like a wild beast beserking.

The air feels thick around me, strange. As the vibrations of the machine reaches a fervour, time seems to stand still. All around us, reality seems to tear. The air shredding, as miniature Rips open all around us, like a cosmic claw has scarred the dimensional fabric.

My immediate instinct is to try and go through them, to find the human world on the other side. But these are too small, and they're unlike any other Rips I've seen- instead of glimpsing the human world on the other side, they shine with an eerie golden light. I can't help but feel a sense of foreboding about what really may lie on the other side.

"HANNA!" I roar. "Find the off switch!"

Scowling against the unnerving radiance, I raise a foot and try to slam down the levers with a talon. Instead I smash the controls completely, the interface shattering under the power of my claw. The humming of the machine dies, the robotic arms slowly going limp and lifeless. All around us, the miniature Rips in the air suddenly congeal, sealing themselves shut, withering into nothing.

Was that a mistake? If we'd left it longer, would a Rip have opened that was big enough for both Hanna and myself to get through into the human world? No. There was no way I could have just left those two innocents in there.

Thinking of the helpless human and Shadow who went into the machine I feel sick for a moment, wondering if Hanna was right. What if by interrupting this process, I've somehow injured them both irretrievably?

With a final tremendous convulsion, the machine seizes and is still.

A moment passes, the tension building. Then I make out panels on the base of the pod unfurling, like a cocoon being laid open.

Something drops down into the tank, too fast to see in the darkness. There's a splash as it lands in the red liquid below.

I move closer, wary. Lights come up on the tank automatically. The fluid is a bright, devilish red like toffee apple. The liquid is still for a moment, then something dark moves inside it.

Something is swimming in there. Something alive.

Its movement is slow, as if the liquid in the tank is made of thick egg white. For a moment I'm blind to the world except for what lies in that tank.

Then the crimson fluid starts to drain away, just as the creation inside the tank rises to the surface, levitating into clear view.

I inhale.

Hovering luminous and serene above the glass tank is... an angel.

She's kept aloft by fluttering leaves for wings. She's humanoid, and her skin is blue, her ears pointy and elfin. Flowers adorn the branches growing through her hair. She wears a skirt made from a blue flower blossom. It pulses with phosphorescent light. But those are all surface details. What is commanding is her aura. Beautiful. Captivating. Not of this world.

"Half human, half Shadow," I say in shock. It feels as if we're witnessing something religious. I look to Hanna. "She's a Majestic, like you told me about. This machine is birthing Majestics."

Hanna shakes her head, disturbed.

"That's impossible. They're a myth."

Suddenly robotic arms fly out from either side of the tank, grasping and restraining the Majestic. She flinches, shocked - but then one of the arms injects a syringe of black fluid into her neck.

The change is immediate. Harsh bark starts to grow along the Majestic's skin, covering her like a carapace. Her bright eyes blacken into hollow points of darkness. The blue glow of her flower morphs to poisonous green.

We watch as an angel transforms into a demon. Placed under a dark thrall by whatever fluid is now spreading through her veins.

The altered Majestic slowly extends an arm, reaching out toward us. We back away. She snarls demonically, then she screams. It's a terrible sound that cuts to my core. She screams, and screams, as if she's being torn apart from the inside - then she disintegrates, breaking apart before us. The Majestic dissolves into grey ash, falling softly and chillingly to the laboratory floor.

Hanna and I don't even breathe.

"Was that... meant to happen?" Hanna asks, clearly haunted by what we just saw.

"A failed experiment," I say slowly, more traumatised by what we just witnessed than I want to let on. "Whatever that chemical was, the Majestic couldn't take it." I shake my head. We have other worries right now. "We need to find the passage to the Underworld," I say unsteadily, searching for an exit. "This is wrong. Whatever is going on here…"

A sharp, violent pain explodes in my back. I cry out.

I can feel the stinging barb arching up into my back muscles, can already feel the full blast of toxic venom flash-flooding through my system. For a moment I'm confused. I know who can cause pain like that, the sensation is too familiar. I stagger.

"Galvanize," I thunder through the pain. My body is losing feeling, disobeying me. My vision swims.

"Hanna," I cry, my tongue numb. "Run!" The last word dies in my throat as my assassin steps into view. It's not Galvanize I'm staring at.

But it *is* the Empress.

Hanna is standing there, alone, her face pale as chalk. She's clutching Galvanize's stinger, the one she tore off the insectoid when we were escaping the student flat.

So she was concealing it all this time. How? Disguised beneath those wide violet wings perhaps, or literally hidden up her sleeve. Hiding the instrument of my doom all this time.

"No…" It's hard to get the words out. My body is moving too slow. I fight it with everything I have. I stare at Hanna as her promise breaks. All my quiet, unspoken hopes for her vanquished as easily as she drove that stinger into me. My worst suspicions confirmed.

"You don't have to do this," I gasp at Hanna, face burning. I struggle against the poison. "This is not who you are."

"It's already done, Eclipse," Hanna says, sounding dead inside.

"I should never have trusted you," I whisper. For one moment my old commanding fury lances through me, the smouldering rage of a king, of an alpha predator. My feathers burst into flame. "I should have left you to rot in that cell!"

Then the anger passes, and instead I just feel weak and used. Lonely. The flame in my feathers sparks, then goes out. Like the candles blown out on a birthday cake.

"Help me," I urge her, my voice breaking. "We're *so* close. There's still time. We made it, Hanna. We're right on the brink."

"What, like either of us ever really believed we were on the same side?" Hanna demands, her voice high-pitched. There are dark bags under her eyes, and her voice is tortured. "I was awake that night in the hold of the ship. I saw how much you wanted to murder me, but didn't. Part of you will never forgive what I did to Cirrus. What you've experienced in his memories. Admit it."

I want to speak, but no words come to me.

"I'm not a freak," Hanna mutters fiercely. I can't tell if she's speaking to me or herself. "I'm the Empress. And I was born to rule."

"But your human... you want her more than anything," I say, not understanding.

Hanna stares at me earnestly, as if she is finally laid bare and naked before me.

"I want *him* more," she says honestly.

My insides sink. I know now, even without the twisted machine being a hideous giveaway. Still. I need her to say it aloud.

"Whose palace is this?" I say slowly. She does not answer. "Empress?"

"I told you. This palace is ancient." Hanna presses her lips together. "But since you destroyed his old home, Aeyu is home to someone new. Raven."

Everything that's happened between Hanna and me was a lie. I thought in some way we were making each other into better Shadows. That there was hope for both of us. But it was just a story, and Hanna made sure I felt I was making all the decisions as she manoeuvred me here. She played the part perfectly. She's hand-delivered me to her dark master, so she can replace Galvanize as his favourite once again.

I turn from Hanna and stagger back through the laboratory toward the open palace doors, where rain is whirled by freezing winds. Back toward my only chance for survival. I flap my wings hard, trying to pump the stiffening muscles hard enough to achieve lift... but then I stumble and fall on the wet rocks of the shore instead.

I'm finished. A sad mockery of myself.

She must be laughing at me.

As the end draws near, I desperately delve deep into Cirrus' memories for courage, memories that vastly outnumber mine.

I see Cirrus as a child, perched in his clock tower as the only place he could get away from Zephyr, wishing he could escape. Afraid that everything he remembered from his childhood was a lie, a fantasy, that Griffin might never come for him. Living in an Empire that saw humans as a disease, who told him he was insane. That's what Cirrus' feelings for Griffin were. Unyielding, crazy and dangerous, a loyalty like fire that could eat everything in its path. Not even the rain that night could have doused it or numbed his belief in his human.

Lying prone, I still drag myself toward the river, away from the palace doors.

Closer. Closer. My body feels so weak.

The toxin is making its final passage through my system. The corners of my vision are turning dark, as I realise I have been truly alone this entire time.

"Not long now, Eclipse," I hear Hanna says quietly. Distantly I'm aware of her kneeling beside my head.

Remember what Griffin told you, I order myself, desperately trying to find some light to cling to in the darkness. *We are part of each other.*

I am him.

He is me.

Feverish, I try to imagine Griffin. Really imagine him, physically, to make him solid. He feels so faint, and the delirium from the poison makes the memory of my human hard to grasp. But I try to focus, to pour my heart and everything I have left into it.

Until it is as if Griffin is here with me, holding my wing. Keeping me company until the end.

I can't feel the cold anymore.

"Griffin?" I whisper, dazed. "I am... sorry. I failed."

This Griffin smiles at me. He's a hallucination I created, I know that. But I realise that even not knowing how the real Griffin feels about me, whether he still wants to know me or if he's still angry at me for replacing Cirrus... it doesn't matter to me. Because wherever he is in the universe, I'll always carry him with me. Right to the end. I'll always believe in him. And in this moment... knowing he's here inside of me, knowing that nothing will be able to take that away from me... that's enough.

Lying dying from the toxin beneath the dark clouded

sky, winds howling, I no longer feel as if I am a freak. I feel like as much a piece of nature as any Shadow in this world. This looks like the end. But I still existed. I was here. I mattered.

All of us do.

Hanna's face swims into view.

"I tried to make you understand," Hanna whispers. "Raven is my drug. He's my answer. I have to prove myself to him again, and for whatever reason... right now, you are what he wants most."

"Hanna," I croak. "We can still make it to the human world. To a new start. Don't do this. Not after everything."

"I'm sorry," she says, with feeling. "But I need him. I don't know how to live without him."

8

FAMILY FRIEND

Griffin

Chills run down my back. I'm sitting in the palace's kitchen, feeling very vulnerable and exposed in nothing but pyjamas. The wide, stone-walled space is everything you would expect from a medieval kitchen. Except since moving into this place Raven seems to have made a few adjustments - including a fully equipped modern kitchen with a stone island to sit at on swivel-chairs. The air is filled with the sound of spitting butter.

There are signs of other life here - abandoned dirty implements and half-chopped cabbages across the counter spaces - but Raven has cleared the space of his staff especially for my visit.

I stand on the other side of the stone island, feeling paralysed. I can't help it. The sight before me is so bizarre, so mundane. Raven is standing before me, his back to me. His black robes are hanging over a chair at the kitchen bench. He's leaning over the stovetop, humming to himself, flipping a pancake with a spatula. He's wearing a black collared shirt edged with gold. He could easily just be an ordinary person, someone just home from work. He passed convincingly as the confident and likeable Toby. He looks youthful. It still makes me feel sick, remembering how quick I was to warm to him in his disguise. Now I understand some of what Phoebe may have seen in him once.

Raven turns to look over his shoulder, and grins, "Come on, sit down. The pancakes are almost ready. I think I got this one to look a little bit like Cirrus."

I just stare.

"There's some orange juice in the fridge. If you want some." I'm still standing there, ridiculously. I'm confused. My eyes stray around the kitchen, searching for a kitchen knife within reach, some kind of weapon I can use.

Raven has washed since he played the part of Toby. His matted hair is clean and combed out of his eyes. The burned flesh down the side of his face is more on display now, but other than that he looks like a friendly, grinning young guy. Darkly handsome, I guess Sophie would have said. Now that I know who he is, I can see clearly the boy I saw in the photo of when Raven was Taylor, and worked with Calvin and Phoebe.

Before he killed my parents.

Even with his hair long, he doesn't look disarrayed, but effortlessly in control. It hits me that the burns down the side of his face must be from when Phoebe banished him. She used Ember's fire to knock some debris into him, blasting him through the portal into this world.

Something else occurs to me suddenly. That dark, humanoid bird who blasted us with ice when we tried to escape the prison room... that must have been Winter, Raven's Shadow. I should have realised immediately, but there had been so much going on. I recall the memory of Winter attacking me and Cirrus when we were children, the night of our Mum's death. I shudder. Even if Winter had been disobeying Raven's wishes, it had still been terrifying.

I don't need a weapon to take out Raven right now, I conclude. If I get my hands around his throat I'll break his neck before he has a chance to call for help. I move silently toward Raven, making my way around the kitchen island.

I rush forward suddenly...

Casually, Raven's free hand flips a tea towel spread out on the bench, revealing a gleaming knife.

I stop myself. It looks razor sharp, and his hand is right beside the handle. I have no doubts that he could disembowel me without having to look away from the pancakes. Slowly I back away, smouldering. Raven is still flipping pancakes as if nothing has happened.

"Seriously, try the orange juice," Raven says, gesturing. "It's worth it. You have no idea the hoops we have to jump through to get food delivered here."

Raven flips the pancake, once, two times... on the third he gets it stuck to the high ceiling.

"Dang," he says, sounding impressed with himself.

"Where's Eclipse?" I say tightly. If Raven made it out of that battle in Sanctuary... does that mean Eclipse didn't? Something tells me Eclipse wouldn't allow Raven to live if he could help it.

"We both made it out alive. Wherever Eclipse is, he's not your concern right now."

There's a chess board sitting on the kitchen island. I have a feeling Raven has deliberately placed it there for me. He's presented me with the black side, with the white pieces elegantly arranged at his own end.

"I hear you like games," Raven says conversationally.

"I don't want to play," I say.

"You're a gamer. Of course you want to play." He smiles. "You want to know if you can beat me."

Taking a footstool, Raven drags it over beside the stove, stepping up to dislodge the pancake. I consider rushing him to knock the stool out from under him. But he could still leap down and get the knife first, depending how fast his reflexes are. I hesitate. The opportunity passes, and I know Raven was flaunting it at me like bait to a shark. Raven doesn't take chances unless he's certain of the outcome.

"This isn't you," I simmer. "I'm not sure what you think you're doing, but I know that you're not this... *normal*. This is not what you were like when I first met you in Sanctuary City."

"You wanted a more theatrical villain? Sorry to disappoint."

"You were wearing those hooded robes, and your voice was..."

"I was wearing a gas mask I invented. It's meant to just protect from weaponised toxins, but I realised early on the way it altered my voice had a pretty intimidating effect on any Shadows I had dealings with."

"You gutted me," I say shakily. I can feel the pain in my stomach like it's fresh, even though after Zephyr healed it there wasn't any physical scarring left. The trauma is still there. "Like a fish. I was bleeding out everywhere, it was so cold..." The memories of our confrontation keep coming back to me. "You told me that you killed Mum. That you put her down, like a dog." I bare my teeth. I'm shaking, physically shaking. I have to stand here while he makes me freaking Cirrus-shaped pancakes. Mocking me.

"That was a different me," Raven says quietly, solemn for a moment. As if with regret. "Do you remember what else happened?"

"You set your mutant Shadow, Ammut, on us," I say. "You tried to stop me returning through the portal. You tried to take the Oracle away from me; the one thing Calvin needed to connect the worlds."

"Correct," Raven says, snapping his fingers. "A sixteen-year-old gamer escaped the most powerful being in the entire Shadow world, all on his own."

"I wasn't alone," I whisper.

"Of course. You had Eclipse too. But the two of you still had to stand up against one of my best creations. Ammut, a host of the most powerful Shadows I could find, combined into one body. No one should have survived the first few seconds, let alone have been an even match for him. But Eclipse is something else. And *you* got away." Raven laughs, sounding genuinely amazed. Like he's impressed, as if I'm a friend of his who just pulled off a crazy card trick. "Grif, I watched you belly-crawl your way up onto that podium. Bleeding out everywhere. It was incredible. You fought tooth and claw and managed to take that Oracle back home to your brother. To try and finish the project that Melissa and I started."

"Don't talk about Mum," I say quietly. "I beat you that time, *Raven*."

"My name's Taylor."

"No. Not anymore."

I'm livid, but he shrugs like it's of no consequence. He even winks at me.

"Believe what you want. But know this. I was in an ugly place when I met you in Sanctuary. I'd been in the darkness so long since Phoebe exiled me from your world. I got lost in it. So many things happened that I regret."

I snort with derision.

"*Really*," he says. "I forgot love and I forgot what the light felt like. I was all alone over here, in a world of strange creatures who hated humans. With my best friend to blame for it, but more so, myself. I was a shell of hate and resentment. When I met you... you brought it all rushing back. Memories of the old times, they came rising back up, echoes that haunted me after you left. What I'd done to you in Sanctuary began to eat away at me, the guilt and the pain excruciating. But when word reached me across the worlds that you'd survived... the relief, Griffin. Since then I've found I can even laugh again. Life feels like a game once more, something to be enjoyed and savoured, instead of a private hell. When we met six months ago... you saved me."

"I don't want to save you!" I shout, losing it. "I want you to *die!*"

Raven meets my eyes, and they shock me. They're full of tears.

"Griffin..." he says, choked up. He takes a step toward me, earnest, his arms hanging helplessly at his sides.

"Why did you kill my Mum?"

"I never meant for you to lose Melissa. I don't know what Calvin has told you, but it's not the full story. Your Mum cornered me one night, put me in an impossible situation. I panicked. My entire life I've been subject to... these compulsions. There are lines that others obey, lines that I cannot even see. I've always looked at the most rational way to obtain what I need, to do whatever is necessary. It's just the way I am. But when Melissa said she would tell Phoebe what I'd been doing, the experiments I'd been conducting..." His voice breaks. "I thought Phoebe would hate me. That she could never love me again if she knew. Suddenly I was facing a lonelier future than I could comprehend. I pushed Melissa. It was in the heat of the moment. I... I panicked, Griffin. I just panicked. But she fell wrong... and she struck her head against the frame of the portal. It made this horrible sound."

I'm crying, gasping for breath at the table. Calvin had never described the actual moment, what the experience must have been like for Mum. All Calvin had told me was that Raven had murdered her.

"And then she was lying there, and there was blood. I was so surprised to see *blood*. And Silvaluna, her Shadow, just collapsed... and it was over. They were both gone. Because of me, yes, but I never wanted it."

Raven leans on the bench, clasping his hands together like a silent prayer. His face is etched with agony. "Melissa gave me everything. She took me off the streets, she believed in me. She taught me how to work on the portal, she pushed me further than I ever thought I could go. Everything I am, I owe to her. She was a mother to me too. And if I was ever to face her again..." He exhales and looks away from my gaze. "I don't think I could," he admits. "Everything, *everything* changed that day."

There's silence. I don't know how to react to this. I don't know what I expected, but it wasn't this.

No. I need someone to hate. It can't be the accident

Raven is making it out to be. He murdered her in cold blood. It was calculated.

"Your pancakes," Raven says, "are getting cold. Don't worry, there's more on their way." I realise he's placed a plate on the kitchen island. A fork and a knife are neatly laid out on either side. Raven was right. The pancake is in the shape of Cirrus. It's very convincing.

I *am* famished, I know it, even though I don't feel like eating. I can't remember when I last ate. I walk around the island, so I can seat myself but still keep an eye on Raven. I start slicing up the pancake, ignoring the man in front of me. I try not to let my hand shake as I move the fork to my mouth.

I chew. The fluffy texture is pretty on point.

Oh my God. It hits me suddenly. *Raven knows our plan.* I told Toby what I was trying to do beside the river. Now there's no way Raven's going to release me, knowing what I'm trying.

Did I mention Phoebe to him? I think suddenly, feeling a bolt of fear. No. I feel a wave of relief. Not by name, anyway. I just mentioned a girl with blonde hair to the others, which would only throw him off further. Raven mustn't suspect she's alive. It has to stay that way, or Phoebe will be in danger. She banished Raven forever from the human world, and he still bears the scars to show it.

"Did you already know about Melissa's secret station on the other side, before I told you?" I ask quietly. There's no point denying it, or hoping that he somehow didn't hear me by the riverside.

"I may have suspected," Raven admits.

"Well, why else choose to retreat to a ruined palace

exactly on the other side from Mum's station?" I say bluntly. "You and coincidences don't go together."

"There's an entrance to the Underworld beneath us. It's made the experiments I'm doing easier to perform here."

I feel my stomach turn.

"Experiments? Like the ones on New Redemption, conversion therapy to turn Shadows away from their humans?"

Raven just smiles.

"Have you heard the legend of the Majestics, Griffin? Angelic beings. Shadows used to believe we were all Majestics once before we were cleaved in half, each Majestic becoming a human and a Shadow. And that if human and Shadow were joined together once more as a whole... they would evolve into a Majestic once again. With powers beyond measure, to whom the rules of time and space are more like... guidelines."

I stare at him.

"You can't be serious. I mean you've done some insane things, but that... it sounds like a fairy tale."

I stop suddenly, forgetting everything else for a moment. My eyes have strayed to a photo frame I hadn't spotted until now, propped up on the stone bench beside a fruit bowl. I stop, and stare in shock.

It's a photo of Raven, back when he was called Taylor, and of me. I don't know how Raven came into possession of it. It's a photo just of Taylor, grinning and holding up a little boy. A boy with wild blonde hair.

I stare at the surreal photo. Baby Griffin is grabbing a handful of Taylor's hair playfully. I look at the smile on Taylor's face, trying to reconcile it. It's at odds with everything that Calvin has ever told me about Raven. Everything he described Taylor as.

I place another mouthful of pancake in my mouth, almost on autopilot.

"Calvin hates you," I say thickly. I swallow. "You two were friends. And you betrayed him."

"I made mistakes," Raven nods gravely. "But did it ever occur to you, that your brother might be just as bad?"

"My brother is a good man," I say, seething.

"You don't really believe that. Not anymore. We're all grey, Griffin, none of us are just light or dark. Your brother hid the truth about Shadows from you for years, letting you suffer. I, however, will never lie to you. I promise."

I stare down at my pancakes, thinking of Calvin. The cold, egotistical tyrant who made it perfectly clear that he had never wanted to be saddled with the responsibility of a little brother to care for. I loved him more than anything in the world and I hated him just as much for not returning those feelings.

"I won't sit here while you keep pretending to be the good guy," I deflect at Raven angrily. "You created the horrors of the Empire. You are responsible for creating the Empress and New Redemption. So many Shadows suffered and died for your experiments. You taught them to fear humans, to hate them, and you used that fear to control them."

"Guilty," Raven says. It makes evil seem almost inane, that this mastermind can be chilling in the kitchen, chewing on his own mouthful of pancake. He's right about at least one thing - I preferred him as the hideous villain who I confronted beneath the Melder Justice Division six months ago. *That* was a villain I could believe in. This one is animated, gesturing like a theatrical showman, his voice friendly, courteous. He's intelligent, but he takes me seriously too. As if he's genuinely excited to have me here.

I don't understand him. I don't know what he wants from this.

"You know that there are several times throughout history where enormous change has necessitated small-scale evils. The deaths of a few justifying the whole. I know, I know, it's not what the Hollywood films advocate, killing is supposed to be wrong… but I don't believe that. You don't either. The two worlds are a game, a simulation that can be adjusted accordingly. Understand that sometimes doing a great good can require a great evil. That's what makes life so complex. It's a system, a balancing act."

I glare at him.

"How many times during your journey through the Shadow world did you do things that your friends," Raven presses, "even Cirrus, thought were evil? But you had seen what they hadn't: the clearest route to victory. Just like when you struck a deal with the Empress to try and save the dying at Winghold. You were doing whatever was necessary to win. You were playing strategically. So don't call me a monster, Griffin. Face it, I just took your game and went pro."

Any retort I was getting ready dies in my throat. Is Raven actually touching on some edge of truth?

"It was Hanna who tried to take Cirrus from you. That was something I never would have done. I am sorry for what she put you through. But do you still think you're the reason that Cirrus died, the reason that he changed that night on New Redemption?" Raven asks calmly. "When you nearly killed the Empress in revenge?"

I flinch. He's cut right through me, like he knows every-thing that's going on in my muddled subconscious. The guilt.

"Aren't I?" I demand. I'm glaring at Raven defiantly, but he's right. Inside I'm crying out for answers. I also wonder how he found out what happened on New Redemption, but somehow it isn't the most pressing thing. "I've tried," I say. "I've tried to understand how I lost Cirrus and how he became Eclipse. I know I keep telling myself they're the one and the same, just like I'm still Griffin, no matter what I go through. But I'm not so sure anymore. It's hard… it's hard to keep faith in that, the longer I'm without him. To believe that Eclipse is really still mine. I miss Cirrus so badly. And I'm scared that when I find Eclipse… things won't feel the same." I have to force the final words out, my voice bitter at myself for even having the thoughts. But, strangely, it's cathartic talking it out. It turns out your worst enemy can really be the best person to confess to. No matter what I say, I can say it with the certainty that Raven's sins still far outweigh mine.

"You're not a monster, Griffin," Raven says. I look up. He's smiling, and there's warmth in it. "You're capable of far more good than you know. But Eclipse isn't Cirrus. He never was."

"You're lying," I say fiercely. "Playing on my fears. Cirrus was my Shadow, and now Eclipse is. I know it. He's Cirrus transformed."

"Yes, Cirrus was your Shadow," Raven allows, "but Eclipse is not." He gives another pancake a flip. "You can project onto him all you like, you can wish to have Cirrus back, but it won't make it real."

"I can feel Eclipse's thoughts when we're together," I say feverishly. "I can hear him in my head."

Raven shrugs.

"Residual connection. Eclipse is using Cirrus' body still, but he's an entirely new entity. You have to learn to let go."

"And accept I don't have a Shadow?" I demand. Raven blurs behind a shield of tears.

"And move on," Raven says simply. "Accept that Cirrus is still inside you, and always will be. He's in your heart. But don't shame him any longer by pretending he's inside Eclipse."

"You don't know anything," I say, simmering. "You don't even know Eclipse. Cirrus is a part of him. And no matter what he is... he's my Shadow. He always will be."

I need to believe that. More than anything. My cheeks are burning. I grip the glass of juice in front of me, prepared to throw it at Raven in anger - when I look into the liquid for the first time, and spy something at the bottom of the glass.

A note is stuck to the base of it, its words just visible through the liquid. It's... a map. A sketchy map of the palace. I squint. There's a drawing of a chamber labelled 'kitchen' where Raven and I are... and an arrow, a diagram leading to another chamber in the palace.

Quickly, I memorise it. All while trying not to breathe too loud. I act like I'm brooding into my glass, so as to not give away to Raven that anything has changed.

Who left this here? Is it another trick?

I wait until Raven turns around to flip another pancake. Then I hurriedly remove the note from the bottom of the glass, and turn it over.

'Underworld can take you home,' is scrawled on it. *'Destroy this.'*

Raven turns back around. I put the note in my mouth without thinking, chewing it down like a piece of pancake.

'Underworld can take you home.' Does that mean there's an entrance to the Underworld here? And that it can somehow take me back to the human world?

And who left the note?

Suspicion nibbles away at the back of my mind. But for the first time in a while, I feel the blooming of hope. I try to remember every detail from the map.

"You had a lot of similarities, you and Cirrus," Raven is remarking with mild fascination. "Both of you had brothers who were cold to you at best, and cruel at their worst. Brothers who took care of you when you lost everything, while secretly blaming you for their loss. Brothers who you and Cirrus treated as idols, while they made you work and work for approval and attention that never came."

"I don't understand why you're saying all this. Why you care."

"Because, I'm invested in you. We're both far more similar than we are different, Griffin," Raven says intensely. "We both know darkness begets light. We accept that order is seeded in chaos. We have both been through so much to stand here in this palace. I just wonder, if we hadn't been separated all those years ago, if you had ended up in the Shadow world with Cirrus and me instead of stranded in your own world with Calvin... how would we both be the different for it? If we'd had each other. If we hadn't been alone?"

I stare at him, at a loss for words. Not for the first time, I reflect that this is not how I had expected this meeting to go.

"Why not work together?" Raven presses, excited. "Together we could design two worlds of perfection. We could end violence and pain."

That's what I'm trying to do, arsehole, I think. I'm so close to changing the world, so close that it's excruciating. *Phoebe, why haven't you opened the portals yet? What's gone wrong?*

Is she the one who left the note?

"What makes you think I need your help?" I try. "You're the one hiding in a broken palace so the Shadows can't find you. Your Empire, your little dictatorship project, has figured out you're the one pulling the strings. That's why you're hiding here in this ruin on some forsaken island, right? Hard to be the puppet master once the puppets grab the torches and pitchforks."

Raven laughs, short and sharp.

"The bravado, I love it. Trust me, Grif, this is a temporary set-back." He smiles. "The Shadow world is still very much mine. Come on. I have something to show you."

He takes his robes from the back of a chair, slipping them effortlessly on as he strides out through the doorway. He takes the knife with him too, casually flipping it by the hilt as I watch.

He just expects me to follow. I hesitate. Then I get up and walk after him cautiously, leaving the kitchen behind us.

I follow Raven out along a dark corridor, which opens up into the wide ballroom from earlier. Pillars encircle us. Low, cold light illuminates the space from the flickering blue flames in the grand chandelier above, leaving only the corners of the space in darkness. Suspended beneath it is a large crystal ball.

Suddenly a strange suspicion creeps over me. Something has been badgering me at the back of my mind since Raven mentioned my brother and Cirrus'. Something about the way he said it.

With a flash I think of the human soldiers who took out Mr Falco and Zephyr, who dragged Calvin away screaming. The strange way the soldier behaved who ambushed Phoebe and me as we escaped the hideout.

Griffin Cameron, the soldier had smiled. *Don't fight us. He has been waiting for you.*

"The soldiers back in Auckland," I say, slowly, not daring what seems too impossible to believe. "The humans who attacked us at the safe house. Were they somehow working for you? Did *you* take Zephyr and Calvin?"

Raven seems to almost smile. He clicks his fingers, and the hanging crystal orb suddenly blooms with colour, like a spherical television.

For a moment it shows a flicker of a wide meeting chamber, where seated human representatives are taking part in some sort of vote. I can make out the logo of the United Nations up on the wall.

Raven clicks his fingers again, before I can properly take in the scene. The image in the sphere changes. I cry out.

I'm staring into the orb at a three dimensional image, like a hologram within the crystal. Inside it are two glass tanks of crimson amniotic fluid. Like a live feed from a security camera. Zephyr is floating inside one tank, asleep, frozen in stasis. In the other one is my brother. Naked, like a cadaver trapped in a lava lamp. His hair floats in the fluid creepily. Watching him feels wrong, seeing him this vulnerable. It feels terribly personal, like seeing my brother before his birth. Or after his death, pickled and displayed for the world to see.

"It was you," I whisper, shock crashing inside me in waves. "You had humans working for you, who captured Zephyr and Calvin… and brought them over here. To the Shadow world, to this damned palace." I turn on Raven, seething. "Let. Them. Go."

"Why? You never mattered to Calvin. Why do you care?"

"Release them!" I shout. "Don't you dare experiment on them, you… *animal!*" I advance on Raven, but he raises his knife, smiling. Whatever my past grievances with Calvin or Zephyr, they're blown away in this moment.

"They're not hurting, just in a very deep sleep."

"The experiments you mentioned," I mutter, a horrifying comprehension dawning as I examine the machine they're in. "You're going to try and turn them into one of those things, aren't you? A Majestic."

Raven just smiles. It's not a smile of confirmation. It's the smile he wears when he's playing a game, like Toby when he was waiting for me to guess his identity. And thinking of Toby, I remember my capture at the side of the river. I think of myself running with Phoebe, and seeing the being chasing us in just a flash, a lithe draconic predator of white…

"Yes?" Raven prompts, still waiting.

"You can't turn them into a Majestic," I whimper, feeling a million miles away. My eyes are still on the sphere. "You can't hurt Calvin and Zephyr."

"Why not?"

"Because," I say, broken-hearted. "You already have. This isn't live, is it? It's a recording."

Raven grins, and actually whistles.

"I told you, Grif. You *are* good."

A whispering fills the air suddenly, a creeping, layered voice that echoes off the walls.

A phantom ripples in the corner of my vision, the hairs on the back of my neck standing on end. I turn slowly, trying to catch a glimpse of it in my peripheral vision. A monstrous form that levitates up beside the chandelier. The air there compounds and pales until it forms a serpentine tail that undulates terrifyingly above our heads.

I watch the vaguely human figure that the tail is attached to slowly take shape.

"Calvin and Zephyr are gone," I whisper in horror. "They've been a Majestic this entire time."

9

KING OF ANYTHING

Eclipse

I gaze hazily upward, hypnotised by the gold tapestries dangling from the stone dome far above. My lavish accommodation is littered with empty wine bottles. The platters of grapes and glazed meats that have been left out for me are untouched.

I've been here for hours, though time has ceased to have any real meaning. I'm lying in a luxuriously comfortable nest of blankets and velvet cushions within a depression in the floor. Stone steps lead down into an adjoining chamber, with a steaming pool wide enough for me to stretch from tail to beak in.

Whatever I expected… what with the betrayal by my only acquaintance and being passed as a bribe to the Number One Big Evil…. it was not this.

I'm in one of the towers of Aeyu. From one side of my

quarters a stone balcony juts out into the open air, and from it gentle winds come blowing in from the forest outside. The storm's ferocity has died. Its wild power broken, now tame and docile as it dissipates.

I am not caged, I have the freedom to leave whenever I wish it seems. Still, these islands are a cage all of their own. This entire world is a cage - with nowhere for me to go.

The comfortable quarters resemble a very grand royal bedroom. Chambers fit for a king. No, fit for a god. It makes me strangely uncomfortable. Disturbed. I recall the poster of the Empress I saw in Sanctuary City. How I had imagined it depicting my own image, imagined crowds of admirers and followers chanting my name. My surroundings bring that back, invoking my old hunger to rule. To force this world to accept me. To adore me.

Hanna and I were never so different after all.

A fiddly... *thing* is strapped to my leg. Some sort of invisible worm. An *IV*, yes, that... that is the word. It must be administering to Galvanize's toxin in my system, and already I feel lucid. Further from death's door. I imagine that death will not claim me until Raven gives death permission to do so.

I hear a door open from the room beyond. Then a figure strides up the steps into my chambers, his black robes swishing out around him. He rises into my vision, smiling. For the mass murderer who created the Empire, the architect of so much suffering, he looks weirdly anxious behind the smile. As if he's some dorky kid trying to make friends in the schoolyard when he doesn't know how. Bizarrely, he even waves.

"Hey there, Eclipse," Raven says. His voice is warm,

respectful. He sits down on the edge of a large, velvet foot stool. Only a few metres away.

I knew Raven was human. That's not what shocks me. It's his face.

I see glimpses into Cirrus' murky memories from his childhood. A smiling human teenager, his dark hair untameable and wild. Gently pulling a warm blanket up over Cirrus as he rests sleepily on his perch.

"Taylor," I say, my throat dry. "You were Raven all along."

One of Silvaluna and Melissa's own team. A friend of Zephyr, Ember and Griffin. Did he betray them? Is Taylor the real reason why Cirrus was separated from Griffin as children? Cirrus' memories of that night are so distorted, uncertain. But parts of them are creeping back into shape. Including the dead body of his mother. A painful riddle with no answer, one that Zephyr had always refused to discuss.

"I'm tired of games. What do you want from me?" I ask tiredly. "Why hold me prisoner?"

"You're not a prisoner, Eclipse. You're here as my guest. As you can see, you can fly away, leave anytime you choose. I've even come here as a gesture of trust." He gestures at the lack of any wall or barrier between us. "If you want to finish what you started last time, I can't stop you."

I strike, lashing out with my claw and pausing it just before Raven's insufferably confident smile. To his credit, he doesn't flinch.

"Oh, didn't you hear?" I smirk at him with lopsided loathing. "I don't kill anymore."

"Hanna did tell me," Raven says softly.

"Yes, she sucks like that," I say. My feathers spark warningly. "Still, I could hurt you in a great many intriguing ways without killing you."

"Something tells me that wouldn't be in the spirit of your vow."

"*'Something tells you?'* How the hell did you get this far by parading around in front of overpowered Shadows who have already tried to kill you once? It's pretty inconsistent."

Leering, I stalk forward, circling around him. Breathing down the man's neck, wanting to see him break in fear. My scaled tail encircles him, emphasising how small he is. How worthless.

"I suppose I'm at your mercy, then," Raven says.

"Yes, well. My mercy's pretty inconsistent too these days," I say, thinking of the dead humans. "Besides, you've murdered thousands."

"But you don't want to become me, do you?" Raven says, smiling crookedly.

"You are just one life," I point out, raising a claw. "I have thousands yet to go for us to be equal."

But I do not move to murder him. I've lost Hanna. Honouring Griffin is all I have left. The last shred of me, blowing in the wind.

Stepping away, defeated, I settle myself back down on my cushions. Dead-eyed.

"So, can we have a civilised conversation without any death or bloodshed?" Raven asks me.

Petulantly, I hurl an oversized goblet with my talons. Dark wine splashes over Raven's robes. He wipes some of it off, his expression sour.

"As I was saying," Raven continues tightly...

I hurl a whole chicken at him from a nearby platter.

Raven narrowly ducks as the naked bird sails over his head, landing with a wet slap on stone tiles.

"What are you, chicken?" I taunt him, raising an eyebrow.

Raven sighs.

"Where is your little pet?" I demand. "Ahmit? Amoot. Am... mut?"

"Are you..." Raven hesitates, uncertain. "Are you drunk?"

"Hmm?"

"Have you been drinking?"

"You left me a lot of wine," I say secretively, my tail noisily sweeping the empty bottles out of sight. I raise a talon to my beak. "Sssssh."

"I have no use for Ammut any longer," Raven says. "He served his purpose. I've been wanting to meet you for a very long time, Eclipse." A dark smile plays at the corner of his lips. "A proper introduction."

Raven strokes his chin, seemingly unaware of the absence of a beard, staring at me with an unfathomable expression. He's a surreal contrast to the cloaked, vicious being who tried to have me killed. His eyes survey me admiringly in a way that makes me feel exposed. It's more than just scientific interest. He's looking at me as if I am a prize.

"I hadn't thought there was a Shadow that could give Ammut a run for his money. You, you rare beauty, are so much more than he was. A Shadow without limits."

"A Shadow brought low by your psychotic bug Empress," I counter broodingly, "a Shadow who can be easily tricked by a faerie."

"Still," Raven grins, "there's potential."

I breathe in, trying to still my foggy thoughts enough to stab at the one thing that still matters to me.

"I came to you. Before our battle, and Griffin getting away... I came to you with a question," I say, my voice serious now.

"And you may ask it."

"Who am I?" I ask my captor, my voice breaking, betraying me.

"What I do know is that what happened to you hasn't happened to any other Shadow," Raven replies. "Not in this world's recorded history, anyway. Cirrus and Griffin were connected in so many ways... their mothers were counterparts. Their brothers are counterparts. Cirrus and Griffin were born side by side and spent their childhoods together. Their bond is closer and more powerful than any human-Shadow partnership I've studied." Raven's face goes still. There's a flicker of darkness across it. "Even more than hers," Raven says quietly, and I'm not sure who he is talking about. "Cirrus' body changed: accelerated growth, rapid new physical developments.... a new ability in place of his old one. A new identity, a new mind replaced the old one, and you were born."

"So you're saying that I was right all along, that Griffin *did* do this to me?" I ask impatiently. "When Griffin nearly killed Hanna aboard New Redemption that night in vengeance, did he change the essence of who he is? Of who I am?"

"No. Forgive me, but you believe Griffin has far more power over you than he really does. No, think of what Cirrus himself had been through: tortured by Hanna. Disowned by his brother Zephyr for fraternising with humans. Cirrus even tried to kill his own brother just in order to save his human."

We are interrupted as another Shadow comes crawling up the stairs behind Raven. Something about him looks vaguely familiar. Something that makes me uneasy.

He looks like a crow, but one that's seriously malnourished. He's hunched and skeletal with beady eyes and withered wings. Something about his movement seems to suggest he's hurt, but trying to hide the fact that something is broken. I can't say why, but the sight of him makes my feathers bristle.

Then I recognise him from Cirrus' memories. The Shadow that attacked him and Griffin, the night Cirrus was sucked out of the human world.

The new arrival makes his way to a decorative table in the corner of the room. He raises himself up on his talons - he's taller than he looks - and starts to arrange the pink pansies in an ornamental vase. The skeletal crow casts a forlorn glance back at Raven. But Raven only has eyes for me.

"I'm saying that the cause of your transformation may not have come from Griffin, but from Cirrus himself."

"So you're saying you believe... what?" I say cautiously, averting my gaze from the strange and creepy servant. I know that the answer to my question to Raven is going to be more difficult to swallow than anything I've ever heard.

"I believe Cirrus *made* Eclipse," Raven says. "Cirrus changed so much that he couldn't go on as he was. Either he needed a new form to reflect his growth on the inside, or it was some kind of defence mechanism to suppress the trauma of what had happened... I can't say. Griffin and Cirrus' powerful connection made the metamorphosis into

Eclipse possible. But it came from within Cirrus as much as from Griffin. Cirrus was eliminated, like old data being erased. Cirrus is truly dead, gone forever."

"But I can *feel* him."

"Phantom pains. It's all imagined, in your head. In Cirrus' place something completely new was born, his code completely rewritten. You. Accept your new existence, Eclipse, and let Cirrus die. Let the weakness die. You have no real ties to Griffin, to Zephyr or Cirrus' old life. You just *believe* that you do, and what you believe creates your reality. Your only destiny is the one you choose to make for yourself." Raven leans forward, his gaze fixed on me. I feel uncomfortable under the focus of those ice blue irises. "You're not Cirrus. You never were. Eclipse, you're magnificent, formidable... and something completely new."

There is silence. The skeletal crow finishes arranging the flowers and admires them, smiling brokenly.

Raven's words burrow into my consciousness like aggressive maggots. I feel tears in my eyes. I'm shocked to realise that I feel... sad. I've strived so hard to separate myself from Cirrus, to prove I'm my own person. I resented being judged by the actions of another Shadow. But now... I feel closer to Cirrus than ever. I care about Griffin, and about Zephyr, no matter how hard I deny it to myself. All of Cirrus' memories, they feel like *my* memories. Whether I intended it or not, they've come to define me. And now Raven tells me that Cirrus is gone forever? That the connection between him and me means... nothing?

I thought after what Hanna did to me I could not feel any more lost, that I was safe in simply not caring anymore. But I realise now that there was a last inch of myself I still had yet to lose. Now the resulting hollowness is eating away at me from within.

Why? Isn't this the news I wanted to hear all along? Wasn't I furious at Ember for thinking that Cirrus was still part of me?

"I see so much of myself in you," Raven whispers. "Just like I do with Griffin."

This new direction of conversation catches me off guard.

"Griffin is nothing like you," I say, my response sharply barbed.

"No?"

"You want to control everything and for everyone to know it. Griffin is full of love. He actually cares about other people."

Raven laughs.

"Don't kid yourself. Griffin and I are the same. We both only play the game for the joy of the game itself. For the challenge. Calvin has been suppressing Griffin all these years, hiding him from his real potential."

"No," I say, vehement. "You can take me, but Griffin is not a part of this. You won't touch him."

"Eclipse, I've taken this world as my own. I've risen from sleeping in the gutters of Auckland and trawling through dumpsters for dinner to ruling an Empire." He smiles. "There's nothing I ever want that I won't eventually have."

"Griffin isn't some... mini-Raven for you to toy with," I scowl.

"No," Raven admits. "He'll be greater than I could have ever dreamed. I believe in him, Eclipse. Just like I believe in you. But for a thought exercise... if a Shadow could choose their human, then would that change things for you?" He watches me carefully as I wrestle with the strange new question.

"What do you mean?"

"What if things weren't written in stone just because you heard Griffin's thoughts? Things are so much simpler when you believe every human is destined for a certain Shadow, their soulmate. But if you got to choose who your counterpart was, it would complicate things, wouldn't it? Seven billion humans. How could you be sure that Griffin is the best human for you?"

"Leave," I growl, a low dangerous sound that shakes the room.

There are more footsteps from the stairwell. When I see who it is, I clam up. My feathers stand on end.

'But I want him *more,'* she had said.

"Oh, finally," Raven says, pleased. "Come, Hanna."

Hanna flushes, avoiding my gaze. Withering under it. I hurt as I look at her. She has washed and changed from our travels, now she's wearing a bright violet gown. The resplendent outfit she wore when she was Empress, the one that matches her wings.

Her eyes are cast downward. Dark hair falls across her face.

"Hanna," I whisper, my voice constricted in pain and regret. "How could you do this?"

She doesn't respond. Her skin is pale as ice.

"You can at least look at me," I say. She doesn't respond. "*LOOK AT ME.*" The stone shakes around us from the force of it, and Hanna jumps. "Did all our time travelling here together mean nothing to you? I thought you were finished buying into Raven's lies. I didn't think you were this weak."

"So, I see you two have struck up a bond. Don't be rude ignoring our guest, Hanna," Raven says, amused. "I hope you don't judge her for bringing you to me, Eclipse. I've wanted to meet you again for such a long time now." He raises a goblet to Hanna in a one-sided toast. "I reward loyal service. And I can be... *merciful*, when it comes to past betrayals."

Raven moves around Hanna to stand behind her. She freezes, so still, eyes towards the ground. Raven steps into her and softly lays his hands on each of her bare shoulders. I can see her shudder slightly, like a leaf shivering in the wind. Hypnotised, as if she's unable to move away from him. I can't tell if she wants to run for her life, or embrace Raven so tight that he can never make her let go.

"You've done well, Hanna," Raven says softly. "And you will be rewarded." For a moment there's something different in his voice. A danger that flickers darkly in his eyes. "I'm so glad you came back to me." He leans into her neck, his hand raising as if to caress it. It's unclear to me if he is about to kiss her or strangle her, or both in the same movement. Hanna looks up and her eyes meet mine. Her eyes are dark and rueful, bloodshot. She trembles, like prey caught in the claws of a predator.

"I've agreed not to slay you both on the spot," I say distastefully. "But if you don't leave me alone, I will start shattering limbs."

Ignoring me, Raven tightens his grip, forcing Hanna's head forward. Hanna cries out, then stifles it. It comes out more like a whimper. Raven breathes against her bare neck, then releases her. Hanna bolts for the door, terrified, vanishing out into the stairwell.

Raven is smiling as he turns his eyes on me.

"You wanted me to see her," I say bitterly to Raven. "Or is this your way of punishing her too?"

"Punishing her?" Raven seems genuinely taken aback. "Hanna has done the best thing she ever could - she guided you to me. More than my other disciple Galvanize ever managed. I have big plans for you and Griffin. And you returned Hanna safely to me, for which you also have my gratitude. She is... family. I don't forget my debts."

"What you did to Hanna was monstrous. Transforming her into the Empress."

"You didn't see her when I found her," Raven says sharply. "She could barely speak. She was so starved that she was eating spiders from a basement floor. I saved Hanna. I raised her up further than she ever dreamed."

"But she stopped being *Hanna*," I say with feeling. "You killed the girl inside, you killed the good in her, in order to raise up an Empress."

Raven stares at me, perplexed.

"You feel for her," he says.

"No," I answer. "I just believed in her. Which is worse."

"Am I wrong to believe in you?" Raven asks carefully.

I stare at him incredulously. I draw myself up to my full impressive height, only to totter slightly due to the wine.

"My intelligence and your strength are equal," Raven presses, his voice passionate. "Work with me and just imagine what we could create together."

"Are you serious?"

"This could be yours. These spoils, this power. You could make a difference with me."

I look around at the quarters, at the luxury. The room's commanding position high above the island, high over this world means it almost feels safe up here. It's a small taste of what I could have. If Raven is serious about finding Griffin, about us working together as some sort of team... it sounds like madness, but what if Raven has a point? I could have my human and convince all the Shadows of this world to obey me, to respect me. Not as a beast but as a god. I feel an old thirst rising within me, my bruised and broken ego savouring the thought of sharing Raven's total power. This is what I had once longed for more than anything, or at least close to it.

"You caused suffering throughout the entire Shadow world with Hanna as your instrument," I say, lost. "And with Galvanize you are continuing it."

"I brought guidance," Raven says. "Structure. Enlightenment."

"Because of you Cirrus grew up without Griffin. Because of you Hanna became a monster. You set us all on the path that ended with Cirrus dying in Griffin's arms."

"I told you that Cirrus is no longer your concern."

"He will always be my concern," I snap, surprising myself.

"So is this a no?" Raven asks, the corner of his mouth twitching. When I don't respond he shrugs, standing.

I remember when I first became Ember's prisoner, how I held so tightly onto my pride. My ego was so enormous, and yet so fragile.

Maybe it's a sign of how far I've come that I'm not afraid of anything anymore. Not for myself. But I fear for Griffin. I fear for the Shadow world if it has to live under the spectre of Raven one moment longer. I fear for the surviving members of Joni's people that she'd tried so hard to protect, I fear for Celeste and her flatmates.

They looked at me and made me real. They saw me as I really was. In the same way I thought Hanna had.

My dreams and longings for my former glory suddenly taste like dust in my mouth.

Raven turns away from me. The skeletal crow scuttles unevenly after him, cowering at his master.

"Make yourself at home, Eclipse." Looking back at me, Raven smiles. "I'm going to go make some pancakes for another guest. I'll bring some up for you. You'll come around, I'm ever the optimist... but don't take too long." He says it lightly, but it hangs between us as a very real threat. I remember the fear in Hanna's eyes.

"I've seen what you're doing to the humans and Shadows." I say, stoic. "Fusing them into Majestics, placing them under your control."

"And?"

"You must have cells where you keep the Shadows and humans for your experiments. Where are they?"

Raven frowns.

"Separate, and safely contained. Why?"

"I want to see the other Shadows," I say quietly.

Raven laughs.

"Why? So that you can copy their powers for yourself?"

"It's not for their powers. It's just... I belong with them."

Raven studies me. He looks troubled.

"You don't even know them."

"No, but they're my people," I say with conviction. "You're the human who has spent his life manipulating Shadows."

"Eclipse. Don't make the mistake of thinking they're your own kind. You're not one of them. You'll give and give, until you're a hollow shell. Don't try and fit in when you can be extraordinary. I'm the only one who sees the real you."

"I won't sit on a throne while others suffer for my privilege," I say, seething.

"You're special," Raven whispers. "You've always known it."

"No, I'm not." I shake my head, smiling bitterly. "I'm just another of the seven billion Shadows in this world, wishing his life meant something."

10

STRANGERS LIKE YOU

Griffin

A giant, serpentine tail flowing into a white humanoid torso. Powerful reptilian legs. Arms with giant scraping claws. A slender neck rising up into...

"No." I cover my mouth, feeling tears of horror in my eyes.

I'm staring at Calvin's face. My brother's face, but with unmistakable features of Zephyr's as well. White scales for skin. His eyes are completely black and opaque, staring emptily back at me. I look back in shock at the Majestic that is Calvin and Zephyr made whole.

A single being, part Shadow and part human. Everything I thought I knew is crumbling away, all over again.

"How did you get them here?" I whisper.

"I had the soldiers fly them directly to the island in the

human world," Raven answers calmly. "Then they crossed over to this castle through a Rip. Just how you arrived, I'm guessing."

"Calvin. Can he... can he still hear me?"

"Yes. But with every minute, Calvin and Zephyr become less themselves. They are becoming one. Who they were always meant to be, before they were split into two individual fragments, left to always crave completion through their other half."

"How many... how many more have you made?"

I can't take my gaze from Calvin and Zephyr's hybrid. They don't seem like themselves. They're so still. It's unsettling. Like nothing but a ghost.

"Most of the other Majestic experiments have failed. So many sacrificed for the cause, with zero results. Only the very strongest of Shadows it seems can survive the process. Zephyr was a worthy candidate."

This is what Raven has been doing - or experimenting on doing - with each prisoner he has removed from that holding room in the middle of the night.

"Do you even feel for any other lives?" I say, shivering. "Those others you have penned up in that room like a battery farm... do you understand that each of them has their own world in their heads?" My anger flares, powered by my sense of helplessness. "If these Majestics are meant to be all powerful, why are Calvin and Zephyr following your every command?" I say fiercely. "Like your faithful dog?"

"Majestics aren't earthly beings. To keep your brother and Zephyr tied to this dimension, instead of just phasing out of reality, I've been having to dose them. A side effect is it ties them to my voice. My command."

"How could you do this to them?" I ask quietly.

"Are you kidding me?" Raven says incredulously. His voice grows passionate, triumphant. "I've made them into a god. They're serene, enlightened. An advanced lifeform existing beyond life or death."

"It's a power trip for you," I say, glowering. "What you always dreamed of. Gecko and Zephyr are your faithful servants now, answering your every beck and call."

"You're right. I should give the authority to make decisions for them to a member of their own family, while they're still gaining a grip on how to exist as a Majestic." Raven locks eyes with the white terror above us. "Griffin is your master now, understand? You will obey him no matter what. His every wish is your command, etcetera, etcetera."

The Majestic inclines his head in acceptance. Calvin's black eyes are still opaque and unknowable.

"What are you doing?" I mutter. I'm frozen rigid. There's a roaring in my ears.

"Getting you to trust me. Now you can ask them anything you want. Everything you've ever wanted to really ask Calvin, if only he'd wanted to give you the time of day."

"This is a trap."

"That's up to you."

"What the hell is that meant to mean?" I demand. I point up at his creation, spitting. "You abducted my brother and his Shadow, took them hostage and turned them into this... *thing!*"

"Your whole life your brother was a strict ruler over you. Always keeping you on a leash, even if sometimes it was invisible to you. He was a cold father figure, someone you could never please, could never be enough for. Calvin took out his own demons on you, even though he was all you had. He lied and lied to you, hid the truth about Shadows from you, hid the truth about your family."

"How do you know all this?" I whisper.

"You hold the power now, not Calvin Cameron. So don't give in to the fear that's inside you because of him. Ask him what you need to ask him."

Somehow, I find myself approaching the Majestic. Slowly, like you would with a traumatised animal. Or something feral you don't want to freak out in case it mauls you to death.

"Calvin?" I whisper. "Is that you in there?"

The Majestic doesn't respond. I feel like a possum caught in headlights, waiting anxiously. Small and alone. Little Griffin again, only five years old, stranded with my older brother, my new guardian who can't bear to look at me. The Majestic slowly descends through the air, its clawed feet touching the stone. Finally, it speaks.

"*Yes.*"

I gasp. It's Zephyr's voice and Calvin's, perfectly overlaid together. Speaking as one. But unmistakably them.

"Prove it's you," I say fiercely to that strange Calvin face, scaled in white. "Zephyr, what did Cirrus say to us when we rescued him on New Redemption?"

"*You came back for me,*" is the Majestic's reply.

I feel a spasm in my chest.

"Calvin. What was my favourite picture book for reading at bedtime?"

I realise too late that's a dumb question, because even my real brother wouldn't remember the answer.

"*The Sneetches,*" the Majestic answers, surprising me.

I blink. I didn't think Calvin had really known that.

"It's you," I whisper in terrified awe. "It's really the two of you." I fight back tears, not wanting to cry in front of Raven. But then the wave of relief is replaced by an unexpected tide of anger.

"You left me," I accuse him. "You abandoned the rest of us, at the safe house. You gave up. You just gave up and let those soldiers take you. We needed you, and you just chose to quit without thinking about the rest of us."

"You left me to be tortured," the Majestic hisses through Calvin's scaly lips. *"To die."*

"No!"

"You wanted to be free of me at last."

"You know that's a lie," I shoot at him, trembling. "I'm going to save you."

"You're. Too. Late."

There's a black tide of turmoil crushing down on me, making me feel far away and alienated from everything around me. Anxieties and old memories are crowding in at me, inescapable.

Calvin coldly appraising me across his desk at Cameron Technologies. Reading me a storybook in bed, only for me to wake up and find him crying against the wall in the middle of the night. Calvin hitting me as we fought in front of the portal in the lab, shoving me so that I was sucked through and had to suffer everything I suffered over there. Calvin telling me constantly when I was growing up that I had to move on, and leave these fantasies of magical creatures and dragon-parrots behind. Telling me that I had to join the 'real world.' A world that he had never lived in.

Calvin who lied to me about our Dad, when he'd promised to finally start telling me the truth.

Lies. Lies and lies and lies...

"You have to answer whatever I ask," I say to the Majestic, feeling strange. "Right?"

"Yes," he breathes.

"Why didn't you tell me the truth about our Dad?" I ask brokenly. "What he did to Taylor?"

In my peripheral vision, I see a flicker of shock in Raven's face.

There's a beat before the Majestic responds.

"To protect you."

"Liar. It was to protect yourself," I bite back. "Tell the truth."

I think of how Calvin manipulated me, how my brother hired Mr Falco to toy with my brain. How he used me as a puppet for his plans, keeping me blind to our family history. Worse, how he made me think that finally we were united as brothers, as friends, only to use me to further his ends and hack the Oracle for him.

When all I ever wanted was for him to love me as much as I loved him.

"Say one good thing about me," I say in a small voice.

"What should I say?" my brother's voice asks me.

"Just say something! *Anything!*" There's no response. It's like a computer overloading without a specific enough request. I bite my lip.

"Say that I'm smart, like you."

"You're smart, Griffin," my brother's voice answers me from those reptilian lips. *"You're like me."*

I close my eyes, wondering at the feeling of hearing Calvin's voice saying those words. I'm not going to deny it, as guilty as it makes me feel… I enjoy it. I know I shouldn't, but it feels good hearing it after all this time. My one wish all through growing up was to hear those words.

"Who do you care about more," I whisper, remembering our fight back at the safe house. "Phoebe or me?"

"*No.*" The Majestic shakes his head, anger entering his voice. Fighting the command to answer. So the Calvin and Zephyr I know are still in there. There's still some fight in them.

"What, are you ashamed? Answer me!"

The eerie being stares at me impassively. An ocean of darkness behind each of those pupils.

But now Raven has come within reach of the Majestic. He draws something from his belt of equipment. A syringe. Using it, he extracts a substance from a vial in his belt, raising it toward the Majestic.

Instinctively I jerk forward to protect what's left of my brother, but Raven holds up a knife and I stop cold. I've recognised it now. It's the same blade that he slashed me with six months ago.

"Don't get yourself hurt, Griffin. I like you, but I won't warn you again. This won't harm them."

I stare at the thick, dark liquid inside the syringe that he holds in his other hand. So that's it. That's what Raven is using to control Calvin and Zephyr. To keep their Majestic under his command... no. *My* command, at least for now.

Raven injects the substance into the Majestics' bare, serpentine neck.

"Will it work?" I ask tensely.

"Yes," Raven says. "The effects are instantaneous. He'll obey you without question."

My hands are tightened into fists. I keep forgetting to breathe.

"Raven used to be your friend, didn't he?" I ask the Majestic.

"Yes."

"In what way?"

"I looked up to him," my brother responds. *"Taylor was everything I wanted to be. I'd never had a human friend before. We clashed, but I still wanted him to be my friend. I hoped we would always be friends."*

"You'd do anything I asked you to, wouldn't you?" I ask, my voice fracturing.

"Yes," the Majestic answers calmly. The famous Calvin Cameron, obeying me like my own servant. *"I have been instructed to do as you command."*

"Then..." I wet my lips. "Kill Raven."

The Majestic flies through the air with lightning reflexes, striking at Raven like a snake. His demonic claws freeze an inch from Raven's bare neck.

Raven whistles, then laughs at me.

"That, was a damn good try. You're a cold-blooded bastard when you need to be, aren't you?"

The Majestic dematerialises. Slowly his body melts away on the air, dispiriting until he's needed again. I watch my brother and his Shadow fade as one and wonder if he's still conscious somewhere in there, and how he would feel about what I just did.

"You tried to play me," Raven says. "But you didn't really think I wouldn't have some kind of an override, did you? Still, if I hadn't... I'd be lying dead on the floor of this palace right now."

I'm hunched on the floor, rocking, like a prisoner huddling in the corner of his dark cell. I'm seeing myself in a way I never have before.

Something dark and ugly has crawled itself to my surface. An instinct for punishment and pain over forgiveness.

Not many things scare me. But this does.

There's an evil inside me. A twisted evil that my Dad passed to me, tainting me.

Is this how he'd felt? So lonely, so lost that he'd do anything to erase the pain? Anything?

But he'd had Mum. He had Calvin, and me. A family. Was really being the only one of us without a Shadow enough to throw that all away?

"Oh," Raven says, struck dumb. "I'm sorry, Griffin. Sometimes I forget that you're a decade younger than me. I didn't mean to scare you. I just wanted to help you. To show you the truth."

He crouches down beside me, reaches to me.

"Leave me alone," I scream. I lash out at him, striking with my hands, wanting to kill the man in front of me.

"No," Raven says strongly, grabbing my arms. "I know you're used to abandonment. To losing everyone, to being pushed away. But so am I. None of them will ever understand you, but I do."

And I stop striking him, and I'm sobbing. Wrapping his arms around me, Raven pulls me into a hug. Tight and fierce. And before I know it I've gone from striking at him, wanting to tear him apart with my bare hands, to clutching him like he's a life raft, the only thing keeping me from drowning as my lungs fight for air.

"Question everything," he whispers. "Your hopes and mine, our dreams, may not be as far apart as you think. You're so much stronger than you know."

I look up at him, and I see the belief in his eyes. His smile. It's like staring into the face of the big brother I'd always wished for. The brother I wished that Calvin had been.

"What do you want?" I say, hushed.

"I want you to realise we're just the same. I want us to put aside our differences. I can show you the full potential of who you are. The greatness that's locked inside of you.

You're not just a tool to me. I care about you, I want to teach you everything I know. We'll be partners. Family, again. That's more than Calvin ever offered to you. All I'm asking is for you to agree to try. Let's try to get to know each other again."

Something about this is calling to me. Something dark and strange and deep within me. The need for family. And I know the terrible things Raven has done. But I'm feeling the void opening up beneath me again, all I can think is... I want to be with someone who knows me. Who sees some kind of worth in me.

Like Mum did. Like Cirrus did. Like...

"Taylor!" a breathless voice rings out. I go still.

An overwhelming bright relief floods through me.

She's alive!

But the relief quickly changes to shock and fear. No, I beg inwardly. No, you were meant to run.

Raven has gone still too. I don't think Raven even *breathes*. He looks like he's deciding whether it was a distant shout from a dream. Fear is transfiguring his face. He looks pale, haunted. As if hope is whispering to him, hope he fears might be a lie.

She steps out from behind one of the pillars near us, planting her feet firmly apart. And as she does, I know that she saw what just happened, and I'm filled with shame.

She's swallowed by darkness. But as she takes some

small defiant steps forward, there's no question that it's her, even with her dyed blonde hair.

Raven gasps, a sudden, shocking sound. And I watch all of his mastery and all of his well-laid plans and machinations breaking apart, as he stares with utter dumb shock at Phoebe like he's a teenager all over again.

Phoebe's alive. She looks scratched up, but she's here in the flesh. Even though I know she's in greater danger than ever before, I can't help but feel a surge of relief. She didn't get taken in the forest. She's still alive.

"Griffin's not the one you want, Taylor," says Phoebe, and I can see the fear in her eyes as she faces the greatest nightmare from her past. "I am."

Phoebe's attention is fixed on Raven. Her once best friend, who she turned on and banished forever. A genocidal dictator being confronted with the girl behind the trauma of his past. There's no knowing what he'll do to her. By coming here Phoebe risked everything, all in a long-shot attempt to save me. I would know if she'd somehow connected the worlds already - we would have heard the portal opening above this very palace, linking to the station on the other side. A gateway between the two worlds. So she hasn't done it yet. She's throwing away our only hope - everybody's only hope in two entire worlds - to try and save me.

Slowly, I turn to look at Raven, afraid. He is staring across at his old friend, who looks exactly like she did when he last saw her.

"It can't be, it can't be you," Raven mutters nonsensically, feverish. "You died. You died and you're not coming back."

"It's me, Taylor," Phoebe says quietly.

"This is cruel," he whispers, and it almost sounds like Raven might be about to cry. "This is the cruellest trick in the world." He staggers, overcome. Phoebe hurries forward to help him, then stops herself, clasping hands to her chest, like she's torn in indecision. For a moment Raven looks like a scared teenager. Less Raven, and more like the Taylor from the photo of the two of us in the kitchen.

Taylor who grew up on the streets of Auckland, with Phoebe as his only friend.

Then slowly, Raven raises his head again to face Phoebe. I can see the fear and suspense on Phoebe's face. And an acceptance. She's come here, no matter what the consequences. She's finally facing her fear of meeting who her old friend has become. Ready to face Raven's vengeance.

"Pheebs?" Raven whispers. It hits me hard. I thought that was just my name for her.

"Hello, Taylor," Phoebe says with a shy smile.

And then tears are falling down Taylor's cheeks - *Raven's* cheeks, and he's running forward as Phoebe steps toward him too. With each step Phoebe becomes less and less part of the shade, the cold light defining her more and more with each step. So that when the two friends finally fall into each other's arms, Raven can already see she's as solid and real as the Phoebe he lost. Stunned, I watch the evil mastermind crying and burying his head in the teenage girl's neck, her now blonde hair interweaving with his midnight black locks. Light and darkness.

Raven's back shakes, and he hugs Phoebe tightly. She squeezes him back even harder. I watch, frozen, as she softly traces the burn marks along the side of Raven's face, burns which mirror hers. I see her hand shake.

Then Phoebe looks up and meets my eyes. Hers are still dark and full of tears.

Very slowly and carefully, as if not to stir a dangerous beast, she brings her free hand to her mouth. Raising a finger to her lips, she mouths: '*Go.*'

11

JAR OF HEARTS

Eclipse

Sleep eludes me. The flames are low in the lamps illuminating my kingly quarters.

Then I hear light footsteps on stone.

I don't even bother to look up. I stare dully down at the wine-soaked rugs beneath my talons.

I am still reeling from knowing who I really am. Raven has offered me what I always wanted: vindication that I am my own person. But one with no history, no connections to others. A blank slate. Only days ago I had thought that was the one thing I most wanted to hear in the world.

There's a small knock against the door in the chamber beyond. The sound is almost too small, too silent to hear... but I do not mistake it. It's followed by footsteps on stone.

Finally I look up. I squint through the low light to see Hanna standing at the entrance to my chambers.

"Eclipse?" she whispers. There's something strange about her voice. Then Hanna notices the full state of my chamber.

Wine is spilled across the rugs, food scraps flung around the place along with feathers from the bedding. The hanging golden tapestries are incinerated, as well as various black husks that used to be items of furniture. I stand with my head pressed against the wall, in the middle of the devastation.

"I redecorated," I say with dark humour. "I told Raven I don't want it. Any of it. I don't belong here. I don't know where I belong."

Hanna stares at me, at a loss of words for a moment. I think of her hanging helplessly in the Resistance's prison, I think of her shivering from the rain in our shelter on the island, I think of her saving my life, and of telling her things that no one else knows.

Hanna still doesn't say anything. Suddenly I notice her red eyes, the glistening tears on her face. A face contorted with emotion, even as it fights to stay impassive. The life, the vibrancy, the fire that sometimes showed through those emerald eyes on our journey has been quenched. She looks dead inside. Broken. It's like staring at a mirror. As much as I want to gain joy from the fact, I don't.

"You don't look so good," I say, my voice just as dead.

"Raven is going to reinstate me as Empress," Hanna says, sounding choked. "This world is mine again. Well, however much of it the Empire controls right now, anyway. Raven will tell Galvanize to step down, and she'll be harshly punished for trying to kill me against his orders. She was acting alone. Raven had asked her to rescue me, but he had underestimated her jealousy issues."

"So you get what you wanted," I say, mirthlessly. "Congratulations. Why did you come here, Hanna?"

Hanna's lips tremble.

"I just... I just wanted you to understand. Why I did what I did. Raven is my..."

"Your everything, I know," I scowl. "And he's emotionally abused you, and taken advantage of you in ways no one ever should. But only you can break the cycle. Instead you chose to destroy everyone in your life except for him. You exist only as long as it makes him happy. That's the only use Raven has for anything. He never gives back."

"You're disappointed in me," Hanna says with a tight smile.

"I'm sad that the girl I thought I got to know is lost forever."

Hanna shakes her head, like she pities me. Like I couldn't possibly understand.

"You don't know what it takes to break free from him," she whispers.

"I don't know?" I explode, and she looks truly scared. "I suffered! You tore at my connection with Griffin and left me to die! I've paid the price for your obsession with a human once already, and I only got past that because I believed in you! *That* was hard! If I could do that for you, why couldn't you at least do the same for me?"

Hanna just stares back, aghast and shell-shocked; like she's seen something she never thought she'd see.

"Cirrus paid the price," she says quietly. "Cirrus, not you."

"What?" I snap. "That's what I said."

"No... it's not. Do you know why I really came here, Eclipse?" Hanna asks me softly. When she first arrived she'd looked like she'd been crying, like she'd run all the way to my cell. But she looks calmer already. I suppose nothing I've said is getting through to her. "I just saw Raven meet someone. Someone who he thought was dead. And..." she chokes up again. "And it made me realise that whatever I do, it will never be enough. He'll never care about me the way he does about her. I don't think it would even occur to him to mention me to her.

'I thought if I tried hard enough, he'd love me. Raven would see me the same way I saw him. Shining, brave, magnificent. I thought one day we could be married, Emperor and Empress. Just him and me, like it had always been. But it was always her. She banished him to this world, she was dead to him for a decade, and her memory gave him more warmth then I ever could... and I was so *alive*. And as soon as it happened I rushed right here, without even thinking. Because apart from Raven, you're the only person I really know. You're the person I wanted to tell about it, to confide in."

Hanna's face is conflicted, anguished. She falls to her knees, sinking into the rich carpet. But then she looks up at me, and as she does she her shoulders relax. She traces the pattern of the carpet with her fingers, as if feeling texture for the first time.

"Why did you come here, Hanna?" I repeat coldly.

She's silent for a moment. Then she raises her chin with conviction.

"To free you," she says, as if just realising. "Come on. We're getting you to the Underworld."

I cock my head.

"Very convincing."

"Excuse me?"

"You're a right little drama queen. But I didn't ask for another show. I'm not playing any more of your games, Raven!" I declare loudly, so he can hear me from wherever he's listening in. "I'm done."

"You're kidding me. Eclipse, you giant dolt-head, I am *saving* you."

"Please leave, before I pop your skull like a grape."

"You're impossible. We need to leave, right now."

"Why?" I grin lifelessly. "I'd like to see him try. And what more could Raven possibly take from me?"

Hanna strides forward. Her face is anxious and desperate.

"Eclipse, if you're ever going to listen to me again, just listen to this. *You don't want to find out.*"

I study her. I see the deep fear in her eyes. How much will it is taking for her to do this.

Or at least, that is what she wants me to see.

"I thought you loved Raven."

"I do." Her voice hardens. "But Raven doesn't under-stand love the way others do. It's like hearts are something he collects and keeps imprisoned in a jar. Just like a serial killer collects trophies. Hearts are something he enjoys owning and having power over. My heart, Galvanize's heart... he took mine from me. And maybe he didn't mean for anything to happen between him and me, maybe that was unplanned. But he took out so much of my heart that sometimes I feel like nothing but scar tissue." She sees my expression. "You still don't believe me, do you?" she asks, exasperated.

"That this is a genuine jail break? No. I've been stung once too many times. And why should I run away with you, even if this was the truth?"

"Hey, Raven is all I have left," Hanna says heatedly. She stares up at me, fearless. "I'm throwing that away, and... and I barely know you. This is *it* for me, you are my only constant now. Imagine... imagine having to turn your back on Griffin. Raven was my entire world. After this, you are all I have. You are my family. You're the one who showed me it was possible to make a promise to yourself, a promise to be someone better than you are, and to keep that promise. I've never trusted anyone, never had to try to live up to anyone's trust in me. I was raised to see everyone as a potential enemy. But you trusted me with not good reason, you just... *did*, and now I want to live up to that. Now, I'm ready to start trying to live up to what you see in me. Okay?

I look at her, but it's still with resentment, suspicion. She senses that, and seems to make a decision.

"Eclipse. Griffin is here. He is here in the palace."

I stare, emotions crashing through me. I reach out with my mind, trying to feel for any sense of Griffin's consciousness here in the palace with me. There's nothing. Perhaps he's too far away. Perhaps the cold walls of this palace block thoughts, like New Redemption did. Or perhaps it's just another part of Hanna's deception.

"If you're lying...." I say warningly.

"You'll break your vow and it will be worth it, yeah. He's here. Apparently he just turned up here in the Shadow world, wandering around the island."

I raise myself up so quickly that Hanna flinches.

"GRIFFIN!" I roar.

"Shut it!" Hanna hisses, looking terrified. "I got a message to him. He'll meet us in the Underworld. Raven is... occupied, for now. I can get you and Griffin back to the human world but we have to move quickly. There's a

Majestic in this palace, one that Raven successfully created with that machine we found. One that didn't spontaneously combust."

"He succeeded?" I whisper.

"Yes. And its power is terrifying."

"I'll judge that for myself," I say calmly. "I have a lot of rage I need to work through."

"You need to listen to me. You can't," Hanna says, and it almost sounds like real concern in her voice. "The Majestic is far beyond Ammut. It can bend rules that Shadows can't. Let me get you to the Underworld, to Griffin. Without stirring up any more crap in this castle."

The thought of being tricked again with this Griffin ploy is almost too much to endure. But if there's the slightest possibility that this is real and not Raven toying with me... I owe it to Griffin to at least try.

"The other Shadows are being held here too," I say, "the ones being made into Majestics. We have to get them out of here."

"I know," Hanna says, surprising me. Strangely, she smiles, and there's a something about it, a peace that hasn't been there before.

"Their humans too."

"Then let's get to it. There's a few routes through the palace to the Underworld entrance. I know one where we should be able to get past Raven unseen."

"Also, if this is another trap," I add, flexing my talons, "I'm going to have to break my promise to Griffin again."

Hanna smiles.

"I know."

. . .

Hanna scans her security card, and we push open the door disguised as a mirror, revealing the cell beyond. I crane my head down to stare through the crack, suspicious that she has led me astray.

We are staring in at a large wooden room, lit by chandeliers with a fireplace in one end. On either sides are bunk beds with white hospital sheets. There are no doors.

Filling the bunk beds around me, staring at me with wide, disbelieving eyes, are young Shadows.

"No. Freaking. Way," a voice whispers, surprised. "Hanna? Eclipse?"

I feel my chest lift at a voice I haven't heard since exploding into a student flat in Midnight Crafters. I blink back, stunned.

"Celeste?"

12

GSA

Griffin

Raven and Phoebe are still hugging.

They stand there for so long, I feel like I've gone from facing off with my psychopathic archnemesis, to being the awkward third wheel.

Phoebe slowly looks up over Raven's shoulder toward me. She looks overwhelmed, petrified, like a possum caught in a trap.

Run, she mouths again, angry that I haven't already. Her eyes are full of tears.

Instead I make explosive gestures at her.

'What the hell are you doing here?' I mouth, furious enough to be hopping up and down, if I wasn't trying to be so deadly silent. Phoebe had a clear shot, she could have tried to find a way back to our world and the station, to

finishing this on her own. She shouldn't be risking herself coming here to save me.

Me. She's doing this for me.

Or did she? From the way she's holding onto Raven, it's enough to make me suspect that the real reason she came here was for him. Maybe after waking up, and seeing how the world changed from her decision to banish Raven a decade ago, she's wondering what her life would be like if she'd made a different choice. And this is a taste of that.

Phoebe widens her eyes at me meaningfully, seething. Yeah, okay Phoebe, I get the message. She wants me to get out of here, to find a way to complete our mission. She's planning to keep Raven occupied while I try to connect the worlds.

Is she freaking serious? She's putting herself in a crazy amount of danger. I grit my teeth, but I have to follow her lead. If I even manage to get away, then I can finish this. The Majestic has vanished now that Raven is preoccupied. But as he has the ability to summon my brother's Majestic back at any moment, I don't think two teenagers are going to be able to escape on their own.

But there's one more thing I have to do first. A second mission I can't leave undone, not when they're in danger of being subjected to lethal experiments at any moment.

Tiptoeing closer to Phoebe and Raven's embrace, I sneak up behind Raven. I can see it there in his belt, slotted into one of the sleeves amongst the vials - a white key card.

A key card like our guard used for the room where the teen prisoners are being held. If Raven has one, it has to be a master key.

Phoebe's outrage and disbelief is pretty easily trans-latable.

'What the hell are you doing? Save yourself you idiot! How did you possibly misunderstand me?'

I gesture to the card. I don't even know if Phoebe can get a good angle to see it from where she is with her chin over Raven's shoulder. But adjusting slightly - to the ever-lasting embrace - she spots it. I can see her trying not to audibly sigh.

I sneak still closer up behind Raven. I hesitate, a new thought coming to mind. It's such a perfect moment. If I can get the knife from his belt, then Phoebe and I might be in the clear...

But if we fail, we're dead meat. It will be like waking a lethal predator. An enraged Raven will realise he's been tricked and call the all-powerful Majestic and all of this will be over for us. For everyone.

I don't know how instantaneously Raven can call on my brother's Majestic. But even without that, I'm not an idiot. I'm sure Raven has plenty of guards somewhere in this place, staying just out of sight. He doesn't take chances.

Sweat beads on Phoebe's forehead, extending her fingers for the card just out of reach...

...she snags it out of the belt pocket, and she's clear.

It occurs to me that as Raven was a pickpocket too once he may have noticed the theft. But he's too wrapped up in his blissful moment of reunion, blind to the awkward hand-off that's happening behind him.

Trying not to breathe too loudly, I lean so close to Raven that I'm almost spooning him... and I grasp the card off Phoebe.

Then I step slowly away, trying to keep my feet soft as they press down on stone.

I take one last look on Phoebe's face and I don't think

I'm going to be able to do it. I can't leave her. She's my... she's the only person I have left. The thought of leaving her with Raven makes my blood boil, is maddening.

But we always save each other.

I'll come back for you, I mouth to her, locking eyes with her for another moment.

Then I turn toward the stairwell, ascending from the ballroom as fast as I can.

I don't expect to survive as far as getting back to the room with the prisoners in it, but somehow I do. It's a struggle to retrace the path that I ran with Toby - I mean, Raven - in the cold lit halls of the palace. But we kept a fairly straight route, and I manage to find my way there. I scan the card on the pad.

There's a barely audible click. The mirror swings open an inch.

I exhale with relief.

Slowly, I push open the mirror...

The kids explode out at me, sharpened wooden weapons held in hand, roaring. Someone throws a blanket over my face, and before I know it I'm being weighed down on my back, suffocated under a barrage of pillows. The kids are still screaming.

"Cut it out!" I gasp, managing to find a gap between the pillows. The attack ends as quickly as it began. The pillows are removed from my face, and I have a group of familiar stunned kids staring down at me, surprised I'm not a Shadow.

"Wait," someone says. "It's the mystery dude who escaped with Toby!"

"You came back for us," one of them says in awe. They look so shocked, so relieved to be outside the room in the cold light of the corridor.

I grin sheepishly.

"Sharpened wooden stakes, pillows and blankets to subdue and disorientate - I'm pretty impressed, guys. I trained you well."

I'm leading the others back toward the ballroom, hurtling down the palace corridor when I come to a sudden stop. The others bowl into me nearly knocking me over.

A pair of tall, ancient wooden doors are on our left, with a scan pad beside them. I pause for a second, thinking about the off-chance that there's more human kids being kept prisoner behind them. I slip Raven's white scan card from my pocket and try it. There's a click as the doors unlock.

Exchanging glances with the others apprehensively, I pull open the doors. They're stiff, so the others lend me a hand pulling them open. I'm hoping there are going to be allies and not enemies behind them.

The ancient wooden doors creek aside to reveal a deep steel room with shelves and wall hangings decorated with a wide array of Shadow world weapons. Crossbows, long bows, swords. The swords look like they were liberated from Winghold, sparking with multi-coloured light, forged in a way that Ember herself designed to do more damage to Shadows in combat. I also spot some human weapons - an AK-47 and what might be a rocket launcher. I'm guessing the crates down below the shelves are stacked with ammo.

"That should do it," I say, amazed at our fortune. "It's time we upgraded you all from pillows."

"What exactly are we up against?" asks one of the girls. Ula, I think. "More things like that crow monster?"

"Trust me," I say. "You'd rather not know."

I survey the weapons, feeling another wave of foreboding.

"Raven has a well-equipped armoury, but where's his army?" I wonder, then shake my head. "Let's get out of here before we find out. Everyone, grab a weapon you think you can handle. Who here's actually ever fired a gun?"

Only April puts up her hand. "My Dad taught me," she says. The one I'd thought was the spoiled princess of the bunch. This lot are just full of surprises.

"Okay, you take the rifle. Seriously, Marty," I say to the small boy from London, "I think that's going to be too heavy to run with, even for us big kids."

Little Marty sadly wrestles the rocket launcher back onto its bracket.

I pick up a crossbow. I like the feel of it, and take some bolts from the crate below it.

This is it. I load a bolt into the crossbow, then help to hand out weapons to the rest of the kids, showing them how to operate them as they get a hold of how their weapons work. All of them are just teenagers like me, and the little kid Marty. They're scared, afraid and alone. Taken by Shadows by force to a world they don't understand.

"Listen," I say gently, so that all of them can hear me. "I'm going to show you Shadows aren't as bad as you think they are. They're going to change everything for you, in the best possible way." I grin cockily. "Kids, welcome. You are now each officially a member of the GSA."

"GSA?" Anke asks.

"Griffin's Shadow Academy. Now for your first lesson: breaking the hell out of this creepy damned castle."

Raven and Phoebe are still in the ballroom. I can hear Phoebe speaking about how she was brought back, as Raven listens with rapt attention. Transfixed by her.

Signalling for the other kids to stay at the top of the stairwell out of sight, I cautiously make my way down the steps down toward the ballroom. The decorative pillars arranged around the space offer me a chance of not being noticed by Raven.

Grab Phoebe. Make it into the Underworld. Cross over to the station in the human world and activate the portals.

I talk through the steps in my head, maybe to avoid the fact I have no idea how to get Phoebe away from Raven. Especially when he has the power to summon a Majestic.

I slowly slide myself behind a pillar to get closer to the pair of them. Phoebe is facing with her back to me, which makes it harder with Raven's attention directed to my side of the ballroom.

But I'm close to them now. I can hear every word.

"And now look at you," Phoebe is saying. "Your own palace. Your own... Empire. Everything you ever dreamed of when we were sleeping on cardboard, trying to scrounge enough coins just for a Burger Max value meal."

"Except that this life was meant to be for the both of us," Raven says softly. I shiver at his voice. "You and me, King and Queen of the Universe. This palace is lonely on its own. And all this time I was still a King in Exile. Unable to get back to our world."

"Have you been... happy?"

"Without you? What do you think?" From Raven's voice, I can tell he's smiling. "But things are beginning to change. Griffin and Eclipse are here now. And now... you. It's a miracle."

Slowly, I tighten my grip on the handle of the crossbow held at my side. I'm clutching it so tightly I think the handle will snap in my hand. I try to quieten my breathing.

"Taylor," Phoebe chokes suddenly. "I'm so sorry I... what I did... I didn't want things to go this far."

"Me neither. But the past is the past. Everything is forgotten, Pheebs."

I sneak another look around the corner of my pillar, see a flash of Raven. He's facing me, and Phoebe is standing far enough aside. A clear shot. It's my moment.

I step out from behind the pillar, turning to face Raven and Phoebe. I see Raven's expression of shock. I aim the crossbow, my blood pounding in my ears...

Can I do it? Can I really do it?

In that second, I want to more than anything in the world. But with another beat, I think if I do it, if I fire the bolt... I might lose part of myself I might never get back.

"You even *try* to summon their Majestic," I say, "and I'll shoot."

I hear footfalls behind me. Turning, I see the other kids all stepping in with me, spreading out in solidarity to encircle Raven. Their weapons pointed at him from all sides.

"Come on, Phoebe," I say, grabbing her arm, pulling her away from Raven. "We have to get out of here."

I look back at him. I wish he could look more evil, this man standing opposite us. This man I hate more than anyone else in either of the worlds. He ruined my life. But right now he looks shocked, dazed. Surprised to see weapons aimed at him. I saw his face when he was talking to Phoebe a minute ago. He had looked so... happy. It makes me sick.

I've only just met Phoebe, it's ridiculous, but she's already the best friend I have.

"A trap," Raven mutters, his voice distorted as he surveys the armed kids. When his eyes finally move back to Phoebe and me, it's with hurt and confusion. "You tried to lay a trap for me?" he asks, his voice dangerously quiet.

Phoebe seems to detect something in him that I don't, because suddenly she grabs my hand, gripping it tightly. It's strange, how she seems to constantly exude warmth.

"Griffin," Phoebe says, her voice firm. "*Run.*"

"*Folks?*" Raven booms.

On each side of the ballroom, the stone walls between the archways begin to move. The palace seems to shudder as they slowly rise upward, revealing what has been waiting behind them this entire time if needed. Standing there waiting for their commands are ranks and ranks of armoured Shadows. Countless personal guards. A hunched demon of blue ice. A mummified zombie tiger with dull glowing eyes. Scores of other menacing visages.

Maybe the rocket launcher wouldn't have been such overkill after all, I think numbly.

Raven steals the moment of surprise to relieve one of the American girls, Julia, of her own crossbow. I grab for him but then his weapon is raised, aimed at me as he slowly backs away, merging into the ranks of his ghoulish guards. I keep my own crossbow aimed at Raven for a moment, in a stand-off. Slowly, me and the other kids back away toward the exit furthest from the stairwell.

"If any of you attack," I say, my raised voice echoing throughout the ballroom. "Your Master dies." My hand shakes, my crossbow still poised toward Raven.

"You wouldn't do that, Griffin," Raven says calmly. "Or you, Pheebs. We're family. You both know it now."

"Don't break rank until I say," I tell the others through tight lips. "We have to run for that exit behind us. That's the entrance to the Underworld, to our way back home. To the station, to ending all of this. At least, let's hope it is."

"Ah... Griffin?" Georgia asks nervously as we back away from Raven's people, who are approaching us from all sides. "Are these some of the good Shadows you talked about?"

"Ah...no," I say carefully. "No, these ones definitely look evil."

"What do we do?"

"Freeeeaking *run!*"

"Stop them!" Raven screams. His voice echoes through the palace, maddened, deranged. "Capture the girl alive, no matter what the cost!"

A shivering wind sweeps up around us, stirring the atrium. Shoot. The Majestic is being summoned.

"Toby, why are you being so freaking evil?" I hear little Marty crying. Phoebe scoops him up in her arms, and we're running, pushing through our gap of escape before Raven's people can cut us off entirely.

I hear the clatter of metal boots on stone as suddenly hordes of Shadow soldiers thunder after us.

We hurtle down a corridor of cracked stone, leading us ever downward. Phoebe shoves little Marty into my arms, stealing my crossbow to fire a bolt over our shoulders. I hear a pained cry behind us.

Marty is wriggling, trying to strangle my face in a hug, temporarily blinding me.

"Stop moving, Marty," I gasp, struggling to hold onto him.

"I love you, Dad," Marty says happily.

Sprinting beside me, I see Phoebe grin despite everything.

There's the sound of water splashing around our feet, and I realise there's some kind of leak. A small river flowing down the corridor around our feet, gravity dragging it downward...

Then we burst out into a dungeon. All around it are various other alternate entrances, presumably leading from other places in the palace. But it's before us, right there in the centre of the dungeon in which a crazy sight meets us.

The entire stone floor of the underground chamber is cracked and caved in, revealing a gaping wound, a cave that leads into darkness. At the entrance of the cave is a pair of warped gates of black iron, the tops of the metal bars spiked with arrow-heads. But they hang wide open, looking older than the palace itself. The current around our feet flows down into the wound in the stone, and water leaks through the cracks in the palace walls to dribble and gush downward, forming a river that flows into the hungry maw. It looks less like a steep drop, more like the river flows along a path. A path down into the Underworld.

Dark vines like creeping tentacles reach out from the gaping, cavernous hole below. It's hard to see but the inner walls of the cave look black and leathery, as if they're organic instead of made of rock. I swear they seem to swell and deflate before us, in a kind of rhythmic breathing. Alien, spore-laden plants emerge demonically from the cave to decorate the strange entrance, with dark creeping vines like tentacles reaching up from below and flowering in blooms of blood red.

It looks like the jaws of hell open up beneath the palace. But it's also our only way forwards, and in fact we barely even hesitate.

"Everyone in, now!" I shout, launching forward, the sounds of the army hunting us right behind us.

"You better be right about this, Grif!" Phoebe shouts. Phoebe helps to pick up April who slips on the wet stone, then charges ahead. "Everyone, follow me!"

We escape into the mysterious depths of the Underworld, hunted by a spurned and furious Raven and his bloodthirsty army of Shadows.

We descend. I've been to the Underworld once before, with Cirrus. We floated along an underground river on our way to Winghold, while glow worms sparkled like stars overhead. But here the Underworld is different. Tunnels branch and change in every direction, the earth hollowed out like Swiss cheese. We're trying to navigate catacombs that feel like living, breathing darkness. A strange, pulsating black flora covers almost every surface. Its tendrils undulate as if we're outside in the wind, but no wind exists. The only light we have to guide us comes from the luminescent algae - if that's what it is - which is scattered occasionally throughout the tunnels. It glows a ghostly green.

The branching catacombs may be good for losing the army of hired killer Shadows behind us, but without a map of the right route, how are we meant to find this supposed way back to the human world, if it even exists? Do all the tunnels lead to the same point, or are we getting more and more lost with every left or right turn that we take? Twelve scared human kids in pyjamas clinging to their stolen weapons, with me and Phoebe taking up the rear.

After running for I don't know how long, Phoebe holds up a hand for us to stop, and shouts to the kids in front.

"They're exhausted," she says to me. "Take a minute everyone! Keep an ear out, though."

"Yeah," I say, wheezing. "Give them a minute. Amateurs."

Right now the Underworld is eerily quiet. The algae casts a sickly green glow across our diverse party. Phoebe's right that the distant thunder of boots and claws throughout the tunnels has disappeared. I imagine them spreading out, searching for us, and shiver. I don't know what they'd do to the other kids. They're ruthless killers. And Raven made it clear that Phoebe is all he wants. Maybe he's gone off having me as an adopted little brother after all?

"The pyjamas are very fetching," I hear Phoebe say. "Were you all having some kind of haunted castle slumber party without me?"

Blinking to make out her eerie green outline, I press my back against the tunnel wall beside her. I speak in a low voice so the other kids can't hear us.

"Phoebe. What was that about, back there in the ballroom?" I whisper angrily. "Did you forget how dangerous Raven is? It's like you're still treating Raven as Taylor, when he's this... monster."

"You're welcome. Glad I could save you."

"He made Shadows sick and delusional just to gain enough power to form the Empire. He did twisted experiments on Shadows and humans that he locked up on New Redemption. He had the kids at Winghold slaughtered, had the place burnt to the ground. He *gutted* me, and then with Calvin and Zephyr…"

"I know, all right?" she hisses, then lowers her voice. She fights down a sob. "He told me what he did to them, and no, I don't understand how he could do that. How it all got so… twisted. I know all the terrible things he's done. He was hugging me, defenceless, trusting, just like my Taylor. Just like before all this. And still then, I was going to do it."

Phoebe draws a knife from the back of her jeans, showing it to me in the dim light from what? "I was going to use this to stab him. To end… all of this. Everything I started, everything I unleashed on this world. But I couldn't do it. It felt so wrong. He's still Taylor, and I'm responsible partly for what I did ten years ago. I'm responsible for making him this way, turning him into Raven."

"No," I whisper. "You tried to save him."

Phoebe ploughs on as if I haven't spoken.

"And in just one moment back in that ballroom, I decided to go with my own feelings over all of those lives. I care about him, and just because of that, hundreds have died. Now maybe even more will."

Raven is actually responsible for far more than just hundreds of deaths, I'm pretty solid on that, but I don't think it's a great time to bring it up.

Phoebe's shoulders shake as I pull her into a sudden hug, unexpected for both of us. "It's okay," I say, holding tightly, protectively. "You've done enough. This isn't on you."

"Yes," she says in a low voice. "It is."

"You faced your worst nightmare for me," I say. The idea seems almost nonsensical. Crazy.

"You already risked yourself to save me, you dork." She punches me in the arm. "Still. Don't, like, expect it to be a regular occurrence. Anyhow, I didn't come here to rescue you. I'm not stupid. I was trying to find a way back to our side, I didn't know this is where you'd been taken. But... I was hiding behind the pillar, and I saw what Raven was doing to you... you were in so much pain, and I couldn't just stand there and watch." She stares at the ground. "I couldn't lose another friend to his own demons."

Trying to lighten the mood, I bump my shoulder into hers playfully.

"You did good. Rumour has it there's a passage somewhere in this Underworld, a way back to the human world. To Mum's station. We still have a shot. All of us. Of course, it could be a trap."

"Great. If it is, we fight our way out. We race the guards there, cross over to our world, activate the stations, and all live happily ever after."

"Wow, it really sounds like you have a handle on things," I grin. "Almost like you could do it without me."

"I could," Phoebe says nonchalantly. Then she smiles. "But it's more fun with you."

Suddenly I hear footfalls from further back in the tunnel. Alarmingly close.

Phoebe and I lock eyes.

"Move!" we hiss to the others, and we're running for our lives again, hurtling to a mythic-seeming, uncertain destination.

I hear snarls behind us. Turning, I loose a bolt into the

dark. Reloading as I run, I fire again, and again. I think I hear curses behind us. Hopefully that's a sign that I hit something.

The ghostly green of the algae grows scarcer and scarcer, then vanishes completely, plunging us into darkness. I squint, waiting for my eyes to adapt more to the total blackness. I can't even make out the others in front of me...

"*Ooof!*"

I slam into a wall and bounce off, hitting the floor of the tunnel. Winded, I fight for more air to re-enter my lungs. I must have reached another fork between tunnels. If the stone hadn't been padded with the weird fungi down here, I could have knocked myself out completely.

Shoot. Raven's guards. I hear them right behind me, and drag myself to my feet. My night vision is fractionally better. Maybe running into a wall jumpstarted it somehow.

I was right about the fork. I have no idea what way Phoebe and our newly-minted GSA ran down. I'm lost. But behind me, a large boulder sits in the middle of the expansive tunnel. It's a miracle I didn't knock myself out on it. I flatten my back against the rock, sinking to the ground just in time before the footfalls behind me come to a stop.

Did they see me? I don't know. I force myself to hold my breath, even as my winded diaphragm is struggling to breathe in new oxygen as fast as possible.

Oh, crapbasket, I dropped my crossbow when I had my little collision. I'm unarmed, helpless. Playing hide and seek in the dark.

And very alone.

I think I hear footfalls from behind me. Coming around the boulder.

I'm alone. Lost. For a moment I feel like I'm back in the

family cemetery in the Domain. Where I was near the start of all this, after Cameron Technologies fell. When I felt more lost and damned than ever, and asked for help. It had come in the distinctive shape of a Phoebe.

But now Phoebe and the other kids are alone somewhere up ahead where I can't find them, where I can't protect them. A hungry horde is hunting us through the tunnels. I have to make it across to the station, to finally make peace between the worlds and end the bloodletting. The answer lies in here, somewhere deeper in the Underworld, I can *feel* it.

I hear something. Heavy breathing, close. Only feet away in the dark.

Slowly, I look to my left.

A pair of crawling jaws emerge around the side of the boulder. I try to quietly slide myself away. Then the creature the horrible maw belongs to comes fully into sight. It's one of Raven's guards, a fearsome tarantula; spines like blades and needles jut out from her... him? I can't always tell the genders of Shadows. Thick, viscous white saliva spills from her mandibles, or maybe its web fluid.

I can make her out, sniffing the air. Peering ahead toward where the tunnels fork.

Quietly, very quietly, I crawl backward around the opposite side of the boulder. Out of her range of sight. Turning, I mosey my way around the rock. Wait for her to move, so I can then retrieve my crossbow and follow. Make sure she doesn't get to Phoebe and the others. That's the plan...

Suddenly I'm face-to-face with the tarantula.

She grins, knowing she tricked me. She must have snuck around the other side of the rock, and now I'm prey.

Spidery goo drips from her mandibles. I hear a hiss from where the saliva lands, the sound of boiling acid eating solid matter.

I hear the sounds of other Shadows coming down the tunnel as well. Looking past the tarantula, I can see them. Raven's guards. My stomach drops. The catacombs are overflowing with them.

Rihäm, Georgia, little Marty, all the others... they'll be killed or imprisoned again for experimentation. Phoebe's might be an even worse fate depending if Raven plans to brainwash her to be his queen, or punish her for turning on him.

Slowly, the arachnid before me prepares to devour me, clearly savouring the coming moment when I'll try to run...

Suddenly I can hear a mind inside mine, my own internal world expanding beyond its normal boundaries. Another being's memories, our feelings and sensations flowing together as one.

A giant claw descends on the tarantula. Talons like scimitars clench around her like a claw machine in an arcade, snatching her up, then hurling her into the air. She flies up and away, screeching as she vanishes into the darkness. I turn behind me, squinting upward, even though I already can feel the being who's standing there, as real as anything.

A giant dragon rises up through the blackness, with the feathered wings, head and shoulders of a mighty cockatoo. Crest raised high like a battle headdress, sticking out his broad chest in challenge. Terrifying and magnificent.

"Eclipse?" I whisper.

He turns his attention down at me, his expression

darkly thunderous. Locked in a stand-off, we stare at each other for a moment, and I barely breathe.

"Griffin," he says slowly. His voice is rich and powerful. Like velvet thunder.

Then he cranes his neck down toward me and I step forward, breaking into a run before I grab hold of his head in both hands, bowing mine to press my forehead against his.

"Eclipse," I say again, joy leaping through me.

I hear the insidious footfalls of Raven's guards creeping up behind me, spreading out through the tunnel. Pulling away from me, Eclipse raises himself back up to his full towering height.

He takes an imposing step over my head, his talons slamming down on the ground between me and the guards. Eclipse leans toward them, leering.

"No one harms my human," he says. His feathers and scales ignite without warning. Blinding golden flames flow from his plumage. He stands like a tall, terrifying spectre, part phoenix and part dragon.

The flames erupt forth, thundering forth in a searing display of power. I flinch, awed.

Raven's guards throw themselves backwards. There's an explosion of flame and I shield my face from the scorching heat. Then there's a roar as the roof of the tunnel caves in, an avalanche of rocks crashing down. When the noise stops I take it we're still alive, but there's no way those guards can reach us now without backtracking.

Eclipse bends down to a near-huggable height. Then, wordlessly, he encases me in his glowing wings. His feathers resemble shards of honey-coloured magma, but they don't burn me when they brush me, just feel snuggly warm and soft to the touch.

I laugh in wonder and with a deep, deep relief. I can feel his mind, as real as my own. I didn't hallucinate it.

We're still connected. Counterparts, forever.

My Shadow, I smile, blinking back tears.

13

IN HELL WITH YOU

Eclipse

"For such a small creature," I smile, amused, "how do you always manage to get yourself into the most dramatically far-fetched situations?"

"I suppose some people would say I'm compensating," Griffin grins back. He looks up at me. I can feel him in my mind, a sensation like nothing I've experienced. The colours, the images and feelings are more intense than last time. His reaction and mine mingling so that it's hard to tell one apart from the other. Ecstasy and fear emanate and blend from both of us.

The tunnel is entirely illuminated by the golden, flickering firelight from my feathers.

Slowly, I bow my head down to Griffin. Taking my head in his hands, he presses his head against mine.

"I'm so relieved you're here," I say, my voice strangled.

"Me too. And that you're alive."

I feel tongue-tied. It's unreal, being face to face at long last. We're strangers, who barely had any time to get to know each other last time we met in traumatic circumstances. But at another level, we also know each other as well as we do ourselves.

Finally we part to better see each other. I smile down at him shyly.

"I'm happy you're still alive too, since that means that *I'm* definitely not dead. That is how this whole counterpart thing works, right? Even if it sort of looks like we've stumbled into hell." I examine him closer. "Your hair changed."

"Yes."

"It's disarming."

"Eclipse," says Griffin, still dazed, still encased in my wings. "Why are you here? *How* are you here?"

"I took a leisurely trip from Sanctuary City to the Underworld to try and visit you."

"Wow," he says, digesting this. "Any good road trip stories?"

"No, sadly it was a piece of cake," I say. I eye him shrewdly. "What about you? Six months, Griffin. Why didn't you join the worlds like you meant to? Why didn't you come back for me?"

"I'm so sorry," Griffin says desperately. "I wanted to more than anything. I tried to be smart enough to make it happen, to be who I had to be to get it done as soon as possible. But Raven threw us a curveball." He hesitates. "Cameron Technologies is gone. Calvin and Zephyr… do you remember who they are?" Griffin's voice breaks.

His sudden fears and doubts swim through my brain. The cause of his anxiety is laid out plainly for me to see, even as he tries to hide it for my sake. I can hear the small voice inside Griffin's head which asks:

How much of my Shadow is still my Shadow?

"I know who Calvin and Zephyr are," I say softly, calming him. "I have all of Cirrus' memories now. They just needed some time to come back to me." Suddenly his words break through to me fully. *Cameron Technologies gone. The lab, gone.* "Was Zephyr hurt?" I demand suddenly. For some reason I feel a slow dawning of panic, a nameless terror in my gut. "Is he..."

"No," Griffin shakes his head. "Not dead. But... I'll fill you in later."

"Did you... did you tell Zephyr what I did?" I say self-consciously. "Helping you take the Oracle back with you?"

Before Griffin can struggle to come up with an answer, I see the answer in his mind.

"Eclipse is a killer," I hear Zephyr's voice saying darkly. *"The parasite who stole Cirrus' body. And if I find him, I'm going to kill him."*

"He just needs some time to come around," Griffin says.

I feel a strange pain deep in my chest. I nod wordlessly.

"I can fill you in on everything as we go," Griffin says, sparking with determination. With belief. "But right now what matters is I need to get back home. There's a station on the other side in my world, a station that can open all of the portals. We can finish this now. Together, like it was always meant to be."

I stare down at him. An unseen inner conflict is warring somewhere inside me, so distant that all I can hear is a dull roar. It is like... the sound of the ocean from a shell when you press it against your ear. With that distant rumbling comes an uneasy, unspeakable notion of dread.

But the excitement, the joy in Griffin's eyes is something that Cirrus is overjoyed to see there as much as I am. I know for a fact that Cirrus would follow his human anywhere, do anything for Griffin, to keep Griffin this happy forever.

"Then let's finish it," I say. Turning, I lash my tail to shatter a nearby rock with restless energy. I spread my wings as far as the tunnel allows. "Have you missed flying at all?"

Griffin rolls his eyes.

"*Have you missed flying at all?*" He grins widely. "Are you freaking kidding me?"

I have to scuttle, using my wings to walk on as front legs while an elated Griffin rides atop my neck. I try to avoid scraping his head on the cavern roof. Wouldn't want to hurt his new carrot-coloured hairstyle. But soon the tunnel widens, and I launch myself out into the open air, relishing the wind in my wings, feeling on top of the world. We sail through an enormous underground tunnel, both feeling weightless, my glowing feathers illuminating our way. I feel Griffin pull himself down closer into my heated plumage. He places his hands against the feathers on either side of my head to steady himself against the beats of my wings.

"Is that... is it okay like this?" Griffin asks tentatively.

"Yes," I say gently, entertained by his awkwardness. "It's fine."

"Some other human kids are down here," Griffin says. "I rescued them but we got separated. I'm not sure where they ended up. We have to make sure they're safe."

"We rescued the Shadows Raven was holding too," I tell

him. "Hopefully they're safe, Hann...." I stop myself, remembering Griffin's complicated history with Hanna. "The Shadows we rescued are further ahead," I say instead. "I came back to find you first."

"Cool," Griffin says wryly. "So we both performed successful rescue missions... and then lost the kids somewhere in the Underworld."

"I didn't *lose* them." I scoff, ruffling my feathers, affronted. "I just... misplaced them. I saved your life, why are you complaining?"

"Hey, I totally had that handled," Grif says. "I was just acting as bait, strategically. So that Phoebe and the others could make a clean getaway."

"Phoebe?" I say, incredulous. "Not... Ember's human?"

"Oh, yeah! She's alive still!"

I remember Ember's seizure before we left Sanctuary. She really *had* heard her human. I feel a strange pang of guilt for leaving Ember there, even though I know it was that or be captured by her again. Knowing that Ember's human is down here somewhere in these tunnels with us brings back memories of the flaming Shadow that I'd tried to keep suppressed. Hard to do, when my burning feathers are a constant reminder, her power still flowing through me.

Still. Despite all the bad blood between us, part of me yearns to tell Ember that her human is still alive. That what she felt in Sanctuary when Phoebe was revived was real. And surely if Phoebe is alive... that means Ember still must be too.

"Cirrus turned Phoebe into stone which preserved her," Griffin is saying. "He kept her alive all this time."

"And somehow... you reversed it?"

"Yeah. I just... touched her. I don't... I don't know how, if I used Cirrus' power somehow, or what it all means."

The idea of there still being such a tangible connection between Griffin and his ex-Shadow... is troubling.

"Just don't get ideas above your station," I say, trying to play it off lightly. "Powers is my thing. As a human your thing is making jokes and eating burgers."

"Harsh. Wait, did I just see some new memory with Ember in it?" Griffin says, and I feel his flicker of curiosity. "Did you run into her?"

"We may have been acquainted," I mumble.

"What's happening with the Empire? With the Resistance? With..." Griffin stops, sheepish. "You know what, just show me everything that's happened since I left. And you said *'we'* rescued the Shadows. Who's *'we'*?" Then Griffin frowns, and I feel how unsettled he is.

"Hanna?"

"Sorry?" I say lightly.

"Why is there so much of the Empress in your head? I mean all that anger you're feeling at her, that I get, but why are you thinking of her?"

"Ahhh..." I hesitate, unsure what's the most painless way to tell him I've been working with his first love who violently betrayed him. "Well..."

I'm not too sure how he will deal with that one. My mind goes carefully opaque. Luckily, a distraction presents itself in the form of an army of evil.

The tunnel opens, and our breath is stolen away by the sight that meets us.

We're in a gargantuan cavern. Its roof stretches high, high over our heads, a reminder of how far we've already descended. Down below, a thin, cracked bridge of stone stretches between two cliff-faces, across a chasm of eerie green mist. Fireflies spiral through the air of the cavern, as if they are floating stars, or the fragments of dreams.

But what is occurring below is even more mesmerising than our surroundings.

On the cliff directly below us, Raven's guards charge across the cliff toward the bridge, more and more of them pouring out from the tunnels to swell their ranks. It's clear now that this isn't simply a mild collection of palace guards. It's an army.

Still running, about halfway across the bridge through the gaping space, is a group of thirteen young humans in pyjamas, armed with swords, bows... and a couple with human guns.

There's Phoebe and the others, down there! Griffin shouts in my mind, unnecessarily. I'm already flying over the heads of the army, pulling in my wings to descend down toward the bridge.

A handful of winged gargoyles are flying in pursuit of Phoebe and her team. With a casual swing of my tail, I stun a few of them, sending them spiralling down at the green mists to try and right themselves just in time. Raven's other winged guards balk at the sight of me, wisely retreating to rejoin the rest of the army.

"Tell me you don't enjoy doing that," Griffin laughs.

My talons cautiously set down on the stone. For a moment I wonder if my weight will collapse the ancient walkway, its fragments crumbling into the abyss below us with the others. Fortunately, the bridge holds.

I turn to face Raven's army. The guards closest to the bridge come to a halt, sizing me up. They all look demented, mad. Not like real people, but primal predators, hungry for the taste of blood and the joy of killing.

"Why aren't they firing at us?" I say, uncertain.

"I'm guessing they don't want to risk hurting Phoebe," Griffin says tightly. "Raven must still want her alive."

Assessing the enemy, I smirk. While I might struggle to take on all of them at once - at least, while trying to practice Griffin's code of not harming any of them - none of them wants to be the first to face me one-on-one on the bridge. We're in a stand-off.

Golden flame ignites from my feathers, and I conjure swirling blasts of fire through the air. A fireworks show of withering heat, a display of my power and control.

The guards look suitably shocked. They come to a total stop, fanning out across the cliff. Buying the humans time to escape over the long bridge.

"Why are you following Raven?" I thunder across at the army of Shadows, frustrated. "What did he do to all of you? Has that human threatened your families, is he... controlling you in some way?"

They stay silent. Attention fixed on us, like predators fixated on their prey.

"I bet Raven just pays them obscenely," Griffin says grimly.

"Or he controls them like a cult," I brood. "Cuts them off from the outside, living in this palace. The way they all look at him... it's like some kind of religious worship."

Where's the Majestic? I wonder. Why hasn't Raven summoned him yet? I mean, I'm not complaining. Otherwise we might be dead already.

Griffin slides down my neck and clambers over my wing. Using the back of my leg as a step he drops down onto the bridge. Through our mental connection, I can hear his quiet pride at how cool the dismount looked.

Turning, I have a clue to his sudden self-consciousness. Phoebe is walking right up to us, staring up at me in open fascination. Her hair isn't the flaming red Cirrus remembers, but is now dyed gold. As if... she and Griffin swapped hair.

But it *is* Phoebe. It's really true. Ember's human is back from the dead.

With a soft, aching heart I remember Phoebe and Ember reading Cirrus and Griffin stories, and tucking them under the blankets after they'd finished watching human movies together.

"You're Eclipse?" Phoebe asks. "You're the Shadow Cirrus mutated into?"

Griffin and I both look at her apprehensively.

"Oh, okay," Phoebe says, awkward. "We don't talk about that. My bad."

Then to my surprise, she extends a hand out to me, seemingly not intimidated by me in the least.

"I'm Phoebe," she says, smiling. "I used to know Cirrus. It's a pleasure to meet you, Eclipse."

For some reason I can't explain, the simple gesture of friendship, of acceptance, means everything.

"Well met, Phoebe," I respond, inclining my head. "If you're anything at all like your Shadow, I would much rather have you as a friend than an enemy."

She cocks her head.

"Did you peeve off my Shadow?"

"Perhaps a little bit," I admit.

Phoebe takes one of my talons in her hand and we gently shake. Looking over her, I see that most of the human teenagers are almost off the bridge onto the other cliff, escaping into the dark tunnel there, continuing downward into the Underworld.

"Pheebs," Griffin begins, but is cut off when Phoebe punches him in the shoulder, hard.

"Ow!"

"Keep up next time, derp-brain," she says angrily. "You gave me a heart attack. We thought we'd lost you for good."

"You need to run, now," Griffin urges her. "Eclipse and me can hold the army off. Once you and the others are clear we can break this bridge, stop them following."

"Really?" Phoebe raises an eyebrow sceptically. "You two can hold off an army?"

"Raven," I warn them, looking back toward the cliff.

Raven emerges from the ranks of guards, wearing his long, sweeping black hooded robes. Waddling along after him is his ever-present servant, the crow Shadow. The humanoid bird bows so low that he's constantly staring at the ground, shuffling obediently behind Raven as if in a permanent state of shame. As Raven walks forward away from the ranks of his guards, the Shadow tries to follow him - but Raven barks something at him and he cowers, retreating to stand with the others.

"That's his Shadow, isn't it?" Griffin says, troubled. "Winter."

I look at him sharply.

"Raven's Shadow?" I demand. Raven hasn't shown the slightest ounce of warmth that would indicate Winter is his counterpart. How could he possibly treat him that way?

"Yeah," Phoebe says tersely. "That's Winter. Looks like Raven still treats him like crap."

"Eclipse, Griffin.... Phoebe," Raven calls out, striding out from the ranks of Shadows. His voice echoes through the massive cavern. His tone darkens. "Playtime is over."

"I didn't agree to that," Griffin mutters, and I laugh.

Raven's patience is clearly cracking. Something dangerous looms in his voice when he next speaks.

"You're running from the inevitable, all of you. The Neutral Zones of the Shadow world will vote to join the Empire. They'll vote for fear and protection from the strange humans, like they always do. Soon I'll have full control of this world again. We could work together to continue my work, building a better world. Or... worlds." He lets the implication hang ominously in the air. "Why work at cross purposes? Why not join our talents?"

"Perhaps because you're a genocidal dictator who tried to kill us," I offer fairly.

"Or because of your weird obsession with Grim Reaper cosplay," Griffin adds, gesturing at Raven's robes.

Raven just shrugs, which I don't believe constitutes a proper apology for genocide.

"Phoebe, come back to the palace with me," he says. Even from this distance, his eyes seem to pierce us. "We can talk this out. All of the others can go free. You and me are all that matter right now. That's all I care about. Just... come home. I don't want to hurt any of you. You're family, Griffin. And you, Eclipse... your destiny is far too great to die here in the Underworld. I'm not giving up on any of you. But make no mistake. I'll do whatever it takes to get Phoebe back."

"Raven... I mean, Taylor," Griffin says determinedly. Raven falls silent. I can tell that Griffin using his true name has given him pause. Griffin's forehead is mopped with sweat. "I'm sorry for what my Dad did to you. Stealing away your Shadow."

The entire cavern is silent. I digest this, reading through Griffin's memories of his conversation with Phoebe as he relives it.

"I'm sorry for what my Dad did to you," Griffin continues, and I can see how hard it is for him to get the words out. How much it takes for him to say what he believes is right. "I'm sorry that he wasn't the person I wish he had been. But you strayed from the path of what's right on your own, just like him. You abandoned Mum's mission she entrusted you with. But we're going to finish it."

"Were you behind the attack on Sanctuary City?" I challenge Raven, flaring my wings. It somehow hadn't occurred to me to get the confirmation. "The humans who came in their aircraft through the Rip in the sky. Was that somehow your doing?"

"Yes," Raven answers simply, without any sense of defensiveness. Without any regret for the lives that were lost. "I found some humans that were... persuadable. It made for helpful propaganda."

"And Cameron Technologies," Griffin says, his voice increasingly dangerous. "The Shadows that destroyed it.... that was you too, wasn't it?"

"Yes. To be fair I mainly sent them to bring you and Calvin safely to me, which they failed at miserably. It would have made your journey here much more straight forward, Griffin."

Phoebe has clapped her hands to her mouth, staring at her old friend in wordless horror.

"Why?" Griffin says, his voice breaking in shock. "All the people who died. Our staff, faces I'd seen my entire life... why Cameron Technologies?"

"What if I told you they had to die for a reason? A few to save the lives of many?"

"You're broken," I accuse him darkly. I'm remembering the innocent Shadows slaughtered in Sanctuary. My vow to not take life is feeling more and more like an impossible weight to bare. "You've crossed a line where the lives of people means nothing to you, as if it's just some... game."

"For God's sake. Do you know how much violence occurs across the worlds every day?" Raven says, incensed. "The invisible suffering embodied in the system, that goes unseen, unpunished? What I'm doing is an insignificant fraction of that, and I'm doing it to end the suffering once and for all. We're family. Griffin, Eclipse, don't act appalled, as if you're like the others. You know that neither of you are."

"Phoebe, run," Griffin hisses. "Go look after the others. Find the way back to the station."

Phoebe stares at the army for a moment, pale, then back at Griffin. She shakes her head tautly.

"I'm going to go with Raven," Phoebe says firmly.

"NO!" Griffin and I explode at the same time. Phoebe winces under the force of my voice.

"It will give you and the other kids all a chance to escape, unharmed," she presses, determined.

"I won't leave you," Griffin says fiercely, gripping her tightly.

"I thought you were the one who could always see the clearest path to victory?" Phoebe says, almost teasingly. There's tears in her eyes. "You told me you could always see the logical moves, especially in the chaos. You're choosing *now* to be irrational?"

"I'm not leaving you," is all Griffin says, stubborn.

Phoebe just shakes her head.

"I'm doing this," she says, as if she is daring him to stop her. "I can't run from this any longer. I've put off having to face my actions for ten years. If I give myself up, maybe he'll let you all escape."

"Stop blaming yourself, like you need to sacrifice yourself for Taylor's mistakes," Griffin says softly.

"But that's just it. He's my responsibility. This was my mission, but I don't really have a happy ending. I was kidding myself before. I don't have an after."

"Yes, you do. Ember needs you. *I* need you," Griffin says urgently, flushing. "Your family isn't all dead and gone, Pheebs."

"Ember's lived for a decade thinking I was dead," Phoebe says in a low voice. "She's already grieved."

"*They* need you," Griffin fires at her, pointing at the other side of the bridge, where the kids are entering the tunnel there. Phoebe looks taken aback at his change of voice. "You need to catch up with the other kids, and take care of them. Lead them, show them the way. They need you. Just... trust me in that. Trust that you're important. Okay? It's easy to keep sacrificing yourself, but choosing to live and fight is harder. Finish your mission. Be the hero."

"I don't believe in heroes."

"I do," Griffin says. "You made me believe in them."

Phoebe stares at him. I had a feeling she was too stubborn to be talked out of anything, but her expression is inscrutable. Then:

"Okay," she whispers. "But be right behind us."

I wolf-whistle through my beak, somewhat unsubtly.

Crush on the babysitter much? I ask Griffin through our connection.

Shut up, Griffin retaliates, going red.

Why shut up when I can tease you about it? I say candidly. *If we're going to die making a stand as heroes, I might as well get in a few zingers first.*

"Take them," Raven's voice carries across the chasm, ordering his army forth.

"Oh, damn," Griffin says.

But before the others can even move, an armoured guard at the very front lunges forward...

...and grabs hold of Raven. Drawing a rapier, the guard brings it around to hold it straight to Raven's unsuspecting neck.

The entire army freezes, transfixed as the traitor in their midst holds his sword to Raven's vulnerable throat. Griffin, Phoebe and I freeze as well. The whole of the Underworld is silent.

"What are you doing?" Raven's snarl echoes. He struggles for a moment, but the guard holds on tightly. All Raven succeeds at is freeing the Shadow's helmet from his head, which falls to the stone with a clang. We all stare in shock at the individual who managed to take Raven by surprise. He stands there in a pirate-like outfit, a long plum cape hanging from his shoulders.

It's a human. An old man.

He looks gaunt, the dark bags under his eyes pronounced even from here. He looks like an escaped prisoner. Dirty, starved, like an escaped rat from a maze.

But the strangest thing of all is when Griffin asks:

"Is that my therapist?"

"Mr Falco?" Phoebe exclaims at the same time, incredulous.

The man called Mr Falco backs toward the bridge,

holding Raven out as a shield against the immobilised army.

"Anyone tries to touch them, he dies!" Mr Falco roars. I can hear the fear in his voice, the trembling he's trying to suppress. I hear Griffin thinking with shame how he always thought of Mr Falco as a snivelling coward, a 'creep.' But right now Mr Falco is fighting through the fear, to save us.

"Phoebe, Griffin, run!" Mr Falco yells, keeping the sword edge close to Raven's throat. "Finish this for Melissa, for Calvin!"

Raven is facing away from us, but something about his body language tells me that he has been genuinely taken by surprise by the situation.

"Nobody move!" Mr Falco yells at some of the Shadows surrounding him. Some of them are trying to edge closer, claws reaching for the swords in their sheathes. "If anybody moves, your master dies!"

"*Mr Falco?*" Raven laughs, delighted. He is seemingly unconcerned with his life on the line. "So you've grown a spine since last time we met, so very far from here. Griffin, tell your pet dog to put his weapon down. I don't want to hurt him."

"Don't listen to him, Griffin!" Mr Falco yells desperately. "Just run, both of you!"

"You'll die!" Griffin yells, confused. "Calvin will kill me if I don't even try to save his only friend."

"Clearly, this man is a hero," I cut through to Griffin. "But we have to honour his sacrifice. Climb on, both of you. I'm getting you and the others to safety."

But Griffin doesn't move.

Phoebe rests her hand on Griffin's shoulder, looking just

as shocked as him that Mr Falco is risking his life for them both.

"Griffin... we have to run, there's nothing we can do. He's buying us a chance. Connecting the worlds is bigger than all of us."

"Run, you damn idiots!" Mr Falco bellows at us. The old man angles his sword toward Raven's neck. "This is for Melissa!" Mr Falco cries.

When suddenly Raven twists out of the old man's grip.

We watch as Raven disarms Mr Falco with ease. Retracting a knife from his belt and spinning it by the handle, Raven grabs the old man's shoulder and drives the blade through Mr Falco's heart.

"Nooooooo!" Griffin screams.

14

MAJESTIC

Griffin

Mr Falco is appraising me over his notepad.

"Tell me, Griffin, are you happy?"

"Are you?"

I watch Mr Falco's body as it falls to the ground.

"Griffin," I hear Eclipse saying distantly, breaking through my memories. My head is swimming, the air thick around me. Everything feels unreal. *"Griffin!"*

I come back to my senses just in time.

"Run!" I scream to Phoebe. "Trust me!"

Phoebe stares at me, and looks like she wants to say something, but then changes her mind.

"I trust you," is all she says. "Slow them down, but be right behind us. Promise me."

"I promise," I tell her, and then Phoebe is running,

following after the teenagers toward the safety of the tunnel.

Smirking over his new kill, Raven turns to his guards.

"Never forget!" Raven screams out at his watching army. He holds up the knife wet with blood, as if he's performing in a play. "I am untouchable! I do not bleed!"

So many confusing emotions are turning inside me. Shock at the sheer violence of what we just saw. That Raven... this guy I've hated for so long, who almost had me trusting him after a single moment of vulnerability - could kill someone so savagely that I've known most of my life, with zero weight on his conscience. I'm grieving, confused by what to feel about the sudden loss of Mr Falco in the world, a man I'd spent so long detesting, and I'm hurting, feeling betrayed by Raven... and wondering why I feel so betrayed by a man I already knew to be a murderer anyhow.

Taking Mr Falco's body, Raven drags it toward the edge of the cliff. He's getting ready to throw it into the chasm beneath us, letting Mr Falco's body fall into the ethereal green mist below.

Not on our watch.

Clambering up Eclipse's leg I pull myself up onto his neck, swinging my leg over.

KILL RAVEN, I shout fiercely to my Shadow, spurring him forwards like a horse. *Go!*

I feel Eclipse's shock through our joined minds. As if he can't believe what I've said, sure that he's misheard.

"What?" I demand. "You're scared of that army? You can take on anyone. You're the most powerful Shadow in the world."

"I thought we didn't kill?" Eclipse says reproachfully. He seems strangely upset, disturbed, but I can't make sense of that right now. "I made a vow not to take lives. A vow to try and live up to who you wanted me to be."

"And I'm so proud of you for that, but sometimes... violence is necessary," I urge him, barely aware of our conversation. Everything is red. All of my focus is on Raven, imagining watching him die just as Mr Falco just did. "You know all the bad things Raven's done. It's time he faced justice."

"This is revenge, not justice."

"What's the difference?" I cry.

Eclipse shakes his head, overwhelmed.

"Who *are* you?" he asks me, as if I'm a stranger. Distantly I feel his confusion. His hurt.

Raven has nearly dragged Mr Falco's body to the cliff edge.

"Eclipse, it's me," I beg. I run my hands through his neck feathers, grasping at them, smoothening them pleadingly, anxiously. "It's me, I'm right here. And I know this is messed up, and confusing, but I need you right now. I need you more than ever. I can't... I can't let this pass. I need you on my side."

Eclipse is silent. Then...

"What do you want your Shadow to do?" he asks quietly.

"End him," I say, temper flaring. "GO, ECLIPSE, *NOW!*"

Eclipse launches himself forward, formidable, wings catching the air, zeroing in on Raven. The entire army bristles before us, raising their weapons. Arrows deflect from Eclipse's wings like twigs, and I press myself lower into his back, staying out of the range of fire.

We're metres away from Raven...

...when suddenly the Majestic is hovering in front of us.

Eclipse flaps hard in shock, killing our momentum. Surveying the floating hybrid of Calvin and Zephyr, human and reptile that hovers eerily unmoving before us.

No. We were so close.

"There you are," Raven says to the impassive Majestic, relaxing. He drags Mr Falco's body along the final stretch, dropping it just short of the cliff edge. So close that a single kick will send Mr Falco hurtling through the green mists below.

"Where have you been?" Raven commands the Majestic with cold fury. "I've been calling you. When I summon you, you answer. Understood?"

The Majestic just floats there, as creepy as ever. A monstrosity, leering at us.

"Answer me! I gave you an order." Raven is uncertain for a moment, but the uncertainty quickly breaks into fury, his face contorting. "You will obey me! Capture these two. Bring me the girl. Phoebe."

Very slowly the Majestic twists his pale, reptilian neck, until he's staring at his master. Then he screams, a sound that's part human cry and part reptilian hiss.

Raven pales. Even his guards retreat away from the chasm and the Majestic that hovers there. A Majestic that exudes ethereal evil.

Eclipse's wings are still beating the air, keeping us aloft. Me and my Shadow, facing off against Calvin and Zephyr as one dark super-being.

"Eclipse, are you okay?" I mutter.

His presence... Eclipse answers, perturbed. *He feels like no Shadow I've ever witnessed, or heard of. Like a primeval death God. An avatar of ancient darkness.*

That's not Calvin, or Zephyr. That's whatever Raven did to them, I think at Eclipse. *We have to protect Phoebe and the others. We need to give Phoebe the time she needs to end this, whatever it takes. I'm sure Calvin and Zephyr will forgive us for roughing them up a little, if it buys us time.*

The Majestic turns his attention back toward us, descending through the air to match our height. Green mists whirl down below us. We could be in a tableau, a mythic oil painting of a great battle. Calvin against his younger brother, Zephyr against the Shadow that was once his. I'm perched on quite possibly the most powerful Shadow in existence, facing something that may still be at another level entirely.

And as we watch, the Majestic starts to grow. Shifting, larger and larger, his growth only coming to a stop when he's undeniably more giant than Eclipse, a white leviathan suspended effortlessly in the air.

Weirdly as we stare across at the Majestic, I feel a pang deep inside me, and I wish Calvin was here right now. I wonder how on earth I'm going to explain to my brother if I ever get him back that Mr Falco, his only friend, is dead, and that I let him die?

I feel Eclipse recoiling, reacting to my own train of thought, shock and confusion, his mind recoiling at my words.

"This Majestic..." he says, horrified, "is Zephyr and your brother?"

"Yeah," I say, simmering.

Eclipse is speechless, and I feel him struggling with that realisation. As Eclipse stares into the black eyes of the pale leviathan, I hear him fearfully wondering if Zephyr is the one hatefully staring back at him..

Raven did this, Eclipse seethes beneath me. *He's been*

trying to do it to those Shadow prisoners too. Perverting them. Twisting them. You're right. Raven needs to face justice.

There's a sound like a sudden gale, even though we're far underground. The sound seems to come from the Majestic, shaping itself into a single word.

Abomination, it breathes. I feel Eclipse stiffen.

"Don't listen," I tell him. "It's that Majestic, it's poisoned by Raven's influence. Calvin... Zephyr! It's me, Griffin. This is Eclipse. We're on your side." I stare back at Calvin's scaled face. Appealing to those black, unfeeling eyes.

The Majestic spasms suddenly, his claws flexing, neck and face contorting.

"Griffin?"

I freeze. The words are torn from his scaled lips, as if from deep within him, with great effort. Zephyr's voice, and Calvin's voice at the same time.

They're still alive in there. Somewhere. Then:

"I can't... control it," I hear Calvin gasp, just his voice, sounding in intense pain. "It wants to kill you. Run!"

Then, with a cry of rage, the Majestic surges toward us. Eclipse roars and flies to meet it, talons outstretched.

I grab on tightly for my life before I'm thrown free. Eclipse attacks, but his claws snatch at empty space. We swerve smoothly in mid-air, turning back around to see the Majestic floating exactly where he was before.

Eclipse bursts into flame, his feathers elongating into golden fiery tongues. He blasts a surge of flame at the Majestic, hot enough to melt metal. But the fire splits and flows harmlessly around our opponent, like the parting of the Red Sea.

Murderer.

"Silence!" Eclipse roars at the Majestic, his voice tormented, as he makes to attack again.

Suddenly Eclipse screams and so do I. Through our link I feel every muscle in my Shadow's body as if suddenly stabbed with white-hot knives, his nerves on fire. Slowly we're lifted higher into the air by an invisible force, Eclipse's limbs locking into his body, his wings forcefully pinned against his back, trapping me. A force field that keeps tightening, squeezing the life out of him. Eclipse writhes, growling in fury. I growl too, echoing his pain and anger.

This is more than Ammut, more than Galvanize, Eclipse thinks to me in awe and fear. *Raw, unbridled power.*

Suddenly the pain ends, and he gasps for air.

You wanted power, the Majestic whispers. His voice is all around us, eating at the very air. *But you are a pretender.* This *is power.*

A dark substance blooms out of the air between the Majestic and us, not gas or liquid but somewhere in between. A black, dark bubbling mass which segments into two before us.

The first mass of darkness moves into definition, solidifies, lightening until individual colours come to the fore.

I swallow, truly rocked this time. Eclipse seems even more shaken for some reason.

We're staring at an elegant faerie with violet wings.

The second dark mass rises up, the blackness peeling away to reveal the shape of a massive golden beast covered in scales and feathers. In the space of seconds the darkness conjured by the Majestic has manifested into perfect replicas of Hanna and Eclipse.

Eclipse shivers beneath me. As uncomfortable as it is

seeing even just a copy of Hanna, it's the copy of Eclipse that draws my attention the most. It's an Eclipse the exact same height as my own, who shares the same features as my own Shadow. But I stare into the eyes of my Shadow's clone, and all I see in them is darkness. Instead of hearing his mind, feeling what he feels, there is nothing but a silence so great it aches. He's an illusion. Nothing more.

But why Hanna? Is the Majestic somehow drawing up memories of ours to torture us with? Creating living weapons that are psychological as much as physical?

Faux-Eclipse roars at us, and his voice, even though identical, sounds fiercely alien coming from another Shadow's beak.

"Don't let him get to you," I urge my Eclipse, but I can see how shaken he is. "We can do this! We just have to slow the Majestic down. Distract him. If he wants to play these games, let him."

But the games aren't over yet.

Slowly, the Eclipse and Hanna copies slide toward each other. As they touch, they pass into each other's body. The faerie and the giant dragon-parrot darken for a moment, their bodies twisting, undulating, two patches of darkness merging into a single cohesive shape. When the darkness falls away, there's only one Shadow before us, and it towers high above us.

It looks like Eclipse, but its eyes are wild. Its feathers are as black as Hanna's hair, and from its back sprout four wings - at the top are the giant wings of a cockatoo, and beneath them sprout insectoid wings that are violet and translucent.

"Impossible," I breathe.

The new Eclipse/Hanna roars. The entire cavern shakes. Even the army behind it moves restlessly with unease.

This Majestic can create a Shadow from nothing. A Shadow made from the most powerful aspects of Hanna and myself, Eclipse thinks, haunted. I'm shocked at how he sounds. I thought nothing spooked him. Even when he faced down the monstrous Ammut last time we met he showed fierce and unwavering courage.

There has always been a stain in you, the Majestic condemns Eclipse from behind its monstrous creation. Its dark eye-sockets stare into our souls. *A sickness that will never come out.*

"You're wrong," Eclipse hisses.

Finish them.

The ferocious Eclipse-Hanna hybrid lunges forwards to kill us. Before Eclipse can even react, the mutant snaps his beak down on my Shadow's wing.

Eclipse screams, blood spraying from his wing, and suddenly we're in free-fall. I yell out, clutching onto my Shadow's neck feathers as tight as I can... but then he barrel-rolls and I'm throw clear of him. Out into empty air.

I *just* miss the abyss below, sailing past it onto the cliff. Raven has just rolled Mr Falco's body toward the edge of the cliff, with his foot, before I literally collide with him.

Raven and I hit the ground, struggling. I reach out to grab hold of Mr Falco's body only to watch it sliding off the cliff.

"No!" I cry, grasping for it. But I watch as it falls out of sight, into the abyss below.

Turning back to Raven I throw a punch at him, but he catches my fist in his hand. I struggle.

"This ends here," I say murderously through gritted teeth.

"Come on, Grif," Raven says, amused. "We both know that you're not a fist-fight kind of guy."

Behind him, I can see his guards breaking their lines to run toward us again.

"Stay where you are!" Raven shouts over his shoulder. He grins dangerously at me. "This is just between us!"

He knees me in the stomach, winding me.

"This is wrong, Griffin. We're on the same side."

With surprising force Raven throws me free of him. I hit the ground again, rolling... and slip right off the edge of the chasm.

I feel a bolt of panic as my legs kick at empty air. My fingers grapple at the edge of the cliff, dragging me to a halt. My legs dangle above the darkness from an unimaginable height, and it takes everything I have to hold on to the edge, my fingers slipping on loose dirt. I barely have enough purchase to keep holding on, and I don't have the strength to pull myself back up onto the cliff no matter how hard I strain.

I suppose part of me has always known that one day my life would depend on my ability to do a single pull-up, and on that day I would fail.

I hear a massive roar. Turning I see Eclipse blasted backward by the foul Eclipse/Hanna chimera. Eclipse falls and slams back-first onto the stone bridge.

No.

Eclipse is... losing? That's impossible.

The shockwave runs through the ancient structure, cracks riveting through the stone. Eclipse flaps his wings uselessly and I feel his pain. His wing is hurting, badly. He can't fly on it anymore.

Still hanging desperately to the cliff-edge, I look away from my Shadow, searching for Raven. He's run a few metres away from me, frozen at the start of the bridge. He's the only person anywhere close to me. No one else can make it in time to save me, not even any of Raven's heinous guards. My fingertips slide another inch and I cry out.

Raven's eyes are locked on the tunnel where Phoebe vanished on the opposite cliff, and the fracturing bridge between them. It's his only way across the abyss.

I can see indecision in Raven's face. Some kind of internal struggle as he stands there, frozen. What is it? What is he waiting for? It looks like every atom of his being is willing him onward toward Phoebe. The girl who used to be his everything.

Raven still has time. He could make across the bridge before it collapses. He's staring at the direction Phoebe ran like a man dying of thirst who's only just discovered water exists. Only to have it robbed from him.

He looks across to where I'm struggling against the cliff edge, further along from the bridge. It all happens in a split second. Some of Raven's guards are running toward me, not wanting a hostage of their master to die on their watch. But none of them will make it in time.

This... might be it for me. But even in my final moments, I can't seem to move my gaze from Raven. We lock eyes for a moment. I watch his face contort, as he sees my impending death. Then he looks back across the bridge, to where Phoebe escaped. At any moment she could be crossing over to the human world, and further from his reach.

The cracks are spreading through the bridge. It won't hold much longer.

One of my hand slips free from the cliff-edge and I cry out.

Eclipse, please! I scream, begging, but then my other hand slips and I'm falling.

I jerk to a halt. Someone has grasped my arm, keeping me suspended above the swirling green mists.

It's not Eclipse who saved me. The arm grasping mine is covered in the sleeve of a black robe. Fireflies weave through the air around us. They cast a low glow over the burn marks across the side of Raven's face.

The bridge finally collapses, fragments of stone hurtling down through the mist into emptiness.

"No," Raven whispers, seeing his chance to follow Phoebe fall away.

I stare up at him, as angry as I am stunned. Confused thoughts crash around in my head.

Raven saved me. He risked losing Phoebe again to save my life.

Why? What makes me worth that sacrifice?

"All right, Griffin?" my life-long nemesis grins down at me, flashing the same grin that he had when he was Toby. When I'd thought he was someone I could look up to, someone who might be a new friend.

I look up into Raven's face, furious at him for killing Mr Falco. But also burdened knowing that I now owe my life to the man I've hated for so long. And as much as I resent it, the two of us are tied in this moment, Raven's hand the only thing keeping me from oblivion. The only thing tying me to life.

Before he can start heaving me up back onto the cliff,

there's a screech. I crane my neck behind me to see that the Eclipse/Hanna mutant is gone. Maybe it's dissolved back into the black oblivion from whence it came. Eclipse must have beat it. I feel a rush of victory, of hope.

But suddenly the Majestic is hissing and diving straight at me. A pale nightmare of reptile and human, his massive serpentine tail undulating behind him. Calvin's face is disfigured with murderous rage, the seething darkness inside him filling him with a frothing desire to kill me and my Shadow.

Has the chemical Calvin was injected with inverted Calvin's feelings toward me into the opposite? I wonder. Or is this a hidden part of my brother that's finally been brought to the surface? Calvin's hidden, simmering resentment at me, given free reign?

That's stupid. I know it is. But knowing doesn't seem to help.

"Raven!" I scream. There's a madness in the Majestic that not even Raven can control anymore. He's gone fully rogue. But still Raven doesn't release my hand to run, when he could so easily to save himself. Arrows and Shadow powers hurtle over our heads from the army, but they don't even touch the invincible Majestic, dissipating against an invisible shield.

"Hold on!" Raven shouts...

But then a claw snatches me from behind and pulls me backward out into the abyss. I scream, Raven's hand jerked away as his grip breaks. For a moment I'm sure it's the Majestic who's claimed me.

I've got you, Eclipse whispers. Then we're falling, and he pulls me into him, great, feathered wings folding around me like a shield. I try to scream as I feel the drop in my stomach, but it comes out as an animalistic grunt torn from my insides.

We fall back-first, and I can see the cavern receding as we fall deeper into the chasm. The Majestic swims downward through the air after us, gaining on us. His white serpentine tail rippling. Calvin's reptilian face sniffing the air, hungry for the kill, closing in the gap to destroy his little brother and his brother's Shadow.

Eclipse folds his wings tighter around me like a protective egg, and then the Majestic is hidden from sight. Eclipse flips, at the mercy of gravity. I feel nauseous, like I'm on a theme park ride from hell. Eclipse favours speed over control as we try to outstrip the Majestic hunting us through the air. We hurtle downward and I can glimpse lurid green mist through Eclipse's feathers, like chlorine gas. We plummet through the substance so fast I think we might suffocate on it. Then we break through the mist, and we're sailing through inky blackness. It feels like being at the very bottom of the ocean. I hear Eclipse cry out, his roar stolen by our descent but mentally burned into my mind. He manages to get his good wing out and catches the air, killing our momentum.

Then there's an impact so abrupt it stuns us. Eclipse's talons release me and I roll out, carried by the force of the impact. I hit wet stone, landing hard and grazing my palms. I lie there, gasping for breath.

Eclipse?

Struggling, I turn myself over onto my back. Up above us, I can see the surreal green mist, separating us from the cliff with Raven and his army of cronies. I can't believe we survived the fall. Staring up at the mist from down here feels like watching the slowly undulating surface of a green sea, all the way from the ocean floor.

High above us I hear the approaching scream of the Majestic. Turning to Eclipse, I can just make out a giant mound of golden feathers, darkly lit by shifting emerald light from above.

"Eclipse?" I urge him, feeling sick. I worm my way in a belly crawl towards him. His mind is silent, his behemoth form scarily still. "Come on Eclipse, please. Wake up!" I shake him, tears in my eyes. "Wake up, wake up...."

The scream from the Majestic comes again, but this time he sounds more outraged. Looking desperately up at the green aurora above us, I wonder why we're still alive.

"He can't get past the mist," I say aloud, feeling a lifting in my chest with the realisation. I'm proved right as the Majestic's thwarted screams continue without him making an appearance. "The mist is a... shield of some kind. Eclipse?"

Placing a hand on Eclipse's leg, I stroke it fervently, desperately.

"Eclipse, wake up."

There's nothing. Then slowly, very slowly, Eclipse raises his head. His eyes open, dark and groggy. He blinks them erratically.

I exhale, exhausted and sick with relief. I throw myself down into his side, wrapping my arms around him as I best I can.

"You're alive," I say into his feathers, muffled. "I'm sorry. I didn't know the Majestic was so strong. I mean, you could have taken out that entire army... how is that thing so over-powered? Are you hurt?"

"I'm fine." But his voice is low, pained. Like he's trying

to hide the true damage from me. The fall took a lot out of him. He tries to move the wing where the Majestic hurt him, but flinches. "I won't be flying again for a while. Looks like we're stuck down here. Where's the Majestic?"

Another scream comes from above. Eclipse looks up at the green mist.

"It's trying to break through, but I don't think it can," I say.

"But it let us through. For some reason."

"Yeah. I guess whatever Raven did to Calvin and Zephyr in making that thing... it isn't allowed down here," I say, my voice changing from relieved to troubled. But I wonder about the bloodthirsty army high above, and if they'll find another way down now that the bridge has collapsed.

I squint through the darkness, trying to get our bearings as my eyes adjust to the dark. An underground river rushes past the shore we landed on, water black as night. The area is littered with some rocky debris from the collapsed bridge. But behind us...

...is the entrance to a temple.

Statues stand on each side of the entrance. It takes me a moment to realise that they're Majestics. But they're depicted far more angelic than the demon currently trying to find a way to tear us apart.

Then I see something else. In Eclipse's other claw, gently clutched in his talons, is Mr Falco.

Eclipse must have snatched his body from the air during his fall, trying to save him.

Thank you.

I gather the nerve to examine Mr Falco. His front is stained with blood, as is the cape spread out beneath him. His eyes are closed.

I'm sorry, Calvin. I failed you. I let Raven take you and turn you into this... thing. And now your best friend is dead because of me too. I bow my head.

Mr Falco lurches upward, wheezing, and I nearly have a freaking heart attack.

Eclipse swears too.

"Mr Falco," I say urgently. Eclipse unclenches his talons, gently placing Mr Falco down on the ground. I study the amount of blood coming through the old man's shirt, and feel sick all over again. "Are you okay?"

It's a stupid question. He isn't okay.

Mr Falco doesn't even give me a scathing reply. His breathing is erratic. He coughs. A wet cough that wracks his chest. It doesn't sound good.

Mr Falco turns to look at the statue of the Majestic. The being that's half human and half Shadow.

"Do you think we meet our Shadows when we die?" he whispers. There's no doubt in his voice. He knows his time is up. Zephyr isn't here to save him.

"I don't know," I respond helplessly. He's shivering.

"If there's one thing that can heal our world, it's Shadows," Mr Falco breathes, looking up at me. "Finish this. Finish it for Melissa, so she can be at peace."

"If you see her... tell her I miss her," I say, my voice catching. Mr Falco is still for a moment, and I wonder if he's already died. My knees are sticky with his blood.

"Don't you wish sometimes I'd convinced you that you really were insane?" Mr Falco murmurs. "That you had never gone to the Shadow world, that you had never suffered through what you did?"

I think of Hanna's betrayal, of Cirrus dying in my arms.

"No," I say, my voice level. "It's still been worth it to find out the truth. To meet my Shadow."

"Never let each other go," Mr Falco rasps. "Never. You and Eclipse have been reunited. You don't know how lucky you two are."

I nod, wiping away tears.

"Don't... cry for me. You never liked me. Nobody did."

"That's not..." I trail off helplessly.

"Just learn one thing from me. Don't be an arsehole. Don't tell yourself it's all right to live your life alone. Find yourself a family, and defend it with your life. Like I tried to do with the Camerons."

I open my mouth, not sure what to say, anything that comes to mind sounding trite.

"My family thanks you for your service," I say finally. It sounds stiff, formal, but somehow I feel it's what Mr Falco needs to hear.

"Get... Calvin and Zephyr back. Find a way."

"I will," I say, voice cracking, hoping it's a promise I can keep.

His breathing is getting weaker.

"No one will cry for me, no one will mourn me," Mr Falco coughs. "I'll die alone, like everyone does." He closes his eyes. "But soon... I'll be with my Shadow." Mr Falco smiles faintly, and then he goes still.

I feel an oversized claw gently settling on my shoulder, Eclipse sending comforting thoughts. Shock crashes through me like an avalanche.

He's gone. Just like that, Mr Falco's body is empty. The man I've been seeing week after week for most of my life, having to talk about the innermost workings of my mind... he's just a body. Suddenly it's like I'm clutching Cirrus in my arms again, watching the light in his eyes die.

"Are you all right?" Eclipse asks quietly. Awkwardly. "Griffin?"

"I didn't even like him," I say thickly, staring down at Mr Falco's body. "And he died for us."

"Griffin..."

I hesitate, then softly untie the plum cloak from Mr Falco's neck, slipping it slowly out from beneath him. I wrap it around my shoulders in tribute.

It may not be Mr Falco's, but I can't help but feel the cloak has his stamp on it. Even when dressing to blend in, I'm sure he would have been drawn to the cloak that made him the most dashing and impressive. It looks like something an elegant, seafaring knight would wear in a fantasy film. And in his final moment, he was every inch the hero he wished he was.

"We should bury him or something," I mutter. "Or make a pyre. I don't... I don't know what he'd want. What Calvin would want." But Calvin's not here. He's part of that *thing*.

Gently, Eclipse picks up Mr Falco's still body and places it down in the water. The dark current takes hold of him, and I watch as he floats down the river away from us. Slowly submerging beneath its surface.

"This is the land of the dead," Eclipse says. "Wherever his soul goes... his body will rest here."

I nod, a lump in my throat.

"He must have been held prisoner here since he and Calvin were captured," I say. "Somehow he broke out, and impersonated a guard amongst an army of Shadows without being found out, so he could try and take out Raven himself."

"He was courageous," Eclipse says.

Rubbing the tears from my eyes, I turn to study the entrance to the temple. Eclipse follows my gaze.

"What is this place?" he murmurs, suspicious.

I think of the green mist up above, shielding this temple entrance, and I start getting excited.

"Maybe it's what we've come all this way for. Maybe this is it, Eclipse. What Phoebe and the others are searching for."

I hope Phoebe and the kids are safe. I hope they made it away, that we bought them enough time.

Eclipse stares fiercely ahead into the temple. It seems brighter through there, some source of weak illumination coming from inside, like the flickering of flames.

"Are you ready," Eclipse asks me, stretching like he's spoiling for another battle, "for whatever's coming?"

I'm still feeling broken. I can't bear to stare at the river where Mr Falco's body vanished. But I nod, trying to match my Shadow's fierceness.

"Things have to get better after all this crap, right?" I say.

"Why are they trying to kill us?" Eclipse says suddenly, sounding broken. "Zephyr and Calvin. Why have they gone so dark?"

"Raven gave him an extra injection of whatever chemical is letting him control them. Whatever it was, it looks like it spun them out big time. Turned them into this... negative copy of themselves. Pure rage."

"Griffin..." Eclipse pauses. "What if that's just what Calvin and Zephyr are really like deep down? Their aggression, their instinct to dominate... both of them had a dark side. What if this is just them exposed as who they really are?"

"What, deep down Calvin wants to kill me?" I challenge him, then shake my head. "Even our relationship wasn't that dysfunctional." I wish I could feel as certain as I sound. Something else is also gnawing at me though. "Raven mentioned some kind of vote taking place in the Shadow world, didn't he?"

Eclipse nods.

"We're in the midst of civil war at the moment," he explains. "The Empire and the Resistance controlling portions of it, and most of the population having no idea which way to sway, or who to side with. Raven must have organised the attack on Sanctuary in order to try and make the Shadows turn to the Empire."

"He's relying on their paranoia and their worst instincts," I say, "but I have to believe that people are better than that. We need to make it to the station and end this. Unite them all with their counterparts."

"Agreed," Eclipse says. "Let's get the hell out of hell."

Together, we enter the temple.

The interior is cavernous. The brown stone is worn, green plants sprouting out of cracks in pillars. Water pours down through some of the walls in rivulets to form shallow pools in the floor. Ceremonial plates cover the ground on either side of the path, covered in grapes, piles of fruit and golden coins. Offerings of some kind. The fruit looks fresh as if it was just placed there, though I can't think who would have been down here for hundreds of years. The rest of the caverns felt positively untouched.

A descending series of floating platforms carved with detailed mosaics lead steeply down to a giant under-ground lake stretching out down before us. Flaming torches illuminate the path formed by the floating platforms. On the way to the lake the levitating platforms wind around an enormous statue, three or four stories high. It's another depiction of a Majestic. The face is humanoid, nearly elfin, smiling serenely. The statue is cupping its hands as if in a form of prayer, palms open and facing up towards the sky. And crouched in those stone entwined hands each the size of a car... is a Majestic.

We freeze.

That's not good, Eclipse says.

I can't immediately say how I know she's a Majestic and not a Shadow. But there's something about her, just like there is about my brother's one. An aura, a *feeling* that she's not of this world.

She looks like an angel, her entire body glowing blue. Deep ocean blue toward the chest and the warmer centres of her body, and shining silvery white along the tops of the wings and her limbs. Her eyes shine with light, like windows to a divine source beyond them.

Griffin, get back, Eclipse hisses. But for some reason I don't. I don't move. I can't take my eyes off of her.

"I don't think it's one of Raven's experiments," I say, transfixed.

"What? What do you mean?"

"I... I don't know," I say. "She just doesn't have the same *feel.*"

The new Majestic stands slowly, strands of silvery glowing hair falling across her face. Eclipse and I watch in awe as she spreads her wings wide, crouching before she launches herself into the air. She glides from the ancient statue down past the platforms and flaming torches, softly descending toward the lake edge.

"She's not attacking us," I say, frowning. "Should we follow her?"

"Are you mad?" Eclipse asks, incredulous. "You want another Majestic trying to off us?"

"But she might not be one of Raven's. What if she's *part* of this place? A clue to where the entrance to the human world is? She might be the key. Besides, the other Majestic couldn't make it down here. So something is different about her."

Eclipse hesitates.

"I'm trying to keep you alive," he reminds me.

"I know."

"You're making it difficult."

"That's my specialty. But to finish this mission we need to get back home. And this Majestic might be the clue to finding this passage between worlds we're looking for."

Finally, Eclipse nods.

"Get on."

I hoist myself up onto Eclipse's back, holding onto his feathers as he launches us forth. His massive golden wings beat us in the direction of the new Majestic. We see her light down at the far end of the lake, against the back wall of the temple. Eclipse and I glide down to meet her, drawn by our hypnotic fascination, as much as our desire to find a way out of here.

Eclipse's talons touch the ground. I jump off his back, getting ground shock as I land into a crouch. He's landed us some distance still from the Majestic, further along the lake. He's still being cautious.

"Eclipse, I can feel it," I whisper, looking around us, excited and scared all at once. "I don't know how, but I just can."

"I think I can too. We must be close to the passage."

The way home to the human world is here somewhere. Burger Max here we come. Plus, you know, activating the station and changing the worlds forever and all that jazz. Priorities.

"Look," Eclipse gestures suddenly and harshly with his beak. His voice is dark. "Over there. That's another one of those fusion machines. What Raven uses to make the Majestics."

At the back of the temple, a machine is set up against this very back wall. It looks entirely out of place. Raven must have put it there recently. The dark contraption spreads out, two pods hanging like black spider eggs from a dark web. Below them are basins of vivid red liquid. The machine is gathering dust, but from its dull glowing lights, I'm guessing it's still operational.

"I wonder why this one got placed down here?" I say.

"Maybe he was testing if it worked better closer to the entrance to the human world. Why else place one all the way down here? Wait. It's missing something else." Eclipse's crest rises slightly. "The other one had a mechanical arm lying in wait beside the tank, to inject the Majestic when it was created. To place it under Raven's control, I suppose."

"Maybe he hadn't perfected his control over them when he built this one," I muse, hypnotised by the machine. I drag my gaze away from it, surveying our surroundings. The machine is placed at the back of the temple. A little further along the edge of the lake is the Majestic, still looking out over the water, seemingly oblivious to us. We're at a dead end, the temple doesn't seem to continue beyond this.

"Maybe this is the very lowest point of the Underworld," Eclipse murmurs. "In which case... the portal to the human world should be here."

Cautiously, we make our way toward where the shining blue Majestic is standing. Her arms are folded behind her back under her wings, and she stares out across the expanse of the underground lake, across its dark, still surface. Slowly the shining blue light that infuses her dies away, revealing a Majestic standing there who looks solid, corporeal. A long cat-like tail swishes gently back and forth behind her. It ends in a blue tuft of fur.

She looks so solid. A living, breathing being in front of us. Her two powerful legs are covered in white feathers, and they end in feline paws. Above the waist her body is humanoid, except the hands are large bestial claws, and her torso is covered in soft white fur like starlight. A long whip-like tail coils out from her tailbone, ending in that plume of blue fur. From either side of her spine, a shining wing flows outward. Her shoulders are protected by silver plates of ceremonial armour, and a breastplate covers her chest.

She's a feline angel.

Finally, I look to her face. She wears a half helmet, and beneath its rim we can see that she's smiling. Two long cat ears protrude upward through slits in the helmet. From the rear of the helmet flows long hair the colour of pikelet mixture.

"Hello?" Eclipse says, cautious. He's tensed for a fight if it comes to that. I take a step toward this new Majestic, then another, trying not to spook her. I have a strange feeling as I approach, heart in my throat, skin prickling all over. Eclipse feels the same, I can tell through our connection. I think part of me knew since the moment I saw this

Majestic, who I believed it was. But I don't say anything out loud, not wanting my impossible hope to be proven wrong.

My body is trembling. It can't be her. It doesn't make any sense. But it looks like...

"Mum?" I exhale shakily.

The Majestic turns to me. She smiles.

"Mum!"

It's impossible, but instinctively, I know it's true. Running forward, I throw myself at her in a hug of joy. I expect my hands to pass right through her like she's a ghost.

Instead I wrap my arms around a living, breathing person. Dazed, I squeeze, and she squeezes tightly back. Her starlight fur feels strange at first, but through it I can feel her warmth.

She's real. She has a heartbeat.

I hang there like a stunned koala, amazed, not wanting to let go in case the dream ends.

And then we're both laughing, and I'm crying too and it's full of happiness and acute aching sadness and childlike confusion.

"How can you be here? How can this...?" I stare up at Mum, at a dream I've had my entire life now made real. At a death that's always defined me suddenly undone. I try to imprint her in my memory, so I can hold on to her forever. What I always regretted most growing up was how many memories from my childhood were blurred or had turned so faded they'd been lost.

The Majestic is Melissa Cameron and Silvaluna, made whole.

I can feel Eclipse's confusion, his doubt that what is happening can be real, and his fear. Even though I call

Eclipse my Shadow, he's not Cirrus. Silvaluna was Cirrus' Mum. How can we explain to Silvaluna that her child is gone? Replaced?

"Mum," I say tentatively, "I want you to meet someone."

"It's a great honour to meet you... both. My name is Eclipse," he says slowly, chokingly.

"Of course we recognise you," Silvaluna/Mum laughs softly, tears streaking her cheeks. "You've grown so much. My hatchling. My baby boy."

Eclipse stares at her, confused. I am too.

Have they confused him for Cirrus, or do they genuinely believe that he's still the same person? But then, Eclipse doesn't question it, which is probably the best thing to do in the surreal situation. He simply bows his head, and my Mum and Cirrus' Mum smoothens his feathers with a furred hand. I can see that he's crying.

"My boys," she says, tears in her eyes, smiling brightly. "My two little boys."

She has the expression of utmost joy. It's been so long since I heard my Mum's voice and the voice of her Shadow, but they're so familiar. Both of their voices perfectly laid over each other. As if they were always two halves of one voice.

"Is it really the both of you?" Eclipse whispers.

"It's us," Mum says serenely. "But we're also just a memory. We're content, but we're still just an echo of what was."

"But you're alive!" I protest.

"No, I'm not Griffin," she says gently. "Just an echo. What I was, what we were, preserved forever. It's the longing in both humans and Shadows for something more, that desire to find and discover each other that allows life to exist. It's that longing which forces the dimensions of existence into being. That's what life is. When we died, we continued on in another place. Silvaluna and Melissa, finally together, two halves joined. We're happy, we're at peace, but we can't change. That's what Majestics are."

My brain swims, the truth of it hitting me deep.

"When we die… we become Majestics with our Shadows?" Faces flashes in front of me. "So Mr Falco is a… a Majestic now?"

"I believe he will be, yes."

"I think… I think he'll like that."

I stare at her in wonder and awe.

Is this the answer? Is it the answer to the question my Mum herself didn't know to ask, the secret at the heart of what my family has been doing for so long? We always thought Shadows and humans completed each other, that they're both one half of the same soul, and that reuniting them would fix the emptiness so many of us feel inside us. But is the answer really to combine the Shadow and the human together into one form?

Into Majestics?

I have another question, but I almost don't want to ask it. Don't want to bring darkness and pain into what's one of the happiest moments of my life. But I can't not ask it.

"Is Dad one too?" I whisper. "A Majestic?"

"Yes. He's here too," Mum says gently.

I absorb this slowly.

"I'm so angry at him," I confess. "I don't understand. The things he did. They don't make sense."

"He loves you. He's sorry he couldn't come. There was so much he wanted to explain to you in person. But even I shouldn't be here. Majestics aren't meant to interfere in the lives of mortals. But this temple, and the nature of the Underworld, they allow me to project myself into the realm of the living."

"I miss you so much," I say, tears staining my eyes. "Was it... bad? The night you died?"

"Only for an instant. It didn't bother me much before then, and now that I'm gone I don't even think on it," she says gently. I nod. That question has been troubling me for a long time.

"I miss you," I choke. "I think of you all the time, what it would be like if you were alive..." I feel a tear fall from my cheek. "I couldn't remember anymore what you used to sound like. Just... stay," I say. "Please stay." I'm holding onto her hand so tightly. I can smell apple crumble, though I know I must be imagining it. I could be imagining all of this, but that thought hurts too much. If this is a dream, I don't want to ever wake up again.

I'm remembering being a boy who is being tucked into bed by his Mum. Her gold hair falling across her shoulders as she smiles and kisses me and Cirrus good night in the spare room of our lab in Cameron Technologies. I remember how she was when I last saw her, fizzing with excitement over how her team was just on the verge of connecting the worlds.

I went to bed in a dream and woke up in a nightmare.

I'm not letting her go. Not like I did that night.

"Stay, Mum. Please. Come with us."

"I can't. I can't even leave this temple or I'll fade. I can watch you, but you won't see me. I'm not corporeal like the Majestic pursuing you. Just a projection. But I promise I'll always watch over you two, even if you don't know it."

"I just want to be with you," I say, my voice cracking. "I just want to be wherever you are."

"I know."

"Where... where are you going?"

"Home," Mum says simply.

I step forward as she tries to gently pull away. I hold her close.

"I'm coming with you," I say, my voice sounding muffled. "I want to be with you. I'm ready, to go through." I shut my eyes tight, trying to memorise the feel of Mum and Silvaluna against me. So much warmth. I can feel Eclipse staring at me, can feel his shock at my words, but I don't care. I'm so happy right here. "I'm ready, Mum." I look up to her face. She's smiling like we're the only two in the worlds. My voice catches. "I'm ready to cross over with you."

"Oh, sweetheart," she says, running a hand through my tangled hair. She leans down to kiss me on the forehead. "You have so much more to love and live. Open your eyes. Listen to your Shadow. You're both going to become someone great. I can see it. You have so much further to go before you join me."

"I'm not good," I say, cheeks flushing. "I'm not great. I've done things. Terrible things that maybe you don't even know about. I'm not a boy anymore. I've seen... so much suffering."

"Look at who you are, how far you've come," she says. "You're alive, and you have people who love you. That is enough."

"Do I?" I ask humourlessly, thinking of my brother and Zephyr trying to kill us right now. They should be here to see this, to be with Mum, but they're not.

"Yes, you do. I wish I could just make you be at peace,

Griffin. But for now, trust me. You will always have a family. Sometimes it can just take a while to see it."

"We need to get back to the human world," Eclipse says softly. He's entranced, still unsettled and confused of what to make of this. There are tears in his eyes, but I don't think he knows why. "Do you know how we can cross over?"

Mum smiles.

"Better. I can take you there."

"You can do that?"

"Time and space are nothing more to Majestics than a mildly intriguing knitting pattern. All it takes is..."

Suddenly, the entire temple shakes. There's the sound of stone cracking, and an unnatural roar that turns my blood cold.

Before us, Mum flickers, and for a moment I can straight through her as if she isn't even there.

"Mum?" I whisper, scared.

"It's the Majestic!" Eclipse deduces. "It's breaking in."

Before us, Mum looks like a ghost. She's becoming more and more transparent, and I cling to her like I'll never let go.

"I'm sorry," Mum says quietly. "It's breaking through. The Temple can't sustain me here any longer."

"But, the portal..."

"You'll have to find another way. I love you both." Tears appear in her Majestic eyes. "Goodbye."

I don't want them to leave us behind. I want to stay here and talk to her, forever. But I have to try and be brave for her...because I'm the one who's still living.

"Mum..." I whisper one last time.

"Go," she says to us gently. "And never forget how much we love you both."

Then she vanishes. She's gone so quickly that it would

be easy to think that we imagined it. Her sudden absence leaves a longing panging in my chest, one that's almost too painful and bittersweet to bear.

"Mum?" I ask, my voice cracking.

I wipe my eyes, still barely believing what just transpired was real.

Could it have been a hallucination? An illusion of this place, showing me what I wanted to see? Now with her gone, it feels it so easily could have been a dream, or a mirage, no matter how real I wanted it to be. But I believe it was real. I believe it was her.

Beside me, Eclipse is swaying. The giant, powerful Shadow looks distraught.

"I'm sorry, Griffin," he manages.

"I'm not," I whisper back, and smile.

There's a rumble through the temple like the entire place is about to cave in. I jump at the terrifying roar of the Majestic. The sound of something... demonic.

Eclipse readies himself for a fight, but I can see his trepidation.

I stare up at Eclipse, and suddenly my brain just lights up. It all comes flooding into place. I look across at the discarded machine against the wall. I look at Eclipse, at my Shadow who I've just finally gotten back... and I feel a leap of joy. Like my insides have just been flooded with light. There's this sense of peace, of certainty. The conflict, the doubts, my fear since we went on the run from Cameron Technologies... it all just falls away.

"We can't defeat the Majestic," I say. "Together my brother and Zephyr are far more powerful than we are."

"Thank you, Griffin. That is *very* helpful," Eclipse says darkly.

I smile at him, suddenly sheepish and ecstatic all at once.

"What?" Eclipse says, frowning at the excitement bubbling out of me. Trying to make sense of my thoughts.

"I have an idea," I say breathlessly. "I know how we can defeat the Majestic. I know how we can get back to our own world to the station and finish this once and for all."

"How?" Eclipse says, his face perplexed. He still doesn't understand, he doesn't *see* it.

"Look," I say quickly. "Raven injects the Majestics after they come out of the machines, doesn't he? To make sure that he could control the Majestics, that they don't turn on him."

"I believe that's how it works, yes," Eclipse says hesitantly.

I gesture at the machine.

"Well, what if this one couldn't? Inject them, I mean? You said it's missing that part."

Eclipse folds his ginormous wings closer, staring at me incredulously.

"Griffin," Eclipse says softly. I can feel him trying to burrow into my thoughts, to know what I'm thinking. "What is your plan out of here?"

I point up at the machine against the temple wall.

"This," I say. "This is the path."

The air is very still all of a sudden. Even the Majestic trying to break into the temple seems to have fallen silent.

"I don't understand," Eclipse says, but from his widening eyes I feel like it just hit him. Suddenly Eclipse steps back. He sees it in my mind, in my soul. He knows what I'm thinking, and now there's nothing left to hide.

"You can't be serious," he says, shocked. "What..."

"You're my Shadow, Eclipse," I say, and Eclipse snaps his beak shut. "I've been so trapped in my own fear, so desperate to hold on to what I know, what I'm used to, that I was scared that by changing, that I would lose what made me special. What made me *me*." I remember Sophie calling me a monster as she broke up with me, what feels like an age ago. "I was scared I'd lose who I was. But now I understand. You can be connected with someone else and still hold onto who you are. But when you find the right person, when you join together you can become something... greater. Something greater than the sum of the parts."

"Grif, you're not making any sense," Eclipse says, incredulous. "You want us to go *into* that thing? You want us to join together and become a Majestic?"

"That's what humans and Shadows are all about," I say, my heart bright. I gesture animatedly, trying to make him get it. "Every Shadow and human counterpart are pulled toward each other like magnets, filled by a desire to be together. Maybe that's because they're meant to be - because at one point, Shadows and humans were the same being, before they were separated. Before they were split in two."

"Haven't you seen the Majestic out there?" Eclipse demands. "You did not see what Raven's machine did to those innocents. It was not anything beautiful. Far from it."

"That's because Raven tainted it. He used that chemical injection to force the Majestic to serve him. That's not what the machine did first, though. Right? This... fusion machine, it's not evil. It's just a way of merging us together. It's the only way we can be powerful enough to subdue the Majestic, until we can find a way to get Calvin and Zephyr back.

We can do it, Eclipse. Not separately, but together, as one. You and I can become a Majestic."

"We wouldn't be ourselves anymore, Griffin," Eclipse says. "I wouldn't be Eclipse. You wouldn't be you. We would be something... else. We can hear each other's thoughts now, but at least we have our own space, our own identity. We go in to there, and we really do become just one being. We won't be friends anymore. We'll be the same person."

"I know!" I say, looking up at him, pleading. He has to understand. He needs to realise this isn't the horror he seems to think it is. He needs to understand that this is *us*. "But we'll be someone who is whole. The best bits of each of us. And I'm telling you, this is what I want. I'm not scared anymore. You're my best friend, Eclipse. You *are* me. I won't let anyone separate us ever again. We're stronger together, you know that. And I'm ready to prove that to you. To everyone."

Eclipse looks from my eyes to the fusion machine against the wall. I try to reach into his mind, to unveil his real feelings... and when I do, it's a tornado of fear, of doubt.... and something else.

"I can't," Eclipse says.

I don't speak for a moment, feeling a sudden attack of anxiety.

"Eclipse," I manage, trying again, "we won't end up like the Majestic. Our end result isn't darkness, it's light. Without Raven's influence, we would be something beautiful. Like Mum and Silvaluna. We'd be an angel, not a demon. You just have to have faith. Come on. We can do this."

"No!" my Shadow says, fierce now. I flinch at the force

of it. He shakes his head and turns away. "I'm sorry, Griffin. I'm so sorry. But I can't."

"Why not?" I ask, my heart breaking.

"Because that's not what I want," he says vigorously, and it's as if he's realising it as he says it. "I don't want to lose myself to something more. If that's what being human and Shadow means..." he trails off, and I can sense how helpless he suddenly feels. I can feel how he wishes my face would stop falling. I can feel how much it hurts Eclipse to see how he's hurting me. "There has to be another way out of here," he says determinedly. "There has to be."

I'm silent, at a loss. I'm just so sure this is the way forward. And his response isn't what I expected at all.

The temple trembles again. We can hear the predatory scream of the Majestic, the temple shaking as he tries to break through whatever mystic force field it is that's protecting this place. Rubble falls from the ceiling, littering our soon-to-be grave.

"If we don't do this," I say, as calmly as I can muster, "then this is where we die."

Eclipse stares at me.

"I can defeat him," he growls.

"The Majestic will kill you. You know you're no match for one. He whipped your arse up there. No offence."

More rubble falls. We hear the unnatural cry of the Majestic, the sound that makes me shudder. It's almost through the defences.

"Your call, Eclipse," I say tensely. "I offered a solution. That was my idea of how to get out of this mess alive. What's yours?"

Which is when suddenly one of the walls of the temple opens up with the heavy grinding of stone. Eclipse and I swing around to face it, to see a section of the wall rotating open. Rushing out through the temporary gap, looking disorientated, is a gang of twelve young Shadows. And leading at their front...

I freeze. I take in the long dark hair, those emerald eyes. Those violet wings.

It's Hanna.

Hanna finally sees me too, and her eyes go wide. She comes to a stop, holding up a hand. The other Shadows all halt behind her.

"Griffin," Hanna whispers.

"Eclipse," I croak, when he doesn't react. "It's her."

"She's not the enemy, Griffin," Eclipse says slowly. He raises a feathery eyebrow at Hanna. "Not for now, at least. These other Shadows are the ones we rescued." He seems relieved to see them alive. All of them.

"Wait, you've been... you've been working with the Empress?" I say to Eclipse, disbelieving. My face feels hot. Seeing Hanna brings back all of the trauma. I can feel the knife plunging into my back again, my fall through the sky toward the dark ocean below. "Why didn't you mention that?"

Which is when Phoebe and our gang of twelve human teenagers in pyjamas with raised weapons erupt through another secret passage, trampling out to find themselves directly opposite Hanna and the Shadows.

The two sides see each other, and everyone starts screaming.

Suddenly Eclipse and I are facing what could quickly escalate into a teenage gang war of humans and Shadows.

15

SCARS

Eclipse

The air explodes with shouting. Everyone is yelling, the tension in the air spiking exponentially. At any moment one of the humans might shoot one of the Shadows unknowingly, or a Shadow could unleash a barrage of high-powered darts from their scales, and then the two sides will obliterate each other in seconds, turning the temple into a death trap.

"Everyone, calm down!" I hear Phoebe shouting at her humans, while on the other side Hanna hollers pleadingly: "They are not your enemy!"

I only spent some time with these Shadows with Hanna when we were escorting them into the Underworld. Some of them have harmless powers. There's two wolves, a flying one who apparently can ease chronic anxiety, while the black one can turn himself into an opossum at will. But there's also a spider-monkey spider (half spider-monkey, half spider) that can spit acid, and a feline unicorn with a projectile horn that can induce terrifying hallucinations. Meanwhile, the humans facing them are holding weapons that could kill the Shadows with zero discrimination.

It will be a massacre.

No more Shadows are going to die because of me. These prisoners, Celeste and her friends from Midnight Crafters included, trusted me to protect them. I told them I could get them out of this place alive. This promise, I intend to keep.

"No!" Griffin screams, running into the middle of the two sides. "Stop!"

The Shadows swivel toward his voice, jumpy, prepared to let loose their attacks at Griffin. I plant a leg down on either side of Griffin, looming above the humans in their ridiculous pyjamas. I raise myself to my full height, spreading my wings and declaring with thunder over the chaos:

"Everybody. STAND DOWN."

Vibrations run through the stone beneath us from my voice. Suddenly a whole lot of bows and guns are pointed up at me, faces widened in fear. Well, at least that's an improvement on the situation. At least the human teens are just aiming at me now.

Griffin and I stand in no-man's land between the opposing sides. Just the two of us, human and Shadow, living shields between the Shadows and the humans who want to obliterate each other.

It's a stand-off.

Hanna and Phoebe both rush forward to join Griffin and me. The four of us stand in the centre between the two lines, holding out hands and talons out in a gesture of peace. It seems to get through to the two sides, most of who lower their weapons or claws. But they still look wary.

"Hey, Grif!" Hanna says brightly, waving at him, even though he's right beside her.

Griffin freezes up. Painful, wild emotions radiate from him.

"Ah... so you two are old friends or something?" Phoebe asks awkwardly, looking between them.

"Oh, we're more than friends," Hanna says, winking at Griffin.

Phoebe looks between the two of them, frowning.

"Who's that?" she asks Griffin determinedly. "Is that your girlfriend?"

"Kind of," Hanna says, upbeat.

"No," Griffin says, his voice hard. "*That* would be my crazy ex."

"Griffin," Phoebe says, taken aback. "Calling girls crazy is supporting a sexist stereotype and reinforcing systemic misogyny. I'm sure Hanna has her own side of the story."

"She literally stabbed me in the back and threw me into the ocean to die," Griffin says.

"Oh. Well yeah, that probably counts." Phoebe looks between Hanna and Griffin again, strangely amused. "Oh, so this must be awkward."

"Fairly," I agree with her from above. Phoebe looks up at me, and we exchange a grin. I suppose it's not really that funny, but there aren't a lot of laughs to be had right now otherwise.

"I kept an eye on your Shadow while you were away," Hanna says to Griffin. "I'm reformed now. We're on the same team."

"Eclipse, can we trust her?" Griffin asks.

"Not for a second," I say casually.

"I'm on your side now, Eclipse," Hanna says, rolling her eyes exasperatedly. "So let's figure out how to get out of here before Raven's army skewers us all. Or before his Majestic makes our insides implode with the power of its mind or something."

"How did you two even…" Griffin's brain seems to be combusting. He looks between me and Hanna. "Why have you two been spending time together at *all*?"

"We were travel companions on the way here," I say. I hear the coldness in my own voice, and realise I still haven't gotten past the pain of her last betrayal. Even if she has now given everything up, for me. For her human. "Now our alliance is finished. Trust me, the sooner we part ways, the better."

"Oh, Eclipse," Hanna says delicately. I see tears in her eyes, even though she hides her feelings well. "Does this mean we're not friends anymore?"

"You can't be anyone's friend, because all you are is an acid, and you eat away anything you touch," I say. "You'll never be happy."

Hanna smiles sadly.

"I hurt you pretty good, didn't I?"

"We don't have time for this," I thunder. "There's an extremely angry Majestic about to break in here at any minute. When he does, we'll all die. We need to work together to find another way out of here."

None of the teenagers around us seem to grasp my words. All the humans see is that there's a giant feathered dragon shouting at them. There's the fresh bristling of weapons amongst them, while the Shadows respond by prepping their powers once again. A bird who looks like a slightly smaller version of Ember spreads wings that burn with blue flame.

"Hey, hey," Phoebe says hastily, putting out her hands again in peace.

"Eclipse?" Griffin says. I look down at him.

"Move out of the way."

"Are you serious?" I say, incredulous. "My people and your people seem pretty skittish. I don't know if they're ready to have their giant Eclipse-shaped shield removed."

"They need to see each other. Properly," Griffin says, his voice strangely soft. "They need a chance to realise what they are to each other, like we did."

I struggle for a moment. The humans and Shadows still look ready to shred each other, paranoid after their sub-par experience in Hotel Aeyu.

Trust me, Griffin begs me. *Please. I've got this.*

Slowly, reluctantly, I drag my talons along the stone, stepping aside so that the two sides can see each other better. If anything happens to either side now, it's on me.

The humans and Shadows stare at each other, ready to fire at a moment's notice. Another shower of rubble falls from the roof to the temple floor. Our time is growing short.

"Can't you see?" Griffin says to the two sides emphatically. "Raven was holding you prisoner so he could experiment on you. He was trying to make these powerful beings called Majestics by combining the Shadow with their human counterpart. You're the counterparts of each other. You're facing *yourselves*."

The human and Shadow teenagers are staring with shock across at each other. I see a range of emotions cross their faces. Fear, suspicion... and something that looks like hope.

"Put down your weapons," Griffin says. "You're not alone anymore. And we're going to need to work together if we're all going to make it out of here alive."

Slowly, ever so slowly, the humans lower their weapons. The Shadows relax their stances, still watching their counterparts warily.

"Well, everyone seems like they aren't going to kill each other, for the moment," I contribute. "That's an improvement. May I mention though that there's a supernaturally powerful Calvin-Zephyr hybrid about to break in, intent on killing us all?"

"We need to find a way out of here, now," Phoebe agrees.

"Everyone, see if you can find a way to open the entrances you came through," I command. "This can't just be a dead-end."

All the Shadows and humans set about trying to find a way to reopen the entrances and get us out of here.

Except for one.

I lower my gaze to see a human who looks like a petite doll. She hasn't lowered her weapon. Instead her lethal looking human rifle is aimed directly at my head. She looks like she knows how to use it. She has it pointed at me like I'm the biggest threat in the room, not the Majestic of darkness trying to break into the temple at this very moment, or the horde of Raven's soldiers who could arrive here through the tunnels at any second.

I feel a coldness settle over me as I stare at her weapon. I remember the agony of metal slugs tearing into me back in Sanctuary City. I know that I'm not fast enough to dodge human bullets, and they seem to pass through my feathers where more powerful Shadow attacks wouldn't. My only weakness, aside from Galvanize's toxin.

Even if I try to move out of the way of the bullets, then the young Shadows behind me that I'm still shielding could die in my place.

"Griffin," I say slowly, feeling lightheaded. Suddenly everyone is looking at what's happening.

The human girl is trembling, staring at me with tear filled, bloodshot eyes. The other humans step away from her uneasily. Her gun is aimed straight up at my face.

The temple is very quiet, except for a distant rumbling of the Majestic, still trying to break into the temple.

"April, put the gun down," Griffin says quietly. His voice is gentle, like he's talking to a spooked deer. But I can feel how scared he feels. How suddenly powerless.

"We can't trust them," the girl whimpers. "It's a mind game. They're just going to stick us back in that room again. Or worse."

"You don't have to do this," Phoebe says, exasperated. "We just told you. Shadows are our friends, not our enemies. Those arseholes hunting us right now are the exception, not the rule. We can't afford to fight each other."

"I didn't abduct you," I say quietly. "I want to get you out of here safe. But I can't if you don't let me."

"Listen, April, this is just the PTSD talking," Phoebe says. "Trust us, you're overreacting."

"You weren't kidnapped," April cries out, traumatised. "You weren't torn from your world, taken by one of these twisted creatures and stuck in a room for five days, while you wondered what happens to the kids taken during the night, not knowing if you'll be taken next and killed, or worse. Too scared to get attached to the other prisoners because they're taken each night by monsters."

"April, please. That's Eclipse." I hear Griffin begging. "He's my Shadow."

April's finger tightens on the trigger.

"You've tricked them into thinking that you monsters are their friends," she hisses up at me. "You brainwashed them somehow. Who are you really? What do you want from us?"

"April," Griffin says in a calming voice, taking another step toward her. I can feel he's scared, but he hides it well.

"If you kill me," I say thickly, "Griffin will die at the s..."

April fires.

Something moves like a blur, flickering through the air in front of me. It all happens too fast to really notice it, I just know that suddenly Phoebe is tackling April her to the ground. Phoebe removes the gun from her, holding the girl's hands behind her back. Griffin looks up at me, shocked and pale.

"You're all right," he says, dizzy with relief.

It's true, I distantly realise. I'm standing. Upright. I heard the gun fire, the rifle aimed directly at me. Why is my brain still functioning? Did the human girl somehow miss?

But then my eyes move down to the floor of the temple... and I see Hanna.

She's lying there, clutching her side. Blood is seeping through her shirt and pooling on the stone beneath her. I remember the violet flash I saw pass in front of me just as April fired.

Hanna was too far away to take April out. So she used herself as a shield.

"Hanna?" I cry, crouching beside her. My God. There's

so much blood for such a small thing. She gasps, her face more pale than ever, eyes looking like she's in shock.

"What the hell did you just do?" I whisper, feeling like I'm not in my own body. "No, no. I don't understand, what do you get out of this? This is another of your tricks. How are you planning to survive this?"

"Eclipse..."

"No, no. TELL ME," I roar at her, furious. "What does this mean?"

"It means *something*." Hanna weakly reaches up to grasp me by the feathers of my head. There are tears in her eyes as she smiles painfully. "It means something, Eclipse. Finally."

Everyone else is in total silence. Watching her pain, and mine.

"Hanna?" I say with dread. Her eyes are still open, but she looks weak. She's fading fast, the life leaking out of her onto the floor. I crane my head down toward her, wretched.

"You saved me," I say.

"Yes."

"I didn't... I thought it was all another con of yours."

Hot tears sting my eyes.

"You're crying," she breathes.

"I don't want you to die for me." A sob escapes me.

"Yeah, well... that's exactly why I want to do it for you."

"No," I mutter. "No, no, no!" The last one is a roar. I'm afraid. I don't know how to save her. The blood is everywhere.

Hanna's dying, and I'm powerless to stop it.

"Stay with us," I plead, afraid. "You owe me."

Hanna tortured me, she betrayed me twice, and now she's here, at my mercy. I could have killed her, not brought her back to life.

But I need her too, and I curl my tail around her protectively. I tighten it around her waist, putting pressure on the wound to slow her blood loss. Hanna cries out, a horrible rending sound.

The temple, the watching humans and Shadows, they all seem to swim around us in our peripheral vision, while this one moment of time stretches infinite.

"You should have seen Raven's face," I hear Hanna say faintly, "when he saw Phoebe again."

Crying, she buries her face in my talons. Like there's nothing of her left, and she has to hold onto me just to be anchored to this world.

I bow my head, crest extended, and touch my forehead gently against hers. Both us waiting for her end.

"I really thought Raven might be my human," Hanna whispers.

"I know."

I remember Hanna chaining Cirrus to that table in New Redemption. The agony of images flooding his mind, as Hanna tried to strip Cirrus from Griffin so he could be her human instead.

And then I think of her hanging helplessly in the Resistance's prison, I think of her lending me her power to take out Galvanize, of unleashing that mutant Shadow on Galvanize to save me when she could have run. I remember her attacking Ember to prevent me being captured, of showing me where Raven found her. I remember how I told her things that no one else knows.

"Eclipse!" Griffin warns. "The Majestic is coming."

Blood is pooling through Hanna's violet gown, expanding on the floor beneath her.

"Save the others." Hanna's voice is so weak. "Make this

all worth something."

"I thought you didn't care about saving a few lives. You always believed it didn't make a difference."

"People... can change," she breathes, laboured. "They can be better. They just have to make a promise to themselves, and decide to keep it."

Something makes me feel like those are the last words I'll ever hear her say. She closes her eyes. She's still breathing, but it's laboured. She no longer seems aware of her surroundings.

I feel a boiling in my blood, a rage singing in my veins. Turning, I lay eyes on the girl who did this. She's kneeling, staring dully at the floor. Phoebe has taken her weapon away, keeping watch.

With Hanna still coiled safely in my tail, I lift up April in one claw, dragging her screaming into the air.

Eclipse, no! Griffin shouts, shocked.

I bring the human girl up to my face, staring down across my beak into her eyes. She looks terrified. She strains against my grip, kicking, trying to scratch at my talons with her nails, before breaking down into sobs. She sounds like a child. I do not want to think of her as a child.

"Hanna matters," I hiss. Rage is overcoming me, rage I have never felt this intensely. Thinking how easily I could kill her with a single squeeze. Imagining her ribs cracking. "She's someone who matters. What right do you have to take her life away?"

"Please," April cries. "Please, don't kill me. Oh my God."

"It must make it so much easier for you," I breathe. "Believing I'm the monster you fear. It would be so nice to believe that killing you would be justice. An eye for an eye. So *easy.*"

April shivers, her face contorted. I look down over the other humans below.

"I don't know you," I whisper. "You're all... *strange* to me. You humans have so much fear and anger in your hearts, just like us. Your fingers twitch so easily at the triggers of your weapons. Weapons of steel and death. It's so easy to blame strangers.

'But even at my worst, I won't kill you," I tell April. "Remember that, human. Remember that next time. Because if you don't, death will find you. I promise you."

The temple explodes at the far end where we originally entered, in a shower of stone and dust. We turn to hear the howling of wind, rippling across the underground lake.

I drop April, who slumps to the temple floor, probably unable to believe that she's still alive. I whirl to face the oncoming threat.

He comes at us, winding through the air, monstrous. His tentacle tail wavers behind him, as if tasting the air. Hungry. Once again parts of him remain invisible, brief impressions showing through before vanishing again. Always growing closer. And closer. His face screaming, equal parts Calvin and Zephyr.

"We're too late," I hear Phoebe shouting, "there's no other way out."

"Attack!" Griffin screams, and surprisingly the other humans and Shadows echo his cry. Suddenly, everyone is on the same side. Humans loose their arrows, whizzing out toward the Majestic. Blue flames, lights like shining stars and an explosive horn fly from the Shadows - but the attacks freeze in mid-air, disintegrating into black dust.

Showing immense bravery, the teenage Shadows charge forwards toward the enemy, the humans drawing their weapons to charge alongside them. Maybe they're just finally happy to have a foe they can fight instead of feeling trapped. I can understand that all too well.

But the Majestic will kill them all.

Hanna is dying, even as I try to staunch the blood with my tail that holds her. I can't fail these other Shadows too. They have no one.

The humans and Shadows charging at the Majestic scream suddenly, levitating up off the ground as if they've suddenly hit zero gravity. They struggle, rotating through empty air. The humans and Shadows cry out as if invisible bonds are tightening on them, squeezing them...

I spread my wings, raising myself up to my fullest intimidating height, crest fanned out. I roar, the power of the sound echoing through the temple. The Majestic turns his cold dead eyes on me.

"That's right," I growl. "I'm the one you want. Leave them alone."

But suddenly, Phoebe is walking through the ranks of struggling Shadows and humans. She holds no weapon, just runs straight up to the Majestic, completely undefended.

"Phoebe!" Griffin and I both cry in warning, but she ignores us.

"I'm sorry," Phoebe shouts at the demon before us, striding toward him.

"Phoebe!" Griffin screams again. I pursue her, reaching out with a claw to grab Phoebe back, but she dodges me, and something about her bearing convinces me to let her go.

"Gecko, I'm sorry you felt abandoned," she says determinedly to the Majestic. "That you were by yourself all this time. But you did so *good*." She chokes up. "God, I'm so proud of you, Gecko. You raised a kid on your own. None of us were ready for that back then, but you did it."

Zephyr/Calvin's black eyes blink slowly at her. Then the Majestic plunges a claw down toward her, grabbing Phoebe by the neck and lifting her into the air. Her legs kick and flail. Griffin cries out, outraged, and runs forwards, but I block him. If whatever Phoebe is trying doesn't work, we're all dead anyway. The Majestic might as well be a cat toying with mice for sport.

"You led Melissa's company to new levels," Phoebe manages, gasping for breath. For whatever reason, the Majestic still hasn't killed her, even though it could with ease. "You never gave up. You didn't have your Shadow, you didn't have your friends, or any family apart from Grif. But somehow you did it. And I'm so proud of you. You told me once that I was a hero. But you're the hero here, Gecko. This isn't you. You're not a villain, no matter what you believe. You're not dark and twisted. You're just a guy who did his best. Come back to us. Be *here* with us. I want... to get to know the new you. You and Zephyr deserve your happy ending."

I steel myself, hoping that Phoebe is onto something, hoping that she hasn't made a suicidal decision. If Phoebe dies right now, Ember will die too in the Shadow world. And seeing Ember's human here before me reminds me of how despite everything between us, I don't want that. I want her to live.

Instead Phoebe is thrown backward, hurtling across the temple. Griffin runs forward to catch her, and she lands into him, hard.

"My turn," I say fiercely. I feel the pain, running deep

inside me. And I'm determined to use it.

I stride forward to meet the advancing Majestic, my talons digging into the stone of the temple floor to steady myself. All around me float the struggling bodies of the human and Shadow prisoners, writhing, helpless...

"Zephyr," I say, facing off against the horror before me. He's in there, I know it, his mind buried inside that undulating white body. So is Calvin.

"How much of you is still *you?*" I wonder aloud. I'm thinking of Melissa and Silvaluna, finally at peace. A bright, shining deity. I remember the sense of peace, of home that came over me as I stood before her. That feeling of family.

She had looked at me with the love of a mother.

"My hatchling," she had whispered. *"My baby boy."*

I am Cirrus again. Screaming, strapped to a slab as Hanna tries to forcefully break the ties between him and Griffin. I remember gasping as I found Hanna in the prison cell on New Redemption, how I struggled with the urge to kill her in the hold of the ship, overcome with emotion. As if Hanna's crimes weren't against Cirrus, but me.

I remember how Cirrus lay on the dais of the chapel, jerking, contracting, mutating. A deeper more powerful force than he could have understood blooming inside him, consuming him, transforming him out of death. His code being rewritten. The same energy reshaping itself. Nothing truly ever dies.

I see Cirrus killing a soldier in Sanctuary without even thinking about it. His joy at the thrill of battle beneath Winghold, not feeling a sense of shame or fear or horror, but a sense of play. That battle was a giant game for him and Griffin as far as he was concerned.

Perhaps I am not the darkness. Maybe it's Cirrus who

was the true psychopath.

'It's the only way we still know we're the good guys,' Griffin had said. *'Because we care. Because we don't want others to hurt.'*

All that time apart, with me living by Griffin's code of morality. Trying to live as if he was here with me, trying to live up to be his moral code. Trying to be a better Shadow than I was. Griffin helped open my heart to the suffering of others. To see beyond myself.

I see Griffin in Cirrus' memories, standing over Hanna, raising a sword in rage as he prepared to murder her in revenge.

Griffin had shown himself to be just human too. All of Cirrus' expectations, the hero Cirrus had dreamed of and loved in his heart all this time... is imperfect. Volatile.

I think of Cirrus' urge to be greater than his brother Zephyr, to be more powerful instead of always living in his brother's shadow. Just as Griffin had wished for with Calvin. I recall Cirrus' urge to be loved by the people of his world, rather than being something dirty, something infectious.

I AM ECLIPSE.

All this time wondering if I'm evil. If I have a darkness in me, one that can't be cleansed. An instinct to dominate, an instinct for blood.

I think of sitting with Celeste and her flatmates, that magical experience of an ordinary life. I think of Joni and her tribe, who have lost everything but carved out some happiness for themselves on these tiny islands, embodying hope. I remember ending the human soldiers who slaughtered those innocent families.

This is revenge, not justice.

What's the difference?

I've seen the beauty of the Shadow world. I've watched as the humans bombed Sanctuary City, I grew up watching the stranglehold of Raven's Empire corrupt the beauty of this world. Shadows living their lives at the mercy of a human, and at the mercy of each other.

Hanna risked everything for me. She threw away the only constant she ever had. She was able to redeem herself, to determine who she really wanted to be.

Our happiest moment, the one moment with Hanna I want to hold on to, is the two of us sitting on the sand dunes beneath the full moon. Laughing. As if the evils of the world cannot reach us there.

Raven told me that Eclipse replaced Cirrus, that I'm something completely new. That I have no history, no loyalty to this body's last owner. A blank slate.

But Raven was wrong. No matter how we try to tear parts of ourselves away and give them different labels, to set apart the good parts from the parts we're ashamed or scared of, we are still one single person. Each of us is a universe. Each of us is legion, host to a thousand aspects of ourselves.

I am the before, and the after.

The Majestic rises up before me as I move to meet him. Writhing through the air like an eel through water. That scaled face leers at me, a mockery of Calvin and Zephyr both. A human face with reptilian fanged jaws. I see it relishing the chance to finish me.

"Zephyr," I say with emotion. "I am not your enemy. I am not the thing you hate. Don't you recognise me?"

I lean in closer, and I smile softly.

"Don't you recognise your little brother?"

16

SAY SOMETHING

Griffin

I strain my ears, frustrated that I can't make out what Eclipse is saying to the Majestic. He's hiding it from my mind too, somehow. But there's a stillness from the Majestic after Eclipse speaks. Slowly, That reptilian face with shades of Zephyr and Calvin seems to stare into Eclipse's eyes. As if searching for something.

Then the Majestic spasms, startling everyone. I back away as the floating Majestic jerks, his pale limbs contracting inward and twisting at unnatural angles. He screams silently. Tiny cracks thread across his skin like fractures in ice. And the cracks are lit gold, a bright light like the sun shining through. Beams of light lance out of the Majestic from multiple angles. He still hisses, straining, his entire body convulsing.

Eclipse lets out a cry and starts to float off the floor. He struggles, wings and muscles fighting against the psychic control levitating him. His chest is forced outward by an unseen force, exposed and held there at the pale demon's mercy.

I'm staring at Eclipse as he hangs there, paralysed. I stare at his exposed, vulnerable chest, and I swear I can hear his heart, beating in sync with mine.

In and out, in and out.

And as I see Calvin and Zephyr's enraged Majestic about to kill my Shadow, I'm suddenly six years old again.

I bound through the carpark of Cameron Technologies, chasing the happy red balloon at the end of the string. I'm scared. I didn't mean to let go of it but now I'm going to lose it, the wind pulling it away from me, and as fast as I run I still can't grab it in my hands...

There's the blast of a horn, really loud, and the 'SCREEECH' of tyres. All I see is a blur and then...

Hands snatch me up, pulling me back and away. A car flies past, super close. The driver looks really angry.

My feet touch down on the sidewalk and then Calvin is there and he's shouting at me, looking really scared. Like I was when I lost the balloon, but much worse. Then he grabs me and he's just squeezing me tightly.

"It's okay Calvin, I'm okay!" I tell him.

"I'm sorry," he says, his voice muffled in my hoody. "I'm terrible at this. At being a... at looking after you."

"No, you're not. You're the best!"

"If something happened to you because of me..." Calvin pulls away, wiping his tears on the back of his sleeve. "Hey," he says suddenly. "You want to get out of here?"

"Don't you have meetings?" I ask, blinking.

"Screw them," Calvin says. "How about we go to the zoo? We can get ice creams."

"Can I see the sparrows there?" I say excitedly.

"Seriously? You can see sparrows anywhere, Grif. But yes, they'll have those too, and they won't even be in cages. But this doesn't mean I'm rewarding you for putting your life in danger, all right?"

"I lost my balloon," I say sadly.

"I know, buddy." Calvin hugs me again. "I know."

The bloodthirsty Majestic with Calvin's face raises his claw. He's poised to tear into Eclipse's chest and drag out his beating heart. Ending Eclipse, and ending me with him. Two bright lines of existence in the universe withering away into nothing.

"Calvin, no, don't do it!"

I'm running toward the hideous creature, the being that my brother's trapped within. The Majestic moans, a strange sound to come from the lips of that terrifying visage. It's almost like he's fighting himself, trying to disobey whatever foul drug Raven injected into him. The poison running through his veins is driving him onward, no matter what he really wants. An evil voice whispering in his ear.

"Calvin, I know you can't understand me, but you... but you've got to!" I plead, coming to a stop just short of him. Bodies float around our heads in orbit. Eclipse's. The teenage Shadows and humans. "Don't ruin everything. You don't want to be like this. I know you're mad, and you're scared. So am I. Look at you, you're Calvin Cameron. Everyone in our world used to look up at you the way I did. You showed them that anything was possible, technological dreams that nobody had been smart enough to come up with before. They trusted that you'd show them a brighter future. And I always knew you would. I know we were orphans, but I grew up thinking I was the luckiest little brother in the world. Each day after school I got to come back to see you and all the amazing things you were working on, dreams you made real. It was like magic."

I take a breath. Then, stepping forward, taking a huge risk, I throw my arms around him into a hug.

"I know you think you and Zephyr have changed," I say, squeezing tightly, refusing to let go. "I know that you think you can't come back from the darkness. But that's small thinking. Don't be small, because you're not. We're so close to changing everything. Come back to us. Be here. Put Eclipse down, put these kids down. Don't just spoil the way the worlds can be. Don't make me lose my Shadow all over again. Please, put them down! Please."

The luminous cracks widen, then start to spread across the Majestic's skin like wildfire, burning with light until I have to jam my eyes shut. I can feel his body changing, shifting, the wide reptilian body receding, the scales hardening into armour.

For a moment, I'm too scared to open my eyes. But I do, and I look up at the Majestic I'm hugging.

The great reptilian monstrosity with Calvin's face is gone. Standing before me instead is...

...a *knight.*

He shines with light, ethereal, as if not truly belonging here. As angelic as Mum and Silvaluna's Majestic had been.

His plates of armour are smooth, flawless and white - making him look like an android from the future. Stormy eyes shine through the cracks in the helmet. He looks like he could have been designed by Cameron Technologies - smooth beautiful design, cutting edge, kick-arse. I wonder if Calvin and Zephyr got to consciously choose how their true Majestic form would manifest, now that Raven's drug is out of their system. Now that they're a real Majestic like Mum is, in the truest sense of the word, a puppet no longer.

All around us, bodies are floating back down gently to touch the temple floor. Our new human and Shadow friends. Eclipse. They're safe.

The knight draws a sword from his sheath. Silvery wavelengths of light flicker around the blade like needles. He slashes it through the air. There's a sound like thunder crashing, and light explodes suddenly. The very air has torn, rippling like a curtain in the wind. Where the sword slashed through the air is now...

A Rip!

I'm staring into a wide crack in reality above the temple floor, and through it I can see a metal, futuristic corridor illuminated with amber lights.

We all stare, stunned.

"That's... that's it," I hear Phoebe breathe in disbelief. "That's Melissa's station over in the human world."

"Pheebs," I warn with a stab of shock. Calvin and Zephyr's shiny new Majestic form is blurring around the edges, as if they're vibrating, growing brighter. And at the same time, more transparent. More spirit and less... living.

I go to grab him but Phoebe catches my arm.

"No! It might not be safe."

The light increases, and suddenly I can feel it in my gut, see it with my own eyes. Calvin and Zephyr's Majestic is slowly vanishing, phasing out of this world. Moving on, or simply evaporating, I don't know. I don't even know if Mum's Majestic was really real, or if this temple just somehow project to me what I most wanted to see. But whatever Calvin and Zephyr are now, we've all come too far for them to simply... *vanish*.

"Zephyr!" Eclipse cries.

"Please stay," Phoebe begs Calvin. "Gecko, don't go."

"Calvin," I choke, the words dragged from my lips. I'm scared in case speaking somehow jinxes this process and makes my brother vanish faster, scared that more begging will do nothing at all. "We're not ready to lose you. People need you."

The light intensifies, and I feel my stomach drop - but then as we all watch in awe, the knight's body starts to divide.

It's like watching one pulsing cell separating into two through mitosis. Very, very slowly, the separate forms of Zephyr and Calvin emerge. It's grotesquely fascinating, like watching both of them being born.

Matter is flowing out of the knight's blurring form, knitting himself back into the individual forms of Calvin and Zephyr. Drawing away from the original outline of the Majestic until finally he's gone, and in his place is just a velociraptor and a human.

All of the other humans and Shadows arrayed around the temple just stand dumbly, having just watched the unbelievable events unfold before them.

"Nobody back home is going to believe half the crap I've seen in the last ten minutes," I hear Sien mutter. The cat-unicorn standing near her nods in agreement.

Calvin is gasping, his back arched as he struggles to press himself up from the temple floor. His bare back is slicked with sweat.

"Zephyr," Calvin manages, scared.

Eclipse is already there, leaning over Zephyr's body a

few metres away. I watch him gently rocking the velociraptor with a claw, whispering urgently for him to wake. Hanna has still been carefully cradled in Eclipse's tail all this time, through all the chaos, and he gently lays her down on the temple floor beside Zephyr. Eclipse's mind is retreating, turning in on itself. All I see in him is his fear for Hanna and Zephyr. Eclipse needs Zephyr to wake so he can heal Hanna, bring her back from the edge of death, if it's not too late. Zephyr's her only chance now.

But I still don't understand. Why is there so much fear in Eclipse for Hanna? A Shadow he's barely met?

Calvin struggles to his feet and staggers across to where Zephyr is lying. I move forward to help him.

"Griffin..." he murmurs. "Little brother."

"I'm here, Cal," I say. I squeeze him. "You're going to be okay."

We reach Eclipse and Zephyr. I release Calvin as he falls to his knees. I watch as he feels for Zephyr's pulse. Then, relieved, Calvin throws himself over Zephyr, wrapping the unconscious velociraptor in an emotional hug. I stare.

Last time I saw Calvin and Zephyr their relationship was in tatters, both of them convinced they had done too many terrible things to regain the friendship they'd had as teenagers. Maybe that one moment as that shining knight, perfectly being two beings made one... it changed something. It did for Calvin, by the looks of it.

Sniffing, in relief I think, Calvin pulls away from Zephyr. He looks slowly up at Eclipse, craning his neck in awe, as if only just aware of the gigantic creature towering over him. I put a hand on Calvin's shoulder.

"Calvin..." I say, oddly shy. "This is Eclipse. My Shadow."

"I'm honoured to meet you, Eclipse," Calvin says. "Damn, you're big. Look at you."

I watch them both with a weird tingling of apprehension and excitement. Having my brother finally meet my new Shadow actually means more than I knew it could. And even with the lives at stake I feel proud, perversely proud right then, of how tall and formidable Eclipse looks. How magnificent this other half of me made real is, this mirror of who I am on the inside. Meanwhile Calvin's counterpart, usually so fierce and intimidating, looks so small and fragile beneath Eclipse, a skink lying at the feet of an eagle.

Eclipse and Calvin stare together down at Zephyr.

"He'll be okay," Calvin says softly. All the rest of us are respectfully silent. "He'll wake."

"She doesn't have long left," Eclipse chokes, staring down at Hanna where she lies beside Zephyr. "Can't you... do something? Wake Zephyr up through your connection?"

"I can feel him," Calvin says grimly, "but he's distant. Still regaining his strength, like he's gone into an emergency power-down. Being a Majestic... it took a lot out of us, but I feel like Zeph took the brunt of it." Then, quieter: "Thanks for looking out for my little brother." He looks at me, and smiles with feeling.

"It means a lot to meet you too," Eclipse says in a low but respectful voice. "There's so much of Zephyr in you."

Again something rings strangely at the back of my mind. Eclipse has never met Zephyr, except for when he was born aboard New Redemption, when Zephyr wanted to kill him. How does he know what Zephyr was like? Why is he talking as if he knew Zephyr personally?

"Ah, anyone got spare pyjamas?" Phoebe asks the

pyjama-clad teenagers around us, awkward. It suddenly strikes me that Calvin is still entirely naked.

"Oh, hey, nobody... nobody needs to see that Calvin," I mutter. It's as intimidating as it is mentally scarring.

Phoebe just raises an eyebrow, a smile playing at the corner of her mouth.

Searching for some kind of sheet or garment of decency for my brother, I become aware of Mr Falco's cloak still tied at my neck. A heavy weight seems to fall on my shoulders, like the cloak is made of lead. I realise with dread that Calvin may not know that his closest friend is dead.

"Calvin," I say weakly, untying the plum cloak from around my neck. "This should be yours."

"Is that...?" Calvin chokes, sounding broken.

"It was Mr Falco's. He... on the way into the Underworld..."

"I remember." Calvin's face curls up in pain, and his lip curls for a moment in hate. "I remember now. What Raven did to him."

"I'm sorry I was so mean to him," I say, my voice strangled.

"Well, you had good reason to, Sebastian *was* an arsehole, after all," Calvin says. He sniffs. "It's just strange that... that I'll never get another chance to remind him of that."

"This was his," I say. Ceremoniously, I tie the cloak around my brother's neck, then step back. The cloak is long enough to keep him warm, and long enough to give him some measure of modesty with all the Shadow and human prisoners who are trying not to stare.

"Thank you, Griffin."

"I was there with Falco when he died," I whisper. "His

last wishes were for you and Zephyr to be brought back somehow, and for us to finish this together."

Calvin stares at the hanging amber crack in reality. The Rip that he made with his own sword as a Majestic. Even saying it in my head, it sounds made up. Too farfetched to be real, if I hadn't seen it with my own eyes.

"Then let's finish it," Calvin says. He looks at Phoebe and me. "Though it looks like you two have done pretty damn well on your own. This is your party now."

Calvin smiles at Phoebe. She's wringing her hands, looking super uncertain as to what to do or say. The intensity of her nervousness mingled with forlorn hope makes me look away.

"I'm so sorry," I hear Calvin say, emotional.

"Don't be."

"I'm so, so glad you're back. I just didn't take the surprise well. I'd grieved for you, for so long."

"It's okay, Gecko," Phoebe says, as tentative as he is. "You thought I was dead. It's not fair that I went dredging all that pain up again. I'm just glad you're not still a mutant hybrid trying to murder us all."

"I don't..." Calvin sounds overwhelmed with shame. "I can't ever apologise enough..."

"It's okay," Phoebe cuts him off. "It wasn't you or Zephyr, not really. We all knew that. Now let's just get out of here alive, like Grif said."

I sneak another look at them. Phoebe's smile, her joy at having Calvin back, causes me to feel a falling sensation deep in my stomach.

I look up at Eclipse, my mind reaching for his. Carefully, almost scared, like I'm approaching a wild lion. Because I don't know what to say to him. I want to help him, I want to comfort him, to make him feel like everything is going to be okay. But his mind is dark and unknowable, filled with fear... and guilt. He's standing watch over Zephyr and Hanna like a catatonic sentinel, wishing for Zephyr to wake, for Hanna to hold on to life. I look at Hanna's face, so still as if in death. It triggers a new storm of emotions. I remember my time with Hanna running through the forest of Kashlak. I remember my very first kiss, and feeling like we were invincible. I remember the good that I'd seen in her, how much I'd cared about her, when she was our friend.

Phoebe grabs my arm, startling me.

"Griffin," she whispers, "Look."

I do, and I shiver. It's like all the hairs on my arms are standing upright, pricking with the magic in the air.

The Shadow and human teenagers have spread out in a V, apparently completely subconsciously. Every human is facing a Shadow, even their body language mimicking each other. It's like each group is facing into a mirror.

Marty is standing opposite the spider-monkey with spider legs. Nam is facing the blue winged phoenix, and Woo-Min is facing the curious looking dragon-dog. The American girls are ogling a trio of Shadows across from them - one of whom looks like a cross between a flamingo and a meerkat.

"Look at each other," I address all of the human and Shadow sides emphatically. "They're *you*. Your counterpart. Can you hear them, inside your mind? You're not each other's enemy."

There's silence for a moment. The Shadow and human prisoners still look nervous, sheepish, or outright cynical.

"Oh, for God's sake," Phoebe says. She marches

forwards, taking the hand of one of the New Zealanders from the human side.

"What's your name?" Phoebe asks.

"Jade."

"Great, hi Jade!"

Seeing what Phoebe's doing, I instinctively cross over toward the Shadow who's mirroring Jade on the other side. He's a graceful-looking buck with folded feathery wings. Vines decorate his antlers, and long peacock feathers trail at his sides.

I extend a hand to him, in an invite. Cautiously, he trots forward, and I place my hand against his fur as I lead him into the divide between the two sides.

"Jade," Phoebe says, marching the girl forward to meet us, "this is your Shadow." Jade's mouth is hanging open, gaping in an 'o'. Jade stares into the buck's eyes and he stares back at her. They're both trembling, torn by curiosity and trepidation.

Slowly Phoebe takes Jade's hand and raises it gently toward her Shadow. My hand brushes Phoebe's. I keep it there for a moment, heart beating hard.

"What's your name?" Jade asks shyly.

"It's Arian," the buck replies. He scuffs the temple floor with a hoof.

"Do you mind if I...?"

Arian shakes his head.

Jade's hand slowly strokes Arian, entwining her fingers in his fur.

"Your whole life you wanted there to be someone out there watching your back, but you gave up on them when they never came," I say to Jade and Arian, to all of them. I'm thinking of my lonely childhood. How much I'd longed for

Cirrus, without even remembering that he existed. I look up at Eclipse. I feel tears in my eyes. Happy ones. "But trust me, when you least expect it, your counterpart will be there. They're here now, and they'll be your friend for life. They'll give you hope when you don't have any. They'll make you laugh when you were sure you couldn't. And you might fight it. It might not make any sense. But it's real."

Phoebe and I meet each other's eyes. I don't think either of us is breathing.

The Shadows and humans are silent, speechless, staring across at each other.

Nothing happens for a moment. Then Arian gasps, and Jade's eyes widen.

"I can hear you," Arian whispers in awe.

"Me too!" Jade says, smiling. "I can..." she looks overwhelmed as a barrage of information telepathically crosses between the two of them.

I didn't know if it would work, it was a gamble, but somehow the two of them have realised that they're connected. They've started to hear each other in their heads.

Then all at once the rest of the Shadows and humans break into a run toward each other, fear and awkwardness giving way to curiosity as they weave past Phoebe and me like a river breaking over rocks. I watch the humans and Shadows launch into each other in tight embraces, or simply smile shyly and kind of goofily bow to each other.

I watch as the meerkat with the bright pink plumage of a flamingo wanders up to April. April is pressed against one of the temple pillars, hugging her knees. She looks petrified, tormented... lost.

"Hey!" the meerkat says brightly. "Are you doing okay?

This has all been pretty freaky, huh?" She holds out a small paw toward April, and smiles encouragingly. "I'm Celeste. What's your name?"

"We did it," Phoebe says to me, and turning to her, I see happy tears in her eyes. I know I have ones to match hers.

"Oh, of course. We're only the best school of Shadow-human matchmaking around. The GSA."

"The GS - what?" Phoebe asks, grinning.

"I'll explain later." I look around us at the mingling Shadows and humans. All they needed was a chance to listen, or they could have ended up killing their own counterpart. I shudder at the thought. But now it's like they're all little kids who've just gotten puppies for Christmas. It's like people-watching at an airport, where long separated couples and family members embrace, where you can feel that acute outpouring of love. People long separated reunited, frayed connections made whole.

It feels like my soul is on fire. It's as if I'm finally coming alive, filled with soaring hope.

Everything Mum talked about, everything our team at Cameron Technologies had hoped for... here it is in front of us. The joy, the relief on each of the prisoners' faces that they're not alone in the darkness anymore is overwhelming. I feel choked up just looking at them. Seeing it is making it real for me. Our mission. My true purpose that I've been building toward my entire life.

I grin at Phoebe, and she grins back. Everything's going to be okay.

A rumble runs through the temple. I guess I jinxed things again. Dammit, Grif.

The rumbling doesn't stop.

I survey our surroundings. The humans in their pyjamas, united with their Shadows. Phoebe. Calvin. Eclipse bent over Zephyr and Hanna, his entire focus on those two individuals. The giant underground lake is behind us, the enormous interior of the epic temple illuminated by countless flaming torches. Water leaks and pools over cracked temple stones, fresh greenery sprouting up between them in a stubborn bid for life.

And right beside us all is that shining amber Rip in mid-air. It's like a permanent stroke, a cut in the fabric of this dimension. It shows no sign of wrinkling or dissipation, and the glow from behind it is a glow of promise. Of the better future that lies beyond it.

The shaking is growing. It's unmistakable now. Boots and claws on stone. Lots of them, enough to shake the foundations beneath us.

I look to the walls of the temple along each side of the lake. Walls which the human and Shadow prisoners had come tumbling through, where sections of the walls had rotated open. How many other concealed passages into this temple may there be that we don't know about? Secret entrances where soldiers could come flooding through at any moment?

"Run!" Phoebe screams. "Everyone, into the Rip!" The Shadows and humans with us run toward the amber crack in reality. The ones at the front show just the slightest ambivalence before vanishing through it.

There's a rabid growling, a fevered howling that reverberates through the stone. Like crazed zombies. Animals. The bloodlust, the thrill of the hunt is driving Raven's army into insanity.

"Eclipse?" I say with a smile. "I think we need to give Raven's guards a warm welcome."

But I get only silence. I turn to him. He's still bent over Zephyr and Hanna, muttering feverishly under his breath.

This is bad.

"Eclipse," I say, incensed, "We need you." He doesn't respond, mentally or out loud. I follow his gaze down to the unmoving faerie. I don't know how I'd feel about the news of Hanna dying or managing to hang on to life. Both are painful and problematic in their own messed up ways. "I'm so sorry. I don't understand what's happened between you two, but I get that she means a lot to you. But you have to take them with us. You have to move them."

"That might be bad for them," Eclipse mutters, almost like he's sleepwalking. "They're both only just holding on. Zephyr just needs to wake up, and he can save her..."

"*We* matter too, right?" I say, placing a hand against his feathered leg. I don't know if he even notices it. I wonder what he said to the Majestic to get through to Calvin and Zephyr, what he said to make the Majestic start falling apart. I know he's hiding something. It's okay for us to have secrets, I just want us to live long enough for us to get to know each other again. For him to trust me.

"I do trust you," Eclipse whispers. But he sounds so far away.

I feel a rush of fear. The army sounds so close. If Eclipse really has checked out for good, there is quite a high possible likelihood of us all dying.

"Griffin, Calvin!" Phoebe snaps. "Eclipse can take care of himself, and he's clearly not going to let them hurt Hanna or Zephyr. We need to go through the Rip, come on!"

The last members of the GSA, as I've dubbed them, vanish through the glowing Rip, like sprinting through a flapping curtain.

Suddenly along two of the temple walls, parts of the stone suddenly explode inward. Multiple sections of wall detonate, and the clouds of dust which follow quickly give way to hordes of Raven's soldiers streaming into the temple, a ravenous army pouring around the lake down toward us.

"Come on!" I shout. I help Calvin as he struggles to his feet. It feels weird to have my big brother so weak. To have him leaning on me. I guess I've never thought of him as mortal until now.

"Zephyr..." Calvin groans.

"Eclipse has him," I reassure him, wishing I was as certain as I sound. "He'll be all right."

Slipping my brother's arm across my shoulders, we move as fast as we can to the Rip. The army is gaining on us fast. I'm powered by a wild terror in me, a primal instinct for survival. I move with Calvin as fast as I can. His movements are stiff and weak, like he's been in cryogenic sleep for millennia.

I hear the stampede of Raven's army, alien cries and shrieks echoing throughout the temple, closing in. I look over my shoulder again at Eclipse standing vigil over Hanna and Zephyr.

What the hell is going through his head?

Eclipse! I scream.

"Go!" Phoebe yells at us, helping me take Calvin's weight. With her help we hobble through the Rip, leaving the temple... and my Shadow... an entire dimension behind us.

It feels strange, simply stepping through from one world to another. There's a flash like lightning so bright I have to shut my eyes, then there's the sound of metal ringing as I set my foot down.

I open my eyelids to see that we're in a long corridor. It's taller and wider than a subway tunnel, big enough that Eclipse could move here quite comfortably. The corridor is hexagonal in shape, like a honeycomb. The metal walls are the colour of amber and seem to glow with heavenly light. It looks like designed the facility to look like a science fiction imagining of the future. She built this in a time when the future seemed utopian and hopeful, unlike the grim reality of it that we've been living through.

This is Mum's legacy, lying dormant for over ten years. Waiting for the same spark that the prototype beneath our home had been waiting for. The reciprocal love between a human and a Shadow which can open portals.

Ten facilities around the world, designed to open giant portals above ground. Doorways where Shadows and humans could cross between the worlds.

"You don't have to carry me," Calvin pants. "I can do it. We have to move faster."

We speed up. Phoebe has run ahead to the others, who were paused in the corridor, worried that we might have already been lost.

Behind us I hear the first of Raven's nightmarish guards burst through the Rip into the passage. I hear them close in on us unnaturally fast, as if they're possessed. Claws scrape on metal.

Calvin cries out suddenly and falls, his legs dragged backward. I look back to see that a puma Shadow has its claws around his leg, and it's opening its gleeful jaws wide.

Suddenly an arrow buries itself in the puma's head. It dies instantly. I help Calvin clamber back up and pull him with me, to see Phoebe was the one who fired the arrow.

Whatever Phoebe is feeling about the life she just took, she's burying it under a determined expression. Storing it for later, I guess.

An arrow hisses over our heads, deflecting off the roof of the corridor.

"Don't you have powers?" I yell at the Shadows in our own party.

"I can make mountains appear," Anke's Shadow blurts. She looks like some kind of beaver. Spinning around, she focuses, and then the metal floor of the station cracks behind us. Shards of rock like stalagmites jut up from the floor and from sideways out of the walls. I hear a clatter as arrows hit our new shields harmlessly.

"Awesome work!" Phoebe cheers. She frowns. "Those aren't really mountains, are they?"

"Mountains can be many sizes," Anke's Shadow says mysteriously.

"I'm pretty sure they can't," I say dubiously. "I think they have to be like, at least bigger than a rock."

Phoebe elbows me in the ribs.

"I mean, that's a beautiful Shadow," I say to Anke. "You have a talented... is that some kind of beaver?"

"It's an alpine marmot," Anke says proudly.

"Okay."

We keep sprinting, hoping we're headed to the control room of this station. It doesn't take long before we hear the shards of rock break apart behind us like cookies crumbling. Then the soldiers are in hot pursuit again.

"There!" I yell. Up ahead I can see the rest of our group we've just caught up to. And just beyond them, the corridor widens in a kind of circular node.

I can hear Raven's guards snarling, hissing psychotically. Consumed by blood lust. A spiral of crimson lightning narrowly hurtles over our heads.

"Everyone, take cover!" Phoebe orders everyone, falling quite naturally into the role of a military captain commanding her troops.

The humans and Shadows with us obey her, diving to the sides where the corridor widens, out of the line of fire with the others.

Calvin and I finally make it too and I help him over to the curving wall to slide down against it. He's still really weak.

We need to get to the Core of the station. We're so close.

Black feathered arrows hiss past as well as a beam of frost which detonates further up the corridor in an explosion of ice. Our people peer around the corner at the approaching forces, firing arrows, bullets and their powers down at the advancing horde. The good thing about this little nook is at least we have the enemy in a bottleneck - they're having to slow and go on the defensive under the barrage of attacks sailing down the corridor at them. But it will only buy us so much time. The threat of death and dismemberment is all too terrifyingly present.

What happened with Eclipse, why didn't he stop them? Did he get overrun out there, or has he managed to stay shielded somehow, still keeping vigil over Zephyr and Hanna? I can't feel his mind, cut off from me a world away.

He should be here. He could protect us so easily, he has so much *power*... but he's opting out. Just like Calvin did when we lost our home, I think, feeling my heart ache.

I need Eclipse. He'll be here, I tell myself. He wouldn't miss this, our chance to finish this together... human and Shadow.

Ula's Shadow, a fluffy white wolf, spreads her wings. As she fans them outward, her fur starts to shift colour, as if she's a living mood ring.

I feel a strange sense of calm taking over me. My entire body relaxes, and I feel my mind becoming bright and clear. The fear and anxiety that's been festering in me smoothens. The change is so dramatic, I wonder what triggered it - until I see the other's expressions changing too. They all seem to be standing taller, their hands more steady on their weapons as their spirits lift. It's Ula's Shadow. She's helping us all get in control of the fears tormenting us. Everything suddenly seems brighter, more possible. We're going to make it out of here alive.

I peer around the corner of the bottleneck. Raven's guards are sprinting and bounding down toward us, pushing against the onslaught of arrows from our side through sheer force of numbers. A broad snow ogre grins psychopathically, a hunched humanoid of living darkness skitters down the roof toward us, frenzied, and a hundred others are following them. An arrow hisses narrowly past my face, ruffling my hair. I dive back behind cover, hyper-ventilating. Jeez, I need another dose from Ula's Shadow already. How am I going to make it up the rest of the corridor to activate the portals without turning into a human pincushion?

You'd think the other kids would break. After all, we are just an internationally-diverse gaggle of misfit teenagers facing down an army of contract-killer monsters. But something about the rescued humans and Shadows has changed. There's a gustiness and resilience that wasn't there before. It's not just the emotional boost they got from Ula's Shadow. Maybe it's that now that they finally have their counterparts. They're fighting together as one.

"Griffin!" Phoebe yells. "Run for the Core! End this crap! We'll hold them here."

For a moment, I'm too flabbergasted to speak.

"What about you?" I say incredulously. Since I'd brought her back from being a frozen gravelly Popsicle, Phoebe had been adamant that this was her mission. That she was the one on this quest, and I was just the sidekick. It took us breaking into Cameron Technologies in New York for her even to agree that we could work together. Now we're here, right on the doorstep, and she's just handing the victory moment to me? Letting me be the one to make history, and to get all the kudos that go with it?

But it's more than just that. Her and I set out as a team - this moment was meant to be about us. I'd imagined the two of us finishing this together, being side by side when the worlds changed. Our love and connection with Eclipse and Ember was going to be what ignited the portals and made everything okay. At least, that's how I'd imagined it.

Phoebe is shouting orders to the others. Giving them words of encouragement as she looses her own arrows at the enemy. She looks alive. Thirsty for battle. Her gung-ho fearlessness is clearly inspiring the others.

"Go! We can hold them!" Phoebe yells back to me. Then she grins, surprising me. "My place is here," she says, and there's something in her voice that hasn't been there until now. Purpose. Not her usual sense of fiery duty, either. She's glowing with life, even in the middle of the fudgestorm we find ourselves in.

Suddenly I get it. At least, I think I understand. Phoebe has a team again. Shadows and humans to coordinate, to care for outside of herself. We came all this way for Phoebe to realise she doesn't need to be the one to push the big red button, to relieve her guilt for failing Melissa and her team. Her guilt isn't defining her anymore. She just needed a new mission, a new family to protect and fight alongside.

I smile. Even in the midst of this horrible situation, facing these crappy odds, I smile.

But Phoebe is right. There's no time to debate. Blood is going to get spilled. People are going to die. The sooner I act, the sooner the fighting ends. The terrible weight of that responsibility settles on my shoulders.

"We'll cover you, Griffin!" Rihäm says stoically. "Whatever you've got to do, do it!"

"Everyone, get ready!" Phoebe yells. "We've got to cover for Griffin." The army has pushed forwards and their coming up to the bottle-neck. Phoebe and the others put away their bows and draw swords instead in preparation to meet the enemy. "NOW!" Phoebe screams in a war cry. She and the others burst out of our hiding place, to meet Raven's charging forces head-on. I seize my moment, busting out of my hiding spot, risking getting an arrow in the back as I sprint at full speed down the corridor toward the heart of the station.

But even as I'm running, I can't resist having one last look just back over my shoulder, and the sight transfixes me.

Nam flies over the heads of the army on his blue-winged phoenix, spraying cold flame like blistering plasma down at them. Rihäm zips down the corridor on her pegasus at the speed of light, armoured in what looks like colourful, unbreakable stained glass. Woo-Min's dragon-dog is yapping and teleporting excitedly from place to place as if purely out of curiosity, impossible for Raven's guards to pin down.

Sien's unicorn-cat fires her horn from her head, and it sails into the encroaching mass of twisted Shadows. The horn explodes like a guided missile, casting through their ranks what seriously looks like pixie dust. A few of Raven's soldiers cough on the substance - and a few moments later they're shrieking in terror, flailing wildly, fending off nightmare hallucinations in their panic. One of them is screaming something about clowns. Meanwhile a purple ram charges down the enemy alongside Arian, who has his human Jade riding on his back. He causes chaos for Raven's guards as he gallops deeper and deeper back up the corridor into the enemy's ranks.

A squirrel with a body containing galaxies snarls and scratches at the encroaching guards, the enemy's swords passing right through her. Even April makes a stand in a surprising show of courage, seeming shocked to find herself fighting alongside her Shadow.

Marty is cheering happily as his spider-monkey crawls at high speeds on its spider legs around the walls and roof of the corridor, hissing and spitting lethal acid down at the enemy, burning and eating away metal shields and armour to be met with screams from underneath them.

Dark, Marty.

A black wolf growls at the enemy, before transforming into a stunned looking opossum. Trembling, it turns tail and bounces hurriedly back into Georgia's arms.

Of course, the soldiers have their own powers, and their own weapons. Deep inside me I know that blood will spill from our side too. As I bolt at full speed for the Core, I hope our people are still alive when this is done, as impossible as that seems. At least they're not prisoners anymore, subjects for Raven's experiments. At least now they're fighting, free, beside their counterparts. Whole.

So I run to connect the worlds, and to stop a massacre.

The corridor we're all stuck in, a giant, amber-glowing subway tunnel of the future, ends in a circular door. As I reach it the door dilates open like something out of a sci-fi movie, metal blades whirring into the frame, revealing an entrance into the passage beyond. An errant arrow from the battle glances off the fancy doorway and I surge through into the passageway.

Eclipse, I hope you're okay. Please, come to me. The others need you. I need you.

Down the end of a passage on my left is a thick glass door. That's to flood the place in event of a worst case scenario, releasing ground water into the base. A safety measure we probably could have used at the station back in New Zealand, come to think of it. Beside that is the elevator door which can take us back to the surface once everything is set in motion. Back to the open sky of the human world.

I check the blueprints in my memory, the ones I tried to memorise from the folder we obtained in New York. This means the opposite end of the passage should lead into the launch bay. So the entrance to that stairway I can see, the one curving upward out of sight... must lead to the control room. Taking a deep breath, I run up the stairway, taking the steps two at a time.

I feel sick thinking of my friends on the outside, left behind to fight. A single arrow or blast from one of Raven's soldiers could kill someone I love in an instant. They're gambling on me with their existence, but in here, it feels like I'm the only guy in the entire world. The walls muffle the sounds from outside, a silent echo chamber that just seems to send my own frantic, tense thoughts back at me in waves.

They're trusting me to do this.

Last time I tried what I'm about to do, Cameron Technologies was collapsing above me, and the chance was stolen away from us. It feels like whenever I raise my hopes to believe in the future Mum wanted, I'm tempting fate to cheat me again, or deliver something worse on our heads.

I can't think that way. I have to dare to believe. I have to figure out how to work this sci-fi ignition switch before the massacre outside runs out of bodies on both sides.

I hurtle through a wide entrance big enough for Eclipse to walk through, into the control room. Here it is, the central nervous system of my mother's station. Her legacy, her key to changing all of our lives forevermore. A long dashboard of controls stretches across the opposite side of the room, covered in dust.

Above the controls is a wide, reinforced window. I stare through it at the amber-lit launch bay beyond, and my jaw drops in awe. A giant rocket lies there in wait. Once launched, it will open a giant portal on the surface of the island, as well as transmitting a signal that makes the other stations around the globe launch their own rockets remotely. The authorities will have no idea what's happening. No way to stop it, until it's too late.

Stepping up to the controls, I run a hand softly along the buttons and keys, familiarising myself. All our paths have led us to this moment. A shiver runs through me at the thought of the weight on me. The fourteen billion individuals who are relying on me right now to unite them with their other half. I orientate myself. From my pouring over the blueprints with Phoebe, the process to activate this station and turn on all the others remotely is deceptively simple. Taking a breath, I start turning the switches and dials, moving through all of the checks for the launch of the rocket.

Clock ticking, I search the controls until I find a pad fit into the interface awaiting a handprint. I hesitate, my hand hovering above it. My hand almost looks too small for the imprint there. With a burst of fear, I wonder if it was programmed for only Mum to be able to use it. If so, all of this could be for nothing.

A charge running through my blood, I press my hand down.

I yell, in surprise more than anything. Jerking my hand away, I examine the small pinprick of blood. The pad pricked me with a needle. Slowly, all the screens and consuls glow green with life. The system is powering up.

A DNA test. So that any Cameron could activate it.

"Very theatrical, Mum," I murmur softly, smiling. I wonder if she had extended that to include Phoebe. Surely she hadn't expected it would be me turning it on, ten years later than planned.

I hear the rattle of talons on metal. I turn quickly, blood pressure spiking, but then my heart soars. Eclipse enters into the control room, bowing his magnificent head through the entrance. The amber glow of the station sets his feathers gleaming like a pile of treasure.

"Eclipse!" I shout ecstatically, with mind and voice. I grin, relief rushing through me. I'm not alone anymore. I have my Shadow. Finally, any doubts or fears I have are quieted. This feels... right.

I think back to the shaky memories of my childhood:

Cirrus and me cuddling each other as our Mum's switched off our lights, as she went off to work on building all of this. And now here I am. Not with Cirrus, but still with my new Shadow, getting ready to hit the big red button together. Honouring our family's vision. It's a boost of hope. This isn't where things end for us. Our path was always leading us here. This is our destiny.

Eclipse saunters up behind me, keeping his wings pulled closely into his sides. He studies the epic control desk, filled with glowing switches and dials, cables running from it and snaking between our legs.

"Is Hanna okay?" I whisper. I'm uncertain how to feel, whatever the answer is.

"She will be," Eclipse says determinedly, in a voice that leaves no room for doubt. He looks over at the decade-old controls, looking overwhelmed. "Is that it?" His mind is a quiet, ongoing hum, a bee in the background, indecipherable scribbles of anxiety over Hanna mixed with tense anticipation.

"That's it," I say, grinning. "It's just running the final checks. We made it, Eclipse."

"I know."

Something is wrong in his voice, but I can't figure out what. This is such a big moment for us, for all of us, for our universe. I want him to feel he's part of it too.

"Eclipse, I know I've been messed up lately," I say, emotional. "And that asking you to become a Majestic with me was... too heavy. Part of me really wanted to go back with Mum to wherever she is now, and for a moment I lost perspective. But I'm never going to leave you. I promise you that. This is the start of our life together. I really believe that this moment, finishing what our Mums started out with their team to achieve at the beginning of all of this... this is what I was put here for. This is my purpose, and yours." I move back to the controls, my hands racing across them to check everything is in order. I'm on fire. I've never felt this *in the flow* before, perfectly in sync with the task before me. "I know we've come a long way from playing around in the hallways of Calvin's company, but we're here now together." I smile, tears in my eyes. Then I move the final switches and dials to prime the launch, hoping I'm remembering the process correctly. It would be a massive bummer if I started the self-destruction sequence by accident, or you know, if I shifted the coordinates so the portals actually transported everyone to some bizarre hell dimension or something.

Sweat slicks my forehead. I pull down the lever. The entire chamber starts to hum around us, and there's the start of a sound like the grinding of gears.

I turn to Eclipse, grinning with breathless excitement. I take in his proud towering form, bowing his crest to not scrape the very generous roof of the control room.

"This is it!" I gesture down at a pad in the very centre of the controls. "Come on, it just needs someone to touch it. The connection between a human and a Shadow. Are you ready to do this? Together?"

There's no response, just weird silence.

"Eclipse?" I repeat. He's staring down at his tail. It curls slightly at the end, as if mimicking how he was holding Hanna in there before. As if he's still clutching her to him like a ghost, like she's something precious... or a puzzle he's still trying to understand. "Eclipse!" I say urgently. "Snap out of it. The others are dying out there, I need you here! This is our destiny. Are you with me?"

Eclipse slowly raises his golden head. Those dark brown eyes the same colour as mine stare into me, pained and filled with grief. Finally they settle into baleful determination.

"No," he says.

17

MY OWN WAY

Eclipse

Griffin vanishes through the luminous, amber Rip with the others. I stay with Hanna and Zephyr in the temple, checking on their wounds. My tail is still coiled tightly around Hanna, hugging her to keep pressure on her wound, to stop the life from leaking out of her body. Every moment her pulse feels weaker against my tail.

I can't believe it. A shiver runs through me as I look over toward the amber Rip.

"There's the human world, Hanna," I laugh softly. There's wonder and bitterness all in the one sentence. We've given up so much to make it this far. Who were we, when we started this? I don't even remember. "We did it. We found a way through."

It feels strange, after my heart aching for it, after everything we've been through to be here. We're right on the verge.

"Hanna?" She does not respond. Her breathing is so shallow.

I'm dimly aware of the sound of boots crashing on stone, of Raven's army of guards exploding down through the temple toward us and the Rip. Consumed in grief and worry for Shadows other than myself, I barely register as the first arrows fly at me. They combust into golden flame before they strike. As guards charge past me, some of them encircle me to attack. Only to scream as their weapons catch fire or their armour spontaneously burns red-hot. The power flows from me almost subconsciously, Ember's searing flame protecting us. Keeping us in a fiery bubble that separates us from the real world. The army breaks against us like a tide, surging past but leaving us untouched.

Urgently, I turn my attention back to the two lying at my feet. Hanna is entangled in my tail on the temple floor and to her right lies Zephyr. He looks just as lifeless. I'm possessed by a terrible fear. A fear that these two lives may sputter out, with me powerless to save either of them. Being left totally alone. No, no. I can't lose them both. I can't.

"Zephyr!" I whisper, scared. He looks so small. I could hold him in a single claw. I check, but he's still alive. I breathe with heavy relief, tears coming to my eyes.

"Zephyr... I need you to live," I say, voice strangled. "You can't die." I laugh, choking on tears. "I realise you hate me. And that my heartfelt plea to save Hanna, the person who used to manipulate you for her evil purposes, the Shadow who kidnapped Cirrus, is probably too much to ask for all at once. You're welcome to laugh in my face. But I'm begging you. Wake up. Heal Hanna. I need both of you. You came out of the darkness, and so has she. She deserves a second chance too."

Zephyr finally opens his eyes slightly, a narrow gap. I gasp. He lays his eyes on me, the golden monster he believed had destroyed his little brother.

The feathers along the back of my neck prickle in dread.

Slowly, very slowly, Zephyr reaches up toward me. He reaches with one of his tiny, stubby arms, without a hope of covering the distance between us. I bend my head lower, tense with anticipation.

I remember Zephyr trying to kill Griffin in the surf, how Cirrus flew at him and froze him into stone rather than letting Zephyr kill Cirrus' human. I remember back in Sanctuary City, where Zephyr rejected Cirrus just because he had found his human.

But I also remember when Cirrus was a prisoner of New Redemption without any hope. I remember how Zephyr and Griffin looked past their differences and stormed the ship together to save Cirrus. I can still feel the joy in Cirrus' heart as Zephyr burst through those doors, the moment when Cirrus knew that his brother had come back for him. Despite everything the Empire had turned Zephyr into, he still loved Cirrus as his little brother.

He still loved me.

Zephyr's claw reaches out to me and I offer my head to meet it, to accept whatever punishment he deems necessary.

Instead he presses his palm to my forehead.

"I forgive you," Zephyr whispers. I gasp, tears leaping to my eyes, overcome. Then...

"Take it," Zephyr croaks.

There is a full moment before I understand what he means. When I do, I'm overwhelmed.

Zephyr is trusting me. He believes in me.

I try to speak but no words come. I just nod, flooded with gratitude. I feel the static hum of Zephyr's power flowing from him into me. Replacing Ember's power to destroy with the power to heal.

Around us the shield of flames crackles, spits and dies; the last of Ember's power. But Raven's soldiers are still wary of coming any closer to me, flowing around us like a river around rocks, toward the Rip.

"Thank you," I whisper. Zephyr trusts me with this. And that means more than anything ever could.

Hanna looks dead already. Those cunning emerald eyes are closed, her violet wings still and lifeless. I bend down and softly nudge her head with my beak, trying to wake her. To keep her anchored to the world of the living.

Come on, Hanna. Fight it. You're far too headstrong to die.

Taking a breath, I turn my attention internally. I focus on the power that Zephyr has granted me. Channelling it in the same way that Cirrus had seen his brother do countless times when he was growing up in Sanctuary City.

I visualise gathering together my own life energy, just as Zephyr had once described the process to Cirrus. This feels more personal than using someone's power ever has. Whenever I used Ember's flame I felt in touch with her, I could sense her in the fire. As if her soul was imprinted on the flames that flowed from my feathers. But now with the healing, it feels like I'm gathering together my own soul, and allowing it to flow into Hanna. Like I'm giving her a piece of myself.

I understand now why Zephyr was always so reluctant to use his healing abilities on Shadows other than himself. It comes with a cost. But it is a cost I am willing to pay.

Hanna moans, a cry from a deep sleep, as a tiny bullet emerges from her stomach and clatters onto the temple floor. With a leap of hope, I see Hanna's bullet wound stitching itself together. Then Hanna falls still, quiet once more. Her eyes still closed.

"Hanna?" I whisper, scared. "Hanna, can you hear me?"

Usually when Zephyr heals someone, the effect is instantaneous, the subject up and about in no time. Did I-did I do something wrong? Is Hanna too far gone to be fully healed?

Hanna gasps, opening her eyes, and I nearly buckle with relief.

"Are you all right?" I whisper to Hanna tentatively. "Hey there."

"Hey there, yourself," she whispers weakly. I nearly miss her words over the clattering of steel boots. Hanna looks at the troops storming around us, still wary of getting too close and being incinerated. "Huh," is all she says. She looks confused, but I'm not sure if that's due to our surroundings or if she's wondering why she's still alive. Finally realisation dawns as she looks over at Zephyr, than back at me. "You healed me," Hanna says, stunned. "You brought me back."

"It was the right thing to do."

She smiles painfully.

"You know, most of this world would disagree with you."

"Most of this world is wrong."

"This is crazy, insane," Hanna mutters, feverish,

nervous, "but I need you. I don't mean that I love you or any of that crap. I have no *use* for you. But I need you. I need you for things to make sense."

"I think they call that... friendship," I say slowly, the word feeling strange on my tongue.

"Really?" Hanna's eyes widen, as if humiliated. "Ah, hell. Don't let this get out, the whole world won't stop laughing at us."

"Hanna," I say, scared. "There's one more thing I have to tell you. Something I... something I only just figured out. Something I haven't told anyone. I don't know for sure but I... I feel it's real." My heart thrums in my chest. I'm not sure how she'll respond to this, with the history between us. Things have been different, and I don't want to change that.

Slowly, I meet her eyes.

"I'm Cirrus," I choke, my throat dry. "Raven told me that Cirrus was dead, that I was a completely new Shadow who replaced him. But he was wrong, and it took hearing that to make me realise. There's a reason I felt all this anger toward you when I met you, why I care so much about Zephyr and Griffin, and it's not just because I have someone else's memories. My mind got scrambled when I transformed, I did change, but I'm... I'm still *me*. Still Cirrus.

'I always felt so powerless, Zephyr's weaker little brother, at the mercy of the Empire. And what happened on New Redemption, whether it came from all of the trauma, or if it came from Griffin or somehow from both of us... I know that it was the intensity of my connection with Griffin that allowed me to change. I wanted to be a Shadow powerful enough to rule the world, powerful enough to have others love or fear me. I got my wish. So I became Eclipse. And I know that as

Cirrus and Hanna we didn't see... eye to eye, exactly. And I know that the two of us being on the same side seems... like madness. But the world *is* madness. And I want you to know I forgive you. I forgive you for New Redemption. For all of it."

Hanna smiles up at me, tears glistening in her eyes.

"Thank you," she whispers.

"I don't think you heard me," I say, thrown by her lack of reaction. "I'm *Cirrus*. I've been Cirrus all along."

"I know," Hanna says smugly.

"What?" I'm shocked. "You knew? For how long?"

"Since you found me in my cell in Sanctuary. I knew it had to be you all along, even if you kept suppressing who you were into this tiny other voice in your mind. But you're still the same to me, either way. You mad, brilliant, infuriating lizard-bird."

"You could have just told me," I mutter.

"Yeah, because Ember doing that really went down a treat. It was up to you to figure it out for yourself."

"And if I hadn't?"

Hanna shrugs.

"You can't change what you are, but only you can choose who you want to *be*. If you wanted to identify as Eclipse, that was up to you. It was your choice. I wouldn't take that away from you."

I look at the Rip the soldiers are rushing through. Griffin ran through that Rip, to the station in the human world. That Rip is the entry to finishing the project that my family and Griffin's built. Something deep in my bones is telling me that this is the moment. That whatever is unfolding with Griffin beyond that shining amber doorway is where future lives will be made or unmade. This slow dread, the deep, unspeakable premonition that has been building in me reaches a deafening roar.

Within this temple I watched as the humans and Shadows we rescued were united with their counterparts. I watched Celeste and the others that Hanna and I had met on our journey here as they finally met their humans, I saw the wild joy on their faces. The rush, the excitement at discovering they were something bigger than just themselves. That they weren't alone.

But even as I watched the miraculous, historic moment, still all I could see were those dead humans scattered around me, amongst the treetops.

"You know, you showed me how to love this world," I say to Hanna. "Even if you value the big picture, the greater good of your people over individual lives, you still want to steer this world toward a better place. You feel responsible for the Shadows in it. You wanted to be a leader who made her people's lives better. And the pain of not being that good leader you wanted to be was eating you alive. Just like it was with me."

"What are you thinking?" Hanna breathes.

"You know what I'm thinking," I say. "You always do." My voice breaks with sorrow. "You're the one who taught me that inaction can be a worse evil then action. You're the one who taught me that sometimes we have to change when our understanding of what is right changes, and that makes us strong, not weak. I just don't know if I'm strong enough to do it."

I look down at her. She stares back as something unspoken seems to pass between us.

"Maybe," Hanna says tentatively, "maybe all this time we've been wrong about wanting to unite with our humans. Maybe there's a chance... that your Mum and Griffin's Mum were wrong. Both you and me have spent our entire lives wanting to find the other side of ourselves, thinking it would change us for the better, but maybe... maybe..." she seems so shy she's not sure she can get it out. "Maybe having people you care about is enough. Maybe it's enough just to *know* our humans exist, to love them from a distance and imagine them here with us. Maybe it's time we accepted our whole selves, even when we're split in two." Hanna looks up at me, eyes wide, uncertain. "Maybe having a friend could be enough. To not feel alone anymore."

I stare down at her. When I found her in her prison cell part of me had wanted to kill her, even against my promise to Griffin. Now I realise that she's the one Shadow in existence who possibly has a chance of understanding me.

"Where?" Hanna asks weakly. "Where do we go? Where is home?"

"There is no home," I say to her. "We're all there is. But we can't spend our lives trapped in another cell." I look toward the Rip. "I have to go after him," I say. I trace the floor of the temple with my tail, anguished.

Hanna nods weakly, still deathly pale. "I know."

I look at Zephyr, now passed out again on the floor of the temple.

"I'm sorry, big brother," I whisper softly.

"Eclipse!" Hanna says, starting suddenly. "Celeste, Frigga, Merida... the others. You have to save them. We have to get them out of here." The emotion and determination in her voice shocks me, and finally jars me out of my trance.

I'd sunk into such a dark place thinking I might be losing Hanna and Zephyr that the rest of the world had felt grey and unreal. Now I see the last of the soldiers surging en masse into the Rip, after the others. I feel a burst of anxiety. My apathy has endangered them.

Time to remedy that.

I pick Zephyr up in a claw, coiling my tail carefully around Hanna. I look toward the amber Rip. It's time. Time to make a choice.

"Griffin will never forgive me," I say. I never thought it was capable of feeling this much sorrow. Not in my entire life.

"If he really loves you," Hanna says weakly, "he'll come to understand."

"But does he? Love me?"

"Of course he does, you idiot. One time I was so jealous of your bromance that I nearly killed you both, remember?"

I stare down at her, and despite everything, the corner of my beak twitches upward.

"We were so close to having a moment here," I say.

Now I'm standing in the control room of the station. My human is staring at me. Through the window, a rocket waits to be launched in the amber chamber beyond.

"No," I repeat to Griffin.

"What?" Griffin says, blinking.

"I can't do this," I say. The mental barrier I've been holding between us is lifting. All of my thoughts are flooding into his mind now, illustrating my words with my emotions, and the experiences in the Shadow world that are colouring my choice. He's hearing my conversation with Hanna for himself. "I'm so sorry. But I... I don't know if I believe in this anymore, that this is the straight-forward fix you think it is. I can't believe that this is the way forward."

Griffin looks stunned. The silence is deafening.

"But that's what we came all this way for," Griffin says, rocking on his feet. Maybe he's going into shock. "This is everything our family wanted. This is what Ember wanted, what I promised her I'd find a way to do. I mean, we nearly died getting the Oracle from Raven! We need to activate this station and open all the portals between our worlds. Everyone can finally find their counterpart. They can be happy, complete...like we are. *You* changed my life for the better. Are you telling me... are you telling me you really don't feel the same as I do for you?"

"Always," I tell Griffin firmly. "And knowing that you are alive, that you are safe a world away, makes me happy. That gives me strength. I so wanted to see you again, and I'm glad we've had this time together. But you and I have to learn to say goodbye, for all of our sakes. We can love our counterpart, believe in our counterpart, without needing to interfere in each other's world. Without losing ourselves in our connection. It's what your Mum and Silvaluna said to us: life is defined by our longing for each other. I need to learn to let you go, while still holding on at the same time. And one day, when we've lived our lives to the fullest in our own worlds... maybe then we'll have a chance to be together again. We'll have all of eternity. But life is for living. We can't force humans and Shadows to live side by side before either have even figured out who they truly are. There'll be chaos and death. I can sense it. I've *seen* it."

"That's what we're going to fix. We're meant to bring in a new utopia, for everyone," Griffin says tensely, "including those Shadows and humans fighting out in that corridor for us right now. And you're saying it's all for nothing?"

"Our friends are safe, Griffin. I've seen to that. And what we've all fought for, it's not for nothing. But I'm saying that humans and Shadows have a gift of screwing everything up, no matter what. We're not evolved enough to meet each other yet. Look at those other kids, at what April's first instinct was. Look at what longing for a counterpart has done to Hanna… to your Dad." Griffin looks up sharply. "I saw it in your memories," I say quietly. "Griffin, to hold you too tightly is for both of us to burn. Our longing to be united as brothers, as two halves of one self, is what living is. But the worlds weren't meant to mix.

'Shadows are endangered by three threats: by humans, by the Empire who tells them humans are evil, and by the Resistance who promises them salvation. Shadows need to take care of Shadows, and not define ourselves by humans any longer. We need a chance to remember who we really are, to focus on our families. The Shadow world is torn apart by Civil War, and my people are dying. I've seen it." I think of my mother and my brother, how different things could have been if they had not met their humans. "I love my world, and I want to protect it. But we cannot fix humans without fixing ourselves first. We all have to find our own answers. Shadows need to start looking after Shadows."

"Where is this coming from?" Griffin begs me. "Is this coming from Hanna? She took Cirrus from me, she led you to become this… thing!"

"No. She did not. I *chose* to become Eclipse."

Griffin blinks, stunned for a moment.

"What?"

"I'm just discovering and starting to accept who I really am. And Hanna... she's on the same journey," I say softly, trying to help him to see. "She understands what I'm going through. We're going back to our world, we're going to finally stop running. We Shadows need to learn to save ourselves. And Hanna and I will do whatever it takes to bring back peace. Even if it takes everything we have."

"You've talked to *her* about this, instead of me?" His face hardens suddenly, his sadness turning to anger in a flash. "Cirrus would never say this," Griffin says slowly, "this is Eclipse talking." He throws himself between me and the controls, as if he can fight me. "Cirrus wanted this even more than I did," Griffin presses, as if convincing himself more than me. "Cirrus understood. I thought you were my Shadow, but maybe I was wrong. Maybe Raven was right."

It hurts to hear that. Even though I know he's just lashing out in his pain.

"Griffin..."

"You're trying to throw away *everything* Cirrus and I worked for! And I won't let you!" He's crying. "What did you do with my Shadow?"

"It's me, Grif," I say sadly. I visualise a symbol, holding it shining in the space that we share between just the two of us. I imagine two golden curved brackets on either side, with a star of green in between them.

(*)

Griffin covers his mouth, eyes wide.

"A Mental Hug," he whispers. "It was real. You remember it too. Which means…"

"It's *me*, dude," I say with a painful smile. "I'm Cirrus. I'm not someone else, I'm right here in front of you."

"Cirrus?" Griffin whispers, trembling at the revelation. "It's been you, all along?" He shakes his head, overwhelmed, tears streaming down his cheeks. "I was born as your egg hatched, we grew up side by side! Our Mums believed we share a soul! I've dreamt your dreams, we've flown through the skies of both worlds… you can't leave now."

"You know," I say, "back when I was just a kid hiding in the clock tower in Sanctuary… I used to think that if only I could find you again, everything would be better. But I've been through so much in the Shadow world just in the last few days, and I… I've changed. Griffin…" Tears fall down my own feathered cheeks now, and I'm too ashamed to meet his eyes. I bow my head in grief. "Griffin, I killed humans. And they deserved it. They had shot innocents."

Griffin is silent with shock, before he recovers.

"That's okay. It's okay." Shakily, he steps forward and reaches up toward my head to comfort me. But I raise it out of his reach.

"Last time we met I made a promise to myself not to kill, but things aren't as clear cut as they were then."

"Eclipse… *Cirrus,*" Griffin says, tears trickling down his cheeks. "But humans need Shadows to fix *us.* We're so damaged. I swear sometimes it feels like everyone in my world is so lonely and sad, and we're driving the human world into oblivion. We need you."

"Maybe," I say feeling broken, "but we don't need you."

He shakes his head violently.

"You can't believe that."

"We have no idea what opening these portals will do! Anything could happen. Nobody, human or Shadow, truly knows what they're doing. We're all just making it up as we go along. You have no idea what the outcome of your actions will be. How do we know you're not making things worse?"

"Because I have faith," Griffin says firmly, and I can tell he believes he is speaking straight from his heart. "I've seen what Ember and Phoebe meant to each other, and I know that back when Zephyr and Calvin were together it was the happiest time of their lives. You have to choose to believe that people are good, that all anyone wants is to be happy. To be loved."

I move toward the controls, my talons clattering on the steel floor.

Griffin spreads his arms to shield them from me.

"If you turn that on, more Shadows are going to die," I say, a sob breaking out of me. I try to fight through the pain, to force myself forwards. This is not about me. This is my sacrifice for countless others. I feel like greater forces then us are weighing in on this moment, that what we do here in this room is going to cause ripples far into the future for both worlds. I wonder if our mothers are watching and what they are thinking. I hope they understand.

I'm sorry. But I know you trust me to do what I believe is right.

"What are you going to do?" Griffin asks, his voice not sounding like his own.

"I'm going to initiate a sequence that will destroy this station, and then I'll destroy the controls as well."

"You won't," Griffin whispers. "You don't even know how."

"You just showed me. I can see the blueprints in your mind, clear as day."

Griffin stares at me, feeling violated. It's an unspeakable betrayal of our telepathic link. It's always been what made us stronger together. But now he knows I've already started using it against him, using that openness between us as a weapon. He feels like part of himself is working against him. I can feel his shock as everything he believed in comes crashing down around him.

"Your chance to connect the worlds will be gone," I say softly. I feel every drop of his pain and heartbreak. I can feel myself destroying him. Destroying myself. "Then I'm going to take Hanna, and we're going to bring the other Shadows back to the Shadow world with us."

"You're saying..." Griffin says, eyes widening as deeper understanding finally dawns.

"Yes. I'm saying goodbye," I whisper. "You are my human, Griffin. My everything. You're my end, and my beginning. But I have to say goodbye. I have to learn to let go."

18

LOSE YOU

I'm staring at the other half of me. My Shadow who's just told me he's betraying me.

Cirrus. Cirrus, it's still been you. All this time. How could you?

Eclipse moves forward toward the controls. In a single movement I spin around to press my hand against the pad, hoping I can keep it there long enough to trigger the ignition...

Eclipse's draconic tail wraps around me, golden scales tightening like a boa constrictor. I'm torn away from the controls, helpless.

"I'm sorry, Griffin," he says. Then my Shadow softly releases me and I fall to the ground. Springing up, I run at him again from behind, reaching for his mind.

No, Eclipse... I'm pleading him, begging him now, with

everything I am. *Please, just don't do this, don't do this, we can still turn this back, do it for me, please....* But I'm forced to watch as Eclipse reaches down to twist a dial in the controls with a single talon. Then he smashes a glass case and pulls the lever that was inside it downward.

The station's warm lights are replaced by pulsing crimson that bathes Eclipse and me in a bloody glow. An alarm is singing, an artificial cry.

"No," I whisper.

"*Self-destruct sequence initiated,*" a voice says from the speakers around us, and through the glass from the launch bay beyond. It's my Mum's voice. My chest contracts. "*This must mean there is no other hope and there is danger of this facility falling into enemy hands. Controlled demolition in ten minutes.*"

Eclipse looked deep inside me and he stole the knowledge from me that he needed to destroy this place. I feel utterly betrayed.

Eclipse knocks me aside with his wing, forcing me out into the stairwell. Trying to keep me out of harm's way. But I trip, stumbling down a few of the stairs before I stop myself. Springing to my feet, I run back up to the control room, but stop as a tail scrapes by me in a golden blur.

"NOOO!" I scream, tears flying from my cheeks.

Eclipse spins around. He's so massive in the confined space that all he has to do is turn in circles; his wings, his tail, every part of him smashing and destroying the control room around him. Sparks fly, and there's the sound of shredding metal. I need to force my way in, to stop him somehow... I shout into our mental link with all my strength. But in the chaos of the fray, there's no space for me to enter the control room. Nothing to do but stand

and watch, stricken, as Eclipse shreds our hopes and dreams.

My feet are already carrying me forward again. I leap up onto his back, grabbing and pulling on his feathers, punching his oversized body, but it's like he doesn't even know I'm there. I hang on as he swings around in berserk mode. He's violating my family's last hope. The last hope for all of us.

When he finally stops, I drop from him, then fall to my knees in the centre of the control room. I raise my head, cheeks wet, to stare at the loss of all our dreams.

The interface needed to launch the rocket has been obliterated. Torn, hanging cables are sparking. The entire station has started to shake, shuddering. The self-destruct sequence is underway. It's as if the entire station is a body, and it can tell that Eclipse has just exploded its heart.

The golden feathered dragon who looks so much like my Cirrus turns around to face me. But he *is* my Cirrus. He's my Shadow, my best friend in the universe, and he has just hurt me in the worst possible way he ever could.

"I'm sorry Griffin," Eclipse says in a tortured whisper. "You mean so, *so* much to me. I'll miss you, but I have to look after my people. I hope... I hope that one day, you understand this. I can feel it in my heart: this was the right thing to do. Humans aren't a sickness, but they're a drug. And we have to break our addiction."

"How did you get past Raven's army?" I say, dead inside.

Eclipse straightens, standing tall in the confined space.

"You once told me that all killing was wrong," he intones softly. "But I don't believe that anymore. Maybe it is when done in the name of revenge, or anger. But not if it's to protect those who need protecting. I will not stand by and watch soldiers kill innocents like Celeste and the others. You told me once that caring about the lives of others was what made us the good guys. But sometimes, watching and doing nothing is the most dangerous kind of violence."

"So you're going to break your rule."

"Raven's soldiers found out why I had that rule in the first place."

I shiver.

Eclipse offers a foot softly to pick me up.

"You have to get out of here," he says, face contorted with emotion, his chest heaving, "make your way up to the surface. This place is going to…"

"Get away from me," I spit. Eclipse stops. His eyes look torn, like he's been ripped in half on the inside. But this is his own decision. He doesn't get to feel hurt. To pretend he's feeling a fraction of what I am.

The siren is still wailing, a sinister rumbling running through the station. As if signifying the end coming, of this place preparing to destroy any sign that it existed.

"Griffin… I'm not going to just leave you." Tentatively, Eclipse reaches down for me.

"DON'T TOUCH ME."

He jerks back, stung.

"Just… go," I hiss, cold. My mouth barely moves. "You've made up your mind. You don't have any say over me anymore. We're done."

My Shadow hesitates for one last moment. Then he turns and shuffles out of the control room. I raise my head to watch Eclipse leave. His wings tucked into his sides, his reptilian tail flicking out behind him as he vanishes from sight, back to Hanna and the Rip. The Rip which leads to the Shadow world he calls home.

Only when he's gone do I scream. I scream and scream, in anger and loss and pain, until I bury my face in my knees. My dreams and my Mum's dreams are crashing and breaking apart, as the station prepares to destroy itself along with any trace of me.

I don't know how much time passes before I hear a new voice.

"Griffin? Griffin!" Phoebe shouts. She comes running up the stairs into the control room. She feels so distant. All of it, it's all so far, far away.

Phoebe looks out the window at the rocket, then around at the devastation of the control room itself, looking sick.

"Griffin?" she says softly, tentatively. She takes a step closer. "What happened?"

"It's over," I say. "I'm sorry."

Phoebe stares at me, her face falling. She looks around us at the wreckage, illuminated in flashing crimson. She's clearly trying to think of a way out of this. She hasn't worked out that there isn't one yet.

It's like it's just the two of us at the end of the world.

I can see Phoebe is trying to breathe, to be the calm one. In, and out. In, and out.

When she places her hand on mine, I can feel it shaking.

"What happened here? I passed Eclipse on the way in, he said that you needed me..." Phoebe trails off, staring around at what remains of the controls, the light making her look like a bloody ghost.

"I'm such an idiot," I say, wrought. "I wanted to become a Majestic with him. And I couldn't see. I've been losing him this entire time. After what happened to Cirrus, what I let happen... why wouldn't my Shadow want nothing to do with humans? With me?"

"Eclipse *loves* you," Phoebe says, incredulous.

"I did this," I think aloud. "Because of me, I made him destroy everything our family ever worked for."

I look up at Phoebe, imploring, desolate.

"Does this mean I'm turning against myself?" I whisper hollowly. "What the hell am I becoming?"

She stares back at me, at a loss for words. Then she shakes herself out of it.

"No. You don't give up that easy. Come on." Phoebe grabs my hand and then she's hauling me to my feet. I'm dragged along behind her lifelessly like a ragdoll, as we run down the stairs from the control room.

Our feet land on the floor of the passage below with a splash.

I look to our right. The glass door at the end of the corridor has been breached. It must have unlocked when the self-destruct sequence was initiated. Its edges have just loosened slightly, breaking the air-tight seal. Just enough for water to gush through the sides in a torrent, splashing along the floor of the passage, in a swirling, rapidly rising tide around our feet.

"The entire place is going to flood," I say tensely. "That's the self-destruct sequence. This whole place will be under water."

"Let's get the others out of here," Phoebe says, her face drawn.

Almost as if she jinxed us, another door clamps shut, this one blocking off the elevator down the passage. Our only escape route to the surface.

Phoebe swears. We swerve toward the amber corridor where the others are still holding off the guards - just as it closes in our face as well, the metal blades contracting inward to seal it shut.

The rising water splashes up against the sealed door and back at us, like we're trapped in a washing machine. The current is already up to our knees.

I see a burst of panic in Phoebe's eyes. Real, visceral fear.

We're going to drown. And nobody can save us.

"The water," Phoebe says aloud, in an epiphany. The doors are sealing when the water level reaches them."

Immediately she pulls me by the hand, shouting: "COME ON!"

We rush down the passageway, in the opposite direction from the flooding doorway. To our left, the entrance to the control room stairwell seals shut. We race along the length of the passage, toward the only door still open, the water seeping ahead of us - and then we're through, just as the final door clamps shut behind us. We exhale.

We're in the rocket launch bay.

I look around the circular space, at the scaffolding around the rocket. The rocket has just been held there in its cradle for ten years, waiting to be released. We're standing on a metal bridge, one that runs toward the rocket before encircling the rocket's base. Access for repairs and final checks. Down below the rocket itself is a long shaft. It all feels very Apollo 11.

"Okay, okay," Phoebe says aloud, as if she's trying to keep herself sane. I can hear the mania in her voice. High above us, vents open around the edge of the launch bay. Torrents of water start to thunder through them, falling down in miniature waterfalls all around us. Soon this launch bay will fill up as well, turning it into a watery tomb. We've only delayed the inevitable.

"Okay, okay, this is bad. Griffin, I need you right now. We need to think of a way out of this, or we're both going to die."

"There's no other way out of here, Pheebs," I whisper. "Eclipse saw the blueprints in my mind. He knows everything I do. He knew there wouldn't be any other way for me to activate the station."

Phoebe slaps me. Actually slaps me, across the face.

"Shoot, I didn't mean to do it that hard. Are you okay? I'm sorry. Wait, no! I'm not. Griffin, I know you're devastated right now, but we need both our brains to think of a way out of here. Because... right now, I've got nothing. And I refuse to believe we die here."

"If you can't think of a way, what makes you think I can?" I say brokenly.

"You're smarter than you think," she shoots at me. "You're Melissa's son. Act like it."

"I was never as smart as Calvin," I whisper. "Not as smart as Raven, or even you." I think of Eclipse's rampage in the control room. I think of my moment with Raven in the ballroom, forcing my brother's Majestic to obey me. "Eclipse doesn't want me. He knows I'll just corrupt him. Eclipse saw the same evil in me that existed in my Dad. I'm just like him. Useless. Shadowless."

"Your Dad had good in him as well as dark, but you're still a million times more than he was. And if anyone else talked that way about you, Griffin, I'd punch them in the face. Listen to me, because we have zero time right now. I don't think it's any accident that my Shadow's power is fire," Phoebe says fiercely, pointing to the burn scars along the side of her face. "Or that Cirrus could turn people into stone. You lost *so* much when you were a kid, Grif. And you were there with me after I banished Raven, when I was breathing what I was sure were my last breaths. And I think, in that moment, you wanted more than anything to be able to hold on to the people you loved, to stop them from dying. Even if it meant freezing them in time forever, just to stall death. I believe that's why Cirrus has the power he does. You *feel* so much, you care about people so strongly, you don't want to let them go. That's what Cirrus made real, that's what kept me alive. Your sheer force of will. Your refusal to lose the ones you love. So you're not giving up on Eclipse either. We can still fix this together somehow, we can still connect the worlds, and you two still have a shot to come back from this."

I stare at her, like I'm seeing her for the first time. I had no idea she'd thought so much into it. Into *me*.

"Don't let your Mum's dream end after all we've been through," Phoebe tells me. "Be who you were born to be. A Cameron."

"We need another way to launch that rocket," I say slowly, "to open the portal and transmit to all the other stations. If we do that, maybe it will automatically stop the destruct sequence."

I look at the rocket. Phoebe's right. I have to believe that the answer's somewhere inside me, that I'm smart enough to think our way out of this.

It's in my blood. It was in Mum, in Calvin.

It's in me.

I breathe. I imagine giving myself over to a greater force, and I see the blueprints of the facility unfolding before me. I retained more of the information that I realised, and I follow the fine lines and details through the cross-sections as if I'm holding the physical plans.

"We hotwire the rocket," I say, a light bulb going off in my brain.

"*Hotwire* it? Bypass the controls - can we do that?"

"The self-destruct sequence will have drained the fuel from the rocket," I say quickly. "We need to get below it. One of us needs to go down that shaft and pump the fuel from the fuel cells back into the rocket, then start the ignition manually."

Phoebe runs it over in her head quickly, then grins manically.

"Okay. Just... don't confuse the blue wire with the red wire or whatever. I don't want to get fried when I'm down there."

"Pheebs...."

"Please, I'm the only one here who isn't athletically challenged. Let's not fight. We don't have time."

We look around us. The launch bay is hardly in a state of readiness - there's loose cabling draped over scaffolding and equipment and tools still lying around, carrying the dust of ten years.

"We can use this," Phoebe says, grabbing a coil of cable from the walkway. She starts winding it around some of the scaffolding, pulling it tight. I help fasten it to her, checking twice, three times that it's not going to come off.

"Grif. I'm fine."

She starts backing toward the shaft, ready to abseil down.

"Phoebe, wait!" I say, running up to her. I don't know what to say. The alarm has gone silent, but the place still pulses with that bloody hellish glow. I stare into her eyes for a moment, the two of us washed in crimson.

"Don't die," I tell her.

Phoebe descends into the pit. Slowly letting the cable wind through her belt, she abseils backward down into the shaft. Beneath the rocket's giant thrusters.

And all the time the water is rising higher, pouring down into the shaft into which Phoebe is descending.

Now it's my turn.

Hunting through the abandoned toolboxes discarded around the walkway, I manage to find a power drill. I almost don't expect it to turn on, but it does. I can't find any drill extensions for it that will open the star bolts on the hull of the rocket, but eventually I find a flat blade one that does the job. Unscrewing the hatch on the side, I stare in at the wires and circuit boards, reminding myself to breathe. Then I set to work, navigating by the blueprint diagrams emblazoned into my memory.

"The fuel cells are submerged," Phoebe calls up. "I think one of them has caught fire." Something about her voice makes me stop my careful picking through the wires to kneel and peer down at her in the shaft.

Fear strikes into me like lightning. Water is rising up through the shaft, and Phoebe's right that it's submerged the fuel cells beneath. But it's not just that. The rising water is being heated from the burning fuel cell below, causing the water to boil dangerously. Coils of steam drift menacingly upward, wetting my face. If the rising, boiling tide reaches Phoebe, she'll be done for.

"Phoebe, you have to get out of there."

"It looks like there's a fuel cell down there that *isn't* on fire, but I can't attach its fuel line to the rocket. The bracket's broken. I need to weld the other line onto the rocket to refuel it."

"I've looked around but I haven't seen anything that looks remotely looks like a welding torch," I shout down, frustrated.

The water pouring from the vents above is sweeping across the walkway, spilling down into the shaft where Phoebe is. Steam drifts up from below and I hear Phoebe cough.

I squint through thick, hissing clouds of steam. I can make out Phoebe with the head of what looks like a thick hose in one hand, trying to plug it into the base of the rocket. Trying again, and again...

The boiling water is rising below her. If she doesn't want to boil alive I'm going to have to haul her up quick.

"Pheebs..." I say in warning.

Phoebe screams in frustration, trying again and again to connect the fuel line to the broken bracket. Mad, she even starts trying to hammer the bracket with the side of her arm to warp it back into place.

"COME ON!"

The water's too close. Running to where her cable hangs taut over the edge of the shaft, I grab hold of it, straining, trying to pull her back up.

"No! I'm not giving up!" she shouts. "If I come back up we drown anyway!" She fights me, trying hold onto the rocket, trying to resist. The cable stretches dangerously, dangling her over the boiling grave below.

"Phoebe!" I beg her, scared for her. I'm beyond caring about myself. I just want there to be some way for her to make it out of here alive. I need that much.

The crimson light pulses around us. Counting away our last few seconds on Earth.

I can hear her hyperventilating, as she kicks out at the wall of the shaft in a muffled scream. She's losing it.

"Phoebe," I say, remembering the anxiety attack she'd had when we fled the safe house in Auckland, "just... listen to my voice. Focus on me, okay?"

I'm lying down, face over the shaft. My mind is racing for what to say, with everything falling apart around us. I just know I have to get her to pull it together, to not think of our impending drowning or boiling, just for a moment.

"I'm scared that after everything, even if we survive this, I still don't know if things will ever be the same with Calvin," I say honestly. Phoebe seems to quieten, like her breathing has started to calm. Like she's listening. "I can't get it out of my head, that Majestic with his face, trying to kill us... but I'm so glad to have him back, and at least now, I understand him better. I know why my brother was so broken after he lost you, why he was so... so cold my whole life. It makes sense, and spending time with you, I know now how that would have destroyed him. You're... you're a lot to lose."

Phoebe doesn't say anything back. There's only the sound of rushing water.

Suddenly, an idea comes to me. It's farfetched, insane, but so is everything about our situation right now.

I'm thinking of Cirrus. Of how Phoebe told me that Mum had always said that Phoebe and I had the strongest connections with our Shadows. Calvin had told me that Phoebe had been able to channel Ember's powers before.

It would be a miracle, but we need one if we're going to keep living. The boiling tide is rising.

"Close your eyes," I shout intensely.

"What..."

"Trust me, please. Shut it all out. I want you to think of Ember. I want you to feel her here with you."

"I think I know what you're trying to do. But Ember's not here," Phoebe shouts, emotional. "She doesn't even know I'm alive. It can't work."

"She's always with you. I've lost Eclipse. But Ember is still out there and she loves you so much. And I see so much of her in you. But if you want to launch this and see Ember again, you first have to realise that she's been in you all along."

For a minute, I think she's too scared to try, or she doesn't trust me. Then...

"Ember?" Phoebe calls out shakily. I can barely hear her over the water crashing down from the vents above, the hiss of steam from below her. The boiling water is nearly touching her dangling shoes. "I'm here. I came back. I need you, now. Please, don't be afraid. I need us to be one again."

Nothing happens.

"Keep trying," I urge, though my spirits are falling. Maybe this was my hope talking, not my intellect.

"Ember," Phoebe says, and something about her voice is different. Stronger. "I just want you to know... I never left you."

Down below, Phoebe bursts into flames.

"PHOEBE!" I scream. The fuel line must have caught fire, either that or she's somehow spontaneously combusted. "Oh my God, are you okay?"

I desperately try to think of how to use the water all around us to put out my blazing friend down below, reeling

- before I realise that the flames are flowing *from* Phoebe. She's a ghost of pure flame, still in Phoebe's shape.

"*Yeee-hah!*" Phoebe laughs victoriously. "Griffin, it's working!"

I can just make her out past the bottom of the rocket. Tears fly from her eyes in the form of sparks. "I can feel her. *Ember.* She's here with me!"

"You just gave me a goddamn heart attack," I wheeze, clutching my chest.

Phoebe clamps the fuel line beneath the rocket. Sparks fly in a shower as she welds the line onto the rocket with her bare hands. Then she pumps the line, dragging up fuel from the cell submerged below to refill the rockets tank.

"Done!" I hear her cry.

I throw my whole body into the cable, hauling on it, pulling her further and further back up the shaft. Phoebe starts motoring her way up the wall, away from the boiling water. She's still flowing with flame.

Phoebe clambers over the railing. It's hard not to stare at her, a human meteor. Her skin glows with Ember's fire, a translucent flaming phantom. She's still grinning from ear to ear, high on her newfound power, of feeling Ember within her.

And then she joins me, her feet touching the flooded walkway. She leans into me and I steady her. Then she reaches out with one hand to press a flaming hand to the body of the rocket.

A shiver seems to run through the air. The hull glows hot with the heat of her flames. It might be just me, but I could swear magma coloured lights seem to shiver through the body of the rocket, working their way into its cracks and rivets, becoming part of it.

"There," Phoebe whispers. "The love between human and Shadow. Grif?"

"Yeah?"

"Finish this."

I switch my focus back to the wires inside the rocket.

I can show you the full potential of who you are, Raven had said. *The greatness that's locked inside of you.*

I let the memory of the blueprints guide me, my hands working to bypass the ignition sequence. For a moment I pause, about to connect two of the wires. I'm taking a risk that this won't somehow short circuit the entire craft or make the rocket blow up along with us.

No, I realise. It's no risk at all. I *know* I'm right. I believe it.

I press the wires together and from inside the rocket comes a dull roar, the sound of it coming to life.

I did it. I feel a spike of joy at the victory.

Plumes of thick steam and then smoke rise up from the shaft. The rocket and the entire chamber around us starts to shake, as if we're in an earthquake. I'm already fitting the panel back into the hull with Phoebe's help, drilling the bolts back into place to seal the wires away.

There's a grinding sound around us, like ancient gears. Parts of machinery which have been waiting in place since this place was built by my Mum ten years ago. High above the roof starts to dilate, opening a passage to carry the rocket to the surface. The vents gushing water high above our heads stop, like taps suddenly shut off. The water beneath our feet starts to drain away. The crimson pulsing light cuts out, returning to the warm amber glow.

I can't believe it. The launch is overriding everything. We might actually make it out of here alive.

But then the flames explode out of the rocket's thrusters and I realise that the receding water will be replaced by fire. Oops. My hopes die as quickly as they were raised.

I run toward the door with Phoebe and her flames, away from the rocket. In seconds, the very air in the launch bay will all be aflame, incinerating us.

But our only exit is still blocked. I hear a clunk as the door to the passage we entered from unlocks. Slowly it starts to rise open, just a crack at first. But suddenly we hear the deafening roar of the rocket and we know there isn't time.

We both know we're going to die.

"Griffin," Phoebe says breathlessly, and I turn around to face her. Phoebe is a spectre of pure flame before me, her eyes bright. She's smiling like she's at the source of all power, high on the experience of feeling one with her Shadow.

Then fire is erupting through the launch bay. Spilling out from the rocket exhaust, spreading over everything like liquid accelerant. Phoebe pins me to the door blocking our exit. Shielding me with her own body.

Flames spread from Phoebe's shoulder blades, unfurling and then curling inward like Ember's wings to enshroud us both. A shield against the coming wave.

And even as I'm feeling broken over Eclipse, and at my emptiest, the girl of pure fire is looking into me and smiling widely. Like she sees me as if I'm already the person I want to be.

Then Phoebe takes my face in her hands and moves close. I feel her lips press into mine.

The point where we touch is hot as flame, but somehow

it doesn't hurt. I can feel her power, Ember's power, flowing through into me and back to Phoebe again. I'm joined to the heart of that power. And I happily surrender myself to it, despite flaming death dancing all around us. Because, for one glorious moment, we *are* the flame.

I kiss Phoebe back, the parts where we touch making us immortal. Impervious to the thundering exhaust from the rocket as it launches up and out of the bay toward the surface, to change the worlds at long last.

EPILOGUE

Griffin

The station's elevator slowly rises. The lights in it are on the blink; the thirteen Shadows and humans crammed in around me are faint figures in the blackness. The rest of our team took the lift up before us. Everyone in here is sitting or leaning on each other, exhausted from the battle.

But they're *okay*. That's the amazing thing, the thing I've got to hold onto. Calvin and Zephyr are here too, breathing. Living. Everybody made it out alive.

We got our miracle. And that's something to be really grateful for.

"Tell me again," I say into the blackness, dry-mouthed. I feel as exhausted as Phoebe, the adrenaline crashing. Phoebe is leaning on me, and I have an arm around her, each of us supporting the other shakily after our near brush with death. The flames that flowed from her skin have died out. It's almost a shame, it would really be great to have some light right now. Phoebe's back to being regular, normal Phoebe. If there was ever anything regular or normal about her at all. "Eclipse. What…" I swallow. "What happened to him?"

I can sense the others looking at each other.

"Some of us were badly wounded, or dying, and he touched us with his talons," a voice answers me. I think it's Rihäm's Shadow speaking, the pegasus with the stained glass wings. "He… healed each of us."

"I gave him my power," Zephyr says quietly, sounding emotional. "He needed it to heal Hanna. Although why he cares about the monster that tried to…"

"So Eclipse healed you," I cut Zephyr off.

"Yeah," Georgia says, sounding haunted from what they've just been through. "And…" Her voice falters.

"What then?"

"Griffin," Phoebe says softly, trying to calm me.

"What did he do?" I press stubbornly.

"He killed them," Georgia finishes in a small voice. "Raven's soldiers."

"How many?"

"Countless," Calvin says, intense. "It was like nothing I've ever seen. He was a force of nature, unstoppable. He sent the rest of Raven's people scurrying away with their tails between their legs."

"It was horrible," a disturbed voice whispers.

"That's enough," Calvin commands. I know he's thinking of me, trying to protect me. He knows how much I'm already hurting from what Eclipse did in the control room. It makes my face burn with shame, having my brother know what happened. I'd been so proud to finally introduce him to Eclipse. My own Shadow. And now Calvin knows that my own Shadow turned on me. He abandoned all of us.

"Eclipse saved us! It was them or us," Georgia says, defending him. "Without Eclipse stepping in, those evil Shadows would have killed all of us. He gave them a chance to run, to leave this Raven guy and live in peace. It's not his fault some of them refused."

"And then?" I say hollowly.

"He offered for some of us to come with him," Arian says. "Us Shadows. But we wanted to stay with our humans. We didn't want to have to go back through that palace. Then he left the way we'd come from. Back through that Rip to our world."

"He took Hanna with him," Zephyr says.

I digest this, looking at our group of survivors.

"Look, everyone. I'm sorry you all had to go through this," I tell the shattered humans and Shadows around us. "But trust us, it's going to be okay now. Everything's about to change for the better. And that's because of you. It's because you fought so bravely, when you so easily could have given in to the fear."

With a firm click, the lift comes to a stop. Suddenly light floods in at us and we all cry out, the bright beams a shocking assault on the senses. But then we can smell the ocean, and feel the heat of the sun. Our motley gang clambers out of the elevator, joining the rest of our people who are waiting for us out on the sand. Phoebe kicks off her shoes instantly, wanting to feel the warm grains beneath her bare feet. Calvin and me copy her, as well as some of the other humans. It feels so good to have those grains pushing up between my toes. It's grounding, anchoring.

I turn around slowly, disorientated, trying to make sense of the water, the greenery and the sand. Once I get my bearings, I'm amazed. Phoebe sees it too.

"That's where we landed the jet," she says, pointing just down the beach from here, towards a copse of trees a little bit down the shoreline. "If the Shadow world and human one match up more or less geographically... we came all the way back across the island when we were in the Underworld."

Beautiful sunlight shines down on us. I can hear birdsong. The ocean stretches out before us and a warm breeze tousles my hair, carrying the smell of salt and the forest. I breathe it in. It's such an overwhelming relief at a physical level to be outside again, in the light, after our long run below the surface of the earth. Such a relief to feel the warm wind on our faces. Now we're just a collection of Shadows and human teenagers in pyjamas hanging around on a tropical beach. Little Marty and his spider-monkey-spider hybrid have already started building sandcastles.

Then Phoebe is shouting excitedly and pointing up at the sky. It takes a moment for the rest of us to see it too, but then my spirits lift. High above us, I can make out a sphere blooming to life. A portal being born.

"You did it," Calvin shouts at me and Phoebe joyfully, sounding like he hardly dares to believe it. "You actually did it!" He smiles wider than I've ever seen him. "Thank you," he whispers.

Zephyr steps up to stand beside his human.

"Well, there you go," I hear the velociraptor say to Calvin, staring up at the giant portal growing high overhead. "Our mothers' project is completed. Can't believe it was that easy. What the hell do we do now?"

Calvin laughs.

"Remember that joyride you took when you stole a car from Cam Tech that night?" he says to Zephyr. "How about a road trip?"

"And go where?"

"I don't know. Wherever. We make it up as we go along."

"I'd like that," Zephyr grins. "Just not another damn opera, I'm begging you. Feeling cultured and sophisticated isn't worth having your ears bleed. Remember when all we were into was movie and board game nights? Those were the days."

Calvin smiles, and I think there are tears on his cheeks.

"Well, maybe we can fit some of those in too."

I study Calvin. It's such a relief to have him back, but there's still a small voice that can't help but wonder who my brother really is now. What lasting effects will being a Majestic really have had on him and Zephyr? After everything that's happened between us... what kind of a relationship can the Cameron brothers have going on from here? Back in Auckland, Calvin confessed that he'd rather have had Phoebe live than me. Then in that palace I forced him to obey me as a Majestic. In the Underworld I saw my brother's scaled face, the hatred in his eyes as he tried to kill me. Are we past all that now? Is this our happy ever after?

I'm going to trust that it is. Because I know one thing. I don't want to lose him again.

Despite our beautiful surroundings, despite the win, I feel a wave of raw pain. I relive Eclipse turning on me in the control room, trying to destroy everything our family had built. I recall the sensation of staring into Eclipse's eyes and feeling Cirrus staring back at me.

I think of Phoebe revealing the dark truth about my Dad. I relive the tender moment with my Mum's Majestic, and I obsess over whether it was an illusion, a trick of the temple, somehow drawing from me my deepest wish... or if it was real. I choose to believe it was real, and that it means Mr Falco is really one with his Shadow now.

I wonder what happened to Raven. If he's still in the Underworld, or in Aeyu Palace, or if he fled the islands over there completely. Since Eclipse has broken his vow not to kill, does that mean he's tracking down Raven right now to finally destroy him? I don't know. Even if he has, Raven is smart. I wouldn't count Raven out just yet.

I remember dangling over the chasm in that cavern, Raven giving up on his chance of pursuing Phoebe just so he could grab me by the arm and save me from death. What was that? I'm just an amusement to him, not of any real solid value. So why did he fight for my life like he was fighting for his own, when only half a year ago he'd been the one trying to kill me?

So many unanswered questions. We've been through so freaking much in just a couple of days. My breakup with Sophie and running out of my school exams feels like a really, really long time ago.

Phoebe bumps into my side playfully, knocking me out of my troubling thoughts.

"Come on, sour face. We won. Aren't you excited? We'll be eating with Ember and Eclipse at Burger Max before you know it."

"I don't know," I say, revealing the storm whirling inside of me. "I can see me there in Burger Max, and I can see you with Ember. But I can't see Eclipse in there with us. I don't see how we get from where we are to that."

"Eclipse tried to sabotage the portals, and he failed. He can't stop what's coming now," Phoebe comforts me. "He's going to realise that he has to accept that there's a new universe coming. He's going to have to find a way to fit into it, to find a way forward with you."

"What if he still wants to push on with this friend breakup," I smile grimly, "even when every single other human and Shadow is united with their counterpart?"

"Once he sees what a utopia it is? He's going to realise he was wrong. He's just messed up by all the things he's seen, just like we all are. He made the wrong choice. Good people sometimes do." Phoebe grins, breaking the solemnity. "Come on, Grif. We just ran through the underworld of another dimension, coordinated a battle against enemy Shadows, launched a rocket to change the worlds…" Phoebe giggles, actually giggles. "It's insane. I mean, I was in fire. Ember was inside me. You helped me to hear her again." We watch the human prisoners we freed laughing, playing in the sand with their Shadow counterparts, soaking up the sun on their happy faces. "You know, they're together because of us," Phoebe says. "You and me, we did that."

I examine her sideways. I can't stop thinking about our kiss, down below in the station. It's possible that only happened because we were both about to die. Phoebe was in some kind of… altered state, and I'm scared she might not even remember that. Because it meant a lot to me.

"That pep speech you gave me," I say, "down in the station… it really helped."

"Oh, I'm glad," Phoebe says spiritedly. "I actually wrote a lot more than that, thought you'd need more."

"Can I hear the rest of it?"

"Nah. I'll save it for the next life-or-death scenario we find ourselves in."

"Oh, so there's a next time is there?" I say, and it comes out sounding strangely hopeful.

"You're weird," she grins.

I smile at her. Even after everything I've just been through, everything we're all carrying with us... she still makes me smile. She's the only one who always can.

We look up at the sky. A silvery sphere is expanding half a mile above the island. Growing bigger and bigger, like an orb of molten mirror. Through its surface I can see the sky of another dimension. I imagine the same thing happening at all the other stations around this world. Doorways opening from our realm to theirs.

"It worked," Phoebe whispers, as we feel the thrill of witnessing the most monumental moment in history. The moment we set in motion. We turn to each other, giddy. We press our foreheads together, bowed in a moment of intense relief. Everything feels unreal. It's a moment charged with magic.

Pulling back slightly, I suddenly feel myself tracing patterns in Phoebe's hands with my fingers. Tentative, not wanting to scare her off but not wanting to pull away either on the unlikely but glorious chance that this is, in some secret way, maybe what she also wants. I don't breathe. I don't think she does either, as we hover on a line between the past and the future.

I wonder how I can explain to Phoebe all the things that I'm feeling. How scared I am to try and tell her that it feels like all the other pieces of me have been torn out, and how she's the only thing I have left. That I feel like a ghost, just like I felt back before this all started, before I met Cirrus. Suddenly it's like all that change I went through didn't even matter, like I'm unsure all over again what it is I like about myself, what others see in me... what the point of me is. But when I'm with Phoebe, she makes me feel like the person I was. The person that I want to believe I can be again.

"Phoebe," Calvin calls, coming up behind her. We both retract our hands faster than light. Phoebe turns quickly to meet him, flushed.

"Hey Calvin, what's up?"

Adding to the moment is the fact that my brother is wearing nothing but the plum cloak of Mr Falco's, wrapped around him like a dressing gown.

Calvin looks anxious. It's an expression that looks strange on him. More like a nervous school kid then the brother I know.

"Can I talk to you for a moment?" he asks Phoebe quietly.

"Okay... sure."

She looks at me uncertainly. Calvin only takes her a short distance away. I don't mean to eavesdrop, but it's close enough that in the quiet I can still hear every word they speak.

"I'm... I'm so sorry," I hear Calvin say. "For how I reacted when I saw you."

"You were a jerk," Phoebe says.

"Yes, I was."

"A cold, alienating meanie."

"That too," he confesses, and I hear a slight smile in his voice. "I was taken by surprise. I wish I'd reacted better, you have no idea how much I wish we could redo that. But, being a Majestic, at the end there... it changed things for me. It reminded me of who I really am. I don't even know how to start explaining it, or describing what it was like being one with Zephyr... but it opened me. Not the hell Raven put us through by using us, but that one moment when Zephyr and I were free of him." Calvin is adamant, crackling with intense energy. He sounds so alive. "Being a Majestic was like... entering heaven. Just a taste of it. I wish you could have experienced what I did. Zephyr and I, we intersected. He was all around me and I was all around him, and both of us felt connected, to everything. I... *we*... could see strands of space-time moving in all directions at once. And I was being called. I could feel that calling in every part of me. But when I heard your voices, I knew my story wasn't finished. That we had to come back."

I shoot a look over at them. Calvin is gazing down at Phoebe, who looks stunned.

"What I'm saying is..." Calvin tries again, "is that I never forgot the fireworks, on the night we met. I kept living, I did everything I did, because you believed that I could go on. But my duty's finished now." He gestures up at the swelling portal above, like a celestial body. "It's like this unimaginable weight from my shoulders. I finally get to do what I want. I get to choose the path I want to follow.

'When Zephyr and I were a Majestic, I swear I could feel Mum's presence. And I felt at peace, I felt her love. And I swear I could hear her say..." I'm shocked to see Calvin crying. "That there was nothing I needed to be forgiven for."

"Calvin," Phoebe says softly.

"I'm finally ready to try and remember how to be Gecko again. Back when I could see our futures, and they were so bright. And you were in mine."

Phoebe looks down suddenly, away from Calvin's intense gaze, as if scared she'll get drawn into it.

"It's... it's really unexpected," Phoebe mutters with an embarrassed smile. "You were just a Majestic, you're confused... that's a lot to put on me."

"I don't expect anything from you," Calvin murmurs simply. "I just love you. I never, ever stopped. Not even for a moment. And I know there's an age gap now..."

"Ten years."

"Okay, a big age gap. I know things are different than they were back then, obstacles that weren't there before. I know that it might be harder to make things work. But it makes me so, so angry that our chance was stolen away from us, Phoebe. Our chance to discover together what it was between us that was unfolding. And if you ever want that chance too, if you ever want to figure out who we are in this new universe together... I'll be there, waiting. I'll never stop waiting for you."

And that's when I come crashing back to reality. I feel like I'm sinking into the sand, vanishing from sight. Phoebe and me just had two days together. She has an entire history with Calvin.

Ever since Mum took Phoebe into Cameron Technologies, since she met Calvin, they've been falling for each other. This thing has been growing between them. For Phoebe, all of that was only two days ago. Maybe what happened between her and me only happened because of the adrenaline, because of the intense emotional stuff we just went through. Because it was suddenly just the two of us all alone against the world. But I don't have any right to come in to try and be with the girl that my brother met first.

Even if I have been falling in love with her since we first met.

Phoebe turns from Calvin to lock eyes with me for a moment, upset and torn. Her gaze is almost pleading. I can see her shock, but also... that a big part of her is longing for what Calvin is saying. I nod to her, just once, like a spasm. Then I turn away.

Devastated, I look back up to the portal far above. Suddenly I'm feeling this is not all the reward I had imagined it being.

I want to look at Phoebe but I don't. So I just stand there alone, churning with hurt and longing.

At least we finished this. But what's my purpose, my place in the new universe we're making? I feel utterly alone. I finally got what I wanted and I'm realising... maybe fixing the worlds won't fix everything.

It's not just about me though. This is for everyone else.

The sphere of the portal is now enormous. Its base touches gently down on the forest's canopy further inland, a gargantuan orb resting on the island. All of the other human and Shadows on the beach with us *'oooh'* and *'ahhh'* in wonder.

For a minute I'd thought the sphere might expand to consume the entire island along with us, but I think it's stopped growing now. It's complete.

Staring into the portal means staring into the Shadow world on the other side, the world we just escaped from. I can make out Aeyu Palace looming there, its spires stretching into the air. I wonder if Raven is still there, if he cut his losses and ran. I wonder if Eclipse is there, or if he's still making his way back up through the Underworld.

I shake my head sharply. It's hard to stop wondering

about him. Rethinking what I could have done differently... to make him love me more.

Here it is, made real: a permanent gateway between worlds. One of ten giant orbs around the world. Tokyo, Brussels, London and Los Angeles, one back home in Auckland...

"Holy crow," I hear Phoebe say. Zephyr is staring up in wonder, and the other humans and Shadows are gaping in awe, moving into each other as if to anchor them in front of such a formidable sight.

My brother rests a hand gently on my shoulder, making me jump.

"We did it, Griffin," Calvin says quietly. "*You* did it. Mum would be so proud."

"I know," I say softly. One day, sometime soon, I'll tell him what I encountered down in that temple.

This is where everything changes, I think. *Thank you, Mum. I'm sorry you won't get to see the new universe you created. But I know you're watching. And we all know it's being born because of you.*

I hear a sound, a droning in the distance. I look at the others beside me. Zephyr's brow creases, concerned.

"Something's coming," he says.

"From the portal?"

"No. From the water. Something offshore."

I squint toward the ocean, shielding my eyes from the glare of the sunset. I can make out something big out there on the water. Ships, out on the horizon. Human military ships, I realise, approaching the island.

And now I can make out separate dark shapes, flying low and fast toward us through the sky.

"A welcoming party?" Phoebe mutters.

The source of the droning sound finally comes fully into sight. Countless human fighter jets, aimed directly for the giant orb, the shining doorway between worlds. Zephyr roars, before any of us have really caught on.

As we watch, missiles launch from the jets, sailing into the surface of the portal.

We scream.

But just then the surface of the orb ripples, and scores... no, *hundreds* of behemoth winged Shadows launch outward. Winged lions, forest spirits, glittering insects... some of them carry smaller Shadows mounted on their backs, their steeds screeching as they fly head-on toward the metal human jets. And behind those Shadows, giant, flying sky-ships emerge, sails whipped by the warm Earth winds.

But it's not just the Empire emerging from that portal. Yes, there are a few violet sails that can be seen with the crest of the heart crossed with clawed gauntlets. But the majority of the ships' sails aren't violet at all. I see the flags and coats of arms of countless different Shadow world countries being flown.

It's not just the brainwashed Shadows of the Empire, I realise with dawning horror. It's everyone.

I'd heard about how most of the Shadow world was about to decide whether humans should be trusted or if they were the enemy. We'd had faith that the average, everyday Shadows over there would listen to the good inside them. That, free of the Empire's control, they'd choose peace and unity with the humans instead.

We were wrong. No, we were flat-out naïve.

The people of the Shadow world have voted for fear of

humans over any instinct for compassion and understanding. They've chosen to side with the Empire.

They've chosen violence.

The human and Shadow armies meet in the air above us, and the slaughter begins for both sides.

We watch as a sky-ship's hull is torn apart by machine gun fire, before exploding into flames. Missiles shoot from the human jets at a second sky-ship, only to be deflected from it at the last moment. Shadows stand on the prow, using their powers to shield the vessel with invisible wards.

A flaming djinn flies head-on into a fighter jet, passing through it. The Shadow emerges on the other side, strangling a struggling fighter pilot with its bare hands.

Two choppers are sent spiralling out of the air by a dragon made entirely of glass. Its crystalline scales deflect the bullet fire focused on it, even as its winged comrades are cut down from the air around it.

All above us, Shadows and humans are dying at each other's hands. My head swims. The serene sky from a minute ago is erupting into a battlefield, flaming debris scattering the trees of the island below.

"No, no, no..." I realise the voice is mine, whispering incessantly, madly. It's like being trapped in a nightmare. "Don't fight, why are you fighting? You don't need to do this!"

"Griffin..." Phoebe says helplessly.

"They're your counterparts, you're killing each other! STOP!" I scream up at them, and the other teens are screaming too, waving our arms, as if that can stop what's unfolding.

A rogue missile strikes the shore and detonates, the

explosion sending sand crashing over us and knocking some of us to the ground.

"Come on!" Phoebe screams at us. "Make for the jet, follow me!"

Pulling a shocked Woo-Min back up to his feet, I snap into action, directing our team toward the trees further down the beach. We're so exposed. Bullets strafe the sand around us, but if we're being targeted or if it's just stray fire from above, I don't know. All above us, Shadows and humans are dying at each other's' hands. My head swims. It's madness.

"No!" Calvin cries out, a sorrowful cry that cuts at my heart, as he stares up at the horror at the unfolding battle above.

I grab hold of him.

"Calvin," I say firmly. "*Calvin.* We have to go."

Calvin stares at me, shell-shocked. I pull at him, and I can't get him to move, but then Zephyr is at his side too and Calvin starts running with us. Flaming debris and wreckage rain down from the heavens, crashing past us. High above, the sky is a battleground.

I run madly with the others, diving and racing along the beach. Some of the Shadows with us fly narrowly over our heads, carrying their humans. Sien is cradling little Marty, while Anke is carrying Marty's Shadow, the scared monkey clutching her as his spider legs hug her too.

My vision is blurred. I'm deafened by the screams of human aircraft zooming overhead, the rattle of machine guns, the scream of giant feathered Shadows in the heavens above. But my heart lifts when I finally make out the dark grey steel of our jet's tail, sticking out from the forest.

It's not far. We can all make it. There's just the slight problem of the air being illuminated with flaming death.

Phoebe tears a remote from her pocket and aims it toward the waiting aircraft. In response, the ramp slowly lowers down from the rear of the jet, just as the first of our team reach it.

I watch Georgia's black wolf and Phoebe help to boost others onto the ramp. The Shadows and their humans in bloodied pyjamas scramble into the dark placebo-safety of the aircraft. Until we take off and get away from this place, we're all still sitting ducks.

Me and April are last. A mortar explodes near us, closer than the last. It kicks up a bank of sand, and I shield April, tensing for the sharp burning sting of shrapnel, but none hits.

"GO, GO!" I scream at her. The jet is starting to lift off the ground, ramp still extended. I reach it and help boost April up toward the ramp....

Celeste is there suddenly, taking her human's hand. Heaving with all her might, she pulls April up to safety. But before I can get into the jet myself the ramp is rising out of reach, and I'm still stranded on the beach...

Then Phoebe's dangling down over the very edge of the ramp. I seize the moment without hesitation. With a running leap I launch myself up into the air. My hand grasps Phoebe's.

Then I'm being pulled up into the safety of the jet. I realise just how many people formed an elaborate chain to allow Phoebe to grab me. Working together, everyone hauls me back into the aircraft.

I'm only just inside when something strikes the side of the aircraft violently. Everyone inside screams and the impact nearly shakes me free. But then I'm inside, in an interior that's *incredibly* cramped.

Our jet zooms away from the island as fast as possible, while I stare out the window at the blood and killing in the air.

It feels like the end. We threw everything we had at it, and now we're seeing the apocalypse unfold. There's nothing else we can do, we have no choice but to run. Because this isn't just one isolated battle. Something tells me that this is just the beginning.

A war is breaking out across the worlds.

Wordlessly, Phoebe hands me a phone. It's one of the Cameron Tech burner phones kept on board. I stare down at the screen, scrolling through the breaking news headlines and accompanying photos, any last hopes we might have had turning to ash. The others crane their necks to read over my shoulders.

Armed guards in a cobbled street in Istanbul, facing down a charging triceratops the size of a bulldozer. The blue mosque on fire behind it as ships sail through the portal.

The Old Quarter of Hanoi in Vietnam covered in a river of sticky, burning plasma, a human tank submerged within it.

Full blown combat in Brussels as a fight for the city taking place, a red fox Shadow shown shaking a dead human body while other Shadows lie around it, shot down by human assault rifles.

One headline from the news coverage stands out among the others.

'New vote signals the formation of historic global alliance: United Nations declares war on Shadow World.'

There's a thunder in my ears. Like I can hear my own blood boiling. The crack left by my Shadow is widening, fracturing inside me.

The great peace. Everything Mum had been working toward, gone. We didn't solve the problem when we opened those portals. We didn't connect humans with their Shadow counterparts.

We started a war.

"Eclipse was right," I whisper, the truth of that hurting worse than anything else.

I feel the absence of his mind, of his thoughts, like a chasm inside me, volatile around the edges. All the work he did to journey to my world, to find me... and now he's gone. We failed each other. And now my Shadow and I are stuck on opposite sides of a war.

How far Cirrus and I have come, I reflect, and how far we've both fallen.

Our dreams are about to be shattered by the sound of human machine guns and atom bombs. When the youth of this world are drafted into the battlefield, and see the horrors of war, which Shadow is it they're going to suddenly have dead in their sights, with their finger on the trigger? Will they see their own eyes staring back at them?

"What do we do now?" Phoebe asks brokenly, from beside Calvin.

Staring out the window at the battle we're leaving behind, I feel myself shaking, brow furrowed. I feel a fury rising in me, a wild predatory instinct to destroy those responsible for this. Like a monster stirring inside of me.

I cracked the Oracle, I hotwired the rocket to open the portals. I'm capable of more than my brother ever granted me. Raven showed me that much.

I'm starting to realise something. No matter the heart-break, no matter how messed up things are, I finally feel alive. I feel strangely calm. We'll get through this. I feel like I can see the colours of the world coming into sharper defi-nition, a new kind of determination burning to life inside of me.

I look at the Shadows and the humans in their pyjamas. Most of them are still staring numbly into nothing, reliving the horror of the battle in the sky. Of counterparts killing each other, just like they nearly had. Some of the humans are hugging their Shadows tightly and vice versa, crying into their fur or feathers or clothing.

They're frightened, but whenever they glance toward Phoebe and me, it's with complete trust. They're capable soldiers of their own. They held their own against Raven's soldiers when most kids our age would have broken and run.

This jet is our Noah's Ark. A small sample of the future.

If the worlds are determined to go at it in a suicidal war, then we'll just have to build an army of our own. We're the next generation. And we have to prove there's something brighter to make out of all this. A utopia of humans and Shadows in harmony is still within reach. It has to be. It's inevitable. This war won't be the end of all of us. We won't let it.

I think of Raven. I think of the Shadow attack he orches-trated on Cameron Technologies, and the attack on Sanc-tuary City. This must what he wanted from the start. Raven's secret agenda was using the terrorist attacks to turn the worlds toward fear and aggression. To play the worlds against each other for when the portals opened.

I think of the chessboard on the kitchen table in the palace. Finally, Raven and I actually understand each other.

War is a game. A game I was born for. And I'm the one who is going to end it.

I feel Calvin step up beside me. Phoebe comes up on my other side, clasping a hand on my shoulder.

"You have a plan," she says. It's a statement, not a question.

"I have a plan," I say in agreement.

Because no matter our pasts and our gripes and differences, this oddball group sitting in the jet with me right now... they're my family. And there is still light in this world that we're going to protect.

Slipping the phone back into my pants, my fingers touch on something strange. I pull the object out of my pocket to look at it. A chill crawls down my back.

It's a tiny scroll of paper. The seal is of black wax, imprinted with a raven.

I exchange dark looks with Calvin and Phoebe. They lean into me so we can read it together.

With surprisingly steady hands, I unroll the note. It only says two words:

'Your move.'

THANKYOU
FOR JOINING THE ADVENTURE

Hey There! I'm Sam.

I hope you enjoyed *Majestic* as much as I enjoyed writing it. For exclusive free stories and behind-the-scenes news on upcoming books, you can join my mailing list at:

www.samblood.com

It would be great to have you there!

Wishing you and your Shadow all of the very best adventures,

Sam Blood

ACKNOWLEDGMENTS

Firstly I want to say a special word on the beginnings of this book. I started writing the manuscript which would later be split into *Cameron* and *Majestic* on the island of Dondet in Laos at the start of 2016. There I spent a month on my own in a bungalow overhanging the Mekong River, with only a stray kitten named Tutu James Holly for company. This book was greatly influenced by that time and that place.

A big thanks to Leslie and Dylan for letting me talk out this story and helping me to refine ideas; and to Lynn and Sylvia for being excellent and invested Beta Readers. Thanks so much to Christopher, Porl and Gene, my fondly labelled 'Hacker Collective,' who were required at many cafe meeting consultations with me in the last few weeks to refine the more technical scenes of the book. One of the biggest unexpected joys of the process were the fun new character moments and gags that came out of these technical discussions.

A shout out to the awesome-sauce community around me of those who were the first to become Shadows fans, and who have been such a supportive team in cheering me on to finish this series both online and offline. You know who you are. Thanks for being part of this journey and making it much more companionable!

Massive thanks, hugs and gratitude to Alicia for being such a fantastic and giving editor and putting up with my eccentric creative-minded shenanigans.

Please give a big hand to Lindsey Wakefield for her knockout illustrations of Zephyr and Hanna - Lindsey, you have a knack for nailing my characters. You rock.

Finally, a huge amount of love and gratitude to Patrick and Vanessa for generously providing me with a writer's retreat in their home for the finishing stretch with Majestic. Without it, this book almost certainly would not be finished.

ABOUT THE AUTHOR

Sam lives in Auckland, New Zealand, where he enjoys writing and playing King of Tokyo with his quirky and highly charismatic friends.

The Shadows Series originated when Sam started telling bedtime stories to his Godsister when he was nine; the stories were about magical creatures called Shadows. He completed the first version of Shadows when he was fourteen, and redrafted it countless times before he published it in its current form.

Sam loves hearing from readers, and you can contact him at sam@samblood.com.

www.samblood.com

www.facebook.com/sambloodauthor

www.instagram.com/sambloodauthor